A FOREIGN FIELD

Margaret Mayhew

severn House

This first world edition published in Great Britain 2004 by
SEVERN HOUSE PUBLISHERS LTD of
9–15 High Street, Sutton, Surrey SM1 1DF.
This first world edition published in the USA 2005 by
SEVERN HOUSE PUBLISHERS INC of
595 Madison Avenue, New York, N.Y. 10022.

British Library Cataloguing in Publication Data

Mayhew, Margaret, 1936-
  A foreign field
  1.   Journalists - England - Sussex - Fiction
  2.   Britain, Battle of, Great Britain, 1940 - Fiction
  3.   Detective and mystery stories
  I.   Title
  823.9'14 [F]

  ISBN 0-7278-6191-3

Typeset by Palimpsest Book Production Ltd.,
Polmont, Stirlingshire, Scotland.
Printed and bound in Great Britain by
MPG Books Ltd., Bodmin, Cornwall.

For May

Prologue

It was the oldest trick in the book, but he was too new to have learned it yet. The fighter had come out of the sun and was on him before he'd even seen or heard anything. There was a shadow above him, the shock and thud of bullets hitting the fuselage, and the enemy was streaking on past and upwards, sleek as a shark against the blue.

The bullets had not touched the pilot but his aircraft had been mortally wounded. It yawned and shuddered like a dying animal. The nose pitched downwards and he began to lose height rapidly. A thin line of white smoke trailed from the cowling and the engine faltered and began to splutter. The pilot's legs and feet were soaked with oil and the smoke was streaming into the cockpit, hampering his vision. Automatically, he began to check over the instrument panel, training eclipsing fear. He read his height and his airspeed and saw that the oil pressure had dropped and that the engine temperature was rising fast. He trimmed the stricken fighter, throttling back gently to nurse the failing engine.

It was very hot in the cockpit and the fumes were suffocating. Sweat trickled from beneath his leather flying helmet. He pushed back the hood and wiped his forehead with the back of his gloved hand, licking his lips. He could still taste the vomit he had spewed up earlier in the battle in his frantic manoeuvres to avoid the enemy planes. He concentrated all his mind on keeping the plane flying. He did not let himself think of the possibility of death.

1

He had been heading for home – the straggling tail-ender on his first sortie into combat, clinging erratically to his leader as a lamb to its ewe, and the enemy fighter had picked him out as surely as a wolf goes for the weakest of the flock. He could hear his leader's voice calling insistently in his ears but could not bring himself to answer. Nothing mattered but the controls in front of him. He was on his own and no one could help him.

The aircraft staggered on downwards towards the ground. The white smoke had turned to black and there was an ominous smell of burning oil. Sweat had now broken out over all his body; the white silk scarf round his neck was soaked and his hands were sticky and trembling inside the fleece-lined gloves. He eased the stick slowly back and, at last, the plane levelled out. He shut his eyes in relief and opened them again to look at the rolling green countryside spread out beneath him in the soft, golden September sunshine. England.

At first he did not notice that the enemy fighter had returned. It was nosing alongside his port wing and he realized that it must have followed him down. He reached quickly for the firing button but the fighter hung back, safely out of his sights while he was powerless to manoeuvre, either for attack or escape. He looked back over his shoulder: the enemy was so close that he could see the face turned towards him in the cockpit and even the red scarf worn round the neck. Now he was afraid. He felt the helpless, hopeless terror and desperation of the hunted who sees the hunter aiming for the final, finishing shot. He waited for the end – the horrifying disintegration into flames and fragments which he had twice witnessed in the short battle he had somehow, until now, managed to survive. He thought of Barbara and knew he would never see her again. Today was his birthday and was also to be his death day.

Nothing happened. He looked back again over his shoulder and saw the enemy raise his thumb towards him and jerk it several times upwards, signalling urgently to him to bale out. Then the fighter flipped away suddenly in a fast, climbing turn, outlined dazzlingly above him as it soared like Icarus towards the sun.

The pilot wiped the sweat from his face once more. He had been spared. The hope of life remained. He had understood the signal but his whole instinct was to remain with the plane so long as it could fly, even though there was no longer any chance of returning to base. He could not bring himself to entrust his life to the bundle of thin silk strapped to his body. He stared down, peering through the black smoke, and felt the sick vertigo that he had never quite managed to conquer during his training. He gripped the stick tighter. The land was so near now that he could see it in clear detail: patchwork fields, shaded valleys and glorious verdant woods. He could pick out the sheep grazing – white blobs against the green – and some cattle standing together near a spreading tree. A pond glinted up at him like a mirror. He passed over a farmhouse, a thatched cottage with a white fence and some washing nearby on a line, a narrow lane winding between hedgerows . . . It looked incredibly beautiful to him, peaceful and unreal, untouched as it was by the bloody battle being fought overhead.

At that moment the engine seized. The airframe juddered and the propeller stopped. He searched intently for the landing place he had to find. There was a group of buildings dead ahead – a little huddle of houses clustered about a square towered church. As he came nearer, he saw that beyond the church there was a large house with lawns. Beyond the house stood a smaller redbrick building with some kind of smaller tower on its roof and, beyond that, a cornfield, wide, flat and beckoning. The corn had been cut and the stubble stuck up like old bristles on a worn-out scrubbing brush.

The pilot touched the rudder, put on a little flap and lined up carefully with the field. Wheels up, his fighter glided silently on over the old church, the graveyard and the big house with its smooth lawns. Relief was euphoric. His fingers stopped trembling; he even smiled. He was going to see Barbara again.

Her face was before him in the cockpit and her voice in his ears. *Come on, Martin, you can do it! You're going to make it!*

He put on maximum flap now and the aircraft sank towards the cornfield. The redbrick building still lay between him and his landing ground. He saw that it was a school and that the small tower was a belfry. Between the school and the cornfield there was a playground full of children and some of the children had gone out into the field and were running about in the stubble. They stopped as they saw him and stood frozen still, their pale faces turned upwards towards him. And then they began running again, like rabbits before the reaping machine . . . exactly where he was going to land.

There was a woman in the playground. He could see her frantically waving to the children in the field while she tried to gather those near her to safety. As the fighter cleared the belfry, he shouted futilely and waved as well, trying, like the woman, to make them get out of his way. But the children ran on, scattering in every direction so that there was no way of being sure to avoid them. Jesus Christ, he thought despairingly, I'm going to hit them. I'm going to kill them.

He pulled hard back on the stick and snatched the flaps up. The aircraft's nose jerked upwards sharply as though tugged by a string. It lurched unsteadily into the air and rose over the children, above the cornfield and on until it reached the wooded valley beyond. There, it seemed to hang motionless for a moment in the blue sky. Then the port wing dipped suddenly and the plane spun downwards towards the earth like a falling leaf. Trees billowed like the sea before the pilot's eyes and then parted and closed about him as the fighter plunged deep into the wood.

The impact shook the ground. The woman and the children stood staring in horror and some of the smaller ones began to cry, their frightened sobbing carried across the valley on the summer breeze.

Then there was silence. The trees were still and it was all peaceful once more under the September sun. Gradually, one by one, the birds in the wood began again to sing.

One

Frank Carter stopped the van. He cursed the sudden impulse that had led him to take a cross-country route instead of sticking to the main road. Because the sun was shining and the hedgerows were bursting into new growth, he had been seduced into a crazy rambler's tour. The lush green of early summer still bewitched eyes accustomed since birth to city grey. Now he was lost. And, worse, the van was overheating.

He had driven slowly along narrow, winding lanes, past verges that were white with cow parsley and fields that were yellow with buttercups. He had looked over the hedges at bullocks munching, knee-deep in long grass, and at lambs growing plump enough for the Sunday joint. Names on occasional signposts meant nothing to him so he had simply turned the van in what he had hoped was the general direction of Milton Spa. The road had led him up hill and down dale, turning this way and that, and he had followed equally aimlessly, enjoying the views, until he realized, firstly that he was gradually being taken further and further away from his destination and, secondly, that the temperature needle was in the red. At the next junction, he stopped.

Carter switched off the engine. In the silence that followed, steam hissed gently from beneath the bonnet. He pictured Ken Grant's face if one of his precious newspaper vans was ruined. A scratched wing and the editor had near apoplexy, so what would a cracked block do?

The signpost at the junction had only three good arms, the fourth having broken off at some stage. He looked at the two remaining alternatives to turning round and trying to go back the way he'd come. If he went left the road would take him to East Ham, three miles away; if he continued straight on he would finish up, after five miles, at a place called Mayhurst. If he chose to go right it was Destination Unknown of the missing arm. He could either toss a coin between the first two, or do what he should have done in the first place and consult the map. Carter reached for the glove compartment and found it empty. He remembered then that he had taken the book out himself to use in the office.

A glimmer of white showed in the grass at the foot of the post. Carter got out and found the missing arm of the sign-post in an advanced stage of decay. He wiped it carefully across the damp grass and, from beneath the mud, like magic writing, letters appeared, faint but just readable. AIRFIELD 2. The local terrain was hardly suitable for any such thing. Carter held the rotting wood up to the remaining stump and matched it there with the letter F. So now he knew that if he turned right he would find himself, two miles further on, at a village by the name of Fairfield. Carter looked about him. There was no house or building in sight. Two miles with a red-hot engine, not to mention a fanatical employer, was better than five and a slight improvement on three. Where there was a village there would be a pub and where there was a pub there would be – in addition to stronger liquids – water. It would save him the trouble of banging on remote cottage doors and reassuring old ladies that he had not come to rape them or rob them of their life savings. Carter got back into the van, started it up and turned on to the right-hand road.

The lane shrank as he progressed until there was room for only one vehicle. Moss on the tarmac and encroaching weeds at the sides indicated that it was seldom used. Carter began to wonder if he had made the right choice. Perhaps the rotted sign had been a portent which he should have heeded. Fanciful images of Fairfield went through his mind as he nursed the steaming van slowly onward up a long climb: a ghost village, wiped out by the plague, where only hillocks and hummocks remained to mark the site; a village, wreathed in valley mists, which had vanished and reappeared, like Brigadoon, for one day in every hundred years; or a village, forgotten because it was no longer on the map and where the inhabitants still dressed and lived as in times long gone . . .

Carter smiled to himself. Come to that, Sussex was full of such places. Smug little communities where time *had* stood still, so wrapped up in their own little world they didn't give a damn what happened outside it. News-wise they were unproductive, unless something right out of the way happened. Once in a while someone went mad with an axe and chopped up his wife, or the choirmistress ran off with the vicar, or the squire tried to evict ageing tenants or unsatisfactory gardeners. But mostly they had nothing more interesting to offer than the annual garden fête or the Brownies' Christmas party.

The needle was right in the red now and nearly off the dial while clouds of steam erupted from the bonnet. The last part of the climb was bordered by great beech trees which towered over the van, forming a leafy canopy. At the top of the rise this green and dappled tunnel ended abruptly. The canopy parted before Carter, like curtains opening upon a stage. Below him lay Fairfield.

It existed all right, and it was beautiful. The little group of houses huddled round a square-towered Norman church looked like a picture postcard – the sort that Americans sent back home to show the folks what little old England really looked like. There was a small green, a pond glinting up at him in the sunlight and even the big house, set just at the right distance from the rest to establish both affiliation and yet superiority. A nice touch of class distinction. There was a redbrick building with a small belfry – obviously the school – and a line of four houses projecting outwards like a spoke from the village centre that looked post-war. Otherwise, Fairfield had been spared any ugly development and there was no rash of little bungalows or council boxes.

Carter switched off the engine again and wound down the window. There was no hurry. He might as well let the engine

8

cool off a bit before he coasted down that last mile into the village. He groped in his jacket pocket for a cigarette and lit up. Even now his hand still shook sometimes and it was more than a year since they'd dried him out. He drew on the cigarette. It was hot in the van and he was thirsty – but not for alcohol, the clinic had seen to that. He hadn't craved it once since. No more booze. Not a drop again – ever. Not unless he wanted to slide even further down the ladder, and Christ knows he'd slid far enough. From Fleet Street to hacking on a provincial weekly, from national reporting to being sent to interview local worthies and crazy eccentrics like the old biddy he'd just called on, who kept thirty cats in her terraced two-up two-down and whose neighbours were complaining. The smell inside the tiny house had been appalling and the thirty inmates had climbed all over him, yowling, needling him with their claws and shedding hairs over his only decent suit. It had never occurred to the cats' owner that he might find their proximity anything less than entrancing; in fact, he had been assured several times over that he was highly honoured. The cats, it seemed, did not deign to walk over just anybody. This fact had at least had the merit of gaining him instant credit with their mistress and thereby loosening her tongue so that she had given him, unwittingly, all the material he needed.

Carter was no longer surprised, as he had been in his earlier days, by how willing people could be to talk to reporters. In his experience, the duller and greyer their daily lives, the more eager people were to talk about whatever happening or drama had made them, for once, important enough to be sought out by the press. He no longer felt any compunction at using all the tricks of the trade to get the information he wanted. The people who knew best how to keep their mouths shut were usually those who really had something to hide.

A bee had wandered into the van and was blundering about against the windscreen, buzzing furiously. Carter nudged the insect to freedom out of the open window. As he did so, he could hear the faint chimes of the church clock below striking twelve. Time and the publication of the *Milton Weekly Courier* waited for no man. Carter took off the handbrake to let the van coast painlessly down the hill, only using the engine for the last quarter mile into the village.

There was no sign to say that this was Fairfield, but Fairfield it must be. He passed the lychgate to the Norman church and drove on to where four roads converged on to the small green. There was a very unremarkable stone war memorial decorated with a faded wreath of poppies and, beside the green, not one hundred yards from the church and only five hundred years or so younger, the Bull Inn. The needs of the flesh and the spirit were thus catered for within convenient distance of each other.

There was nobody around. Under the heat and glare of an unusually hot midday sun the English village had taken on the dusty, deserted air of its foreign equivalent at siesta time – even down to a cockerel and an assortment of scraggy hens scratching about at the roadside.

Carter parked the van beside the only other vehicle outside the pub – an ancient Ford saloon. The Bull, he noted with approval, was mercifully unspoiled. No attempt had been made at updating the place to roadhouse specifications. This was a haunt of the spit-and-sawdust brigade with their real ale. The gin and Babycham lot would drive on by, if they ever got here in the first place.

Carter looked the pub over. The woodwork needed repainting and the roof would certainly need retiling within a year or two, while there was a crack in one of the windows that had probably been there for ever. Rather appropriately, a vine sprawled its way across the front of the building, untrained and flourishing. An old beer barrel had been planted with some marigolds and a stone sink contained some thirsty-looking plants that had yet to flower and seemed unlikely to get that far. Two wooden benches stood against the wall, one each side of the public bar door, which was open. Despite the heat, both benches were empty. The patrons of the Bull were evidently not sun-worshippers.

The cockerel and his entourage had progressed along the road and Carter watched in amusement as the fine fellow with his red-brown body and glossy black tail strutted towards the public bar and entered with all the confidence of a regular. His ladies, a strange mixture of colours and breeds, scrambled after him. Carter followed.

It took him a moment to accustom his eyes to the gloom. After the bright day it was dark as a coal hole. The first impression, therefore, was smell: the typical and unmistakable smell of any old pub, a composite of beer, smoke and wood wrapped together in a mellow bouquet. The ceiling between the low, black beams was kippered a dark yellow, the bar solid oak and the floor plain bricks. A huge inglenook fireplace took up almost the width of one wall. As Carter had expected, no concessions had been made inside to modern tastes. There was no hideous fake bric-a-brac, no ships' wheel compasses, no plastic flowers or coloured lights, no dangling Spanish dolls, no jukeboxes or Space Invaders.

There were about half a dozen customers in the bar and they were all old men. Every head had turned as Carter came in and he had been subjected to the close scrutiny that any stranger to a small community experiences wherever he may be in the world. The cockerel and his harem were pecking hopefully at the bricks and no one was taking the slightest notice of them. The landlord was wiping glasses at the far end. Nobody spoke. A match scraped and flared in a dim corner, a settle creaked, someone coughed rheumily. Carter went over to the bar and stood waiting.

The landlord took his time. He dried three more glasses slowly before he hooked the cloth over his left shoulder and came to serve him. He was a large, fat man who seemed to fill the narrow space behind the bar, already overcrowded with crates and barrels and bottles. He had a ruddy complexion, thick white hair and a beard. A change of clothing and he would have looked as medieval as his surroundings. This was Falstaff but without the knight's jovial humour or good fellowship. He put both hands, huge palms flat down, on the bar and leaned forward.

'Yes?'

The monosyllable was a clear message: Carter was not welcome. Drink up quickly and get out.

'Coke, please.'

There was an audible hiss from behind Carter – the shocked intake of breath by the regulars sitting over their pints.

'With ice . . . please.'

'No ice. Sorry.'

The landlord, not looking or sounding at all sorry, uncapped a dusty bottle of Coca Cola, poured it out and set it down, slopping some over the rim of the glass.

'That'll be five shillings.'

He'd been right about Fairfield, Carter thought, as he handed over twenty-five pence. Somewhere along the line it had got stuck in time. He drank the warm, flat Coke. Complaint, he knew, would be a waste of breath. Falstaff wiped down the counter with a dirty cloth. The regulars ruminated into their mugs. Over on the other side, the lounge bar was completely empty.

'Any sandwiches?'

'We don't do food. No call for it.'

'I'll have one of those packets of crisps, then. Cheese and onion, if you've got it.'

'Plain only.'

Carter opened the packet. He was not surprised to find its contents stale and soggy. He dropped a piece of crisp on to the floor and the cockerel, who had been waiting hopefully, moved in. There was a mad rush from the hens but they were too late. Their lord and master had got there first.

'I'd sooner you didn't do that, if you don't mind. It doesn't do to encourage Mactavish. Next thing we'll have him up on the bar.'

'Sorry.' Carter took out his cigarettes and lit up. If it hadn't been for the fact that the bar was already wreathed with smoke, he thought his genial host might have tried to discourage that, too.

'Press, is it?'

Carter turned. The voice had come from the inglenook. An old man in a cloth cap, sitting beside the empty grate, had spoken up suddenly through his pipe. For a moment Carter wondered how on earth he'd known, then he remembered the van parked outside the window with the provincial weekly's name emblazoned on the side for all to see. He realized that everyone else present knew it too and that the patrons of the Bull had closed ranks against him, probably for no other reason than that he might threaten their peace in some way. He was a stranger, and a snooping stranger at that. He nodded.

'*Milton Weekly Courier.*'

'Wasting your time here,' someone else said. 'No news at Fairfield. Nothing happens here.'

'I wouldn't say that.' Carter looked towards the speaker. 'There's always news . . . if you look hard enough.'

He was gratified to see them all shift uneasily. Most people, as he knew, had something in their lives, past or present, that they are ashamed of and which a nosy reporter might, just possibly, rake up.

'After anything in particular?'

The pipe had spoken again from its chimney corner. They were all curious, as well as uneasy, and he was tempted to tease them, to punish them a little for their unfriendliness. But he relented.

'No. Just passing through. The van's overheating. I was after some water.'

There was a collective relaxing and a perceptible defrosting of the atmosphere. Mugs were raised and lowered in unison. Two more pints were called for and another pipe was lit, thickening the blue haze overhead; there was even a rumble of something approaching conversation. The landlord leaned towards him across the bar, his beer belly resting on the edge like a side of meat.

'There's a tap outside, round the back. And a can nearby. You can help yourself when you want.'

Carter thanked him and ordered another Coke. He knew that they still wanted him gone but he felt in no mood to be rushed. He offered Falstaff a drink and the landlord grunted and drew half a pint for himself.

'You're not a drinking man, then? With the Coke.'

'Not any more. I'm off the hard stuff.'

'Hmmm. From up north, aren't you?'

'That's right. Newcastle, born and bred.'

'I thought I recognized the accent. Not as bad as some I've heard, though. I fought alongside a bunch of Geordies in the last war. Cussed lot of buggers. Couldn't understand a word they said. Nobody could. They could fight, though, I'll give 'em that.'

'Where were you?'

'France. BEF. I was captured just before Dunkirk. Spent five years as a guest of Herr Hitler.'

'Not much fun for you.'

'You can say that again. I only weighed eight stone when I came home. Not that you'd believe it now.'

'We don't, Charlie,' someone said and there was a chortling chorus round the bar.

The landlord ignored them. It was obviously an old joke.

Carter said encouragingly: 'You must have found Fairfield a bit quiet after all that.'

'Oh, I didn't come back here then. I only bought this place ten years ago. I come from Kent, myself.'

'He's a newcomer, is Charlie,' the most ancient-looking patron muttered into his brown ale. 'Kentish man.'

'Man of Kent,' Charlie corrected irritably. 'I come from south of the Medway.'

'All the same,' was the stubborn reply.

''Tweren't quiet here in the war, you know,' the man with the cloth cap and pipe said suddenly. 'We'd just as much doing as Charlie. The Battle of Britain was fought right over our heads . . . planes flying round the chimney pots and falling

14

out of the sky. And the Jerries used to drop their bombs on us when they were running for home. Right on the edge of Bomb Alley we were. We had seventy bombs jettisoned over Forge Wood, all in a long line. You can still see the craters. A hundred and eight were dropped, all told.'

'Get on with you, Jesse,' the landlord told him, raising his eyebrows to Carter. 'Quiet as the grave, it was. That Dad's Army of yours had it easy. Spent all your time fire-watching here at the Bull. Saw your planes through the bottom of a glass . . . No wonder you saw so many.'

The indignant protests from all sides that followed this jibe made it clear that Jesse was not the only representative from the old Home Guard. But before any more argument could take place, a figure appeared in the saloon bar doorway, blocking the light, and the talking stopped.

It was not until the new arrival stepped down into the pub that Carter could see him clearly. The man was old, but exactly how old was hard to tell. He was unshaven and his clothes were as shabby as a tramp's — torn, dirty and either too large or too small for him. His trousers were held up by a piece of twine, his collarless shirt had only one button, and both the shapeless red woollen hat he wore on his head and the green mittens on his hands despite the heat, were full of holes. He looked around the company with bright eyes but he had the slack and hanging mouth of the imbecile. A black and white collie dog slunk in at his heels and the cockerel, Mactavish, ruffling his feathers and flapping his wings, made a dignified but rapid exit with his ladies in tow.

There was a general muttering of 'Morning, Tom' from all corners. The newcomer nodded and smiled and gave a little bow in each direction. Then he shuffled over to an empty table and sat down. The dog slid like a shadow after his master and lay down beneath the table at his feet, muzzle on his front paws, eyes shining as brightly as his owner's. Tom went on smiling and, seeing Carter, nodded and smiled the more. Carter could smell him even at a distance.

'He's after a pint,' Charlie warned in a low voice. 'Don't

take any notice. Always on the scrounge, that one. Screw loose, as you can see. He lives in a tin hut in the woods. Has done for years. God know's how he survives, him and that animal of his.'

The conversation took up where it had left off, as though there had been no interruption. A thin man spoke first, from the settle.

'Charlie doesn't know what he's talking about. Quiet as the grave, indeed! Remember that night that Junkers came down over at Fox Green? Went up like a bomb. You could see the flames for miles. Took hours to put that fire out, didn't it, Jesse? Done to a crisp, those Jerries were.'

'Serve 'em right,' someone grunted.

'What about that German pilot parachuted into Ted Barnes' ten-acre at harvest time?' another reminded them. 'Old Mrs Barnes she went after him with a pitchfork, waving it like that Boodiker woman and shouting blue murder. Reckon if Ted hadn't reached him first she'd've run him straight through!'

'She would an' all,' Jesse agreed. 'I was right behind and I had to hold on to her till they came to take him away. She took some stopping. She was a big woman.' He took a puff at his pipe. 'Funny thing, though, when I saw that blighter there on the ground I felt sorry for him – never mind he was a Jerry. Just a nipper, he was, and scared stiff – what with Mrs Barnes and her pitchfork and Ted and his shotgun. I ended up giving him one of my cigarettes.'

The oldest inhabitant had stirred in his corner. He took a long swallow of brown ale before speaking. 'I mind when I was cutting corn at Moat Farm one afternoon when this black shadow came across the field after me. I thought at first 'twas a Messerschmitt and I was off that tractor and into the ditch faster 'n a rabbit.' He took another long swallow. 'But 'twas only a Spitfire, flying home very low. Soon as I saw that I stood up and gave him a wave . . . Good lad.'

'Then we had the doodles,' the thin man went on. 'Bloody cheat, Hitler sending them over. Shot at 'em with rifles, didn't we, but it didn't do no good.'

'Old Ted kept one in his barn for twenty years,' Jesse said. 'Towed it in there with his tractor and left it under some sacks. In the end the Ministry found out and came and took it away. Turned out it could have gone up any time.' He shook his head. 'He never was that clever, poor old Ted.'

They continued to reminisce agreeably among themselves, swapping anecdotes about the war and using terminology that had passed into history. Carter listened for a while, and the more he listened the more he realized that this motley little army would have been incapable of defending their village for more than two minutes. If the Germans had ever invaded they would have crushed these eager heroes under their jack-boots like so many beetles.

He turned back to his Coke. The war had been over for thirty-five years but it might have been yesterday for these old men. They would go on talking about it now until the cows came home. He wasn't that interested. He hadn't even been born until after it was all over. There had been other wars since – ones that did concern his generation, like the ever-present threat of the Big One that would finish everything for everyone, for ever. World War Two was for the history books and for the memories of old codgers like these. He caught the bright gaze of the idiot, Tom, who was sitting drinkless at his table. The nodding and smiling began again.

'Plane,' Tom said in a curious, high voice, addressing Carter. 'Plane. In wood.'

'Take no notice of him,' Charlie growled. 'He's after a drink, that's all. He tries it on with everyone. Anything to get attention.'

'Give him one – whatever he likes. It doesn't matter.'

'Suit yourself.'

The landlord shrugged his big shoulders. He drew a pint and carried it over to the old man. As he set it down on the table the dog thumped his tail.

'There you are, Tom. Your luck's in today. Compliments of the gentleman at the bar.'

The idiot rose to his feet and gave Carter a jerky bow,

17

doffing the red woollen hat. Then he sat down again and, raising his glass, drank with repellent gusto. When he had put down the drink, he spoke again.

'War plane. In the wood.' He tapped his chest with his mittened fingers. 'I saw it.' He lifted one hand and made a steep diving motion through the air, accompanied by a loud whining sound.

'He's always telling that one,' Charlie said sourly. 'If anybody talks about the war he swears he saw a Spitfire come down in Trodgers Wood where he lives. He just wants to be in on the conversation. He's got a dozen cock and bull stories for anyone who'll listen. I don't know why I let him in here. He stinks to high heaven! I must be getting soft in my old age.'

Carter lit another cigarette. He said idly: 'Has anyone ever checked out his story of the plane?'

'No need to. If there'd been one this lot of Chelsea Pensioners would've known all about it. They grabbed every bit of excitement going, stuck in this backwater. Trodgers Wood is less than a mile from here. You don't think they'd miss a little thing like a Spitfire coming down, do you?' Charlie flapped at a fly with his cloth. 'Like I said, Tom's always spinning yarns. He's nutty as a fruitcake. A real loony. The last time he was in he told us he'd just seen the Queen in the churchyard.'

Carter smiled. 'Maybe she was. You never know.'

'The *Queen*! In *this* place! What would she come here for?'

Carter drained his Coke and looked at his watch. 'Well, I must get that water for the van.'

'Help yourself. The tap's round the back.'

He nodded to the landlord and to the rest as he left. Old Tom was still making repeated dives with his right hand at the table in front of him. Carter held his breath as he passed him and gave him a friendly smile. He went out into the bright sunlight.

He found the tap at the back of the pub, as Charlie had said. The landlord's enthusiasm for gardening evidently did not extend beyond the barrel of marigolds and the stone sink of wilting plants at the front. If there had ever been a garden at the back it had long since disappeared under a riot of weeds and brambles. Accumulated rubbish from the pub was scattered about – empty bottles, broken crates and rusty tins. Mactavish and the hens were scratching about industriously.

Carter found the watering can, after diligent searching. He filled it and carried it round to the van. It leaked but enough water stayed with him to fill the radiator. He replaced the cap and shut the bonnet. As he turned, he found that old Tom was standing behind him, the black and white dog sitting at his heels.

'Plane. Spitfire in Trodgers Wood.'

Carter sighed and reached in his pocket for some coins. The quickest way to get rid of him would be to give him the price of a drink.

'Here you are, Tom. Get yourself another beer.'

The old man shuffled forward and his dog crept with him and then sat again. Carter held the money out but instead of taking it Tom put his own hand into his trouser pocket.

'Plane,' he repeated insistently. And he made another diving motion with his hand which ended with his palm outstretched beneath Carter's nose.

Carter stared down at the ragged green mitten and at the small piece of metal which could have been anything – there was certainly nothing to identify it as part of a plane. He placed the coins beside it.

'Get yourself that drink, Tom.'

He got into the van and started her up. As he drove off he glanced once in the rear-view mirror, expecting to see the old man heading double-quick back towards the pub. Instead he was standing just as he had left him, his arm still held out, and looking exactly like a scarecrow.

Two

The offices of the *Milton Weekly Courier* were in the centre of the town. The buildings had started life as a Georgian residence but additions and alterations over the years had left little trace of the gracious beginnings. Inside it was as scruffy and functional as most newspaper offices, where the only object is to get the paper out on time, every time, and there is little mileage in fancy decor or window-dressing.

As Carter walked into the office on his return from Fairfield, he found the usual Tuesday turmoil. Two p.m. on Wednesday was the deadline for copy. The paper was printed and made up on Thursday and on sale on Friday. It was normally subbed and finished by Thursday morning. Tuesday, therefore, was a busy day. The other seven reporters were round the news desk and the clack of ancient typewriters was deafening. Even Mike Tubbs, the chief sub, who normally took a liquid lunch from eleven until three, was at his desk, nose down and stone-cold sober.

Carter sat at his place at the news desk and typed up his piece on the old woman with thirty cats. While he was doing this, Brenda, the office factotum, brought him a cup of coffee. She was nineteen and wore brightly coloured clothes that were usually about two sizes too small for her. Her permed blonde hair stuck out in a frizzy halo around a zanily painted face and everything about her appearance belied the fact that she was hard-working and very efficient. She typed at a rattling speed, she manned the switchboard, she took messages and the money for the small ads and she made tea and coffee for anyone who looked as though they needed it – which was

most of the male staff, most of the time. And she did it all
with a smile. Carter spent a pleasant few minutes chatting her
up and she went away giggling and wiggling her bottom in
its tight red satin skirt. Harvey, the oldest reporter, who would
probably die in harness, scowled across the desk, either from
disapproval or, more probably, envy. Carter grinned and
returned to his typewriter and the cats. When he had finished
the piece he chucked it in the sub's tray and, as he did so,
Ken Grant stuck his head out of his office and called him in.

The editor's door was always kept open so that he knew,
or thought he knew, everything that was going on outside it.
Planning was all to him. The board on the wall behind his
chair bristled with lists, notices and memoranda and the Weekly
Diary was as often to be found on his desk as on the sub's.
In so far as a newspaper's contents could be planned ahead,
Ken had it all worked out. What no editor, however organized, could ever know was the off-diary events before they
happened – the car smashes, the robberies, the fires, the accidents. Ken Grant was fond of calling these 'the cream on the
cake' and when the cream had to be spread too thin he had a
habit of turning very sour.

It was very hot in the small, square office and the sun
poured through an unshaded window. An electric fan whirred
and turned on the desk and neat piles of paper were carefully
weighted against the draught. Carter positioned himself so that
the cool air swept over him pleasantly.

'Do you mind not smoking in here.'

It was an order, not a question, and Carter dutifully stubbed
out his cigarette in the ashtray on top of one of the piles. The
editor had given up smoking two months previously and, like
all converts, was twice as anti as anybody else. A large No
Smoking sign decorated the wall in addition to the rest of the
information on the board.

'Filthy habit. You ought to give it up.'

'I'll give up smoking in your office, Ken. Will that do?'

'It'd be something.' Ken Grant shuffled papers irritably.
'You're late back.'

'The van overheated.'

'Not damaged, I hope!'

'The radiator leaks, that's all.'

'See that it's fixed, then.' The editor unwrapped one of the mints that he now kept in his desk drawer. He folded the paper precisely into four and placed it in another ashtray, which contained several other wrappers similarly dispatched. He looked up at Carter with grey pebble eyes. 'Nothing decent from you for a good while, Frank. Time you came up with something . . . A nice dollop of cream for our cake next week. Any leads?'

'Not at the moment.'

'I thought you Fleet Street laddies could smell a story out any time, anywhere. I'm beginning to think I hired the wrong man. I'll have to put you back on to Parish Councils and Women's Institute meetings if you're not careful.'

Carter looked out of the window and gave himself time before answering. Ken Grant was a Sussex man and a dyed-in-the-wool provincial newspaperman. Not for him the heady heights of the nationals; his fulfilment lay in keeping thousands informed of what was happening immediately around them rather than millions of what was happening in the world. As a matter of principle, he despised and distrusted Fleet Street and rarely missed the chance of a dig. Carter had reached the conclusion some time ago that he had been hired for the pleasure of eventually being fired. For the moment, however, he had no intention of giving the editor that satisfaction – not until it suited *him* to go.

He looked down into the street below. It was full of shoppers – mostly middle-aged matrons going peacefully about their business. Milton Spa was not exactly a hotbed of drama and excitement; the majority of its citizens led routine and uneventful lives. There was no racism, no riots, no violence and scarcely ever a murder. His contacts could seldom come up with anything other than run-of-the-mill stuff that would never make more than the odd line or two in a national. He could hear Ken Grant crunching away menacingly at his mint and knew he must think of something to pacify him. The editor's temper, never sweet, had deteriorated badly since he had given up smoking. Carter debated whether to bring orchids into the conversation but decided against it as he knew nothing whatever about Ken's one other passion in life. He had sometimes wondered whether he grew them because their beauty compensated for the stolid ugliness of Mrs Grant. Carter searched the sky for inspiration. He watched a plane making its way overhead, en route for Gatwick, and leaving a white trail in the blue.

'There's one lead,' he said slowly. 'But it's probably a dead end.'

He recounted the story old Tom had spun at the Bull in Fairfield. The editor grunted and sucked at the mint instead of crunching. A good sign.

'Could be something in it. You never know. Check it out, Frank. Check it out.' He leaned back in his chair. 'It would make a good story.' He sketched an imaginary layout in the air. '*Spitfire found in wood after forty years. Battle of Britain hero's fighter recovered* . . . The pilot almost certainly baled out so we might be able to trace him and get a picture of him beside the engine, or the propeller . . . that sort of thing.'

'Wizard prang! Tally ho!' said Carter before he could stop himself.

Ken glared. 'It may not mean anything to you, Frank, but there are a hell of a lot of people in this part of the country who fought in the last war. A lot of our readers are retired servicemen. I'm one myself, come to that. And the Battle of Britain was fought in these skies. The locals have memories of it.'

'I've already discovered that,' Carter agreed, smiling. The editor had more in common with the patrons of the Bull than he would have guessed. 'I'll check the story out, but the old man was a loony. They say he tells them all the time.'

'Never mind that. And while you're there, see if you can dig up anything else. Those villages are like stagnant ponds.

Stir up the surface a bit and you'll find that underneath they're teeming with life.'

This did not seem a description that really applied to Fairfield but Carter let it pass. He had only mentioned the incident because he could think of nothing else to offer. He did not seriously believe that there was any truth whatever in Tom's story. The Spitfire was as much a figment of the old man's crazy mind as the Queen in the churchyard had been. He considered asking Ken if he should check that out too while he was about it, but decided not to risk it.

Later in the afternoon, Carter saw the chairman of the County Council Planning Committee who had come under fire for throwing out a perfectly good scheme for two hundred new houses without giving a proper hearing to the District Council who had proposed them. Councillor Jackson, who had been accused of irresponsibility by the chairman of the District Planning Sub-Committee, had retaliated angrily with similar compliments. The fur had flown in all directions. The interesting fact had subsequently emerged that Councillor Jackson's married daughter lived in a large, detached neo-Georgian residence immediately opposite the site of the proposed new development. The councillor's statement to the press, categorically denying any connection between his committee's decision and the value of his daughter's property, was lengthy and verbose. The more he protests his honour, thought Carter, scribbling away, the faster we count our spoons. He had yawned his way through a hundred council meetings since his cub days and met many Councillor Jacksons in his time. There was nothing to rival them for pomposity, publicity-seeking and self-interest.

The early evening was spent covering a public meeting held to discuss the building of a new secure psychiatric unit in a local hospital. Two hundred alarmed and disgruntled ratepayers had assembled in a room with seating for sixty, baying for blood. And, as they had failed to be convinced that the countryside would not be overrun with demented, violent patients, the meeting had ended in uproar. Since he was at the back of

the room, Carter was able to exit smartly before he was tram-
pled to death. He made his way back to the van, parked at a
convenient getaway spot. Neither Councillor Jackson nor the
ratepayers would qualify as cream on Ken Grant's cake; they
were, at best, a smearing of jam.

On his way back to Milton Spa he stopped at the Crown
and Anchor, a mile out of the town. The landlord's wife was
a good cook and the landlord himself one of his best contacts.
There is no better listening post than a pub and Carter had
had some reasonable tip-offs from Terry Gordon on occasion.
This time, however, the landlord had nothing of interest to
report. Business had been on the quiet side and with the recent
hot spell a lot of the customers had taken their drinks outside
to the garden. There had been less chat and gossip at the bar
than usual.

Carter ate some of Betty Gordon's steak and kidney pie,
sitting up at the bar. The Crown and Anchor attracted a good
many passing motorists and made sure it catered appropriately. Here were all the plush comforts that the Bull at Fairfield
had so conspicuously lacked: patterned fitted carpet
throughout, red-shaded lights, embossed wallpaper, soft, piped
music and a long menu of hot and cold snacks and dishes both
in and out of the basket. There was no place for Mactavish
and his shady ladies. The rest of the clientele, too, was in stark
contrast to that of the Bull, averaging a good thirty years
younger, well-dressed and with money to spend. The beer
garden through the door at the back had a well-kept lawn,
freshly painted tables and chairs with Courage umbrellas and
there were borders of bright petunias and plastic tubs of red
geraniums and blue lobelia. A notice pinned to the wall in
front of Carter informed customers that the Crown and Anchor
had won the area competition for the best-kept pub garden in
the previous year.

Carter finished the pie, which had been excellent, and lit a
cigarette. The landlord, spare and quick as Charlie had been
cumbersome and fat, served him his black coffee.

'Know a place called Fairfield, Terry?'

Terry Gordon shook his head. 'I can't say I do. Near here, is it?'

'About fifteen miles south, I'd say. Piddling little village in the middle of nowhere. I got lost or I wouldn't know it either. I had to stop when the van was overheating. There's an old pub called the Bull.'

'Still don't know it. Sorry, Frank. It doesn't ring any bells.'

'No matter. I'm not surprised. It's only a dot on the map. Nothing to go there for. You wouldn't think much of the pub.'

'One of the old kind, is it?' Terry said, polishing a glass to diamond brilliance. 'Sawdust on the floor. Flies in the bar.'

'That's it.'

'Mind you, I've nothing against them.' The landlord inspected the glass before putting it away. He took up another one. 'Plenty of old folk prefer them that way. They don't like change. They don't want things too modern. But my customers expect everything up to date, see. They want quick service and good food, and they want it clean and comfortable.' He put the second glass away. 'If I was to run my pub like that old one of yours they'd all drive on past and stop at the Bricklayer's Arms.'

'Tell that to Charlie.'

'Who?'

Carter smiled. 'Nothing. It doesn't matter. You're right about the old folk, though. They were there, all caught in time like in an old photograph.' He let the cigarette dangle from his lips as he spoke. 'Do you know there was even a village idiot – a real loony – who spun me some story about a Spitfire he'd seen coming down in a wood during the last war . . . He tried to make out it was still there. He was just touching me for a drink. Two drinks, in fact.'

'Doesn't sound very likely, I must say. Though you never can tell. I've been told some strange tales in my time and one or two of them have turned out to be true.'

'This pub was full of fossils from the old Home Guard. The landlord swears they'd never have missed a plane coming down on their little patch.'

Terry Gordon shrugged. 'Maybe not. But lots *did* come down, all over the shop round here. I was only ten when the war ended – just a kid – but I can still remember seeing a dogfight overhead. I was in our back garden and I looked up and saw these two fighters diving all over the sky. It was a sunny day and you could see them clear as anything against the blue, chasing each other round and round. One of them came down in the end – I don't know which side – and there was black smoke streaming out behind it all the way.' He made a diving movement with his hand that reminded Carter of old Tom. 'It hit the ground with a great *woomp*. It was a couple of miles or so away but you could feel the thump and see the flames as it went up. I remember being told by my mum to go and sit in the shelter and when I sneaked out later it was still burning.'

'There you are then, Terry. If you saw and heard it that well then this Spitfire would have been spotted by someone.'

A customer hailed the landlord from the other end of the bar and Terry went away to serve a round of drinks. When he had finished he returned.

'Not necessarily. Depends how it came down, doesn't it? And where. If it was somewhere flat like East Anglia where you can see for miles, I'd say you were right, but Kent and Sussex are full of ups and downs. You get it coming down in a wooded valley at a time, say, when there's a lot else going on, and it could have been missed. What about the Spitfire in Epping Forest?'

'What about it?'

'Some schoolboys found it thirty years later, or something like that – stuck in a ruddy tree. Nobody knew it was there. True story.'

'Don't believe a word of it.'

'Cross my heart. There's hundreds of planes still lying about the place – only mostly they're buried in the ground or under water. So they say.'

'So who says?'

'Well, these societies that go round digging them up.

Aviation archaeologists, they call themselves. One of them comes in here quite regular. He was telling me about a Hurricane they'd just dug up. They'd found all sorts of bits and pieces . . . Thrilled to bits, he was. I don't see the fun in it myself. So far as I can tell it's just a lot of rusty metal that'll never be anything else again. Still, it takes all sorts . . .'

He went away to serve another customer and Carter sat and smoked thoughtfully for a moment and drank up his coffee. The piped muzak was playing some unidentifiable tune from a speaker nearby; plastic music to go with the plastic wood on the bar and the plastic flowers beside him. What would Charlie and the rest have made of it all, and why the hell did his thoughts keep coming back to Fairfield? He wished to God he'd never been near the place. Tom's plane did not exist. Checking it out was a waste of time. There was no way those old warriors would have failed to spot a real-live fighter coming down in their midst, however many hours they had passed on duty at the Bull.

Terry reappeared. 'Tell you what, Frank. I'll give you the name of that bloke who runs the local aviation thing. Might be useful. You never know, do you?' He took a pencil from behind his ear and wrote on a notepad. 'He'll soon tell you if there's anything there. They're cagey as hell about where they're digging – never say a word till it's all over and done. But if you want a bit of advice about old war plane wrecks, he's your man.'

Carter thanked him, folded the paper and put it in his pocket. He never passed up any information or any name that might conceivably be of use one day. His opinion of Tom's story, however, remained unaltered.

An hour later Carter let himself into his digs in Milton Spa. As he opened the door of the large Victorian house in Lime Grove, the familiar smell of yesterday's cabbage greeted him. The hallway, hideously furnished with a dark and ugly side table, Anaglypta wallpaper and red and black tiled floor, was lit from overhead by a single sixty-watt bulb in a white glass

28

shade. From behind the closed door of Mrs Eliot's sitting room at the far end came the loud, repetitive jingle of a television commercial. The widow, comfortably installed in front of her idol, was paying it her customary nightly homage from tea-time until close-down. Mrs Eliot was the antithesis of the traditional talkative, nosy landlady. She took no interest whatever in her solitary lodger, so long as he paid his rent on time and did not disturb her viewing. The characters in any of the soap operas and series that she followed with such avidity were far more real to her than the man who actually lived and breathed under her roof. This was just as Carter wanted it. He would have repulsed any attempt at prying into his life; he preferred indifference and privacy and Mrs Eliot provided both in abundance.

He climbed the two flights of stairs to the room he rented on the first floor. It was big and high-ceilinged and the furniture was of the cheap, post-war variety. Drawers stuck, legs wobbled and handles came off. The unlined curtains of horrible hue and pattern barely stretched across the window and had shrunk several inches above the sill, leaving a gap at the bottom. Even if Mrs Eliot had been remotely interested in her lodger she would have learned nothing from snooping through his belongings. There were no photographs, mementoes or private letters or papers, except for his passport. She would have gleaned only the facts that he was a newspaper reporter, that he had been born on the seventh of September, 1948, in Newcastle-upon-Tyne (which made him thirty-two); that he had brown eyes, brown hair, was 1.79 metres tall and had no distinguishing marks, most of which she already knew.

Before going to sleep, Carter lay smoking in bed for a while, looking up at the moulded ceiling – the only elegant feature of the room. He thought, as he did every night, about Jan. Since her death she had been his last thought of the day and his first on waking in the morning. He had left all visible links with the past deliberately behind him when he had come to Milton Spa, but the invisible were as strong as ever. He could conjure up Jan – face, voice, gestures – as easily as if she were still alive and, even after six years, he could not really believe that he would never see her again. Did anyone ever believe it? It was the hardest part . . . That and bearing the burden of guilt for the rest of his days. What was that bit from the prayerbook about sins? 'The remembrance of them is grievous unto us; the burden of them is intolerable . . .'

Carter drew on his cigarette and exhaled the smoke slowly. He stared up at the long crack in the ceiling that wound its way like the Nile from one side to the other, and at the damp patch in the corner which was almost exactly the same shape as Australia. He had thought once of standing on a chair to write in all the names of the cities he knew, like in a geography exam at school. Sydney and Melbourne were easy. Perth was over on the far left and Darwin up at the top. Brisbane was somewhere up on the right. He was a bit hazy about the others. Canberra was between Sydney and Melbourne, inland, but where the hell was Adelaide? Somewhere along the coast from Melbourne, after the bulge and before the Bight? He thought about it. He thought about anything so that he didn't think about the day Jan had died.

He finished the cigarette and stubbed it out in the old saucer that served as an ashtray. *My husband never smoked, Mr Carter, and I'd sooner you didn't, if you don't mind. I don't care for the smell of it in the house.* Tomorrow he would go back to Fairfield on this wild goose chase. After that he'd better start thinking hard about how he was going to come up with something good enough to please Ken Grant. And keep his job.

Three

Carter drove over to Fairfield early the next morning. He lost his way three times and spent half an hour going round in circles before giving up and asking for directions at a farmhouse. The woman who came to the door told him cheerfully that everyone got lost. There were signposts to Fairfield dotted about the countryside, pointing this way and that, but when it came down to it they were no help at all. Strangers always lost their way.

It was after ten by the time he finally reached the village – opening time by country hours. The Bull, however, was firmly shut and locked. Charlie obviously kept his own hours rather than licensing ones.

Carter went round the back and knocked on the door there. Mactavish was pecking about with his hens and they came over and gathered hopefully round his feet. He began to regret his generosity with the stale crisp. He was about to knock again when sounds from within stopped him. A bolt scraped and a key turned and Charlie's face, bearded and bleary-eyed, appeared.

'We're not open yet.'

'I saw that. It's not drink I'm after but directions.'

Charlie grunted and opened the door a little further. 'Oh, it's you again. The one from the paper. Where do you want to get to, then?'

'That old man Tom – the one who said about the plane in the wood – where does he hang out?'

'You didn't believe him, did you? I told you, it's all rubbish.'

'I'm just checking it out like the good reporter I am.'

31

Charlie lifted massive shoulders. 'If you want to waste your time . . . He lives in a shack in Trodgers Wood.' He jerked his thumb over his shoulder. 'That way. Through the churchyard and over the stile. Follow the footpath across the field and the wood's at the bottom. I doubt if you'll catch sight of him though. He's nervous as a wild animal if anyone goes there. They tried to take him away once and he's never forgotten it. Waste of time, but please yourself.'

Carter thanked him for this graciously delivered information. He heard the sharp rasp of the bolt behind him as he picked his way out through the debris. The cockerel ran after him a little way and then gave up the chase.

The church lychgate was very old and bleached by time and weather to a silvery grey, the slate-tiled roof green with thick moss. A noticeboard informed him that this was the Parish Church of All Saints, that Sunday services were at 8.0 a.m. for Holy Communion and 11.0 a.m. for Morning Service and that the Rector was the Rev. Hugh Longman, Fairfield Rectory, Fairfield. Telephone: Fairfield 268.

Carter pushed open the gate, which squeaked on rusty hinges. A brick path led between leaning tombstones up a gentle slope to the north door. There were signs of life and of death. Someone had recently scythed the grass, which lay in yellowing swathes; a mass of bright flowers marked a recent burial. As he passed the tombs he noted the old names from the past – some hardly legible. Ezrah, husband of Sarah; Emma, daughter of Josias and Ann; Florence Mary, sister of the above; Hannah, wife of Bartholomew.

The church was as beautiful as he had expected, close to. Like all ancient buildings it had become part of the earth, growing from it as naturally as any tree or plant. The Norman tower stood square and solid against the English sky and, as Carter stood admiring it all, the clock struck half past and the sound hung for a moment on the air. There was a sudden fluttering of wings and two white doves flew down from the tower and landed on the nave roof where they walked up and down, cooing softly.

Carter had intended to skirt the building to find the stile but decided, first, to take a look inside. It was years since he had set foot in a church – unless the ugly little chapel in south London where Jan had been cremated in a hurried mockery of canned hymns and gabbled prayers could be said to count.

He read the notices in the porch out of a fascinated curiosity. A curling poster for the Church of England Children's Society proclaimed 'God Knows Your Help is Needed' and underlined this with a picture of a sad-looking waif. Another told him helpfully all about the aims and objectives of the Mothers' Union. Two neatly typed lists gave him the names for the fortnightly church cleaning rota and the weekly altar and memorial flowers, month by month throughout the year. This week, apparently, it was up to Mrs Tompsett and Mrs Wenham to clean up, while Mrs Armstrong-Avery and Mrs Rawlings took their turn at the floral arrangements. At Easter, Harvest Festival and Christmas, a Miss Burton and the Festival Decorators stepped in, sounding rather like an old-fashioned dance band. From Ash Wednesday through Lent nobody did anything in the flower line, although they kept on cleaning. There was a stern warning issued in capitals at the bottom of the second list: IT WOULD BE APPRECIATED IF ARRANGERS WOULD MAKE SURE THE OASIS IS WELL SOAKED *AND* STANDING IN SOME WATER.

The latch was stiff and clicked loudly as he opened the door. Out of the sun it was as dim and cool as it had been in the Bull over the way. A carved lectern eagle perched with mighty wings outspread above the rows of empty pews. There was complete stillness. The smell of musty hymn books, lavender and metal polish mingled with the light, sweet scent of the flowers decorating the altar and side aisles – courtesy Mesdames Armstrong-Avery and Rawlings.

He wandered about. There were two rather fine medieval brasses set in the chancel floor. A small lancet window picturing bunches of grapes and sheaves of corn attracted him because it was obviously very old. He read some of the stone memorials and a plaque on the wall above the choir stalls in proud and loving memory of a Captain Sir John Dalrymple, Bart, of the Royal Navy who had been killed in action in the Atlantic in 1944. Later on, he came across three more memorials to Dalrymples who had died less dramatically at home.

The eagle watched him with its wooden eyes.

He opened the door to the belfry tower. The red, white and blue bell ropes hung motionless. There was a faint and eerie moaning sound which he realized must be the wind in the tower overhead. Unless it was the souls of the dead . . .

Before he left the church he stopped by the door to look at the gold-lettered roll of former incumbents. It started at 1195 with a William de Sparle and went on through eight centuries up to the present rector, Hugh Longman.

The brick path continued round the west end of the church and petered out into a mossy track. The grass had been left uncut here and some of the older tombstones had finally toppled to the ground and were almost hidden. Within a generation or two, Carter thought, nobody cares anyway. Names on a grave, on a plaque, on a brass or on a roll, even gold ones, are only just names to those who come after. Unless you're rich or famous, and preferably both, nobody will know a thing about you, except for the few bare facts that have been dutifully, or legally, recorded. Ezrah, Josias, Ann, Hannah et al. had all been flesh and blood. They had walked and talked, lived and died in Fairfield. But across the gap of years they could never be more than shadows. Ezrah sounded a mean old skinflint. Carter could see him with a straggling beard, counting a hoard of money, but for all he knew he might have been a fat, jolly man. He could picture Josias and Ann, parents of Emma who had died at two in 1713, as kind, worthy and loving, bowed down with grief at the early death of their daughter. They could equally well have been unfeeling, harsh and neglectful, the fine tombstone erected more to the neighbours' opinion than to their daughter's memory.

At a space in the trees edging the graveyard he saw the stile and, beside it, the yellow concrete block marking the beginning of a public footpath. He climbed over. The field sloped away downhill towards the wooded valley. To the south more fields stretched into the distance, undulating towards the long ridge of the Downs. In a gap there was the bright metallic glint of the sea. No pylons, no motorways, no factory chimneys, no dark, satanic mills, just a glorious landscape that had probably been unchanged for centuries.

He leaned against the stile and lit a cigarette. This was dream England, as people exiled always imagined it. The reality was not always as good. A hell of a lot had vanished under a great tide of modern development. Hedges thousands of years old had been grubbed to make way for the combine harvesters; the pigs and chickens had vanished into factory farmsheds and the old orchards had been felled because English apples could no longer compete with plastic-packed ones from the Common Market. Stockbrokers in Gucci shoes inhabited the thatched cottages and nobody lay under the greenwood tree any more. They were all elsewhere – gone to Wates and Wimpey houses, bedsits, high-rise flats and bungalows. If any lying about was done it was on a package-tour beach under a far hotter sun. The sweet bird still sang but nobody came hither and its merry note went unheard above the roar of juggernauts and jumbo jets. Except in places like this, *Here shall he see no enemy but winter and rough weather.* It was ironic that this particular bit of the country had apparently seen a good deal of the enemy, forty years ago.

He set off down the field towards Trodgers Wood, side-stepping the cowpats. A group of brown bullocks watched him curiously, the boldest following him at a distance, the rest lagging behind timidly. On his right he could see the back of the big house, its tall windows facing towards the sea. There was a terrace running the width of the house, French windows giving on to it and, below, smooth, green lawns.

At the bottom of the field a three-strand barbed-wire fence lay between him and the wood. He negotiated this with difficulty, tearing his trouser leg in the process. If there was a path he could not see it. The undergrowth was dense, a wild tangle of brambles and thickets. He forced a way through, scratching

35

his hands and face and cursing as he did so. After a while he stopped and called the old man's name but the wood stifled the sound and he felt as though he had cotton wool in his ears. Somewhere near he could hear the faint trickling of water. He looked this way and that. There was no point in going on; he could blunder about all day and get nowhere. Better to give up and go back while he still had some idea of the way out of this place. As he stood debating this, he suddenly had the sensation of being watched and the hairs prickled on the back of his neck. He turned.

The old man, Tom, was standing no more than six paces behind him, the black and white dog crouched at his heels. Man and animal were motionless and stared at him with their bright eyes. Carter did not dare move for fear of frightening them away. Presently, Tom nodded and smiled.

'Plane,' he said in his tinny voice. And he made his odd diving motion with his mittened hand. Then he beckoned with his forefinger and moved off.

Carter followed him. The old man moved with surprising speed and silence, the dog trotting close at his heels. They were on a path of sorts – a narrow footway that led into the depths of the wood. He went after Tom blindly and could have tracked him by the smell of him. They reached a stream, shallow but wide, and the old man stepped across the water on pointed toes as though he were dancing, scarcely wetting his feet. Carter, trying to use the same stones that lay just beneath the surface, missed his footing and soaked his already torn trouser leg.

Charlie had described Tom's home as a shack; this was a euphemism. Corrugated sheets of iron had been leaned together like a house of cards and the roof was kept in place by boulders. It was as primitive a dwelling as any Stone-Age cave and a good deal less weatherproof. For a moment Carter was afraid that he was going to be invited inside but Tom beckoned him on and, a few hundred yards beyond the shack, he stopped.

'Plane,' he repeated. 'Spitfire! Boom!'

And he pointed in front of him and dived his hand again.

It was like having a ghost pointed out by a medium in a trance. Carter saw nothing. Not that he expected to see a complete aircraft sitting in the middle of the wood, but at least something that might have set the old man off – some kind of wreckage, perhaps old bits of farm machinery or parts of an abandoned car. There was nothing.

He went over to where Tom was standing, keeping downwind of him, and saw that he was on the edge of a mini cliff. A steepish incline, about four feet high, led down into a damp hollow full of dead leaves and young saplings reaching in vain for the light. Beyond, he could make out the shine of water and the green of rushes.

Tom had nipped down the bank and was capering about in the leaves, picking them up in his hands and letting them flutter down around him like confetti. The collie dog bounded about, barking. Carter shivered. The loony was a repellent sight. If he'd known the way back he would have left him to his weird dance; as it was, he might as well take a look for himself. He slithered down the incline, adding mud to the wet and the tear in his trouser leg. He walked around the hollow. The ground was boggy beneath his feet and as he kicked aside the top layer of dead leaves he saw a black gleam of wetness beneath. Tom had stopped his capering and was watching him eagerly. Carter kicked about a bit more.

'OK, Tom. Let's go. Show me the way back.'

He started up the bank again and stopped at the top. The old man had fallen to his knees and was scrabbling frantically among the leaves while his dog pawed the earth and thrust his nose into it. Carter watched them impatiently; the joke had gone on long enough. He was very tired of the whole nonsense. He groped in his pocket for a cigarette and lit it.

There was a falsetto cry from Tom and Carter turned to see him still on his knees, eyes shining like a happy child as he held out his mittened hand. The dog wagged its feathery tail and barked again. Cursing inwardly, Carter slithered back down the bank again.

The fragment which Tom held resembled the one he had been offered outside the Bull, except that it was considerably larger – five or six inches in length. Carter took it from him. The metal, whatever it was, was thin, light and crumpled almost like paper. There were blue patches and when he rubbed at these with his thumb the blue came off on to his skin like powder, leaving a silvery gleam beneath. There was no rust. Aluminium didn't rust and he had a vague idea from school-days that it oxidized blue. But if this was a piece of aluminium, what did that prove? Thousands of things were made of that metal – kitchen pots and pans included – and he wasn't even sure that a Spitfire was one of them. He looked about the hollow again. There was no other evidence that he could see. He looked, too, at Tom. It was best to humour him, he decided; to let him think that he believed in his plane. He smiled, nodded and put the fragment carefully away in his pocket, signing to him that he wanted to be shown the way out of the wood.

The old man and his dog trotted off obligingly and when they had reached the field Carter handed over a palmful of coins. He made his way back up towards the stile, past the bullocks who lifted their heads to watch him.

Something flashed brightly in the sun from the direction of the big house. The French windows had been opened and Carter could see a figure seated there. Someone had been observing him closely through binoculars. Presumably a stranger tramping about the field was as rare a sight as a lesser-spotted woodpecker. Or rarer.

He reached the stile, panting after the uphill climb, and retraced his steps round the church. As he walked down the path a sandy-haired young man dressed in jeans and a navy-blue sweater came through the lychgate towards him. He smiled and nodded when they met.

'Good morning. You've been inside our church, I hope? We still keep it unlocked, I'm glad to say – unlike many. People will steal anything moveable these days – even from a church.'

Carter held open his jacket. 'No crucifixes or poor boxes, I promise you.'

38

The young man smiled. 'I hope I didn't give the impression that I thought there might be. Actually, all the valuables are safely locked away in the vestry now, except during services. Still, you might have unscrewed one of the brasses, or even taken out the lightbulbs.' He held out his hand. 'Hugh Longman. Rector of All Saints. Sorry, I should have introduced myself sooner.'

Carter was surprised. He had imagined some doddering country cleric who had been put out to grass years ago. He took the hand.

'I'd never have guessed it. My name's Frank Carter. Of the *Milton Weekly Courier.*'

The handshake was very firm. 'Oh, I don't wear my dog collar all the time. On purpose. I have a theory that it makes me seem more human and approachable to my parishioners – rather like a policeman out of uniform. I could be wrong, of course. Are you doing a piece on All Saints? It's a fine old place. Saxon site, though there's no trace of that church left. The tower is Norman, as you can see, and the chancel early English – about 1190, I believe. You noticed the lancet window there, I expect. Pity about the pews, isn't it? The usual Victorian atrocity. The old box ones were taken out as well as the musicians' gallery . . . Tragic the things that are done in the name of progress. Things swept away that can never be recovered. Lost and gone for ever. What did you say you were doing a piece on?'

'I didn't.'

Carter explained briefly and the rector listened attentively as one whose life is spent doing so.

'You'll forgive my saying so, Mr Carter, but you've probably been had for a sucker, as they say. Poor old Tom is famous for his tall stories.' His eyes travelled downwards. 'I'm afraid you've wrecked your shoes, and trousers, for nothing.'

'I'd already reached the same conclusion. I was just making sure.'

'A good newsman always does make sure, I imagine. Truth,

39

after all, can be stranger than fiction. However, I must say I've never heard of anyone else speak of a plane buried in Trodgers Wood, or any other part of the parish, come to that. And a lot of my parishioners have lived here all their lives. I've only been here two years myself so they look on me as a complete newcomer.'

'The landlord of the Bull has been here ten and they still call him that.'

The rector laughed. 'I know. But a lot of them were born in this village. They've lived here all their lives and they'll die here. You can understand how they feel.'

'It's a nice place to be buried. I'll say that for it.'

'We'll soon be full up, more's the pity. People should be able to lie at rest in their own churchyard, not shuffled off to some municipal plot. Of course, cremation's quite popular now. People seem to feel it's tidier and cleaner. It fits in better with modern belief – or non-belief, I should say. If someone's burned up you don't have to consider the possibility that they might be lurking about somewhere still. They're gone and that's that. Rubber-stamped as dead. Personally, I'm in favour of good old-fashioned burial. There's something rather satisfactory about the "earth to earth" bit.' He gestured towards the new grave with its pall of flowers. 'George Clark's under there. Splendid old boy of eighty-four. He had eight children and sixteen grandchildren. They'd all left the village but they came back to see him off in style and pay their respects. It was done as it should be and there he'll lie in peace . . . at least until this planet's finally blown to bits by the rest of mankind.' He shook his head. 'Sorry. I mustn't ramble on. How is old Tom, by the way? I haven't seen him for a while. He fights very shy of anyone in any kind of uniform. If he sees me in my dog collar he runs a mile.'

'He seemed pretty fit, considering the way he lives. So did the dog.'

'It's the life he likes – that's the most important thing. It's a mistake to try and force people into other moulds. Some well-meaning social workers came and tut-tutted about that hut of his – no running water, no toilet, no heating, that sort of thing. But what does it matter? They quite overlooked the fact that he'd been living there for more than thirty years, happy as a bird and, as far as anyone knows, he's never had a day's illness in his life. He may be simple but he knows what's best for him.'

'I take it he wouldn't go quietly.'

'He wouldn't go at all. He hid somewhere in the woods until they gave up looking for him. They came back a few times but in the end I persuaded them to leave him alone. Sir Phillip has no objection, anyway.'

'Sir Phillip?'

'Sir Phillip Dalrymple. The owner of Fairfield Hall. You probably noticed it. The big stone house beyond the church. Trodgers Wood is on his land. The family have lived there for years.'

Carter remembered the church memorials.

'Squires of the village?'

'You could say that.' The rector had not missed the mocking edge in Carter's voice. 'A bit feudal, I grant you, but even in this modern day and age the system still has its advantages. For people like old Tom, for example. Without the protection of the Dalrymples he would have been locked away long ago. The squire looks after his own.' He glanced at his watch. 'Excuse me, but I must leave you. If you need help at any time, don't hesitate to call on me, Mr Carter. The rectory is at the far end of the village, past Mrs Jennings' shop.'

He walked on up the path and disappeared into the church. Carter wondered what it felt like to be the latest in a line of men stretching back eight hundred years. Did Hugh Longman ever think about his predecessors, or did he concern himself only with the present – the next Mothers' Union meeting or how to keep one jump ahead of the Parochial Church Council?

Returning to the van, Carter found that he was out of cigarettes. The Bull was open now, its saloon bar door wide if not precisely welcoming. Charlie might not run to sandwiches but he would surely have cigarettes. On the other hand, they might be as stale as the crisps. On sober reflection, he decided to try the shop that the rector had mentioned. He left the van where it was and walked on through the village, past the war memorial and the green, past the small pond where two ducks were paddling about and on past a row of neat cottages with small front gardens and wicket gates. A high brick wall enclosed the land on his left and finished in the entrance to Fairfield Hall. The wall was crumbling in parts and the wrought-iron gates could do with a repaint. Things ain't evidently quite what they used to be with the squire. The wall continued for another fifty yards, curving left with the road, until it finally gave way to an iron paling fence. Behind the fence stood a redbrick building with a small belfry on its roof and an asphalt forecourt. Carter awarded himself no prizes for guessing that this had once been the village school – but no longer. There were curtains at the windows, flowers in smart garden-centre tubs and a sports car standing outside the door.

Mrs Jennings' shop looked as though it had been converted from another old cottage. Its bow-fronted window displayed tiers of cream crackers, digestive biscuits and bottles of squash and Ribena, all ranged behind glass shaded with yellow cellophane. A lean-to shed sheltered the entrance at the side and here, as in the church porch, there was a noticeboard. 'Dancing,' Carter read, 'adds pleasure to leisure. Learn to dance at Fairfield Parish Hall with Miss B. Plumb, FISTD, LA, MISTD/BB. Ballroom and Latin American. Every Friday 7.30–9.30 p.m.' Beside Miss Plumb's notice another card, written in a large, childish hand, offered gerbils for sale. Another a reward of £1 for any information leading to the recovery of Bubbles, a pet chinchilla belonging to Jane Roberts of Honeysuckle Cottage. There was an announcement in faded red felt-tip of a jumble sale in aid of handicapped children which had come and gone and, beside it, a notice cleaner and newer than all the rest and boldly printed with black letters on a fluorescent green background:

This village has entered for the Best-Kept Village
Competition. We ask residents and visitors to help us
keep our village tidy and well cared for during June and
July. Judges will pay particular attention to: Greens,
Playing Fields, Churchyards, Verges, Ponds, Schools,
Litter, etc.

Ken Grant had likened Fairfield and its kind to stagnant
ponds – still on the surface but teeming with life beneath. So
far as Carter could judge from the village noticeboards, these
had been strong words. It seemed to him that life in Fairfield
was just as quiet and uneventful as it looked, unless orgies
took place at the ballroom dancing classes on Fridays or the
rector practised black magic at the altar of All Saints when
the moon was full.

The shop doorbell jangled behind him and he turned almost
guiltily, as though he had been caught reading private papers.
The woman who came out was elderly, very thin and gaunt-
faced. She wore a grey skirt to mid-calf, a cream blouse, lisle
stockings and flat leather brogues. She moved briskly and the
brief nod she gave him was as free from artifice as the rest
of her. Her glance was swift and piercingly appraising; he felt
that the pale blue eyes had summed him up in that one look.
There was something of the schoolmistress about her and he
would not have been surprised if she had asked to inspect his
fingernails or ticked him off for sniggering at the village
notices. She was carrying some tins of cat food, a loaf of
brown bread and a packet of cereal and stowed these away in
the wicker basket on the front of an antiquated black bicycle
which was leaning against the shop wall beside the door. He
watched her ride away without a wobble.

The yellow cellophane cast a strange light inside, as though
the shop was caught in a perpetual stormy sunset. It was
cramped and crowded. Every shelf was piled high with goods,
in no particular category. A perilous pyramid of baked beans
towered over a pile of cheap stationery and a box of ballpoint

pens; a Dundee cake rubbed shoulders with some jars of pickled onions. There were even boxes of goods on the floor and a sack of potatoes standing beside an old-fashioned iron and brass weighing machine. An ice-cream freezer rattled away noisily, blocking the route to a separate, grilled counter which was evidently a sub post office.

The woman who stood behind the goods counter was half-concealed by her wares. She was very short and dumpy and wore a nylon overall patterned with dizzy zig-zags in mauve and green. Her frizzy hair was dyed auburn and pinned back into an untidy bun. There was a flourishing moustache on her upper lip.

'Can I help you, sir?'

Charlie, he thought, might take a lesson or two in customer relations from Mrs Jennings. He squeezed between the sack of potatoes and a box of tinned dog food to reach the counter and ask for his particular brand of cigarettes. She swivelled on the spot and rummaged through a crowded shelf behind her until, triumphantly, she produced the appropriate pack. He handed over the money and she depressed the keys of an old till with the concentration of one playing a difficult piano concerto.

'Thought you were going to ask me the way,' she told him with a cheery smile as she gave him his change. 'People always end up in here when they get lost. Sometimes they've been going round and round for hours. Passing through, are you?'

Her curiosity was warm and inoffensive; Carter welcomed it. In his job he always encouraged people to talk. Even if they did not tell you what you wanted to know they might end up telling you something even better. He repeated his story of Tom and the Spitfire once again and she burst out laughing, her plump frame shaking with amusement. One of the tins of baked beans fell to the floor with a crash. Carter picked it up and replaced it on the tottering pyramid.

'He's a caution that Tom, really he is! A Spitfire indeed! Whatever next! I'm surprised he didn't say it was one of those

44

big jumbo planes. Last time he was in here he told me he'd just seen Prince Philip in the Bull. Prince Philip! I ask you! What would *he* be doing in a place like that? I said to Tom, I said, "What was he drinking then, tell me that?" Do you know what he said? Guinness! Prince Philip drinking *Guinness*! Whoever heard of such a thing?'

She roared with laughter again. Carter quickly steadied the baked beans. What with the Queen in the churchyard and Prince Philip in the Bull, the old man certainly had a vivid imagination, or a strange compulsion to tell whoppers. Pity he didn't choose more believable things and get himself a bit more beer money in the process.

'No one else has ever mentioned a plane to you – one that came down in the war?'

'No,' she said, still laughing. 'It's just Tom's way of getting attention. Proper old devil he is!' She looked at Carter with interest. 'Fancy you being the press. You don't look like a reporter, do you? I always picture them something like Humphrey Bogart, you know . . . a raincoat and a trilby hat down over the eyes. I remember that film where he—'

'Were you here during the war, Mrs Jennings?'

'Oh, no.' She shook her head and the pencil she wore behind her right ear flew out and rolled across the counter and over the edge. Carter retrieved it for her. 'Thank you, dear. I've only been here about twenty years. Hubby and I bought this little business then. When he died I stayed on. I could have sold up and gone back to Balham but I didn't want to leave after all that time. It's not really a living, but I like the country. Nice clean air. You can breath proper. Arthur had asthma and it did him a power of good . . . until he died, of course. That's why we came here from Balham in the first place.' She stuck the pencil back behind her ear. 'Miss Burton was here in the war. She could have told you all about it, if you wanted to know. The lady who was in here before you.'

'The one with the bicycle. Elderly. Grey hair?'

'That's the one. She was a schoolteacher here, in the days when there was a school. It's closed down now. They all go by bus to the big school eight miles away. Pity, I call it. It's taken the life out of the village. And they don't learn their three Rs like they used to. Half the kids who come in here can't add two and two together, let alone write and spell decent. It's a shame.'

His instinct had been right about Miss Burton, then. He could easily imagine her holding sway in the village school, sitting at her high desk, feet together, back ramrod straight with those all-seeing blue eyes fixed on the rows of children below her. No one, he had a feeling, would have dared defy Miss Burton. There would have been no back-answers or slacking while she was in charge. And if there had been, he had no doubt that she would have dealt with the matter summarily. No new-fangled nonsense about child abuse or educational psychology – six brisk strokes of the cane and a hundred or so lines and some tiresome little bugger would quickly have come to heel.

He chatted on for a while with Mrs Jennings, who held forth on a variety of subjects without fear or favour. Her customers were included in the discussion. On the whole, he gathered, they were not a bad lot in Fairfield. Some of the older ones were a bit stuffy or difficult – always finding fault with everything – but all in all, she informed him magnanimously, they were all right. It didn't do to grumble. People were the same wherever you lived: a mixture of good, bad and somewhere in the middle. Carter mentioned the rector and she beamed instantly.

'He's lovely, our rector. We're ever so lucky to have him. The last one was a proper so-and-so. Nobody liked him, but we couldn't get rid of him. He was here ten years and by the time he left the church was empty on Sundays except for old Miss Coleman and she's stone deaf. He preached to himself, he did. But Mr Longman's quite different. Everybody likes him and the church is full every week. Ever such nice sermons he gives. Nice and short, if you know what I mean, and something easy to follow. The other one rambled on for hours and Colonel Allen used to fall asleep and snore.'

Carter changed tack. 'I see you're entering for the best-kept village competition.'

Mrs Jennings chuckled. 'It's a scream, isn't it? Bit of a laugh. We went in for it last year but Mayhurst won, so this year we're trying to beat them.'

Carter remembered the name on the broken signpost. 'Is that the village next door?'

'That's right. There's quite a bit of rivalry between us, one way and another. Not much love lost. They fancy themselves, but to my way of thinking Fairfield's much the prettier. More natural, if you know what I mean.'

He knew exactly what Mrs Jennings meant.

'It's a good idea, really – the competition,' she went on, rearranging some packets of prunes. 'Gives us a tidy up. You should see the painting and the clipping and the mowing that goes on these two months before the judges come round. Miss Burton's in charge of the committee and she's at everybody's heels like a sheepdog. She's been on at me to get the shopfront repainted but, as I said to her, how am I going to afford it? And I can't do it myself. *I* can't climb ladders; I go all dizzy. She asked me just now when she was in if I'd mind if she got someone to paint it for nothing. They wouldn't charge a penny, she said, and Sir Phillip would pay for the paint. Well, I don't mind that. Why should I? I'm not proud. And it's all in a good cause. I'd like to see Mayhurst lose for once.'

'That's generous of Sir Phillip . . . to pay for the paint.'

She considered this. 'Miss Burton persuaded him. She could persuade anyone anything. Even Sir Phillip. I expect she's told him to get his own gates painted. I wouldn't be surprised.'

'What's he like?'

Mrs Jennings put her head on one side. 'Not what you might call easy – though perhaps I shouldn't say that. Now, Lady Dalrymple's another story. Kindness itself, she is. Game as anything. And no airs and graces. I feel sorry for her. Mind you, I can't blame him. I mean, who wouldn't be a bit difficult in his shoes?'

47

He was about to ask what particular shoes these were when the doorbell jangled and another customer came in – an old lady with a plastic shopping bag hooked over one arm who settled herself comfortably on the bentwood chair beside the counter and prepared for a nice long gossip. Carter left them to it and walked back to the van. It was well past midday and he felt ravenously hungry – too hungry to be content with stale crisps from the Bull. As he drove away he wondered whether Miss Burton's influence extended to Charlie and his pub, which could also do with some tidying up.

On his way back to Milton Spa he stopped at the Crown and Anchor. He ordered Betty Gordon's shepherd's pie and a tomato juice. The bar was half empty as many of the customers had taken their food and drink out into the garden and were sitting under the Courage umbrellas admiring Terry's handiwork with the petunias and geraniums. Carter could hear the high-pitched shrieks of children running about, creating havoc. Terry had had to fill in the small goldfish pond with its fishing gnome in case, as he had put it grimly, one of the little perishers drowned themselves.

Betty Gordon brought the shepherd's pie to him herself. She was a comfortable, motherly woman and one of the best cooks he knew. Except Jan. Jan had been a natural. The tiny kitchen in their London flat had been crammed with cookery books and she read them as other people read novels. She never seemed to have a failure. Every dish, whether it was French, Italian, Spanish, Chinese or plain old English, turned out just as it should be – or even better. And she did it all in a space not much bigger than a cupboard and without any modern gadgets. When he pictured her in his mind it was as she had so often been – standing over the museum-piece of a gas stove, spoon in hand, stirring, tasting and weaving her magic.

'Morning, Frank.' Terry had appeared behind the bar. 'Pie all right?'

'Great, as usual. My compliments to the chef.'

'I'll pass them on, but we don't want her getting big-headed. She might ask for a rise. That bloke I told you about is in today, by the way. The one who digs up old planes. Want to meet him?'

'Could be useful.'

'Right.'

Carter waited while the landlord moved up to the other end of the bar to speak to a dark-haired, middle-aged man who was drinking there alone. Even if Tom's plane had turned out to be a load of old rubbish, this contact of Terry's might have a real one on the books – something that would satisfy Ken Grant instead. After a moment the man came over and held out his hand.

'Bob Simpson's the name. Pleased to meet you. I hear you think you might've got wind of a Spit.'

Carter took the hand. Simpson had spoken with a marked Sussex accent, soft and mellow to the ear. He was a small man, wiry in build and ordinary to the point of being nondescript. There was nothing about him to suggest that his passion in life was something as out of the way as uncovering the wrecks of World War Two aeroplanes. Carter would have put him down as someone who enjoyed a quiet evening at the local, with perhaps a few hours fishing at weekends or a bit of spadework in the vegetable patch, plus the occasional day out with the wife and kids.

'I thought I might have done, but it turned out to be a false alarm.'

Once again, Carter retold the story. When he had finished Simpson nodded agreement.

'I think you're right. For one thing, I've never heard of a Spit coming down at Fairfield. We dug a Hurricane up at Mayhurst last year – about three miles away – but that's the nearest I know of. We've a pretty good idea where most of them are, you see. It's all in the records.'

'Records?'

'The Public Records Office at Kew. They've got all the RAF squadron operations records books and combat reports.

Margaret Mayhew

Then there's the local office at Lewes. The ARP and the
Observer Corps recorded everything that happened in the
area, not to mention the police. They give date, time and loca-
tion. We can look up the name of a village where the plane
came down and the name of the farm – it's usually in a field.
They even sometimes give Ordnance Survey map references.
Of course, those have all been changed since the war. We've
had to work out a system to convert the old grid to the new
one.'

'So there's no way one would have slipped through the
net?'

'Unlikely. But not impossible. There are planes, from both
sides, still unaccounted for – something like one hundred and
seventy RAF pilots are missing from the July to October
period in 1940, for instance. On September 11th twelve pilots
were recorded missing on that one day alone. We've recovered five of those since, but that's all. A lot of them must
have gone into the sea, of course. Or else the plane hasn't yet
been excavated to identify and locate them. It's all a long,
slow process of elimination, you see. You find the plane and
match the pilot. If you can.'

'Any more planes you're about to dig up?'

Bob Simpson shook his head. He said guardedly: 'Nothing
on the cards at the moment. We did one last weekend – a Spit
over at Newbridge. Bit of a disappointment. There wasn't
much of it left; just part of the prop and a few odd bits and
pieces. The recovery group must have cleared most of it at
the time of the crash.'

'Did that often happen?'

'Depends how busy they were and how easy recovery was.
It was all done by hand in those days, of course, and some of
the planes went in pretty deep.' Simpson held out his hands
wide. 'I could show you a photo of a hole in the ground no
more than a few feet across, taken just after a Hurry dived
into a ploughed field. No sign of the plane except a few small
fragments on the surface. Imagine trying to dig that out with
spades!'

'They must have had a tough job.'

'It must have been murder sometimes. The procedure was to cordon off the site so as to keep away the souvenir hunters and the kids. Then, if it was an enemy plane, the Intelligence boys would come along and have a peek to see if there was anything useful for them.'

'Such as?'

'Almost anything. New weapons. Modifications in the aircraft. Manufacturing labels . . . they could learn a lot from those about where the parts were being made in Germany so they could go and drob bombs on them. When they'd finished the recovery group would clear away as much of the wreckage as they could. Sometimes, though, they'd just chuck it all back down the hole and fill it in again.'

'What about the pilots or aircrews?'

'What they could find of them was removed for burial,' Simpson replied. 'A lot of the fighters were empty, of course. The pilots generally had the good sense to bail out in time.' He drained his glass. 'What'll you have?'

'Thanks. A tomato juice. With Worcester.'

Simpson raised his eyebrows. 'I thought Terry said you were a newspaperman.'

'I'm the only non-drinking reporter in the country.'

Simpson laughed and went away to get the drinks. When he returned, Carter asked him how long his group had been going.

'Ten years. It started more by accident than anything. The way these things often do, I suppose. I was out fishing on the Pevensey Marshes one day when I saw this propeller blade sticking up out of the mud at low tide. I was with a mate of mine and we went and borrowed a tractor from a local farmer and pulled out the engine of an American bomber. There was a bit about it later on in the local paper and people wrote in and said they knew where there was another plane buried . . . that kind of thing. It sort of snow-balled from there. There's quite a lot of us now – all sorts and shapes and sizes. We've got engineers, farmers, lorry drivers, draughtsmen, clerks . . . I'm a surveyor myself.' He smiled wryly. 'And secretary and treasurer of the group for my sins. It's a chore sometimes, but it's kept me out of mischief since my wife died.'

He'd scored a bullseye with the fishing, Carter thought, but there were no days out with the wife and kids. As widowers they had something in common, except that looking at the man drinking his beer quietly beside him, he knew there was no chance *he* could be blamed for his wife's death. She would have died decently in bed, not flung through the windscreen of a car. Carter offered the surveyor a cigarette, which was politely refused, then he lit up himself.

'I'm getting curiouser and curiouser all the time,' he said. 'How do you find these planes? I mean, I know there are records and that you get tipped off, but even so, a few feet wrong and you could miss it.'

'That's right.' Simpson set his beer mug down on the counter. 'But there are usually some good clues. If we're lucky enough to have the map reference we go to the nearest buildings and try and find someone who knows or remembers something about it. More often than not it's a farm and the farmer, or one of the farm workers, remembers seeing the plane come down and knows just where it is. Sometimes it's the farmer's son who was maybe fourteen or fifteen at the time. That's an impressionable age and they never forget.' He picked up his beer again. 'Once we've located the probable site we look for the clues. A crater in the ground, the grass growing differently in one spot, branches broken off trees, hedges with a gap in them . . . it's all still there, generally, even forty years on. We use metal detectors to narrow it down even more and make sure. Then we do an exploratory dig by hand before bringing in the JCB.'

'Sounds like a lot of hard work to me.'

Simpson smiled quietly. 'It can be. But I've got the time. Just the one kid and he's grown up and away from home now. I work odd hours anyway – out and about all over the place – so it suits me. And those old planes were real beauties.

You can keep all your modern bombers and fighters. Give me a Spit or a Hurry or a Lancaster or any of them. Even the German ones, come to that. They're worth saving. All of them.' He finished his beer and put the empty half-pint mug down. 'Well, I must be off. Sorry about that plane of yours.'

Carter put his hand in his pocket to settle up for the shepherd's pie and, as he did so, his fingers encountered the sharp edges of Tom's scrap of metal from the wood. He called Simpson back.

'I forgot about this. The old man gave it to me. He got it from under the leaves in the hollow where he said the plane was.'

The surveyor took the fragment and moved away from the pink glow of the bar lighting towards the window, where he examined it carefully. He even sniffed at it. After a moment he returned, looking thoughtful.

'It's a piece of aluminium all right – the blue corrosion tells you that. And it's been in some kind of shunt by the look of it.' He paused. 'Off the record I'd say it did belong to a crashed war plane.'

Carter tried hard not to look sceptical. 'You can tell that from a bit this size?'

'I've seen a lot of wreckage. You get a feeling for it after a while.'

Carter said slowly: 'You mean you think there *could* be a Spitfire there, after all?'

'Not necessarily. This could just be part of a chunk of plane that happened to fall into the wood while the rest of it ended up miles away.' The surveyor handed it back. 'Tell you what. I'm over near Fairfield tomorrow, checking some land drains. If you like, I could meet you. You could show me the place and I'll have a look for those clues I was telling you about.'

They fixed a time and Carter was left staring down at the crumpled aluminium in his hand. Bob Simpson's pronouncement had not thrilled him that much. For one thing he didn't really believe it. For another it meant a second traipse through Trodgers Wood, and all for nothing. He was beginning to wish he'd never turned right at those crossroads or gone near the bloody place.

Four

They had arranged to meet at the lychgate at eleven. This time Carter found his way without getting lost and parked his van close by. He was ten minutes early and so he got out and walked up and down while he was waiting for Bob Simpson to arrive. The cockerel and his retinue were scavenging outside the Bull. Someone had cleaned the pub windows and replanted the stone sink with bright salmon-pink geraniums instead of the previous moribund plants. There was also a new green litter bin, placed strategically near the wooden benches, although these, as usual, were empty despite the fine weather. Carter detected the hand of Miss Burton and her best-kept village competition committee at work. It was certainly not Charlie's. He smoked a cigarette to pass the time and was about to throw the butt away when, feeling the schoolteacher's invisible presence and eye on him, he crossed the road and placed it carefully in the litter bin.

The church clock struck eleven and the white doves cooed in unison on the nave roof. As the sound died away an old Sunbeam Talbot came rattling round the corner and drew up beside him. Bob Simpson climbed out. He was wearing an old green sweater and trousers tucked into rubber boots. Carter looked ruefully at his own thin-soled shoes.

They walked up the brick path, past old George Clark's grave where the flowers were beginning to fade, past Ezrah, Emma, Florence Mary, Hannah and the rest and on round the church to the stile. As they traversed the field towards Trodgers Wood, Carter glanced up at the big house. No one was watching this time, or if they were it was from behind closed windows.

55

He managed the barbed wire fence better, ducking through after the surveyor between the strands. Simpson was as at home in such conditions as old Tom had been. Once in the wood, however, it was Carter's turn to take the initiative. He set off in what he hoped was the right direction. The trouble was that he had not paid much attention when he had been with the old man, never dreaming that he would need to find the way again without him. He blundered on uncertainly, hoping to see some landmark that he might remember. Where was that path? And where the hell was Tom, anyway? Hiding behind some tree and watching them, most likely. The chances were that the sight of Simpson would scare him off and he'd never show himself. Somewhere in the depths of the wood he could hear a cuckoo calling repetitively and mockingly. Carter stopped and turned.

'I'm sorry, Bob. I'm lost. I can't remember where the hell the place was.'

Simpson looked about him. 'Not to worry. We'll find it sooner or later. There must be some kind of track leading to it if it's near the old man's hut. He must use it all the time.'

Carter was less sanguine. The wood had become so over-grown and was such an impenetrable tangle of old and new growth that it could take hours to find Tom's hut and, from there, the hollow. He was about to suggest that they gave the whole thing up when there was a faint rustle of dry leaves and a dark shape materialized before him. Tom's dog looked up at him with his yellow eyes. There was no sign of the old man but Carter had no doubt he was skulking somewhere close at hand. He spoke quietly to the collie, holding out his hand, but it bared its sharp teeth in a soundless snarl.

'Looks like we're not welcome,' Simpson said. 'Is that the old man's dog?'

'Yeah. And I don't fancy trying to get past him. Where's Tom, for God's sake? He'd better call him off if he wants us to do anything about that Spitfire of his.'

Carter shouted the words out loudly. There was silence for a moment and then he heard a faint whistle from somewhere deeper in the wood. As suddenly as he had appeared, the black and white dog turned and vanished again into the under-growth. After a few seconds he reappeared, looked at them unwinkingly and then disappeared again. He repeated this once more.

Carter laughed. 'I think we're meant to follow him. He's been sent back to round us up like a couple of lost sheep. Tom isn't far off but I doubt if he'll show himself. He's not sure who you are. You might have come to take him away to a home.'

They went after the collie, forcing a way through where the dog had passed easily. He trotted ahead, moving with his low, slinking gait. At intervals he stopped to wait, watching them with his bright eyes, his pink tongue lolling over his teeth. He kept an even distance between himself and them. Once or twice Carter was sure he caught a glimpse of the old man, flitting like some hoary wood elf from tree to tree ahead of them.

Before long they were on a path that Carter remembered and after that they made faster progress, half-running to keep up with the dog. When they reached the stream the collie plunged straight in, bounded across and stopped to shake his coat on the far side. Carter made exactly the same mistake with the stepping stones as before and soaked his trouser leg, while Simpson strode over easily in his boots. When they reached the tin hut the dog went and sat on his haunches outside the entrance. There was no way of knowing whether his master was inside or not and Carter, looking from the hut door to the half-bared canine teeth, decided not to try and find out.

'I think Tom's taken cover in there,' he told Simpson. 'We'd better leave him alone. This is the end of the trail, anyway. The hollow's just a hundred yards or so further on.'

They left the dog on guard. Carter had no difficulty in finding the place and when they stood on the edge of the small cliff he pointed to where Tom had uncovered the piece of aluminium. Simpson nodded. He said nothing but slid down the bank and walked about the area. Carter sat wearily on a tree stump and squeezed the water out of his trouser leg. He lit a cigarette. All the doubts he had always felt from the very beginning had multiplied on seeing this spot again. There was no clue whatsoever, so far as he could see, that a plane had plummeted to earth here. Nothing so cataclysmic had ever disturbed this sylvan grove – he was damn sure of it. It would be easier to believe in fairies. Peaseblossom, Cobweb, Moth and Mustardseed would come forth before any Spitfire remains. As if to echo his thoughts, the cuckoo mocked again, close by.

The surveyor took his time. He looked up into the trees about the hollow, then he moved away to a distance and squatted on his heels, studying the ground. After that he walked about again, kicking over the leaves with his heavy boots and staring at the earth beneath. Twice he bent to pick something up and each time he examined his find closely. For several minutes he simply stood and contemplated the spot in silence.

Carter felt himself losing patience. He threw away his cigarette and stood up.

'Well? What do you think?'

Simpson turned. He said cheerfully: 'Oh, I think there's a plane here.'

Carter stared. 'Are you sure?'

'Pretty sure.' The surveyor groped in his pocket and scrambled back up the bank again. 'Look. Here's another piece of aluminium like the one the old man found before – and this one's got a rivet hole.'

The piece of metal, badly crumpled like the previous find, had a neat round hole near one edge. Simpson delved in his other pocket.

'And this is the clincher.' He held up a transparent shard between thumb and forefinger. 'Perspex. It's part of the cockpit.'

'Are you saying there's a whole aircraft down there? You're sure it's not just bits and pieces that fell off as it went over?'

'I don't think so. A lot of these trees have grown up since, but if you look at those older ones over there you'll see that there are some branches missing – they're all lopsided. The plane did that. And if you study the level of the ground down in the hollow you'll notice a saucer-shaped depression near the centre. That's where it went in. The earth's very boggy down there. We're at the bottom of the valley and there's a marsh and a pond just beyond those trees. This hollow may have been part of that marsh forty years ago and dried out since. I'd guess the fighter sank in pretty deep. The wings would almost certainly have been torn off; they'll be around here somewhere but well hidden by now.' Simpson smiled drily. 'I can see you're still not convinced. Pity I couldn't find some bullets for you. They're usually scattered around near the surface.'

'Sorry, Bob. It just seems incredible. A whole bloody plane here all this time. And nobody except Tom knowing about it. How the hell could it have been missed?'

Simpson shrugged. 'Anybody's guess now. The valley's deep and thickly wooded. Visibility's not too good. It's no surprise that no one's found it since. It's obvious nobody ever comes here but Tom. The wood belongs to Sir Phillip Dalrymple of Fairfield Hall – I looked it up. He's known locally for discouraging trespassers on his land.'

'Is that what we've been doing? I thought there was a public right of way.'

'The footpath skirts the wood. We left it at the edge of the field by the fence. Since then we've been trespassing, I'm afraid.'

'Ah.'

Carter stared at the hollow. The trespassing didn't worry him nearly so much as what to think or believe. Supposing Bob Simpson was right and there really was a long-lost Spitfire buried here? He looked up at the missing branches. The timber was so neglected in the wood that the damage might equally have been caused by disease or overcrowding. As for the faint depression in the ground, who was to say that wasn't just natural subsidence? The aluminium could have fallen off a stricken plane but the perspex was more difficult to explain away. Tails and wings tended to drop off shot-up aircraft, but cockpits generally stayed put. He said at last: 'Well, what do we do next?'

'We can't do anything unless Sir Phillip gives his permission.'

'I have a strange feeling that might not be easy to get.'

Simpson smiled quietly. 'So do I. Still, we can but try. I'll get in touch with him officially and ask if he'd let my group carry out an exploratory dig by hand, at least. No disturbance, no mess. He might agree. Landowners are usually very helpful, but it's true this dig would give us more headaches than most, being so far in the wood.' He put the trophies away in his pocket. 'I'd like to do it, though. It's a mystery. A bit of a puzzler. And that makes it all the more interesting.'

'What about the pilot? Do you think he's in there?'

'More likely bailed out. If they could, they did. If he didn't and we do get as far as excavating, then we could have problems. The Ministry of Defence are a bit touchy these days about disturbing plane wrecks that might have human remains in them. Apart from the landowner's permission, we'll need theirs too. Still, no pilot in his senses would try and land a plane in the middle of a wood when he had some perfectly good, nice flat fields all around – that big cornfield up by the old schoolhouse, for instance. He was either dead already or, much more likely, not in the plane at all. Nobody knows yet what happened for sure, and we may never know.'

Carter looked thoughtfully at the hollow and felt a stirring of interest. He liked mysteries too. Especially ones likely to intrigue newspaper readers. And Frank was right about the Spitfire appeal. Everyone knew about the plane. Strong men had been known to weep at the sight of those elliptical wings soaring through the sky. The plane had a magic and nostaglia value all of its own. In the popular imagination, England's salvation had depended on that tiny fighter alone – the golden chariot of fire flown by the Few against the whole might of

Hitler's Luftwaffe – even though, as he'd read somewhere, there were actually more Hurricanes combatant during the Battle of Britain. And not only the British admired the plane. He'd read too that Germans used to boast that they'd been shot down by a Spitfire. There was a kind of Spitfire snobbery, and to have been nabbed by a mere Hurricane lacked the same cachet. 'Give us Spitfires, Herr Reichsmarschall', or words to that effect, some German war ace had asked rather recklessly when Goering had enquired what was most needed to further the Nazi cause.

Carter shook his head. He was getting as sentimental as Ken and his retired readers. If there was anything under those dead leaves it was no more than a heap of twisted metal. Still, if they could get it out, it wouldn't make a bad story.

Simpson was looking at his watch. Time was running out before his next appointment and, in any case, there was nothing more they could do at this stage. Thanks to his good sense of direction, they found their way back out of the wood with only one false turn, re-passing Tom's hut where there was no sign of either the old man or his dog. Carter guessed he'd been watching them at the hollow and thought it was a pity they couldn't give him the good news. As they walked up the field towards the stile, he pointed out the big house to the surveyor.

'That's the Dalrymple pad.'

'Yes, I know. I looked that up on the Ordnance map, too. Very nice. I think we're being watched, by the way.'

Carter saw that the surveyor was right. The French windows were open and, although there was no glint from binoculars this time, he could see the same figure seated there. It was too far away to make out anything other than a vague outline, but he had a very clear image of a bluff, barking military type with fingers itching for his shotgun.

'I hope we're on the public footpath.'

'We are now.'

They climbed on up to the stile. Simpson paused to look back at the wood. He shook his head as though almost unable to believe his own conviction. They climbed over and went round the church to the lychgate. The surveyor climbed into his old Sunbeam Talbot.

'We'll try our luck with Sir Phillip. Like I say, you never know.' He hesitated. 'I'd be grateful if you'd keep it under your hat. If word gets round we'll have all kinds trampling round that wood with metal detectors and they won't give a damn if they're trespassing or not. Wouldn't do our chances much good.'

Carter nodded. Simpson waved and drove off, the car backfiring once loudly as it vanished round the corner past the war memorial and the green.

There was a family saloon car parked outside the Bull and a young couple with a small child were sitting on one of the benches outside the door. The child was grizzling and squirming discontentedly on his mother's lap and the whimpering turned to indignant wails as she tried to placate him with one of Charlie's stale crisps. Exasperated, the father leaned across and slapped his son hard on the leg at which his wife turned on him like a she-cat. Between them, their offspring screamed at top volume. The joys of parenthood, Carter thought, as he drove off in the van. He turned the corner by the village green. He'd looked forward to being a father once. Jan's baby would have been six years old by now. He'd never known if it was a boy or girl; at four months there had been no chance of independent survival. Anyway it was better not to know. Somehow, though, he always pictured it as a girl – a blue-eyed kid with straight blonde hair like her mother. Jan had wanted a girl. They'd been going to call her Anna after Jan's Swedish grandmother.

The gates of Fairfield Hall stood open. There was no evidence, however, that Miss Burton's clean-up campaign had triumphed here as well; the paintwork was as rusty as before. Carter slowed and stopped outside the entrance. He was curious about the owner. Why was he so difficult and what were the extenuating 'shoes' referred to by Mrs Jennings? Was it he who kept vigil with binoculars at the French windows? What sort of man would Bob Simpson and his group have to deal with? The rector had told him that the family had lived at the Hall for years. There had been Dalrymple memorial stones dotted about the church and he had an idea that one of the brasses had been for a Dalrymple. There might be something of interest if he dug around a little, disturbed the calm surface of Ken Grant's village pond. A line or two, perhaps, for the paper's Town and Country Diary on page twelve. How do you see your role in modern village life, Sir Phillip? *No different from in the Middle Ages.* Have there been many changes in your lifetime? *Not if he could help it.* But things *had* changed, thank God, and the upper classes had lost the upper hand. They could bluster and bray all they liked but it would never be the same again.

It was worth a try. Carter turned the van into the entrance and up a long driveway, bordered with rhododendron bushes and laurels. Gloomy and depressing. Further on the drive divided into two. The right-hand fork led towards an old stable block, now used for garaging. There was no Rolls in sight, just a K-registration blue Mini and a Land Rover. He could see a walled garden beyond the stables and several large greenhouses. He drove on, following the left-hand sweep which took him up to the house and the front door. He stopped the van, switched off the engine and got out. Close up, the place didn't look quite so good as it had done from down below in the field. Like the gates, the windows needed a repaint and some of the stonework was in bad condition. Even so, it was an impressive Georgian pile. A thick creeper grew over the front, softening the starkness of the stone, and a stately porticoed entrance shielded the front door. He tugged at the brass bell pull set in the wall. A high hedge concealed the rest of the garden from prying eyes, but through an archway he could see part of the lawn.

The door opened and a girl looked at him enquiringly. She was no beauty. The hazel eyes, set very wide apart, were partly obscured by a ragged, rat-chewed fringe, which reached almost to her tilted nose. The rest of the hair, which was dark and

63

rather greasy, was worn screwed up into a wispy knot on the top of her head. She wore no make-up, her skin was poor and she looked as though she might collapse from exhaustion at any minute. Her jeans were dirty at the knees and the man's shirt she wore had a grease stain down the front. Against all the odds, it all still added up to something appealing, and Carter composed his face into a practised leer. The overworked, exploited au pair, he thought.

'Is Sir Phillip at home?' he asked slowly and clearly.

Her eyes slid towards the newspaper van and he could see her instinctively pulling up the drawbridge. Even a Heidi or a Gretchen would probably recognize it for what it was. She looked at him again, coolly.

'What did you want to see him about?'

The accent was pure, cut-glass, upper-crust English. Carter did a quick rethink. The daughter of the house, he decided. He would have expected her to appear in a skirt and cashmere sweater, or at least jolly old jodphurs and a sensible shirt, but the Fionas and Carolines today were busy rebelling along with everyone else. Whoever she was, she was becoming more distant every second.

'I'm Frank Carter from the *Milton Weekly Courier*. I'm doing a piece on Fairfield, its history and so on. I'd be grateful if Sir Phillip could give me a few minutes of his time.'

As always, when talking to the top drawer he was conscious of his bottom-drawer accent. The years since childhood had smoothed off some of the rougher edges to his speech, but it was still Newcastle. In a way he was proud of it – he was certainly not ashamed. It never bothered him except at times like this. And what bothered him was that he should ever give a damn.

'Do you have an appointment? I don't remember Sir Phillip mentioning it.'

'Sorry, no. But it won't take long, I promise. Just a few quick questions.'

The distance between them was becoming wider, actually and figuratively. She reached for the door handle.

'I'm awfully sorry, but I'm afraid I don't think he'd want to see you. Perhaps if you wrote a letter . . .'

He smiled at her with as much charm as he could muster, which, when he wished, was not inconsiderable. 'The trouble is that the article's going in the paper this week. I only need a word or two from Sir Phillip – as squire of the village.'

She stared and then laughed quite suddenly; the strained look in her face disappeared for a moment. 'Squire of the village – that's frightfully old-fashioned, isn't it?'

'Not to some people,' he said, with truth. Like half the readers of the *Courier*.

He watched her trying to make him out, trying to decide whether he was going to be a flaming nuisance or whether she could trust him to behave like the gentleman he wasn't. He smiled at her again, winningly. She brushed away the fringe of hair from her eyes in a weary gesture and surrendered the drawbridge.

'If it's really only for a few minutes . . . You'd better come in, Mr Carter. I'll ask him if he'll see you.'

He had never set foot in an English country house of any distinction before. This was small fry by the standards of the great stately homes, but it was still not to be sneezed at. He looked around the big hall with interest. It was a great improvement on Councillor Jackson's mock-Tudor pile outside Milton Spa. The councillor's furnishings had looked as though they had been bought up en masse from the show window of a high-street store. Here, even Carter's untutored eye could see that everything had been part of this house for years and belonged to it as much as the stone fabric. The oak coffer standing against the wall had probably been doing that for a century or more; the Indian carpet, worn in places by generations of Dalrymple feet, was no relation to the patterned Axminster that stretched from wall to wall in the councillor's des res. The ancestor looking down his aristocratic nose from the gilded frame over the fireplace would sniff loudly, if he could, at the skein of geese at sunset flying in rigid V formation over the councillor's electric logs.

'If you'll wait in the drawing room, I'll tell my husband you're here.'

Carter looked at the girl, thinking he had misheard her.

'Your husband?'

'Sir Phillip,' she said. 'That's who you wanted to see, isn't it? I'm Zoe Dalrymple. Sir Phillip's wife.' She opened the door with a small smile. 'In here, Mr Carter.'

The drawing room was even better than the hall but Carter, smarting from his own stupidity, looked around sourly. This was gracious country living, free from the least hint of Councillor Jackson's Dralon and leatherette vulgarities and moon miles from the front parlour he remembered himself as a kid. Everything was classy but understated and it had been put together with the kind of careless good taste that the upper classes hand down but interior decorators can never hand out. The two large sofas, one on each side of the fireplace, were covered in faded chintz and comfortable cushions. The immense Chinese rug was probably worth a small fortune and, from the line marks tracking back and forth, it looked as though someone had been casually pushing a pram across the priceless pile. The furniture all looked antique as hell. What else would it be, Carter thought. It was all treated as casually as the carpet. A pigeon-hole desk was stuffed untidily with papers and letters; a round, leather-topped table was strewn with old newspapers and magazines; a tall glass-fronted cupboard housed a jumbled and dusty collection of exquisite porcelain and, in a window alcove, there was a magnificent grand piano, lid shut, yellowing sheet music on the rack and its surface covered with the family photos of many years. A silver-framed boy in a sailor suit stared coldly at Carter. Next to him there was a sepia print of a thin and elegant woman in a long, Twenties-style dress with feathers in her hair; she had rather a pained expression on her face – probably, he thought, because of the feathers, which looked as though they might be tickling her. He moved on and found himself looking at a stiff studio portrait of the girl who had opened the door to him. He hardly recognized her in her evening gown, two-strand pearl necklace and coiffeur-set hair. She was gazing into the middle distance, somewhere over his left shoulder. He considered the photograph for some time and decided that he much preferred her in jeans and a man's shirt and with greasy, un-set hair. It was nothing to do with his self-acknowledged resentment of the upper classes; it was just that she looked better that way. What was she? A child bride? The second or third Lady Dalrymple? A last try for Sir Phillip before he gave the whole thing up and settled for looking after his roses?

There was a bowl of yellow and pink roses in the centre of the drum table and he could smell their sweet scent. He flicked open a copy of *Country Life*. There was a nice Tudor mansion – real, not mock – going for anyone who could find three hundred and fifty thousand pounds, and a cosy little mews house in Kensington for a mere eighty. He turned the page. The Honourable Annabel Cunningham-Greene was being rash enough to marry Captain Marcus Willoughby at the Guards' Chapel on July 9th. Another English rose picked in the bud.

Carter went over to the open windows. From here the owner of the binoculars must have watched his progress across the field. The tree tops of Trodgers Wood were visible on the right but the boundary of the wood was not, he was glad to see. With luck, he had only been observed on the public footpath. From up here, as at the stile by the church, there was a very clear view of the pattern of fields stretching away towards the South Downs and the sea. The more Carter looked at the landscape the more he saw that Bob Simpson had been right: only a dead or absent pilot would have let his plane go down in that wood.

The garden, like the house, was a bit run down. There were more weeds about than he had expected and some of the shrubs had got out of hand. An elderly man in a flat cap, waistcoat and string-tied trouser legs was mowing the wide lawn with a machine almost as old as himself. He plodded up and down, the motor coughing and spluttering, leaving odd tufts of long grass behind him where the blades had missed their target completely. At the end of one traverse the engine died and the gardener creaked to his knees to coax it into life again. Carter grinned and shook his head.

He stuck his head out of the windows and looked along the terrace. There were mossy stone flags, a carved balustrade and a flight of steps leading down to the lawn. A swing seat that had seen better days stood on the right and, near it, a rickety-looking table and some equally battered cane armchairs. Unlike the weeds, the garden furniture was no surprise to him. To people like the Dalrymples, Hollywood poolside-type loungers would have been both vulgar and unnecessary. He looked down with some curiosity at a wooden ramp fitted from the sill of the French windows to the terrace level a foot or so below. Perhaps the old boy was so doddery he couldn't make steps any more.

To the left he could see the tower of the church rising above its protective ring of trees. The clock chimed one o'clock and, behind him, a French ormolu and marble clock joined in too in an arpeggio of high, silvery notes. Carter looked at his own watch. He hadn't realized it was so late. It had been a bloody stupid time to call.

The drawing-room door opened suddenly and violently, crashing back on its hinges. The man who entered glared ferociously at Carter.

'You've got five minutes. Not a second more. Then out!'

Mrs Jennings' sympathy, the youth and strained look of Lady Dalrymple, the lines on the carpet, the wooden ramp on to the terrace were all explained to Carter as he turned. The squire of Fairfield was not at all the blimpish old curmudgeon he had imagined. He was about the same age as himself and must have been very good-looking once, before the disease or accident that had put him in his wheel-chair had distorted his body and crippled his limbs so that he was now a grotesque and pitiful sight. His hands were crabbed and twisted and his head hunched deep into his shoulders. His face, pale as his wife's, was marked with the ravages of pain and suffering. Beneath it all, Carter recognized the

68

small, fair-haired boy in the sailor suit of the silver-framed photograph.

'I'm doing a short piece for the *Courier* on the history of Fairfield—'

The door crashed shut and the wheelchair was propelled fast towards Carter, leaving fresh tracks on the carpet. Carter stepped out of the way.

'Why?'

'It's an interesting old village, sir. Very little seems to have changed in the last fifty years or so. Your family has lived here a very long time. I'd like to ask you a few questions, if you don't mind.'

'But I do mind, Mr Carter. I mind very much. And it's me who's going to be asking the questions.' The baronet spoke with a curious staccato cadence.

The chair, which squeaked, rolled on towards the French windows. Sir Phillip picked up the binoculars from the table.

'I've been watching you through these. I should like to know what you have been doing trespassing on my land.'

'There is a public footpath across the field, sir . . .'

The wheelchair spun round with amazing force. 'I may be a cripple, Mr Carter, but I've not lost my wits. I know you've been trespassing. There is no public footpath through Trodgers Wood. You have trespassed twice. The first time alone yesterday morning. The second time a short while ago when you were with another man – a fellow news hound, I imagine.' The chair moved closer. 'I'll save you the trouble of explaining. My gardener drinks at the Bull. He's there every evening. He told me all about the newspaper reporter who fell for Tom's Spitfire story. We had a good laugh about it. I was actually quite amused, at first. I thought you must be a complete fool. Any entertainment is welcome here, Mr Carter. Even the sight of you hotfoot across the fields in pursuit of Tom's plane.'

The chair squeaked again as it moved towards the fireplace. 'Now I see you, you don't look quite such a fool. And it's less entertaining to have you here in my drawing room claiming to write some rubbish for that rag of yours. What heading did you have in mind? Crippled baronet speaks of mystery Spitfire? MS-stricken landowner refutes legend of missing wartime fighter? Something along those lines?'

Carter battled for self-control. Years ago anyone who had spoken to him like that would have regretted it. Since then he'd learned to swallow every kind of rejection and insult. It was all part of the job. Newsmen were dirt. Less than dirt, sometimes. Besides, when it came to it the man had a point. He *had* been trespassing. He said quietly: 'I'm not here under false pretences. My editor asked me to get some local material while I was investigating Tom's story.'

'Am I the local material? Barren Baronet of Doomed Dalrymples? Except that men can't be barren, can they? Only women. Men are sterile or impotent, or even just incapable. I thought you wrote for the local weekly, Carter, not the *News of the World*.'

He was so bitter that the bitterness almost polluted the air around him. Carter substituted his resentment for pity, but he knew better than to show it.

'I had no idea that you were ill, sir. I was just digging around. There'll be nothing printed about you in the *Courier*.'

There was a moment's silence. Then the wheelchair squeaked towards the window again. Phillip Dalrymple seemed unable to stay in one spot for long, as though to keep on the move compensated in some way for his real immobility.

'Who was that man with you?'

'Bob Simpson. He's the treasurer of a local aviation archeology group.'

'Don't tell me he was fooled by Tom's story, too?'

'He didn't believe it at first, any more than I did, sir. But when I checked it out alone Tom uncovered another piece of metal in the wood. I showed that piece to Bob Simpson when I met him by chance in a pub. He thought it could belong to a plane. I took him to the spot in Trodgers Wood this morning to have a look. He found another large fragment and a piece of perspex, which he says is part of a cockpit. Some of the tree branches are missing where he thinks the fighter came down and there's a depression in the ground where he thinks it went in. He thinks there *is* a plane there.'

'And what is he proposing to do about it?'

Carter hesitated. There was no point in dissimulation. 'He's going to ask your permission to do an exploratory dig, by hand, to make sure.'

'Kind of him to go to all that trouble,' Phillip Dalrymple said with heavy sarcasm.

'He's been excavating war planes for ten years. I think he knows what he's talking about.'

'Do you? Do you, indeed?' The wheelchair trundled back to the fireplace again. 'So you believe in Tom's Spitfire, after all? I'm disappointed in you, Carter.'

'I believe it's possible. No more than that, at the moment. Do you mind if I have a cigarette, sir?'

'Not if you give me one. Zoe hides them from me. The quacks say I shouldn't smoke. It's bad for my health. Rather amusing that, don't you think?'

Carter offered one of his filter-tips and lit it for him. The crabbed fingers gripped the cigarette with difficulty and determination.

'You sound as though you come from the north somewhere, Carter.'

'From Newcastle.'

'A Geordie! You're a long way from home.'

'It's been a while since I was in Newcastle. I spent ten years in London before I came down here. In Fleet Street.'

'Fleet Street to the local rag! Something of a comedown.'

'My present editor wouldn't agree.'

'And how long have you been with the *Courier*?'

'About six months.'

The baronet's head twisted on its shoulders to look up at him. 'No more big scoops. It must be all flower shows and fund-raisings. Why did you leave Fleet Street?'

'I was fired.'

'Ah!' The wheelchair squeaked to and fro restlessly. 'Well, at least you're gainfully employed now, Carter. Which is more

than can be said of me. I'm unemployable. I can't be hired
and I can't be fired. All I can do is sit here. And I can't even
do that very well.'

Carter took a breath. 'About the plane, sir . . .'

'To hell with the plane! It doesn't exist. Your five minutes
was up long ago. You can get out!'

The unguarded moment of self-pity had gone and the angry
arrogance was back. Carter sighed. Simpson didn't have a
chance. He fished in his pocket to make one last bid.

'This is the piece of metal Tom gave me from the wood.
It's aluminium. You can tell that from the blue powdering.'

'I did do chemistry at school, thank you.' Phillip Dalrymple
took hold of the fragment awkwardly. 'I can see it's aluminium.
But that's *all* I can see. It could have belonged to anything.
Any old pot or pan.'

'Rather a thin pan, sir. Or pot. When you look at it.'

'I *have* looked at it and now I'm putting it where it belongs.'

Carter said nothing as the metal clinked into a waste-paper
bin. If the squire hoped for a reaction he was going to be
disappointed. Carter had specialized since the classroom in
blank looks and, when pressed, in what the army calls dumb
insolence. The wheelchair was on the move again, wearing
the carpet out.

He tried one last tack. 'You can't be so sure there isn't a
plane there, sir. Not without more investigation. And Bob
Simpson's not a fool, I promise you that. He knows what he's
about. Have you thought there might be a pilot there who
ought to be identified and given a decent burial?'

The wheelchair stopped abruptly. 'That won't wash, Carter.
And you've got a bloody nerve. Don't start shedding crocodile
tears all over the place and pretending to be righteous. You don't
give a damn about any pilot. All you're interested in is a good
story.' Phillip Dalrymple squinted up through cigarette smoke.
'My father was blown to bits on active service in the Atlantic
in 1944. He has no grave but he's no less of a hero for that.'

'I saw his memorial plaque in the church. At least there is
that. And you know what happened to him.'

'I know what happened to him, all right. He was murdered by the Germans.'

'Murdered? On active service?'

'Yes, Carter. Murdered. His ship was sunk by a U-boat. Those of the crew who weren't already dead took to the lifeboats, my father included. They might have survived – been picked up by another ship – except for the German plane that dive-bombed them and blew them out of the water. One of the boatloads *did* live to tell the tale. That's how we know what happened to him.'

There was a pause. Carter said doggedly: 'Doesn't that make you think it might be a good idea to find and preserve something like a Spitfire, which fought against the Germans?'

'Not if it's on my land. Even if there were any truth in Tom's story – which there isn't – I should still refuse permission. I've no intention of letting loose a pack of fanatics on Trodgers Wood.' The baronet stroked the binoculars, which he was still cradling almost like a baby under one arm. 'These belonged to my father, you know. Spoils of war. He pinched them from a captured U-boat commander and brought them home with him on leave. His last leave. I was born four months after he was killed. I inherited, in utero, the title, this house and the land on which you have been trespassing – all at the very second when that lifeboat disintegrated into little pieces.'

'You wouldn't remember the war then, sir?'

'I follow your meaning, Carter, but it makes no difference. My mother was here all during the war. So was my grandmother and she didn't die until 1962. My mother died five years ago. They had plenty of time to mention, in passing, a Spitfire at the bottom of the garden. And, apart from school and university, I've spent all my life here in this house. My condition, as you will have noticed, obliges me to stay put. Nobody – either in the family, the staff or the village – has ever spoken of this plane, except for poor old Tom. Satisfied, Carter?'

So that was that. With the only evidence in the bin there wasn't much mileage in continuing the argument with a man

73

who'd made up his mind from the first not to listen. Carter gave up and took his leave. As he reached the door Phillip Dalrymple called after him.

'Leave me a few cigarettes, would you? There's a good chap.'

Carter went back and handed him the rest of the pack. As he left the drawing room and crossed the hall, Zoe Dalrymple appeared. She was carrying a fish slice in her hand and there was a smell of cooking coming from somewhere.

'I hope my husband was able to help you, Mr Carter.'

He looked down at her, feeling distinctly unfriendly towards all Dalrymples and their kind.

'No. He wasn't.'

Grease was dripping from the slice on to the Indian carpet and there was more grease down her shirt front. God, she was a messy cook.

She said suddenly and with an awkwardness that disarmed him: 'It's because of his illness. It's been frightfully hard for him, you see. He was so active before. Marvellous at sports. In all the teams. Victor Ludorum at Eton. A rowing blue at Oxford.' She looked up from beneath the rat-chewed fringe. 'You can imagine how it's been. Awfully difficult for him to adjust.'

He could imagine it only too well. A man born with a silver spoon in his mouth and holding all the cards – talent, good looks, wealth, background – was going to find it a lot harder to adjust than someone who had been dealt all the duds and never counted on anything.

He said more gently: 'I'm sorry I disturbed him, Lady Dalrymple.'

'Oh, you won't have done him any harm. In fact you'll have done him a lot of good. He doesn't get many visitors. It's his own fault, really. He wants people to talk to and then when they do come he gets all bitter and angry and spoils it. So silly, but he can't help himself.'

'I can understand it.'

'Can you?' She looked doubtful. 'I don't think anyone who

hasn't suffered like that could know quite what it's like. People are terribly good in the village, of course, but they don't like to keep dropping in. It would be better really if we lived in one of the cottages . . . And the illness frightens people, you know. They don't know much about multiple sclerosis and they're not sure if they can catch it.'

Carter sniffed the air. 'I think something's burning.'

She gave a wail of horror. 'My God! The fat! I left it on!'

Acrid smoke had penetrated as far as the hall. Zoe Dalrymple vanished through a door at the far end and down a long passage. Carter, following, heard a shriek of fright. He broke into a run.

The smoke in the kitchen was thick as a London fog. Flames leaped ceilingwards from a pan on the Aga cooker.

'*Jesus Christ*! Where's the lid?' he shouted.

She was stumbling about, wrenching open cupboard doors, coughing and choking. A chair went over with a crash.

'For God's sake, woman! The *lid*!'

'I can't find it! I can't find it!'

She was almost sobbing in desperation. Carter, his eyes streaming, swore violently. Through the smoke he had caught sight of a roller towel on the wall. He wrenched it off, soaked it under the sink tap, wrung it out and flung it over the inferno. The flames subsided. He looked about, searching unknown territory for something more, and saw the pan lid lying on the kitchen table. He clamped it quickly down on top of the towel and the fire disappeared as though by magic. Carter dragged the pan off the hotplate and shut down the Aga lid. There was still a sizzling and a spluttering going on but the fire was out.

'Let's get some air in here.'

Both coughing hard, they flung open windows and the back door. Smoke poured out into the yard beyond in great billowing clouds. Gradually the room cleared and they could breathe properly again.

If the mistress of the house had looked a mess before, she was even worse now. Her face was streaked with dirt and was dead-white with shock. Most of the hair had come loose from the topknot and straggled about her shoulders. Carter thought she was about to keel over. He righted the chair she had knocked down in her frantic hunt for the lid and held it out for her.

'Better sit down a minute. You don't look too good.'

She collapsed into the chair. After a moment she said shakily: 'I don't know how to thank you, Mr Carter. How *could* I have been so stupid?'

'Don't mention it. All in a day's work.' He paused. 'Sorry about the language.'

'Oh, I don't care about that. What does that matter?' She clapped her hands over her face. 'When I think what might have happened! The whole house might have burned down!'

'Don't think about it. It didn't.' Carter nodded towards the pan sizzling away on the side of the stove. 'I shouldn't touch that lot for quite a while. Let it cool right down. Was that your lunch in there?'

She let her fingers slide slowly down her cheeks and smiled. 'Yes. It was fish. I'll have to think of something else now. I'm a hopeless cook anyway. Absolutely useless. Would you believe that I once did a Cordon Bleu course and I still can't even boil an egg properly?'

He thought of Jan and her evening classes at the local poly. Then he stopped thinking.

'Neither can I. It's no disgrace.'

The smile widened and some colour appeared in her face. She stood up and began to shut the cupboard doors, left open in the panic. Carter had time now to notice the kitchen and saw that it was chaos. Even discounting the open doors and sundry scattered objects, it was a disaster area. Nothing was tidy and not much put away. The deep, old-fashioned sink was full of unwashed dishes. The pine table in the centre of the room, where he had found the pan lid, was also the repository of a strange medley of items; a reel of black cotton, a bottle of ink, a loaf of bread, a tin opener, several books, a tin of lubricating oil, a bottle of milk, a pair of garden shears and a tin of white gloss paint. It was like Kim's Game set up and ready for play. The shelves of a huge pine dresser were stocked with rows of unmatching plates and a collection of cups and mugs of all colours, shapes and sizes hung along the front of the shelves on brass hooks. The bottom shelf of the dresser contained a number of cookery books, all old, dusty and obviously unopened for years. The nearest title to Carter was *Wartime Cookery: 101 Ways with Dried Eggs*. Above the sink, on the kitchen window ledge, some dejected-looking plants were declining rather than growing. The indoor gardening at the Hall appeared roughly on a par with the cooking and housekeeping.

There was a squeak-squeak from the passage and Phillip Dalrymple wheeled himself through the doorway.

'Trying to burn the house down, Zoe? Or just incincerating the lunch, as usual?' He looked at Carter. 'I thought I told you to go, not come snooping in here.'

'You have Mr Carter to thank for the fact that the house *isn't* burned down, Phillip. Or at least the kitchen. I left the fat on. He put out the fire.'

'I see. How incredibly careless of you, Zoe. But so like you. And how nice for you, Carter. You have a story after all. How I saved historic family house from disaster! I could write the copy for you, if you like. Let me see . . . A lucky chance brought me to crippled baronet, Sir Phillip Dalrymple's home, Fairfield Hall—'

'Don't, Phillip!'

He swung his wheelchair round towards his wife. 'Don't what? Don't mention that I'm crippled? Or don't tease him? Neither will worry him, I promise you. He's been a Fleet Street hack in his heyday. Nothing could possibly shock or embarrass him now. He's immune to every human condition or action – aren't you, Carter?'

'More or less.'

'There you are. I told you. So, where was I? Ah yes. I quote: "I had gone to interview Sir Phillip, the thirteenth and, unfortunately, last baronet, to see what dirt I could scrape up for your entertainment, when fire broke out unexpectedly in her ladyship's pig-pen of a kitchen and I was able to dash heroically to the rescue . . .'"

'*Phillip*!'

Dalrymple ignored his wife. He continued. "'This saved the day, which had so far been a non-starter. I had begun by trespassing on Sir Phillip's land in search of a non-existent Spitfire—'"

'*What* did you say?' Zoe Dalrymple turned from one of the cupboards. She had a tin of Portuguese sardines in her hand.

'A Spitfire, my darling. Old Tom's plane.'

'I'd forgotten about that . . .' She looked at Carter. 'But that's only one of Tom's stories. You didn't believe him, did you? He's not quite right in the head, poor thing.'

Carter explained about Bob Simpson and the evidence.

'Where is this piece of metal you showed Phillip?'

Carter explained about that too.

She put the tin of sardines down on the table with the rest of the Kim's Game set-up. 'Would you fetch it, please, Mr Carter? I'd like to see it.'

Carter hesitated, but Phillip Dalrymple waved his hand in a slow, expansive gesture.

'Be my guest, Carter. I like to indulge my wife's little whims, whenever possible.'

He went and retrieved the aluminium from the waste-paper bin in the drawing room. When he returned to the kitchen, Zoe Dalrymple was sawing at tomatoes with a blunt bread-knife. She laid down the knife at once and took the fragment from him, studying it intently and turning it this way and that as she did so.

'And your Mr Simpson swears this is part of a plane?'

'He doesn't swear it. He just believes it.'

'You said there were some other pieces. A bit of perspex that could be part of the cockpit?'

'That's right. Unfortunately, Bob Simpson has those with him. This was the piece Tom gave me.'

Dalrymple said impatiently: 'It's just a bit of aluminium scrap, Zoe, not Exhibit One at the Old Bailey. You can put

78

it down now. It's only part of an old saucepan or something.'

She shook her head. 'It doesn't look like that to me. It's much too thin, for one thing. And why should it be so crumpled? That must have been done by some kind of impact.'

'Someone bashed a saucepan around. A rotten cook, like you. Give it back to him, for heaven's sake, Zoe, and let's get on with lunch.' The wheelchair squeaked its way round the table. A drawer was jerked open and three knives and three forks tossed on to the table top. 'You may as well stay and take tin luck with us, Carter, since you're still here. Unless sardine salad is too gourmet a dish for you.'

The invitation, delivered with an offhand rudeness, staggered Carter. He had judged that he was about to be thrown out again. He caught Zoe Dalrymple's eye and remembered what she had said about her husband craving company.

'Do stay, please, Mr Carter.'

'That's very nice of you, Lady Dalrymple.'

She smiled at him gratefully. Carter wasn't sure whether he ought to have called her 'milady' or 'your ladyship', or whether that was only for butlers. He wasn't even sure why he'd accepted at all. He had never mixed socially with people of the Dalrymples' class – if this could be called mixing – and nor had he ever wanted to. He had seen too much of their arrogance, their clannishness and their indifference to the fate of anyone outside their charmed and privileged circle. So why *was* he staying, he asked himself. In the end, he came up with the convenient answer that it made good sense to hang around and ingratiate himself with them. Whatever the reason, he certainly wasn't staying for the food.

In the end, as it turned out, the lunch was quite passable. Space was cleared on the table by the simple expedient of shunting the Kim's Game up one end. After a short struggle, during which Carter took over the fight from his hostess, the sardines agreed to come out of their tin and join the home-grown lettuce and tomatoes. Zoe Dalrymple produced some fresh brown rolls from the local bakery, although her husband did not touch these.

It was an irony of modern mores, Carter reflected, that the top and bottom of the scale could eat as they damn well pleased. They could sit round the kitchen table in the midst of chaos and use odd plates and Woolworths cutlery and nobody thought the worse of them for it. While those somewhere in the middle were condemned to serviettes and doilies and cruets all laid out laboriously in chill dining rooms in case the neighbours noticed. Maybe he had something in common with the Dalrymples after all.

Phillip Dalrymple's slow progress with his knife and fork was painful to watch.

'I hope the sight of me eating doesn't put you off your food completely, Carter. But then, as a newsman, you must be used to revolting spectacles.' He succeeded in spearing a piece of sardine. 'This is nothing to what I *shall* be like. Zoe already has to cut up meat for me. Eventually, she'll have to spoon-feed me like a baby. I shall probably become incontinent like a baby, too. A rosy future in store for us both, don't you agree?'

Carter said flatly: 'Isn't there anything they can do these days?'

'Nothing whatever, my dear chap. That's the whole joke of it, you see. You *think* you're getting better. You *do* get better. But it's only one of Mother Nature's little tricks. It doesn't last. Remission is the medical term, I believe. They have names for everything, our quack friends. Names, but no cure. Damn and blast!'

The fork had slipped from his fingers and clattered to the table. Carter made an involuntary move to retrieve it for him then stopped as he saw that Zoe Dalrymple had made no such attempt herself. The fork was picked up again and jabbed at a piece of tomato.

'Are you a sporting man, Carter?'

Carter half-smiled. The phrase conjured up gentlemanly visions of cricket, rugger, rowing, perhaps some squash in the winter at the club ... The back-alley football and bloody-nosed scrimmages he'd known in his childhood had nothing to do with his host's meaning.

'Sorry, no.'

'Surely you played games at school?'

That was another mistake they often made: assuming that all schools had the same facilities as Eton.

'I did some boxing. Played a bit of football. Not much else.'

'Done any rowing ever?'

'Only on the Serpentine.'

Carter saw the drift. He'd been asked to lunch because Phillip Dalrymple was longing to talk to someone, anyone, about the things he used to do in the good old days. Someone who would understand, preferably. It was too bad he'd picked the wrong person this time. He pitied him deeply but he couldn't help him. And he didn't dislike him any the less because of his illness. As Dalrymple himself had correctly assumed, sentiment had gone out of the window with him a long time ago. He'd seen too much suffering and misery and, like a doctor or a priest, he'd learned not to get involved beyond professional limits. The only suffering he couldn't yet distance himself from was his own.

'I did a bit of rowing myself once. At school and university,' the baronet said casually.

The classic understatement of the Oxford blue, Carter thought. There was a fat slug in the lettuce and he tipped it surreptitiously over the side of the plate and on to the floor.

'Did you, sir?'

'Stroked the eight. We won the Ladies' Plate at Henley. I even rowed for Oxford. We lost the boat race that year, unfortunately.' The last piece of sardine was safely skewered on to the fork. 'I was a fine figure of a man in those days, wasn't I, Zoe, my darling? Six foot two of rippling muscle. I wonder what my height is now.' He looked over the side of the wheelchair to the floor and measured upwards with his hand as far as the top of his head. 'Four foot something, I'd say. Have you a tape measure, Zoe? I'd like to know how much I've shrunk. No, of course, you wouldn't have such a thing. Or, if you did, you'd never be able to find it. My mother kept everything in its place you know, Carter. If she could see this house now she'd die all over again.'

Zoe Dalrymple had stood up to clear the plates and Carter rose to help her. She seemed unaffected by her husband's jibing, presumably because she was used to it and understood. It was easy to hurt the one you loved, Carter thought, chiefly because they always happen to be the nearest to hand and the most convenient. Take it out on your wife, or on your husband, or even your children, and keep it in the family. And a man like Phillip Dalrymple would bitterly resent his dependence on his wife. He was not in that category of the disabled who have managed to find compensations in life and even fulfilment of a kind. Many of them succeeded in rebuilding their lives from nothing into something worth living. This one would never come to terms with his illness and would find no peace of mind. Not that Carter blamed him. He wasn't sure he would have done so himself either.

The blue plastic washing-up bowl in the sink was already full and they put the dishes on the side. Zoe Dalrymple ran some water from the hot tap, testing it with her fingers.

'Bother! The boiler's playing up again. I'll have to get that man back to see to it. The water's only lukewarm.'

'It's falling to pieces like everything else in this house, including me,' her husband said. 'Is there going to be any afters or am I asking too much of the chef?'

'There's some tinned peaches.'

'Tinned peaches! Sardines *and* tinned peaches! What gastronomic delights you are serving up today, Zoe. A feast fit for a king! Are you as lucky, Carter? Is your wife a second Fanny Craddock?'

'She was a very good cook.'

'Was?'

'She died in an accident. Six years ago.'

Zoe Dalrymple exclaimed: 'I'm so sorry, Mr Carter. How awful!'

'At least it was quick,' her husband muttered. 'I don't think I'll bother with the peaches. I'll resist the temptation.'

Carter picked up a sodden tea cloth.

'Do you want me to dry?'

She was trying to squeeze the last drops of detergent out of a plastic bottle, which was making gasping noises like a stranded fish.

'Would you really? That's terribly nice of you. I'm sorry there's so much. Mrs Sweet usually comes to help out but her sister's husband has just died and she's gone to the funeral.'

'Nothing like a good funeral,' Phillip Dalrymple said. 'The working classes love them.'

That was true enough, Carter thought, doing his best with the wet tea cloth. He remembered the demise of his grandmother: the laying-out in the front parlour, the wake, the orgy of sobbing and black clothes, the flowers, the bakemeats and the booze. And no one had even liked the old girl.

What with the tepid water and the lack of detergent, as well as the wet cloth, they made a bad job of the washing-up. The finished dishes were smeary and dull. Zoe Dalrymple filled the kettle and set it to boil on the Aga hotplate and Carter fetched mugs from the dresser while she hunted for the coffee. When the jar of Maxwell House had finally been run to ground in the fridge and the kettle had boiled at last, they sat down to coffee round the table again. Carter remembered with frustration that Phillip Dalrymple had his only pack of cigarettes. He picked up his mug, which said Home Sweet Home on it. The coffee tasted vile.

Zoe Dalrymple put down her OXO mug. 'About this plane, Phillip'

'What plane?'

'The Spitfire in Trodgers Wood.'

'There isn't one. And we have finished with that particular topic of conversation, my own dear one.'

'*I* haven't,' she said stubbornly. 'If there's a chance that there *is* a plane there, Phillip, you can't just do nothing about it.'

'Why can't I?'

'Because Spitfires are part of England's history. You can't leave one to moulder away.'

'You are so naive, Zoe, it's unbelievable. Do you seriously imagine that there is a whole shining new machine sitting there in the wood, flaps down, ready for take-off? If there were anything there at all it would be nothing but a heap of old junk buried twenty feet deep. What's the point of digging that up?'

'There's a lot of point. For one thing it must be possible to identify the plane. They have numbers. I remember reading that somewhere. Don't they, Mr Carter?'

Carter nodded. He had been having some difficulty keeping his mouth shut and resisting the temptation to punch cripples for being rude to their nice wives. Her championing his cause again had surprised him.

'I thought you only read *Country Life* and *Tatler*, Zoe,' Phillip Dalrymple said nastily. 'Do stop talking rubbish.'

The crabbed fingers, moving even more jerkily with irritation, slopped coffee on to the table.

She went on, undeterred. 'There might be a pilot with the plane and no one knows anything about him. Imagine not knowing where your husband, or your son or your brother is. Or what happened to him. It must be awful.'

'You've been talking to Carter,' her husband said. 'You'll be burying him decently next, with full military honours.'

'I should have thought you of all people would approve of that, Phillip, remembering what happened to your father.'

Carter winced. He would have steered clear of that particular subject himself. Phillip Dalrymple banged his coffee mug down.

'Will you shut up, Zoe? There is no pilot and there is no plane!'

'How do you know? You can't possibly be sure. Trodgers Wood is deep down in the valley. It's only really visible from our land. It's quite possible, I'd say, for a plane to have crashed there and not been seen at all. And nobody goes there

84

except poor old Tom. It's been neglected for years and years.'

In the silence that followed the telephone rang from the hall and Zoe Dalrymple went off to answer it. Carter said nothing. The baronet fumbled clumsily in his pocket and produced two cigarettes.

'Light us up, Carter, there's a good fellow. And they're *your* cigarettes, don't forget.'

Carter obliged.

'Zoe has a vivid imagination. Like most women. Did your wife have a vivid imagination?'

'I wouldn't have said so. But then I wouldn't say your wife had either.'

'How diplomatic of you, Carter. You're hoping she'll talk me round, aren't you?'

'Since you ask, yes.'

Zoe Dalrymple returned. She sat down again, making no comment at her husband smoking.

'That was Miss Burton. Her sister's been taken ill and she has to go away to look after her. She wanted to know if I'd take her place as secretary at the fête committee meeting here next week.'

'What is the matter with everybody's sisters! First Mrs Sweet's and now Miss Burton's. It's very inconsiderate of them all.' Phillip Dalrymple drew on his cigarette. 'You should see the fête committee in action, Carter. A lot of cackling females, twittering on about strawberry jam and lucky dips and who is to be bulldozed into helping this year. Is Mrs Armstrong-Avery still filling the chair with her ample posterior?'

The name rang bells with Carter. Then he remembered that he had seen it on the flower rota in the church porch. He also recognized the name of the telephone caller.

'I think I met Miss Burton outside the village shop. An elderly grey-haired lady on a very old bike?'

'That's our Miss Burton,' Phillip Dalrymple said. 'One of a dying breed of dessicated English spinsters. The pillar of the community. Keeps us all in order. She ran the village school years ago – a veritable Dame Slap. She left before my time, luckily. Moved away to take care of her old mother. Or it might have been her old father. It was an old something. Discipline was never quite the same again, apparently. I went there for three years before prep school and we ran riot.'

'But she came back?'

'To the village, but not to the school. She has occupied herself with running everything else instead. Amongst a multitude of exhausting activities, she is secretary of this committee. For the past fifteen years, the annual Fairfield Fête has been held here at the Hall. There is a perfectly good recreation ground, but people like to come and nose about the garden, taking cuttings and looking in through the windows . . . As if that were not enough, we now also enter for the best-kept village competition – thanks to Miss Burton and her indefatigable efforts to put us on the map.'

'I saw the poster. Seems like a good idea.'

'It's an appalling idea. We never win. And Miss Burton terrorizes the neighbourhood, making everyone cut their hedges and mow their lawns. She even persuaded me to put up the cash to have that dump of a shop repainted outside. Next thing she'll be after me to paint our gates. Thank God she's going away.'

Zoe Dalrymple smiled into her mug. 'I think Miss Burton is the only person Phillip is really frightened of.'

'She reminds me far too much of the matron at my prep school.'

'But you'd be pleased if Fairfield won the competition.'

'There is no chance whatever of it doing so, my innocent Zoe. At this very moment the Mayhurst Maquis are planning to blow up the parish hall or plough up the green. Don't forget that last year they organized that paperchase straight through the village . . .'

'That was the campers.'

'It was Mayhurst in disguise. They won last year and they'll make sure they win again. You wouldn't believe the backstabbing and rivalry that goes on between Fairfield and

Mayhurst, Carter. It's archaic. I don't give a damn who wins so long as they all leave me in peace.'

Carter laughed. For once he found himself in sympathy with Phillip Dalrymple. He finished his coffee. If he didn't get back to the office soon Ken Grant would be looking out his cards. He said goodbye and was about to leave the kitchen when the baronet said casually: 'By the way, Carter, I've changed my mind. I've decided to give your chap Simpson permission to take another look in Trodgers Wood. You can tell him.'

Carter took a long breath. 'Thank you, sir.'

'Not to please my wife. Or to please you. But for the pleasure of proving you all wrong. As I told you, any entertainment is welcome here.'

Zoe Dalrymple saw him out.

'Thanks for the lunch,' he said. 'And for the support.'

'Thanks for putting out the fire.' She smiled up at him and looked less tired than before. 'It wasn't me, you know. It was you. Phillip likes you, believe it or not. I think it's because you don't crawl to him. Or pity him. He can't stand that. Also, you gave him cigarettes.' She held out her hand. 'You must come to lunch again, if you can stand it. I promise to try and do better than sardines next time.'

He took her hand in his; it was small and rather rough. A lady she might be, but not of leisure. As he walked away, she called after him.

'I do hope there *is* a plane, Mr Carter.'

'So do I.'

He drove off thoughtfully. One way and another the Dalrymples had been something of a surprise.

Five

It was evening before Carter managed to get Bob Simpson on the telephone. He had tried earlier several times but there had been no reply. Back at his lodgings he tried again, using the hall telephone, and was rewarded at last by an answering click and the surveyor's voice on the other end of the line. He gave him the good news about Phillip Dalrymple's agreement. Simpson sounded cautiously pleased.

'I'll get in touch with him myself, of course. I'll try and fix a weekend with him when I could take a couple of my lads over there for a dig around.'

'You'll let me know, Bob? I'd like to be in on it.'

There was a slight pause. Simpson said reluctantly: 'Fair enough. After all, it was you tipped us off in the first place. And it sounds as though you talked Sir Phillip round this far.'

'I don't know what made him agree in the end. He wasn't going to and he doesn't believe there's a thing there. He knew all about me, by the way. Been spying through binoculars and listening to the locals. I wouldn't have mentioned the plane, but he brought it up.'

'Well, no harm done. What's he like?'

'Like his reputation. Bloody difficult. But with some reason. He's got multiple sclerosis. Confined to a wheelchair and he used to be a real sports champion. He's bitter about it.'

'I don't blame him.'

The signature tune of *Coronation Street* blared out from behind Mrs Eliot's sitting-room door. Carter turned his back and stuffed a finger in his free ear.

'He's waiting to prove you wrong about the plane.'

'Well, we won't know for sure until we've done some more digging. I'll let you know when I've fixed the date with Sir Phillip.'

Simpson rang off and Carter stood by the phone for a moment, thinking things over. From his point of view it was all pretty much a dead loss. There was no story yet and there might never be one. Even if Simpson and his lads dug up a few more bits of metal just to prove the plane existed, there was no guarantee that Phillip Dalrymple would give permission for them to go on and dig up the rest. And Ken didn't want bits and pieces. He wanted an engine or a propeller at the very least, and preferably a pilot too – dead or alive. Something for the *Courier* readers to get what teeth they had left into.

He lit a cigarette. To hell with Mrs Eliot and her no-smoking rule. Supposing the pilot was buried with the plane? Would enough evidence be found in a hand dig to identify him? It didn't seem very likely, which was a pity. A dead hero was always good news. Much better than if he'd hopped overboard and was alive and well in Wigan. The recovery of the remains of one of the Few – gallant, young and dashing – would be far more tear-jerking than one of them alive and kicking forty years on, ageing and balding. 'They shall grow not old as we that are left grow old.' That one was always trotted out on appropriate occasions and, so far as Carter could see, it gave about the only good reason for dying young.

Hilda Ogden's voice squawked from the sitting room and was answered by a low, male rumble. Mrs Eliot had not missed a single episode of *Coronation Street* since it began. Carter took himself and his cigarette off upstairs.

The next day produced a useful tip-off from Terry at the Crown and Anchor about a local lad who had just driven to Monte Carlo and back in a forty-six-year-old Baby Austin. The car had made the trip without once breaking down and its proud owner would make a good picture beside it for the cover page of the *Courier*. Ken Grant was grudgingly approving.

'But I want that Spitfire story, Frank.'

'You may not get it.'

The editor unwrapped a mint with ominous precision.

'Just what do you mean by that? The plane's there. The expert says so.'

'The expert *thinks* so. But whether he's right or wrong it's not up to him, or us, whether a proper dig's done. It's up to the landowner, Sir Phillip Dalrymple. And he's a difficult sod. I told you.'

Ken rested his chin on his hands and stared flintily across his desk. 'Then you'll have to make sure he *does* give permission, won't you? Use your natural charm on him. Or on his wife – if he has one. I thought you fancied yourself as a ladies' man.'

The quaint expression was an oblique reference to the glimpses caught through the ever-open office door of Carter with Brenda and the other girls in the office. Carter forgave him. Anyone with a wife like Mrs Grant, a vast Valkyrie in viscose, was entitled to feel resentful of another man's freedom.

'Sir Phillip is an invalid in a wheelchair. Chatting up his wife would be frightfully bad form. Not jolly old cricket, you know.'

'I wouldn't have thought you'd let a little thing like that bother you, Frank.' The editor picked up his pen and crunched the mint noisily. 'You'd better be nice to both of them, then. Call again. Butter them up. Make them feel patriotic about it. "Never in the field of human conflict . . .", all that sort of thing. Once it's established there's a Spitfire there, he's bound to agree. And it's going to make a good story. Forty years lost in a wood and nobody knew it was there except one old man whom nobody believed.' He sketched an imaginary layout in the air. 'We'll have a couple of pictures – say, one of the wreckage and the other of the pilot.'

'Would you prefer him alive or dead?'

'Don't try to be clever, Frank. If he's alive, you find him. If he's dead, you find his picture. Understand?'

Carter understood. Nothing was going to put Ken off the

scent. He went back to the news desk and his typewriter to finish off the Baby Austin story. Brenda waved to him from the switchboard which she was manipulating with dexterous efficiency and long nails the colour of dried blood. Today she was wearing a see-through white nylon blouse with a wide, frilled collar. Combined with the heavy eye make-up and the frizzy mop of hair it made her look like Pierrette.

Carter pecked away at the typewriter keys. Ken had called him a ladies' man. If a ladies' man could be said to be a man who likes ladies, then that was true enough. If it meant only what Ken meant it to mean, then it wasn't true. Not since Jan had died, anyway. There had been brief encounters, of no importance to either side, which did not include cradle-snatching kids like Brenda. As for him charming someone like Zoe Dalrymple, she was out of his class as well as out of his reach. None of which stopped him liking her, but stopped him getting any ideas. He lit a cigarette and held it in his mouth, squinting through the smoke as he went on typing.

It was four days before he heard from Bob Simpson. The surveyor phoned the newspaper office and when Carter heard the slow Sussex voice he sat up and took notice.

'It's on for next Saturday.'

'You spoke to Sir Phillip?'

'I did. On the telephone.' A pause. 'I see what you mean about him. He's not an easy customer. But he confirmed permission for us to do an exploratory hand dig in Trodgers Wood. Nothing more than that, as yet.' Another pause. 'I've also had a word with the Ministry of Defence and they've given us the go-ahead to see what we can find. These days they like to have all the historical background to a crash but, in this case, of course, there's nothing we can tell them. It's a real mystery.'

'Where shall I meet you?'

'Let's say at the church lychgate again. Eight o'clock. An early start, I'm afraid. The sooner we get going the better.'

'I'll be there.'

*   *   *

91

As it turned out, Carter was in Fairfield again before Saturday. An interview with a golden-wedding couple who, to judge by their non-stop bickering, seemed to have endured fifty years of married misery, had taken him within five miles or so of the village. For reasons he could not exactly define, he found himself taking a long way round in order to pass through Fairfield. He came into the village from the north side and passed the rectory – surprisingly, a modern box; the parish hall – a Victorian horror, the playing fields and Mrs Jennings' shop, where a painter was already at work up a ladder. He drove on past the old schoolhouse with its belfry on the roof, the former domain of Miss Burton, alias Dame Slap, and came finally to the open gates of Fairfield Hall. The excuse he gave himself for turning into the driveway was that he was acting under orders – Ken Grant's orders to be charming to the Dalrymples – and that, after all, he had been invited to call again.

As he came near the house, he saw a number of cars parked outside. Either Phillip Dalrymple had a sudden glut of visitors or there was some kind of meeting. He got out of the van and rang the doorbell. He expected to see Zoe Dalrymple when the door opened but instead there was a grim-faced, overweight woman wearing a hideous flowered bungalow apron. This, he realized, must be Mrs Sweet of the defunct brother-in-law, come to help out. She did not live up to her name.

'What do you want?'

Carter told her.

'Sir Phillip's bad today,' she told him with some satisfaction. 'Can't see no one. And her ladyship's got the committee.'

'Committee?'

'For the fête, of course.'

'Of course.'

He remembered now. She was standing in for Miss Burton who had gone away to look after a sick sister. He smiled as nicely as he could manage at Mrs Sweet.

'Lady Dalrymple asked me to call. I'm from the *Milton Weekly Courier*. It's about an article.'

A Foreign Field

She noticed the van for the first time and unbent a little. 'Going to do a bit on the fête this year, are you? I hope you're going to take photos this time. There was none of us last year. A crying shame, I called it, when there was that great big picture of the Mayhurst Fête right in the middle of your front page. Favouritism, that's what it was.' She nodded, as one who knows. '*That's* why they won the best-kept village competition too. Friends in high places!'

Carter moved one pace forward. 'If I could just see Lady Dalrymple for a moment . . .'

The floral bust blocked his way. 'I don't know about that. She's in the committee, like I said. They're all in the drawing room.'

'If you'd just tell her I'm here. Frank Carter, from the *Courier*.'

'I'm just the cleaner, you know, not the butler. I've got my work to do. Still, seeing as you're the press . . .'

She went away and Carter waited in the hall. The ancestor above the fireplace looked down on him coldly. If he could have stepped down from his frame, Carter thought, he'd have been reaching for his horsewhip. He could hear the murmur of female voices coming from the drawing room but the rest of the house was silent. He wondered where its master had taken refuge and whether 'bad' was really bad or just diplomatic in face of invasion. Mrs Sweet returned, shaking the furniture, and jerked her head in the direction of the voices.

'She says to go in.'

He went in.

The furniture had been rearranged to form a semi-circle – armchairs, sofas and hard chairs all grouped together. A solitary male sat in amongst a dozen or so women; a lone cockerel, like Mactavish, in a collection consisting mainly of boilers. Although the day was warm and the French windows opened on to bright sunshine, tweeds were much in evidence and, at a quick glance, Carter counted six sets of pearls. Spectacles were set firmly on noses, pencils or pens poised attentively above notepads. And all eyes were turned towards Carter.

Zoe Dalrymple stood up. She had been sitting at a card table at the centre of the semi-circle, beside a statuesque, elderly woman dressed in pale mauve who could be none other than Mrs Armstrong-Avery. Carter wondered if Miss B. Plumb of the ballroom and Latin American dancing was also present.

'Madam Chairman, may I introduce Mr Carter of the *Milton Weekly Courier* to the committee?'

There was a stir of interest and a gentle clucking; Madam Chairman inclined her head graciously.

'We are very pleased to welcome you to the meeting, Mr Carter. I must say that we are rather flattered that the press should take such an interest in our little fête. I hope that means that you are going to give us a better coverage in your newspaper than last year. One *tiny* paragraph on an inside page!'

'We'll try and do better.'

She smiled. 'Excellent, Mr Carter! Mayhurst village has arranged to have their fête on the same day as us again – they do it on purpose, of course – and we don't want them stealing all the limelight like they did last year, do we?' She looked round the semi-circle for corroboration and received it with a unanimous shaking of heads. 'I think we could squeeze Mr Carter beside you, Mrs Fortescue. Would you make room for him, please?'

A friendly-looking woman with legs like bolsters and hair permed in tight waves shuffled sideways on one of the sofas and patted the small space she had created welcomingly. Carter sat down, thigh-to-thigh with Mrs Fortescue, who smelled strongly of April Violets. The meeting continued under the very capable direction of Mrs Armstrong-Avery.

He had, apparently, interrupted a discussion on the number of trestle tables required for the fête. Each of the ladies present, he discovered, was in charge of running a particular stall and each was asked in turn how many tables she needed. The number available was limited and any greed was frowned upon. Country Larder was allocated two, as were Toys, Books and Garden Plants, but a bold bid for the same number for the White Elephant stall was firmly quashed. The stallholder, who was new to the committee and had not yet learned her place, retired defeated and abashed.

The matter of the tables settled, the meeting moved on to other items on the agenda. The lone cockerel, consulted once as treasurer for his opinion, crowed timidly from his hard chair and then fell silent again. Miss B. Plumb, it turned out, *was* present. She was elderly, with a faded, wispy beauty and very long, thin arms. Carter was not sure that attending her dancing classes would add much pleasure to his leisure.

Arrangements were discussed for providing teas. The local Women's Institute had agreed to lend china and an urn for fifty pence and had undertaken to provide tea, sandwiches and cakes for sale to the public.

Carter took out his notepad and pencil – no easy operation, pressed as close as he was to Mrs Fortescue. The look from the chair that swept the semi-circle like a lighthouse beam included him and he judged it time to appear busy. He wrote a few words, which Mrs Fortescue tried to read and, glancing up, caught Zoe Dalrymple's eye. She smiled and bent her head again to her own note-taking. He would scarcely have recognized her. She had washed her hair and put on some make-up and she was wearing a skirt and blouse. He was finding it hard to keep his eyes off her.

The meeting dragged on. From time to time, Carter ostentatiously jotted something down while Mrs Fortescue, overpowering him with the April Violets, leaned closer and tried to see what it was. He longed for a cigarette but hadn't the nerve to light up.

'Prizes for the raffle,' Mrs Armstrong-Avery boomed, looking expectantly round her committee. 'Contributions, please. We need at least ten good prizes.'

After some hesitation the offers came: a bottle of sherry, a hand-knitted bedjacket, a box of fruit, an unused electric carving knife still in its box, a pink teddy bear . . . Carter did not feel he wanted to win any of them.

Pony rides were next under discussion. The committee

member in charge announced apologetically that the pony in question had gone lame.

'*Lame!*' said Mrs Armstrong-Avery in Lady Bracknell tones. She took off her spectacles to stare at the member. 'How very unfortunate!'

For the pony or for the fête? Carter wondered. Alternative steeds were hurriedly suggested but rejected one by one as too old, too young, too frisky or too slow. A donkey was suggested but turned down as well.

'Donkey rides are *most* uncomfortable,' Mrs Armstrong-Avery declared.

Carter bit his lip. He had a mental vision of her astride a very small donkey as in a seaside postcard. Zoe Dalrymple caught his eye again and looked hurriedly down at her notes.

Madam Chairman had replaced her spectacles. 'And now we come to the last item on our agenda: judges for the fancy dress. We already have one judge – Mrs Fleming has kindly agreed to take on the responsibility – but we need one more. Someone outside the village who can be quite objective. It wouldn't do for it to be one of us. Suggestions, please.'

All eyes swivelled towards Carter. Beside him, Mrs Fortescue wriggled coyly and lifted her hand.

'I propose we ask Mr Carter, Madam Chairman. I'm sure he would do it very well.'

To Carter's dismay there was a chorus of agreement.

'I don't think . . .' he began and then faltered under their expectant gaze. He encountered the treasurer's sympathetic, but helpless, look. This was how a rat felt in a trap. He shrugged. 'I'll do my best, if that's what you want.'

'Splendid!' Mrs Armstrong-Avery beamed her approval at him across the card table and Mrs Fortescue patted him on the knee.

Serves me right, he thought, for coming in here under false pretences. He avoided looking at Zoe Dalrymple.

The French clock chimed midday and, the meeting concluded, he helped pass round the sherry.

'Will you have one yourself, Mr Carter?'

A *Foreign Field*

'No thanks, Lady Dalrymple, I don't.'
'I thought all newspaper men drank like fishes.'
'A lot of them do. So did I – which is why I don't any more.'
'I see. Good for you.' She drank a little sherry. 'I'm awfully sorry about the fancy dress judging. Do you mind?'
'Yes. But I know when I'm cornered. And outnumbered.'
She laughed. 'I suppose they do seem a bit alarming, but they're all terribly kind. They do a tremendous amount of good work, you know, for all kinds of charities and worthy causes.'
'What's this particular one in aid of?'
'The fête? It's for the church bells this year. They need repairing and it costs an absolute fortune.'
He looked over towards the chattering group by the fireplace.
'With Mrs Armstrong-Avery at the helm, I don't see how you can fail. You'll probably raise enough to rebuild the whole church. Who's the treasurer?'
'Mr Whitaker. He's a retired bank manager. Poor man, it's an awful job. Nobody wants to do it.'
'I suppose Mrs Armstrong-Avery got him to volunteer.'
She smiled and started to say something else when they were interrupted by Mrs Fortescue who had sidled up coyly. Zoe Dalrymple moved away and Carter followed her with his eyes, only half-listening to Mrs Fortescue. One or two of the other ladies came over and soon he found himself surrounded. Over their heads he caught the sympathetic eye of Mr Whitaker once again. He answered questions patiently and politely. Yes, he did enjoy being a reporter. Yes, the hours could be long. Yes, he did meet all sorts of interesting people. Yes, he did agree that there should be a speed limit through the village. No, there was nothing he, personally, could do about it. No, he hadn't heard of any scheme to build sixty council houses on the field next to the rectory. Yes, he agreed that they were very lucky to be able to hold the fête at the Hall and yes, it was very generous of the Dalrymples. Yes, he did feel sorry

97

for Sir Phillip. And yes, Lady Dalrymple was charming . . .

After twenty minutes the sherry glasses were empty, refills delicately refused, and the committee members began to disperse. Zoe Dalrymple saw them out while Carter waited behind in the drawing room. He listened to the cars starting up, one by one, and the occasional shriek of clashed gears as they crunched away down the gravel drive.

She came back into the room.

'Well, that's over, thank goodness. I only hope I can read my notes.' She perched sideways on the arm of a chair. 'What did you *really* want to see me about, Mr Carter? It wasn't the fête, I take it?'

He found himself admiring her legs, which were very lovely. 'No. Sorry about that. False pretences. Still, I got my come-uppance.'

She smiled. 'You did rather, didn't you? Straight into the lion's den. So, if you didn't come here to be co-opted as a fancy dress judge, it must be about the Spitfire. Did you know that Phillip gave your Mr Simpson permission to do a dig by hand this Saturday?'

'Yes, Bob told me. It's good of him.'

She pushed her fingers through her fringe. 'Once he's given his word he'll stick to it – you needn't worry about that. But I'm afraid you can't see him today. He had a rotten night.'

'The dragon at the gates told me he wasn't well. I'm sorry.'

'Mrs Sweet? She's not a dragon. She's what's known as a "treasure", although she may not look like it. In the old days when Phillip's parents were alive there were six indoor servants, two gardeners and a boy to run this place. Now we're down to Mrs Sweet on Tuesdays and Thursdays and Harry who mows the lawns and pulls up the weeds when he can see them. He's over eighty.'

It had been tough at the top in the old days, Carter thought. His own mother had gone out charring to make ends meet whenever his father was out of work – which was most of the time. She'd cleaned offices, not homes – up at four, three hours' slog with bucket, mop, broom and duster before she went off to spend another eight hours serving in a shoe shop, breathing in other people's smelly feet while standing on her own. She'd come home more dead than alive and somehow got a meal ready and on the table for a husband who'd had *his* feet up all day, when he hadn't been propping up the bar of the Red Rover.

Carter looked at Zoe Dalrymple. It was a world she knew nothing about. But she did know about suffering and tiredness. He had seen the same exhaustion on her face as on his mother's and the pallor and dark shadows were there beneath the make-up. If Phillip Dalrymple had had a very bad night he didn't suppose that his wife's had been much better.

'Do you look after your husband all by yourself? Don't you have any help?'

'We've had nurses. Several in fact. But they never stay. Phillip doesn't like them. He prefers me to look after him.'

'It must be pretty hard work.'

He couldn't, in fact, imagine how the hell she coped. She was small and slight when she should have been an Amazon with biceps.

'It's tiring, sometimes,' she admitted, but without a trace of complaint or self-pity. 'It's been easier, though, since we turned one of the downstairs rooms into a bedroom. There was a time when Phillip could still manage the stairs – with my help – but he can't do that any more.' She ran her fingers through her hair again and the neat committee image deteriorated still further. 'It was an awful blow for him . . . not being able to go upstairs to bed like a normal person. I can't tell you . . . We thought of getting a lift installed, but it's much too expensive.' She stood up. 'I'm terribly sorry, Mr Carter, but I really ought to go and see how he is. Do you mind?'

'I'm on my way,' he said at once.

He followed her to the door. She shook his hand.

'The fête's on Saturday, twenty-eighth June, by the way. It opens at two o'clock and the fancy dress parade takes place at three.'

'I'll be there. What do I have to do?'

'There's nothing to worry about,' she said kindly. 'You and Mrs Fleming just have to pick out the first, second and third and then present the prizes.'

'Is Mrs Fleming anything like Mrs Armstrong-Avery?'

'Not a bit. You'll like her. She's very jolly. I hope we're going to have some photographs on your front page.'

'I'll do my best,' he promised. 'Tell me, do Mayhurst really pick the same day on purpose?'

She smiled. 'They say *we* do. I'm not sure who's right. It just happens. Neither side will back down and, of course, it means that neither fête does as well as it might.'

'Can't they call a truce?'

'The chairman of the Mayhurst committee is like Mrs Armstrong-Avery, only even more so.'

'Enough said.'

'Are you going to be at the dig on Saturday with Mr Simpson?'

'If your husband has no objection.'

'Of course not. It was your idea in the first place and he wants to be able to say that you were both wrong.'

'What do you want, Lady Dalrymple?'

'I want you both to be right.'

He drove the *Courier* van down the drive and parked it outside the Bull. Mactavish and company were scratching around near the door and, inside, the regulars were sitting behind their pints. Charlie was washing glasses at the sink behind the bar – sloshing them through scummy water and setting them to drain upside down. He took his time before coming to serve Carter.

'Back again? Not still chasing old Tom's Spitfire? Rubbish it is. I should've thought you'd found that out for yourself by now. I thought all you reporters were a smart lot.'

How to win customers in one easy lesson, Carter thought. He avoided answering the question and commented instead on the smartened-up pub exterior with its salmon-pink geraniums and new green litter bin. Charlie looked sour.

'Nothing to do with me. Dratted busybodies! It's supposed

to help us win some competition. They wanted me to tidy up the garden at the back but I told them to take a running jump. No one ever sits out there, so what's the point? As for that litter bin – no one will use that, either.' He leaned across the bar counter and wagged a finger under Carter's nose. 'The way I see it, the last thing we want is to win any bloody competition. All it'd mean is a lot of nosy trippers coming here and messing up the place. What can I get you?'

Carter ordered a tomato juice. Charlie's argument had a certain logic. He was sorry he hadn't seen the landlord and Miss Burton in confrontation; it must have been quite a sight. While he waited, he nodded to the other patrons in the bar, who grunted and nodded in return. He recognized Jesse, the old man in the cloth cap with the pipe who was sitting, as before, in the inglenook beside the cold grate.

'There you are. One tomato juice.'

Carter paid up for the cloudy pinkish-brown liquid as uncomplainingly as he had done for the warm, flat Coke on his first visit.

'Have something yourself, Charlie.'

'Thanks. I don't mind if I do.' The landlord drew himself a pint and stood quaffing it, the mug engulfed by his big fist. He looked more Falstaffian than ever. 'You find Tom that day, then?'

'In the end.'

'Difficult customer, he is. Nervous as anything – like I told you. Thinks people might try to take him away again and lock him up in one of those nut houses. I'm not saying I like him coming in here, stinking like a polecat and making a right nuisance of himself, but when all's said and done he's harmless, and in my book he's a right to his freedom like any other man.'

Carter lit a cigarette, bemused. Charlie had a surprisingly liberal streak in him beneath the gruffness. Life was full of surprises.

He said casually: 'He showed me where his plane is.'

'Where he *says* it is, you mean. I'll bet you a hundred quid there's nothing to see. Is there?'

101

'Nothing at all,' Carter agreed. 'It's just a hollow full of dead leaves. Watch it, though, I might just take you up on that bet.'

'Might as well hand over the cash now. You're wasting your time. Stands to reason, doesn't it? Even our Dad's Army here wouldn't have missed something like that.'

'What's that you're saying, Charlie? What wouldn't we have missed?'

Jesse of the flat cap and pipe had left his inglenook and come to the bar, empty mug in hand.

'A bloody great Spitfire landing in Trodgers Wood, that's what. Mr Carter here thought for a while there might be something in Tom's fairy story.'

'Fill this up will you, Charlie?' Jesse said, getting his priorities right. He waited for the refill before speaking again, sucking on his unlit pipe with a faint whistling sound. When the mug was safely back in his hand again, he said in slow, Sussex tones: 'Spitfires weren't big, Charlie, they were little. Look at 'em today against the modern ones – like fleas against elephants. Makes you wonder how those lads did what they did.' He removed the pipe and took a long swallow. 'I'm not saying it isn't possible, Mr Carter. Anything's possible. I've learned that by now at my time of life. But I was in the Home Guard here from start to finish and we never saw no plane come down anywhere near that wood. Nearest one was a Junkers 88 that crashed at Fox Green a good mile away. There was another German plane landed in a ploughed field a bit further off and they took that one away all in one piece. There was a Hurricane over near Mayhurst – which that lot wouldn't let us even take a look at – and that's all there was at Fairfield.'

'I said it was quiet,' Charlie said scathingly. 'You should've been where I was – right in the thick of it.'

'I'll remind you, Charlie,' Jesse said with dignity, 'that we had more than a hundred high explosive bombs dropped round Fairfield, not to mention twelve flying bombs. We had one warden and one fireman on duty every night, on watch from dusk till dawn, and we had over fifteen hundred raid warnings.

If you call that quiet, I don't. We were in the front line and that's a fact.'

Charlie muttered unintelligibly and rudely into his beard and went off to dry glasses. Jesse set down his mug and began to fill his pipe. The argument was evidently a recurring one which neither side ever won.

Carter said: 'That sounds a lot of bombs.'

'Jerries dropped them as they went home. None of them fell on the village itself, I'm thankful to say, but that was only providence.' He tamped down the tobacco carefully with the end of a matchstick. 'All very well for Charlie to talk about being in the thick of it but he was tucked up nice and safe behind barbed wire for most of the war while we were being bombed. And if Hitler'd invaded, we'd've been right in his way.'

And that would have been that, thought Carter. A few old men and boys brandishing shotguns and pitchforks. He raised the tomato juice.

'To the Few who stopped him.'

'I'll drink to that,' Jesse agreed and did so. Then he scraped his match alight and put it to his pipe, puffing out little clouds of smoke. After a moment he took the pipe out of his mouth. 'To tell the truth I've never given that story of Tom's much thought. Never took much notice, him being a bit queer in the head and telling so many tales. But now I do think about it, Trodgers Wood's right down in that valley out of sight and, as I said, anything's possible. There was a lot going on here during the war, as I'm always telling Charlie, though he won't believe it.' He smiled suddenly, showing tobacco-stained teeth. 'Nice if it *was* true. It'd take me right back to the old days.'

He stuck his pipe back in his mouth and puffed away thoughtfully. Carter wished he could have told him more but, remembering Bob Simpson's warning, said instead: 'You reckon those were the days then, Jesse?'

The pipe was removed and another swallow of beer taken before the old man answered. 'I do. At the start, when we were the LDV, we used to meet up one evening every week

103

---

in the potting shed behind the Hall – with her ladyship's permission, of course. We started off wearing our own clothes with an LDV armband and some of us brought our own shotguns. Later on they gave us First-World-War rifles and we got our uniforms and they called us the Home Guard instead. We learned fieldcraft, map reading and first aid in the week and on Sunday mornings we'd try it all out on exercises.'

'What sort of exercises?' Carter asked, fascinated.

'Well, for instance, our platoon commander would send two men off to a place only he and they knew about. The rest of us had to go off after them and locate and capture them. They were the enemy, you see.'

Carter blinked. He tried not to smile. 'What else did you do?'

'We stood guard over any plane wreckage – British or German – till it was made safe. But, as I told you, there weren't many of those in our area.'

'Did you capture any enemy pilots?'

Jesse said regretfully: 'Not what you could call *capture* exactly. There was that young German lad parachuted down into Ted Barnes' ten-acre, but then Ted got there first with his shotgun and Mrs Barnes was ahead of me with her pitchfork . . . And it was old George, our policeman, who made the arrest, formal-like.'

'Pity.'

'Yes, I'd have liked to have got one of them myself. That would have been something to tell Charlie here.' He puffed a bit more at the pipe and drank some more beer. 'Then we had to do the sandbags.'

'Sandbags?'

'During the invasion scare,' Jesse explained patiently. 'The War Office sent down a whole lot of empty bags. We had to fill 'em all up with sand. Then we took them round with Ted's horse and cart and set up barriers on approach roads to the village. One of us kept watch all night at each barrier.'

Carter said in disbelief: 'Was that meant to stop the Germans?'

'I don't know about that. But if you heard someone coming along you had to shout, "Halt! Who goes there, friend or foe?" I used to think that was a bit silly myself. I mean, did they really think the Germans were going to say so if it was them? Still, that's what we were told to do. And when whoever it was had answered, if it wasn't foe, we were supposed to say, "Advance, friend and be recognized." I don't mind telling you, Mr Carter, that when it came to it, things didn't always go by the book. Often as not we'd just sing out, "Who's that?" and they'd say "Dick Jackson" or "George Clark" or whoever it was and we'd let them through. We had to keep on our toes, though. It *could* have been Jerry invading. You never knew.' Jesse sighed. 'Yes, those were the days.'

He set down his empty beer mug and Carter, bemused for a moment by these revelations, pulled himself together and quickly bought him another pint.

Six

C arter was out at Fairfield by a quarter to eight on the Saturday morning. This time he had taken the practical step of buying some gumboots and of wearing his oldest clothes.

The village was deserted and Charlie, presumably, still slumbered behind the drawn curtains at an upper window of the Bull. Even the cockerel and hens were nowhere to be seen.

The day looked set to be fair and the sun already felt warm. Carter parked the van and walked through the lychgate and sat down on a bench seat beside the brick path. The white doves, at least, were up and about and cooing softly from the church roof.

He lit a cigarette and thought about things. He thought about the probability that some remains of a Spitfire would be found and, if so, he wondered just what had happened on the day when it had plunged down into Trodgers Wood. He looked up at the sun. Had it been a fine summer's day like today, as in one of those old photographs where the fighter pilots had sat about outside on Lloyd loom chairs or lain on the grass while they waited for the order to scramble? And how old had this particular pilot been? What had he looked like? Had he been afraid, or was he one of those wizard-prang types apparently without a nerve in their bodies? More important, where was he now? Buried with his plane in the wood, or alive and kicking somewhere in the world, a man of sixty-odd, still dreaming dreams about the good old days of the war, like Jesse at the Bull? Or a man to whom none of it meant anything any more?

A Foreign Field

The wreaths on old George Clark's grave had been taken away and the mound sported only a jam jar full of some pink and blue flowers. The dew was still on the grass, wet and glistening like a gossamer shroud. Not a bad spot to sleep the long sleep, Carter decided, looking round. He got the impression that the churchyard residents were a pretty peaceful lot and he was inclined to agree with the rector that there was something to be said for good old-fashioned burial – if it could be in a place like this.

The roof and chimneys of the Hall could be seen through the trees. He thought about Zoe Dalrymple. The irony of that was that she was the only woman he had thought twice about since Jan had died and she was strictly *verboten*. He'd done enough harm already in his life without lusting after cripples' wives – even if they were willing. Zoe Dalrymple might have been suitably grateful to him for saving her kitchen and for entertaining her husband, but he wasn't sure that she even liked him.

Bob Simpson arrived with his helpers at eight o'clock on the dot, timing it again as the church clock struck. Instead of the Sunbeam Talbot he was driving an old Bedford van. The two men with him were in their twenties and he introduced them as Glen and Dave. Glen was huge and bear-like and wore a shapeless blue cloth hat, while Dave was small, dark and wiry as a monkey. Carter was surprised to find them so young. He had imagined that people interested enough in old war plane wrecks to spend their spare time looking for them might at least have dim and distant memories of the time when those wrecks had still been flying about the skies.

Tools and equipment were unloaded rapidly from the back of the Bedford: spades, forks, a pickaxe, a bucket and brush, plastic bags and a metal detector. The load shared out, they set off through the graveyard, over the stile and down the hill towards Trodgers Wood. A skein of white mist hung over the valley and the dew was soaking wet in the long grass. Carter looked back once at the big house. The French windows were shut and he could see no sign of life. He trudged on. He wished he had been able to warn Tom about the dig, in case the old man took fright.

They eased their way through the barbed-wire fence, passing the equipment from one to another. Once in the wood and out of the sun, it was cold and dim. As before, Carter felt as though his ears were muffled, all sounds seeming absorbed by the thickness of the growth around them so that twigs and branches popped rather than snapped beneath their boots.

Bob Simpson found the way to the hut and, from there, to the hollow without much difficulty. Years spent tramping about the countryside had taught him to recognize one tree from another. Carter, who would have been lost again within five minutes, comforted himself with the thought that in any city, the situation might have been reversed. He kept an eye out for Tom, but if he and his dog were anywhere near they were keeping well out of sight.

Carter stood at the edge of the hollow and watched as the surveyor swept the ground with the metal detector, holding it out in front of him as though hoovering a carpet. Almost at once the flat disc registered with its high-pitched bleep, increasing in intensity as it homed in on whatever lay beneath the surface. The spot was marked with a peg and the search continued. By the time the whole area had been scanned and marked, Carter reckoned that even Charlie would have had some difficulty in denying that there was a whole lot of metal lying about there.

They began to dig.

The sun had reached the wood and filtered down through the trees. Soon all four men were sweating. The first to strike lucky was Dave, who uncovered another fragment of crumpled aluminium, a little larger than the previous finds. Bob Simpson inspected it before laying it down on one side. Carter, who had been digging as directed, stopped for a moment.

'What do you think, Bob?'

'Same as I always thought. Here, come and take a look over here.'

Carter went over to where the surveyor was working and

Simpson pointed out small blotches of powdery-blue that he had exposed beneath the surface.

'That's where the aluminium fragments have oxidised to powder. You always get that at a crash sight and it's a sure sign you're digging in the right place. That and those patches of soil discolouration from fuel-oil waste.' He bent down to retrieve the new find. 'This bit that Dave dug up's another bit of the fuselage, left near the surface as the plane broke up on impact. The heavy stuff will be down much deeper, of course.'

Carter stared at the ground. The oily pockets of soil were clear enough, but the blue bits looked exactly as though someone had sprinkled a packet of Daz washing powder around. He felt like a doubting Thomas. He saw and yet he still could not quite believe – much as he wanted to. He wanted more evidence.

'How deep would the engine be?'

'Too deep for us to dig by hand. It depends on the speed of impact, the state of the ground, and so on. But you've seen how soft and boggy this place is. I'd say it's at least fifteen or twenty feet down. Possibly more.'

'As much as that?' Carter said, disappointed.

'I'm afraid so. It'd be a JCB job. Meanwhile we go on scratching around near the surface and see what we can come up with.' He looked at the piece of metal in his hand again and wiped away some of the mud with his fingers to examine it more closely. 'Do you know, Frank, I've a feeling . . .' He stopped and shook his head. 'No. Let's just wait and see. It never does to jump to conclusions.'

They continued working for another hour and, as they dug the marked spots, more and more fragments emerged and were carefully gathered together.

'We keep every bit, however small,' Simpson told Carter. 'It could be of value in piecing the whole puzzle together in the end.'

They took a short break, resting on the drier ground above the hollow with their backs leaning against trees. Simpson and the others had had the foresight to bring cans of Coke and lemonade, which they shared with Carter. While he drank his and rested muscles aching from unaccustomed hard labour, he watched the surveyor going through the little pile of finds, one by one. He had an uneasy feeling.

'Something bothering you, Bob?'

Simpson shook his head. 'No. Nothing to worry about.'

Carter swatted away a fly. 'The thing I *am* worrying about is how the hell we're going to convince Dalrymple with that lot. He saw bits like that before and said they were saucepans. We need something better.'

The surveyor looked up with a smile. 'Wait and see.'

'You say anything heavy will be too deep to hand dig?'

'If you're thinking of the engine again, or the prop, or anything sizeable, the answer's yes. Certainly for today anyway.'

Carter looked at the pile. 'Supposing we do succeed in convincing Dalrymple somehow that those jigsaw pieces make up a Spitfire – what then? You'd need a JCB to get the rest up, and how would you ever get a machine through this far into the wood, even with his agreement?'

'I took another good look at the Ordnance Survey map. We could get one in from the north-west side. There's a lane there that passes the edge of the wood and the trees aren't so thick. I went and took a look. If we used a wheeled digger instead of a tracked one it would be more manoeuvrable.'

'And if he refused to let you use a machine – any machine?'

'Then I'd say that's that. To hand dig would be difficult and dangerous. It'd mean several weekends instead of just one and would take far too long. You'd get the hole filling up with water all the while. With a machine there isn't time for it to get flooded and it's a damned sight safer, too. Dig a big hole in the ground with sides twenty feet deep and you can get the whole lot caving in on top of you if you're not careful. With a JCB the men can keep out of the way and let the bucket take the risk.'

Carter was silent for a moment. 'What else might there be fairly near the surface?'

'Bullets. Bits of tail wreckage. If we're lucky some of the rudder, perhaps.'

Carter drank from his can of Coke and looked over at the hollow. Despite the increasing evidence, he was still finding it hard to believe that there really was a plane there. It reminded him of the time he'd stopped to look over the wall at an excavation being carried on at a demolition site in the City near Fleet Street. There had been a noticeboard with helpful diagrams to tell onlookers what was going on and what had already been discovered – part of a Roman wall, Saxon remains, medieval foundations, and so on. He had found it all as clear as the London mud the people were working in below. But, if you knew what you were doing, as the archaeologists had done and as Bob Simpson did here, then you saw the whole thing differently, through different eyes. What was obscure to one man was obvious to another.

He said, thinking of another angle, 'Didn't you say that you didn't believe the pilot was with the plane?'

'I said I thought he was more likely to have bailed out, unless he was dead already. Otherwise he'd have made for the fields, not a wood. If we ever get as far as doing a proper dig, I hope he's *not* here. Like I told you, it only makes for complications. The MoD don't like it. They prefer to treat planes with human remains as war graves. Not to be disturbed. You can see their point of view. It all makes for extra work and trouble for them, let alone the expense of a military funeral – that's another reason they put forward, believe it or not. And they're afraid some eighty-year-old mother will get upset again over something that happened a long time ago. It's understandable.'

'If I were an eighty-year-old mother – or a wife or sister,' Carter said, 'I think I'd sooner know what happened to my son or my husband or my brother.' He was quoting Zoe.

'All the relatives I've ever come across feel that way, too,' the surveyor answered. 'As a matter of fact, I had a letter from the mother of a Hurricane pilot once, and she was ninety-four. It was after her son had been found and buried with full military

111

honours near her home. She said she felt she could die in peace now and that when she did she was going to be able to be buried near her son. It seemed to make her very happy.' He shrugged his shoulders. 'Still, you can never tell, I suppose. And there's other ways of looking at it. Some people believe they should be left where they were – that it's as good as any proper, consecrated grave. The only trouble is, like with this one, you don't always know they're there in the first place, and digging a plane up is the only way of identifying it for certain – and sometimes the pilot, too.'

They carried on digging. Carter had stripped off his shirt and by now the sweat was running down his face and body. He was the least fit of the group. Simpson and Dave had the wiry strength of the small man while the giant-like Glen moved and worked like an automaton. Carter wiped the sweat out of his eyes, paused for a moment and then drove his spade down into the wet earth again. This time, instead of cutting through cleanly, it came up against something soft but resistant, lying about two feet below the surface. He withdrew the spade and probed around cautiously to make sure he had not been mistaken. Then he called Simpson.

The surveyor dug around the find and lifted it carefully out in one piece. Dave and Glen had gathered round and the three of them removed the mud by hand.

Carter looked down at what he had discovered, without much enthusiasm. It was a strip of heavy canvas-like fabric, badly torn and with traces of a reddish colour on one side. When Simpson turned it over he saw that the other side was yellow. He had no idea what its function could be. That it was part of the plane was clear enough from the reaction of the others, and he saw that they, at least, knew exactly what it was. Glen whistled loudly and wiped his hand across his brow, leaving a thick trail of mud.

'Well, fancy that! I'll be blowed!'

The other two had taken the piece of canvas to a clean patch of grass and were laying it out – smoothing it out as gently as though it were fine velvet. Carter watched impatiently, listening to them exchanging comments between themselves.

'What is it, Bob?'

The surveyor glanced up apologetically. 'Sorry. I forgot about you, Frank, for a minute. This took me a bit by surprise – though I did have an idea at the back of my mind that it might turn out like this.' He touched the canvas. 'This is part of the rudder. They were wooden-structured and covered with doped fabric like this and then distempered some colour. This piece must have got torn off when the plane went into the ground – as you might expect.'

'Why the surprise, then?'

'It's not quite what we thought.'

'How do you mean? Tom was right, wasn't he? There's a plane here – just like he said.'

'Tom was quite right about that. But not about it being a Spitfire.' Simpson shook his head. 'It was stupid of me ever to take his word for it. I should have learned that lesson by now and listened to my own instincts. People made mistakes in identifying aircraft all the time during the war – even those with all their faculties, let alone someone like Tom. The pilots even used to shoot down their own side; so did the anti-aircraft people. It was quite common.'

'For God's sake, stop talking in riddles, Bob. If it's not a Spitfire, what is it?'

The surveyor stood up. He considered the length of torn canvas lying at his feet for one more moment.

'It's a Bf 109E. It's a Messerschmitt.'

The first thing Carter felt was a crushing disappointment. A Messerschmitt! Not a glorious little Spitfire all ready to be set on a dainty dish for the delectation of the patriotic *Courier* readers, but a Kraut plane! A plane flown not by one of the brave and gallant Few, fighting 'Per Ardua ad Astra', but by an arrogant, jack-booted member of Goering's Luftwaffe, with all the wrong connotations of sinister black crosses and swastikas. Carter swore beneath his breath. Ken wouldn't like it half so much. Neither would all the retired colonels, let alone the retired air commodores and wing commanders when they looked at their local newspapers. He could see them muttering 'Damned Nazi!' into their clipped moustaches before turning the pages to see who had won the best vegetable prizes. As for Phillip Dalrymple with his hatred of all things German, any chance they might have had of getting permission for an extended dig was almost certainly up the spout once he heard about this.

He said, but without much hope: 'Are you quite sure, Bob? No possibility of a mistake?'

'I'm ninety per cent sure, let's say that.' Simpson crouched down and fingered the canvas once more. 'The 109Es generally had both nose and rudder distempered this yellow. You can see the colour quite clearly still. Sometimes they were red, sometimes white, but more often than not the spinner, engine cowling and rudder were all yellow. A few of the 109s that went on sorties in July and August 1940 still had the old pale blue and dark green paint, but they were rare.' He looked up at Carter. 'The thing is, Frank, that the Spitfire rudder was green and brown. Unless some joker in the RAF painted his yellow – which doesn't seem too likely unless he was aiming to get shot down by his own side – then this one's a Messerschmitt all right.'

Carter swore again, this time longer and aloud.

Simpson said mildly: 'We excavate German planes too, you know. Not just British. We're not fussy. We've even been known to dig up American ones. Last April we recovered a Thunderbolt. It had been shot down by a Spitfire.'

'I'd like to have heard what the pilot said!'

'It wasn't on record. He was too busy bailing out.'

Glen guffawed and Dave grinned. Carter hoped the American pilot had found it half as amusing.

The surveyor stood up. 'What difference does it make if this is a Messerschmitt?'

'My editor was all starry-eyed about the idea of a Spitfire story. He'd got the whole thing worked out . . . "Never in the

114

field of conflict", pictures of the pilot, past glories for the readers, and so on. Besides which, our friendly landowner isn't going to be too enchanted either. His father was blown to bits by a German plane when he was sitting minding his own business in a lifeboat in the Atlantic in 1944. They're not exactly his favourite people.'

'Then maybe he'll be all the more anxious for us to remove this lot,' Simpson suggested. 'And, after all, it was probably shot down by one of our lads. You could look at it that way.'

'I'm trying. But I'm finding it difficult.'

To Carter's increasing depression they later uncovered a number of German bullets.

'7.9mm,' Simpson commented, showing Carter a small brass cylinder in his palm, dull, dirty and squashed nearly flat at one end. 'Better not handle it, Frank. Some of them had phosphorous heads – the tracers – and they can still ignite.' He paused. 'Of course, it *could* have been fired from a German plane and been embedded in one of ours, but I don't want to raise your hopes. We've found several of them.'

The bullets were added to the growing pile. They were joined by two or three more fragments of perspex and some larger pieces of the fuselage skin. The earth became steadily wetter as the work progressed.

A movement by the trees caught Carter's eye and he saw that Tom was watching them from a safe distance. He parked his spade and strolled over towards him. The old man stood his ground. A wooden wheelbarrow filled with twigs and broken branches was set down in front of him and the black and white dog sat at his heels.

Carter pointed at the hollow. 'Your plane, Tom. We've found some more pieces of it.'

The imbecile's bright eyes flickered from Carter to the site and back again. 'Spitfire!' he said and dived his hand through the air. 'Boom!'

Carter moved a little further downwind of him. It was weird to think that this smelly old tramp had been the only witness; that those beady little eyes had watched the last few seconds of the plane's life and, come to that, maybe that of the pilot's too. Just how much had Tom been able to see? Enough to know whether or not there was a man in the fighter – even though he'd got the nationality all wrong?

Carter said carefully: 'It wasn't a Spitfire, Tom. They think it was a Messerschmitt. A German plane.'

Tom's eyes darted to and fro again. He nodded happily. 'Spitfire! Boom!'

Carter sighed inwardly. Outwardly he smiled encouragement. 'Was there a man in the plane, Tom? Did you see the pilot?'

The old man nodded dementedly. 'Man in plane! Man in Spitfire! Boom! *Boom!*'

'What's he saying, Frank?'

Bob Simpson had clumped over, spade in hand, boots clogged with thick mud.

'He says he saw the pilot in the plane, but he's probably just trying to please. He still keeps calling it a Spitfire, though I told him what you think.'

'It's all the same to him, I dare say.' Simpson nodded pleasantly to Tom and spoke to the dog, who wagged his feathery tail. Then his glance fell on the wheelbarrow full of kindling and, suddenly, he laughed out loud. 'Well, there's your final proof for you, Frank. Before your very eyes and no need to dig an inch for it. Pity we didn't see it before.'

Carter looked round nonplussed. 'What proof? And what's so funny?'

Grinning all over his face, Simpson pointed to the white-walled rubber tyre on the front of Tom's home-made barrow.

'That's the tail wheel of a Messerschmitt!'

Later on they broke for lunch. Again, the others shared what they had brought with Carter, who felt both guilty and grateful. He could never be bothered to cater for himself. If he didn't eat out somewhere he didn't eat at all. But now, resting from his labours, he felt ravenously hungry and thirsty.

Tom had gone, trundling his barrow away and clearly

delighted that they had, all four, admired his handiwork so enthusiastically. So far as they could understand him, they had learned that he had found the tail wheel up a nearby tree – one of those with missing branches. Bob Simpson, munching through a ham sandwich, was still amused.

'I came across a Lancaster canopy used for growing lettuces once, but I reckon Tom's wheelbarrow beats that.'

Carter swallowed the last of his sandwich. 'So now we know for sure?'

'No doubt about it. It's an Me109 down there. We've no need to dig any deeper for any more evidence. We'll fill in and leave it all tidy, as we found it. Then I'll have to report to Sir Phillip. He wanted to know the result at once.'

'It won't please him on either count: that we were right about the plane and, still less, that it's German.'

'I can't change the facts,' Simpson said, shrugging.

'I'll come along with you, if you don't mind.'

'I'd be glad of it. You seemed to do all right with him last time. You may be a help.'

'No harm in trying, as they say.'

A bee buzzed past. Somewhere in the wood the cuckoo was calling and to Carter it no longer sounded mocking, but triumphant, as though it approved wholeheartedly. He wished he could think that Phillip Dalrymple would do so, too. Bob Simpson had not yet met him face to face and didn't really understand what they were up against. He finished the can of Coke and stretched himself out on the grass in the shade of the tree. A little way off, Dave lay with his head pillowed on his arm while Glen had propped himself against a trunk and tilted his floppy hat forward over his eyes. Except for the birdsong it was quiet. Carter put his hands behind his head and looked up into the pattern of leaves above him.

'I wonder just what the hell did happen to that plane. How did it manage to end up here?'

'We may never know,' Simpson said matter-of-factly. 'It wasn't necessarily shot down; it might have crashed because of a pilot's error, or simply run out of fuel. The Germans only had about ten minutes combat time before they had to head for home.'

'Christ! Was that all? They must have been fighting with one eye on the clock.'

'All the time. And don't forget the Channel lay between them and home. All those miles of rough, cold sea to get across. They couldn't afford to dilly-dally. In fact, some of them put down on this side rather than risk drowning on the way back.'

'Can't say I blame them. But it doesn't look like that happened here.'

The surveyor agreed. 'No, as I said, he'd have picked a nice flat field. Mind you, he could have been *aiming* for a field and then got it all wrong or had a power failure. A lot of their pilots were as inexperienced as ours, with only a few hours flying under their belts. And Messerschmitts weren't that easy to handle. You should see the figures for crashes when they weren't even combatant. It had a nasty swing on take-off and landing, as well as a weak undercarriage that had a nasty habit of collapsing. A bit hard to cope with if you were only nineteen or so and hadn't quite got the hang of things.'

Carter offered his cigarettes and, when Simpson had declined, lit one for himself.

'Supposing the pilot *is* here? What would you expect to find of him?'

'Not a complete body, sitting upright in the cockpit, if that's what you're thinking. A lot of people imagine it's like that but the only time I've ever found a pilot in one piece was when we excavated a Hurricane that had gone down into a peat bog. When we lifted that one out he still had recognizable features. Gave us a bit of a turn.' Simpson bit cheerfully into his sandwich. 'Mostly, we just find a few bones, perhaps some shreds of skin and pieces of clothing. On impact, the pilot is thrown forward and the skull is usually crushed inside the helmet. It's not really a body, as such, more a question of human remains – and not that much of them. They often have to fill the coffin up with damp sand for the burial.'

Carter watched the smoke drifting up towards the branches over his head. Gruesome details never worried him. He could have told far worse stories from his crime-reporting days.

'How do you identify these remains?'

'If there's more than one body in a plane then it's not easy to sort out. If it's a single-seater fighter, like this one, then the job's a lot simpler. So long as you can come up with the aircraft serial number – not the engine number because of engine changes – then it's just a case of matching the remains to the number through official records. Sometimes there are codes and emblems still visible on the plane, which all help. The Germans were very fond of them; painted them all over the place. If there's any snag in identifying the aircraft, you can still be lucky and find the pilot's dog tag, or some personal documents – letters, papers, photos. You'd be surprised what survives in the ground, even over forty years or more.' Simpson nodded towards the site. 'If there's a pilot in there, we shouldn't have much trouble identifying him. Nothing's been touched since the plane crashed – except for the tail wheel and a few scraps. But I think you'll probably find that he bailed out and is now a prosperous businessman in Stuttgart, or somewhere.'

Carter asked curiously: 'Are you sorry you missed the war? Don't you wish you'd been able to fly the old machines you keep digging up?'

The surveyor considered the question for a moment before answering. 'Sometimes, yes. Sometimes, no. If I'm honest, mostly yes. The ones I come across didn't survive, of course, which colours your thinking a bit. But, if their life was short, it was a glorious one in a way ours will never be. Yes, I think I'd like to have been one of them.'

'What about Glen and Dave? It's strange they're even interested, considering they weren't even born till long after.'

'They're not the only young ones in the group – not by a long chalk. We've got a couple of ex-pilots and a gunner, but otherwise it's people who've never been anything other than

119

Margaret Mayhew

a passenger on a holiday package flight.' The surveyor frowned
a little. 'I don't know that any of us could explain it. I reckon
it's just something that fascinates us all. You never know what
you're going to find and it's a direct link with the past that
gets to you somehow . . . Same as people digging up Roman
remains, I suppose, except that this is something you can understand better.' He paused to finish the sandwich. 'When it comes
down to it, is it any wonder people keep looking back these
days? There's not a lot to look forward to in this world. And
those were the days when England was England and not a
European annexe full of foreigners. Anyway, come to that,
what are you doing here, Frank? You weren't born then yourself, either.'

'It's all part of the job, isn't it? I'll admit that up till now
I've found everything to do with World War Two bloody
boring . . . All those old soldiers and their everlasting memories of the cock-ups they made. But this sort of thing's a bit
different.'

'It's about individuals,' Simpson said. 'It's about what
happened to one man, or a small group of men, not a whole
army.'

'Well, let's hope we'll get the chance to find out what
happened to this particular man.'

They filled in the holes and raked over the leaves, leaving
almost no visible signs of disturbance. Bob Simpson carried
their finds in a black plastic bag. As they toiled upwards across
the field towards the stile, Carter saw that the French windows
at the Hall were now open and that the owner was stationed
there in his wheelchair, watching them through the binoculars.

They found the churchyard full of people and the air buzzing
with the sound of a motorized hedge-cutter. Smoke rose from
a bonfire in an out-of-the-way corner. The workforce engaged
in a tidying-up operation was exclusively male and, with the
exception of one teenager and of the rector, exclusively elderly.
Carter recognized several of the patrons of the Bull, winkled
from their dark corners to lend a hand and to wield scythe

and sickle. Jesse, cutting close by the pathway, stopped work as they went past. His cap was set squarely on his head and his unlit pipe clenched between his teeth. As he saw the tools and the bag, his face lit up.

'Find anything, Mr Carter?'

Simpson cleared his throat in warning.

'Nothing to speak of, I'm afraid,' Carter told him.

The old man looked disappointed; the pipe drooped. 'I'd hoped there'd be something.'

They moved on.

'Sorry about that,' Simpson muttered apologetically. 'But if we don't keep it quiet it'll be all round the village and we'll have souvenir hunters and God know's what else mucking things up.'

Near the lychgate the rector, in jeans and a T-shirt, turned from trimming back some ivy. 'I can see you've been taking Tom's plane story quite seriously, Mr Carter. Did you find anything interesting?'

Once again, Carter was forced to lie – or, at any rate, avoid the truth. He answered much the same as before and introduced Bob Simpson and the others. The rector's gaze rested on the black plastic bag for a moment, but he made no comment.

Carter said brightly: 'Is all this work in aid of the best-kept village competition?'

'It is indeed. I fear God's acre has become rather overgrown, but our little army of volunteers will soon restore order. We have a blitz on the churchyard once a year anyway but since we've entered for the competition we try extra hard.' He snipped away at the ivy. 'The nuisance is that we can't mow the grass by machine because of getting round the graves; it all has to be done by hand. We've rather given up with the oldest part – the bit beyond the west door. We just leave it to grow wild now. Luckily there are some rather rare and beautiful flowers there so we've officially designated it a conservation area and the judges can't mark us down for it.' He smiled over his shoulder. 'Canny of us!'

'I hope you win.'

'Thank you, Mr Carter. So do I. Not that winning is important in itself, of course.'

'Tell that to Mayhurst.'

Hugh Longman laughed. 'You've heard all about the rivalry, I suppose. Ridiculous really, but there it is. If it makes us take care of our villages better, then perhaps there's some point to it. Since they won last year it's been worse, of course. There were some ugly rumours of favouritism, discrepancies in the marking, and so forth ... All quite unfounded, I'm sure. I *say*, just look at this!'

The snipping had uncovered a headstone, masked by the curtain of ivy. Thomas Taylor, who had died in 1734, had been unveiled once more.

They left the rector and the others beavering away and loaded everything into the back of the Bedford van. Carter, in his own mini van, led the way round to Fairfield Hall.

Zoe Dalrymple opened the door to them. She was wearing jeans, a pale blue shirt and a leather belt round her waist. Instead of being twisted into a topknot, her hair was loose about her face, making her look younger than ever. Carter found himself staring at her. It was as though she had suddenly taken on a new dimension for him and every detail and everything about her had become significant and important to him. He pulled himself together and introduced the other three, seeing the astonishment register on their faces as it must have done on his own when he had first discovered who she was.

She invited them inside in her natural, friendly way. 'Good news?'

'Well, there's a plane there all right.'

She smiled at him. 'I knew it. I knew there must be. Don't worry about Phillip. He's coming slowly round to the idea. I think he had an idea he might be wrong.'

Glen had removed his hat and was standing first on one boot and then on the other. Little shards of dried mud decorated the carpet around his feet. Dave had prudently remained on the doormat. Carter was still looking at Zoe.

Simpson cleared his throat. 'I'm sorry about the mess we're making, Lady Dalrymple. I think we'd better take off our boots.'

'Good heavens, no,' she told him, smiling. 'The place is filthy anyway. Come on in and meet my husband.'

They followed her towards the drawing room, Glen tiptoeing as though he was playing Grandmother's Footsteps. Simpson and Carter exchanged glances.

'Over to you,' Carter murmured. 'And I'll do what I can.'

Phillip Dalrymple was beside the French windows, the U-boat commander's binoculars resting on his knees. He swung the wheelchair round and Carter saw at once that he was in vile humour.

'There you are, Carter! And Mr Simpson, presumably, together with his sidekicks.' The baronet propelled his chair rapidly across the room and stopped dead a few feet from where they stood. He ignored his wife. 'Well, Mr Simpson, what have you in that bag? A complete Spitfire?'

The surveyor said quietly: 'Nothing like that, sir.'

'What have you found, then? Since it's *my* land you've been poking about on I feel I have some right to know.'

'That's why we're here, sir. To report to you.'

'Then report away. I'm all eyes. And ears.'

Simpson cleared his throat. He began to open up the neck of the black plastic bag. 'We found a number of other pieces of aluminium – similar to the one you have already seen, but larger – as well as more perspex fragments from the cockpit.' He extracted a piece of crumpled metal, smeared with mud, and handed it to Phillip Dalrymple. 'This is the sort of thing we kept digging up. It's part of the fuselage.'

The invalid barely glanced at the exhibit before returning it. 'Is that all? It could belong to anything.'

Simpson delved into the bag again, as though in charge of some lucky dip. 'We also found this, sir.'

Phillip Dalrymple looked at the strip of yellow canvas. He raised his eyebrows. 'Well? What is it?'

'It's part of the rudder.'

123

'How can you possibly know that? It's just a bit of old cloth.'

'I can assure you, sir, that it's definitely part of a plane. I'd stake my life on it.' Simpson groped into the bag once more. 'And these are bullets.'

The wheelchair squeaked forward. There was a pause. 'I'll admit they look like it. But that's all.'

Carter could see the surveyor taking a long breath.

'They're German bullets, sir. 7.9mm. The piece of canvas belongs to the rudder of a German plane and Tom had used the tail wheel to make a wheelbarrow for himself. It's not a Spitfire in Trodgers Wood. It's a Messerschmitt.'

This time there was a much longer silence. Nobody spoke. Then the wheelchair reversed away from the black plastic bag.

'Did you say a *tail wheel*, Mr Simpson?'

'Yes, sir. A tail wheel belonging to an Me109E.'

There was another moment's silence.

'All right. I accept what you say. You believe there is a German fighter on my land. In which case, Mr Simpson, I categorically refuse to allow any further excavation. I warned you when we spoke on the phone that I wasn't going to have that wood messed up by you and your group of amateur sleuths, and I'm certainly not taking the risk if there's any possibility of it being a Hun plane. So far as I'm concerned, it can stay where it is and rot.'

'It's of some historic interest, sir, and—'

'To hell with historic interest! My only interest is in you getting out of here and staying out!'

Carter stepped forward. 'That would be a pity.'

'A pity for you and your newspaper, Carter, you mean. No plane. No story.'

'I was thinking more of you.'

'That, I don't believe! You're thinking of what your editor will say when he hears you can't deliver. And if you do try to print anything about this, Carter, I'll have you up in court for trespass with Simpson here. Get them out of here, Zoe. The lot of them!' He was very white and trembling violently

124

in his wheelchair. Without another word, Bob Simpson picked up the bag and they left the room. As Carter was closing the door behind him, the baronet cried: 'You can tell him to bring that bag back here, Carter! Anything found on my land is my property.'

Carter looked at him. He shook his head.

'Sorry, sir. It's captured enemy property surrendered to the Crown. It belongs to the Ministry of Defence. Bob Simpson told me. It's all in a directive from them.'

'Like hell you're sorry!' The chair trundled fast forward over the Chinese carpet. 'Don't give me that, Carter!' The chair stopped. 'Have you got a cigarette on you?'

Carter gave him one and lit it for him. He put the half-full pack beside the Zeiss binoculars.

'You could find an excavation entertaining, sir.'

Phillip Dalrymple drew on the cigarette. He exhaled the smoke. He had stopped shaking and looked better. 'Go to hell, Carter!'

Carter pocketed his lighter. He gave a half salute. 'Certainly, sir.'

Out in the hall, Bob Simpson was apologizing to Zoe Dalrymple for having upset her husband. Glen was shuffling his boots uncomfortably while Dave looked at the ceiling, much embarrassed. As Carter joined them, Zoe was being very nice about it all and trying to reassure them. He could see, though, that underneath it she was as upset as Simpson. When she turned to him, he saw the strain and unhappiness in her eyes.

'I'll try and talk him round later, Mr Carter, if I can. It's been one of his bad days. He's been terribly depressed.'

'You look a bit down in the mouth, too.'

She pushed her fingers through her fringe distractedly. 'Me? Oh, *I'm* all right. But I just hate it when he's like this. So bitter about everything and everybody.'

'It's understandable. I'd feel that way myself, if I were him.'

She looked towards the others, out in the drive. 'I hope they understand too. I hope they're not too disappointed.'

125

'We didn't really expect your husband to agree – once he found out it was a German plane.'

'It's all so silly, isn't it? I mean, it all happened such a long time ago, but Phillip will never forgive what happened to his father.'

'We all have our hang-ups. I've got mine.'

She looked up at him very seriously. 'I can't believe that. You seem so . . . so *sane* about things. As though nothing worries you.'

'It's all a bluff,' he told her truthfully. 'By the way, I'll see you on the twenty-eighth. I haven't forgotten.'

'The twenty-eighth?'

'Now *you've* forgotten! The fête. The fancy dress judging. What would Mrs Armstrong-Avery have to say?'

She smiled then. 'Of course. It's awfully good of you.'

He walked away down the drive to join the others, knowing that it wasn't awfully good of him at all. He would have judged a hundred fancy dress contests if it meant seeing her again.

Seven

B ob Simpson was philosophical.
'You win some, you lose some,' was his verdict after
they had left the Hall. 'It's a pity, but there it is.'

Ken Grant was less so.

'A *German* plane, Frank! I thought you said it was a Spitfire.'

'I thought it was. We all thought it was. But it turned out
it wasn't.'

'God almighty! Can't you even get *that* right? I thought
you Fleet Street boys knew all the answers. And now you tell
me there's to be no dig anyway!' The editor crunched furiously at a mint. 'It would still have been a good story. Not
as good as a Spitfire, but we could have used a different angle.
We could probably have found the RAF hero who shot him
down and gone for that.' There was more crunching. 'We
could still print what we have, I suppose . . .'

'And have a whole load of trippers tramping over
Dalrymple land, looking for bits of plane? Let's hold our
horses, Ken. Give it a week or two. I think he might change
his mind.'

Ken rested his elbows on his desk and his chin on his hands;
it was a habitual gesture with him, intended to convey deep
scepticism and impatience.

'On what exactly do you base that assumption, Frank?'

'Just a hunch.'

'A hunch! I can't run my newspaper on your hunches.'

'If you put in even a mention, we'll lose the chance of a
good story for ever. Apart from that, he's threatened to sue
me if we do print.'

127

'Sue you! For what? It's not libellous to say someone's got an old plane on his land.'

'For trespass. Two times.'

Ken removed his elbows. He pulled out his desk drawer and took out another mint, which he unwrapped slowly. When he had put the sweet in his mouth he folded the paper neatly into four and placed it on top of a symmetrical pile of other wrappers in the ashtray.

'Are you telling me that you went barging about on this man's land twice – without getting permission beforehand?'

'There was a public footpath, but it didn't happen to go through the wood; it went round it instead. Those things are very bad for your teeth, Ken.'

'Not half as bad as cigarettes are for your lungs.' The editor leaned back in his chair, arms extended to allow his fingers to drum lightly on the edge of the desk. This was another of his habits: the weary-old-provincial-newspaperman-who-has-seen-it-all one. 'I don't know how things are done up in the smoke, Frank, but in our simple country way, out here in the sticks, we take note of little things like people's private property. We respect it.' The fingers drummed louder. 'So, the long and the short of it is that you've made a mess of the whole thing, from start to finish. Wrong tactics, wrong plane, wrong everything.'

'I haven't finished with it yet, Ken.'

'Oh yes you have! You've wasted enough time on it already. Any more and I'll have finished with *you*.' The fingers stopped and the editor leaned forward again. 'I can't say that our association has been an unqualified success so far, can you, Frank? I've had Councillor Jackson on the phone today about you. He is also threatening to sue. He didn't like that piece you did on the planning committee one bit. He's a very angry man.'

'What didn't he like about it? The part about his married daughter having a house opposite the proposed new development that he and his committee threw out? I was just reporting the facts. He asked me to state that there was no connection between the two. I did.'

A Foreign Field

'Come on, Frank. It was the *way* that you wrote it. I read
the piece again myself and the implication is there.'
'If the cap fits . . .'
'He's no intention of wearing it. Any more than I have of
being sued for libel. I told you when you joined us, Frank,
that it's our policy to tread very carefully where people of
local prominence are concerned. We'll print a retraction and
an apology. And *you* can write it.'
Perhaps it was as well, Carter reflected afterwards, that they
were interrupted at that point by Mike Tubbs, the chief sub,
who had returned from his three-hour lunch break and stood
in the doorway, swaying very slightly. Otherwise, he might
have said things about crooked councillors and boot-licking
editors that he would probably have regretted.
He sat at the news desk, lit a cigarette and put his feet up.
Under Harvey's sour and baleful eye, Brenda teetered over
on three-inch heels to bring him a cup of coffee. Partly to
tease the old reporter and partly to cheer himself up, Carter
spent several minutes chatting to her. She was wearing a
shocking-pink lurex dress with nails to match. She perched
on the side of the news desk and held out the talons for his
approval.
'Do you like the colour? It's new. Pink Panther, they call
it.'
'Very nice, love.'
She had hitched up her tight skirt until it was well above
her knees and crossed her legs. Carter handed her a cigarette
and lit it for her. She leaned back on her hands and shook her
frizzy mop of hair in what he knew she hoped was a close
imitation of Marilyn Monroe. He caught sight of Harvey
watching from across the desk with a mixture of outrage and
lust in equal quantities.

Ken Grant's discontent was mollified later in the day by a fire
breaking out in a basement storeroom of Milton's only department store, conveniently in time to make the cover page.
Carter interviewed the teenage assistant who had discovered

129

the blaze, the manager, the head fireman and several shoppers who had been in or around the store at the time. Meanwhile, the photographer snapped away happily at fire engines, broken windows, the gutted basement and long shots of hoses snaking away down the main high street. No one had been hurt, rather to the disappointment of the onlookers gawping from behind barricades. Carter knew that very well. Bad news was good news, so far as papers were concerned. The people pressing forward to see better, even the kindliest of souls in private, would have relished a body or two. Come to that, so would his editor.

That evening he ate out at one of the Milton pubs, a pseudo-Victorian establishment with a great deal of heavy flocked wallpaper, red plush, brass trimmings and electrified, modern oil lamps. The menus were school slates to reinforce the old-fashioned, good, honest English cooking image, but the steak and kidney pudding had come straight out of the freezer, pausing briefly in the microwave en route.

It was late by the time he got back to his lodgings and Mrs Eliot was well into the final lap of her evening's viewing. As he went up the stairs he could hear the rise and fall of voices, punctuated by a lot of ghostly sounding music. His landlady was very fond of horror films. The more horrific, the better.

He lay on his bed on top of the covers, smoking and staring up at the long crack in the ceiling, which was the Nile, and the damp patch, which was Australia. He'd got the Australian cities all worked out. Now he might as well try and put in the rivers. The only trouble was that apart from the Murray River, which was somewhere on the south-eastern side, he couldn't think of the name of a single one. He must have known them once. He could remember the teacher at school drawing a map of Australia on the blackboard and marking in wiggly lines for rivers with squeaking chalk, and he'd been rapped over the knuckles for getting one of them wrong. But their names had gone beyond recall.

With no rivers to think about, he thought about Jan. And

then, although he had sworn to himself not to, he thought about Zoe. Her image superimposed itself on Jan's image and her voice overlaid Jan's voice. And none of it helped him feel any better about anything.

He must have dozed off, because the next thing he was aware of was Mrs Eliot banging on his door and calling that he was wanted on the telephone, and hadn't he heard it ringing, and some people should know better than to phone late at night and right in the middle of a good programme.

He followed her down the stairs as she hurried back to her horror film, her mauve rabbit-fur mules slapping loudly against her heels at each step. By the time he reached the ground floor the sitting-room door was shut and the volume turned up several decibels as though to compensate for viewing lost. He picked up the receiver.

'Mr Carter? I'm terribly sorry to telephone so late. Were you asleep?'

The wire accentuated the classiness of her voice, just as he knew it would make his own sound even more the reverse.

'No problem. What can I do for you, Lady Dalrymple?'

'I got your number from your office,' she said hesitantly. 'I hope that was all right. The girl on the switchboard said I would be able to catch you in the evening, but you probably wouldn't be in until late.' There was another slight hesitation. 'She seemed to know quite a lot about you.'

Carter smiled faintly. 'Brenda knows a lot about all of us. She more or less runs the paper.'

'She certainly sounded awfully efficient. Are you sure I didn't disturb you?'

'Quite sure.'

'I would have phoned earlier, but I couldn't leave Phillip until now and I didn't want him to hear ...'

'I know what you mean.'

'I just wanted to tell you that I've done my best with him – about the plane – but I can't persuade him to change his mind. I don't think there's any hope of it. I'm most awfully sorry.'

There was a crescendo of horror music from the sitting room. Carter carried the phone further down the hall.

'It can't be helped,' he said. 'I appreciate your husband's feelings.'

'I know you do, Mr Carter. And I'm very grateful. But it's a pity, after you and Mr Simpson tried so hard. And I do think the plane *ought* to be excavated. It seems such a shame to just leave it there.'

Carter was about to say that it was unlikely to stay there for ever and then stopped himself. The truth was that now its whereabouts were known they would not be forgotten. Phillip Dalrymple might refuse permission now, but no actuary would predict a long innings for him and the next owner of Fairfield Hall – presumably his wife – would probably oblige. But to say so would be unforgivable.

'Don't worry about it any more, Lady Dalrymple. There are other planes around. Bob Simpson's always digging them up. He's like a terrier after bones.'

The simile was a bit unfortunate but he sensed her smile and relax a little.

'The trouble is,' she went on, 'a rumour has started round the village. Mrs Sweet says everyone's talking about the plane and Harry told me that yesterday they were all buying poor Tom pints and pints in the Bull and asking him where it was in the wood. Luckily they got him so drunk they couldn't make head or tail of anything he said. It wouldn't matter except that we've already had some people trespassing and, of course, Phillip's furious about that.'

'I can imagine he might be.'

'They still think it's a Spitfire, though. Nobody seems to have any idea that it's a German plane. Not that it makes any difference, but the trespassing hasn't helped with Phillip. After you'd gone, I thought for a while that he might agree, in spite of it being German, but now I don't think he ever will.'

Carter was thinking fast. The trespassers were bad news and needed discouraging. There were other considerations, too.

'Look, I'm sorry about all this. I feel responsible. Would it help if I called by the village? I could stop off at the Bull, say, and the shop, and scotch the rumours.'

'Would you do that? I'd be terribly grateful.'

'As I said, I feel responsible. I'll do my best to put them all off the scent.'

She thanked him and rang off suddenly. He would have kept her talking if he could; instead he was left standing in the empty hall with the instrument in his hand. He replaced the receiver slowly. As he made his way back up the stairs, blood-curdling screams reached him from below.

Mrs Jennings' shop had taken on a new lease of life. Outside, at least. The newly painted woodwork shone, the window glass sparkled and there was a tub filled with yet more salmon-pink geraniums beside the door. Any more of them in the village and Carter thought the judges might deduct points for lack of originality. He pushed open the door and the bell jangled loudly.

Inside, nothing had changed. The yellow cellophane still cast its stormy light and Mrs Jennings was behind her counter, presiding comfortably over chaos.

'Hello, dear. Back about that plane, are you? You could have knocked me down with a feather when I heard it was true all along. Fancy that now! Old Tom and his stories that nobody believed a word of, and one of them turned out to be true. Still, Prince Philip's never been near the Bull – that's one thing I *do* know for sure.'

He asked her for a pack of cigarettes. 'Who told you Tom's plane story was true, Mrs Jennings?'

She was searching for the cigarettes on the shelf behind her as she answered him. 'Oh, I can't rightly remember. I get so many in and out of here all day. I forget who says what some-times. I *think* it was Mrs Coleman, but it might have been Mrs Buss. Not that you can believe all *she* says, any more than with Tom, thought she's all there in the head. A real old gossip, she is. Here you are, dear, I've found them – they were hiding under the custard powder.'

He forked out the necessary change. 'I'm sorry to disappoint you, but that's all it was – gossip. There wasn't a Spitfire there after all. The aviation archaeology group dug the spot and found that Tom had got it all wrong.'

Mrs Jennings looked as disappointed as Jesse. 'Well, now that *is* a shame. I thought it was ever so exciting. Romantic, really. One of them lovely Spitfires hidden away in a wood all this time, just waiting to be discovered all these years.'

No one could deny, Carter thought, that Ken Grant knew his readers. 'Yes, it's a pity about it.'

Mrs Jennings pressed the till keys carefully and the drawer shot open into her stomach; she dropped the coins in one by one.

'He died, you know. The minute he'd finished it. The effort killed him.'

'Sorry?'

'Mr Mickle. The one who built it. Did it in three months flat, from start to finish. A real race against time, it was. He had to get it ready for the Battle of Britain, otherwise they'd have won. But he did it, even though he was ill. Then he died. And *we* won.'

Carter wondered if R. J. Mitchell would have recognized this potted version of his achievement in designing the Spitfire. And yet, Mrs Jennings had got it right, in essence.

'A brilliant man,' he agreed.

'One of the best.' She nodded energetically. 'They don't come like that any more. Nobody would bother to sacrifice themselves nowadays. They're all too busy working for the Arabs or the Americans, earning pots of money. That's all they care about now. That, or they don't want to work at all. Look at them! Long hair, dirty clothes, drugs, on the dole . . . My Arthur used to say that the country was going to the dogs. He fought in the war, you know. He was in the desert with the Rats. Best years of his life, he used to say. If the war had gone on another year, I'd have joined up myself. Always fancied the Wrens somehow. The uniform's nicer than the others. Those ATS didn't look nice at all. Horrible colour, and I bet that material scratched. I get dermatitis, you know, so I have to be careful what I wear next to me. Otherwise I come out in a rash and get great blisters all over—'

Carter was spared more details by the entrance of another customer, greeted by Mrs Jennings with a mixture of deference and familiarity.

'Safely back again, Miss Burton? How's your sister then? All right now, is she, dear?'

'Much improved, thank you, Mrs Jennings.'

The voice was just as Carter had expected: deep, brisk and very clear.

Mrs Jennings patted her auburn bun. 'Well that's a relief. You can't be too careful when you're getting on a bit – that's what I always say. If my Arthur had taken more care of himself he'd still be here today. But he wouldn't listen. Time and time again I used to say to him, Arthur, I used to say—'

'I wonder if I might have a pound of sugar, Mrs Jennings, if this gentleman has finished. Granulated.'

Mrs Jennings was muddled now. 'Did I serve you, dear? I can't remember.'

Carter held up the cigarettes.

'So I did. I must be getting old. I'll be losing my wits next, like poor old Tom. This gentleman's from the press, Miss Burton.'

'Really?' she said politely but without interest. 'How do you do?'

'He's been here about the plane.'

Miss Burton opened her purse to pay for the sugar. 'What plane, Mrs Jennings?'

'Thank you, dear. Of course, you've been away. I was forgetting. You wouldn't have heard about it. Ever so exciting it's been. Except that it wasn't there, after all. A false alarm, so this gentleman says.'

'I'm afraid I don't quite follow you.'

Carter said briefly: 'There was an investigation into a story of Tom's – the old man who lives in Trodgers Wood. He said

135

he'd seen a Spitfire come down there during the last war. It turned out to be untrue.'

Miss Burton had picked up the bag of sugar and stood holding it against her flat chest. She stared at him. 'He said he'd seen a Spitfire?'

'It seems he's been telling the story to everyone for years. Anyone who would listen, that is, and buy him a drink.'

The schoolteacher was still staring. 'I never heard it. How extraordinary! Not a word.'

'He mainly tells it in the Bull.'

'Of course, I never go in there. And I haven't seen Tom for years.'

'Saw him a month back,' Mrs Jennings said, thumping a tune on the old till along the counter. 'Smelly as ever, he was. Have to hold my breath when he's in here. All he ever buys is toffees. I don't know how he eats them, seeing he hasn't a tooth in his head. Beats me what he lives on. It can't just be the toffees . . .'

Miss Burton ignored her. She looked at Carter with her sharp eyes. 'You say the story was investigated? By you?'

'By members of an aviation archaeology group. I was there too.'

'And what did they find?'

'That there were no Spitfire remains.'

Miss Burton continued to look at him and Carter felt as uneasy as if he were still in the lower fourth and had just told a whopper. Except that he had spoken the truth.

'I see.'

'Tom and his tales,' Mrs Jennings said. 'Proper old devil, he is. Leading everyone up the garden path on a wild goose chase.'

Reasonably sure that his job was done, Carter held opened the door for Miss Burton and followed her out of the shop. The ancient bicycle was leaning against the wall; the school-teacher put the sugar in the wicker basket and grasped hold of the handles. She looked over her shoulder.

'What is your name?'

He almost stood to attention. 'Frank Carter.'
'Have you a few minutes to spare, Mr Carter?'
'Certainly, Miss Burton.'
'A cup of tea, then? My cottage is only just up the lane. Follow me.'

She wheeled the bicycle out on to the road and set off at a smart pace without once glancing back to see if he had obeyed instructions. Carter leaped hurriedly into his van, afraid of losing sight of her. He caught her up by the parish hall and thereafter kept a respectful distance behind the upright, briskly pedalling figure. Just before they reached the rectory she turned right down a narrow lane. They passed a line of four post-war council houses and a few yards further on she signalled left with a stiffly extended arm and disappeared into a small entrance at the side of a cottage. There was no room there for a car and so Carter parked as close to the verge as possible. He went through the picket gate. As he had expected, the white clapboarded cottage and its front garden were pin-neat. Even the flowers grew in orderly fashion, lining the pathway to the front door in straight rows. The sign on the gate had said Lavender Cottage and, appropriately, a large lavender bush grew beside the door.

Miss Burton reappeared round the side of the house, drawing off her grey cotton gloves.
'Come in, Mr Carter. Indian or Chinese?'
'Sorry?'
'Indian or Chinese tea?'
'Indian, please.'

He followed her into the cottage. The front door opened directly into a sitting room, which was comfortably but simply furnished with two easy chairs, a circular table and dining chairs and several shelves full of books. There was an open rolltop desk with its contents as neatly arranged in the pigeon holes as the desk at Fairfield Hall had been messy. Everything was clean and bright and there was a strong smell of lavender polish.

Miss Burton had vanished once again – this time into the

137

inner depths of the house – and he could hear the clink of china and the whistle of a kettle. While he waited he looked around the room. On closer inspection, there were some surprises that did not quite fit the spinster's image of olde worlde Englishness. A glass-fronted corner cupboard was filled with a collection of ivory elephants, ranging from large to miniscule and carefully displayed, trunk to tail, in order of size. There were more elephants on the walls in the form of pictures and a David Shepherd print of a trumpeting bull elephant above the fireplace. Beneath this, a row of wood-carved and exotically eastern figures danced along the mantlepiece and Carter was examining these when Miss Burton returned, bearing a tea tray.

'Sit down, Mr Carter. Milk? Sugar? Lemon?'

He started, feeling guilty about nothing. Like all authoritarians she had that effect on people.

'Milk, please. No sugar.'

She had set down the tray on the round table and poured out the tea. The cup she handed him was very small and of such fine bone china that Carter was afraid of breaking it. She poured her own – no milk or sugar – and sat down opposite him, feet together, back straight.

'I spent my childhood years in Ceylon, Mr Carter. My parents were out there, tea planting, and I've always had a particularly good nose for tea as a result. This is an excellent blend, I think you'll agree. Mrs Jennings doesn't stock it, of course. I have it sent from Harrods. It's my one extravagance.'

Carter sipped politely. To him one cup of tea tasted much like another. This one seemed rather weak and a bit scented, that was all. He put down the tiny cup.

'Fairfield's a long way from Ceylon. How did you finish up here?'

'It's a long story,' she said. 'I'll tell it briefly. When I was fifteen I was sent to boarding school in England, with my sister. We didn't want to go, but my mother was afraid we would not be properly educated out there. She thought women's education vitally important – quite rightly. We lived with an

138

aunt in Reading in the short holidays. In the long breaks in the summer we went back to Ceylon.'

'The best of both worlds.'

'So I discovered.' She smiled thinly. 'I did rather well at the boarding school and went on to university – Cambridge. I still went out to Ceylon every summer but eventually my parents retired and came home to live in England. By that time I was a qualified teacher. I worked for several years in various schools before I found that I enjoyed teaching young children best, at the primary stage. At five a child learns so quickly and it is the most satisfying thing to be able to give that child a good start – to set him, or her, on the right path in life.'

'How do you do that?' Carter asked with interest, thinking back to his own early school days. Far from learning quickly, he had spent a good deal of time playing truant and the rest paying as little attention in class as possible.

'It's very simple. You teach them self-discipline and application, and you teach them to enjoy learning. A questing mind is a priceless asset and it *can* be taught. Young minds can be stunted or nurtured, Mr Carter, just like any plant. Children should *want* to learn, not find it boring drudgery.' She raised her cup and drank, then set it down carefully in its saucer on her lap. 'I'm quite out of touch now, but I doubt if children have changed their needs today, although the methods of teaching are quite different. I couldn't agree with them. I was too old to change my ways and so I retired from the profession altogether. I'm told it's all play and no work in a great many of the primary schools now. Such a tragedy for all those fresh young minds.'

'I hear you taught at the village school here during the last war.'

Miss Burton fixed her pale eyes on him. 'Who told you that? No, don't trouble to tell me, Mr Carter. It's of little importance. I expect you already know all there is to know about me. Everybody in Fairfield gossips disgracefully – as in all villages – which is why I didn't want to say anything

139

to you in the shop in front of Mrs Jennings, who is one of the worst offenders.' She leaned forward in her chair. 'Did I understand correctly when you said that the investigation conducted in Trodgers Wood revealed *nothing*?'

Carter hesitated. Then, with those sharp eyes upon him he decided there wasn't much point in beating about the bush.

'They did find something, as a matter of fact. Bits and pieces that they believe are part of a fighter from the last war.'

Miss Burton nodded slowly. She sat back again in her chair. 'I suspected as much. You see, Mr Carter, Tom wasn't the only one to see that plane crash. I saw it too. And so did the schoolchildren with me. But it wasn't a Spitfire. I'm quite sure about that. It was a German aircraft. A Messerschmitt, I believe. Will you have some more tea?'

Carter waited with a dreadful impatience while she refilled his cup and then her own. As soon as she had sat down again, he said incredulously: 'You mean you *knew* it was there all these years but you said nothing about it?'

She looked at him drily. 'I can see you do not approve, Mr Carter. But there is an explanation, although not, I realize now, a justifiable one. I see very clearly that I failed in my duty forty years ago. But you must understand that until today it had never occurred to me that the remains of that plane had not been removed at the time, as well as its unfortunate pilot. When I finally returned to Fairfield after the war I had almost forgotten all about the incident. If I had heard Tom's story I should have guessed that his plane and my plane were one and the same and that the wreckage must still be in Trodgers Wood, but I am not in the habit of frequenting the Bull, which is where I believe he usually tells these tales. And if I hadn't been away looking after my sister until yesterday I should have heard rumours about your investigation and put two and two together. Will you have one of these biscuits? They're plain, I'm afraid, but they go quite well with the tea.'

He shook his head. 'No, thank you. Bob Simpson of the aviation archeology group knows it's a Messerschmitt, not a

140

Spitfire. You were right there. But I still don't get it . . . Can you tell me exactly what happened and what you saw?'

'That is why I asked you here, Mr Carter. You are from the press, aren't you? The *Milton Weekly Courier*. Well, I want you to print this story in your newspaper. It should have been told at the time – except, of course, that nobody had anything good to say of any German then. Things are different today and bravery and self-sacrifice should not be allowed to go unrecorded.'

Carter felt prickles of expectation on the back of his neck. 'Meaning what, exactly, Miss Burton?'

She stood up and reached for the teapot.

'Meaning, Mr Carter, that the pilot of that Messerschmitt – whoever he was – gave his life for my schoolchildren.'

Having said this, Miss Burton vanished with the teapot and Carter had to wait again until she finally came back with the pot recharged. He had not, in fact, touched his second cup, whereas she now embarked on her third.

'I'm still in the dark, Miss Burton. How did all this happen?'

'Have you a notebook, Mr Carter? I should like you to take this down.'

He took the pad he always carried from his pocket and unclipped his biro; if she wanted him to take notes, then notes he would take. Other interviewees couldn't stand someone writing things down like a policeman, while some people loathed and suspected tape recorders as much as others preferred them for speed. It took all sorts. In point of fact he hardly ever needed any aide-memoire on an interview of this kind, preferring to keep it all on the casual level, which often produced the best results. There was nothing casual about Miss Burton, however, and she would probably check through his notes for errors and spelling mistakes afterwards.

'Fire away. I'm ready.'

She took a sip at her tea, frowning a little in concentration. 'It was in September, 1940. About the sixth or seventh, I'd say, but I'm afraid I can't remember the exact date. Term had only just started, I do know that. It was very hot weather. Day

141

after day of brilliant sunshine and cloudless blue skies. Battle of Britain weather, we still call it – those of us who remember. You're much too young, of course.' Miss Burton shut her eyes for a moment, thinking herself back into the past. 'There weren't many children at the village school at that time. There was the threat of invasion and our evacuees had all been sent away to Wales. After France fell, Fairfield became an evacuation area instead of a reception area, you see. We were in the front line, so to speak.'

It was a pity Charlie wasn't there to hear her and Jesse to applaud, Carter thought, jotting down notes.

Miss Burton, continuing her story, allowed herself to wander as she reminisced. 'They were quite a challenge, those evacuees. We had part of a school near Tower Bridge sent to us. They shared our school with the local children and all settled down quite happily together. I found them very intelligent, on the whole, and most rewarding to teach – once they understood my ways.'

Carter covered up a smile with his hand. He wondered how many short hours it had taken Miss Burton to instil 'her ways' into the little perishers. He prompted her gently.

'How did you come to see the plane?'

'It was in the morning – at recreation time. That would have been between eleven and a quarter past. I remember that we had been reading Masefield's "Cargoes" in our English lesson just before. Such a colourful poem! The children always enjoyed it, although they sometimes used to stumble over some of the words.'

Carter said suddenly: '"Quinquireme of Nineveh from distant Ophir rowing home to haven in sunny Palestine, with a cargo of ivory, and apes and peacocks . . ."'

His memory failed him and Miss Burton, nodding her approval, came to his rescue. '"Sandalwood, cedarwood, and sweet white wine." I see you enjoyed it too, Mr Carter.'

'One of my favourites,' he assured her. In fact, he had had to learn the poem as a punishment for drawing rude pictures of his English teacher in class – a lady as well-endowed in her upper regions as Miss Burton had been skimped. 'Did you hear the plane go overhead?'

'We *saw* it, Mr Carter. I told you. We had finished the English lesson on "Cargoes" and gone outside for recreation. The children used to play on a small asphalt square on the west side of the schoolhouse – I believe the new owners have turned it into a very nice lawn now – and there was a big cornfield next door, belonging to the Dalrymples, who own Fairfield Hall. Of course, I never allowed the children to trespass, but the previous Lady Dalrymple always insisted that the children use the field once the corn was cut; she was most concerned because the playground was so small. A most kind and thoughtful person. More tea now, Mr Carter?'

Carter shook his head and Miss Burton continued.

'On that particular day the corn had just been cut and so I allowed the children to go out into the field, although I stayed in the playground myself with one or two of the others.' Miss Burton took another sip of tea. 'I didn't hear the plane coming at all. It was quite extraordinary. The engine must have stopped, because there was no real noise – just a rushing sound like a gust of wind. And a shadow. I looked up and saw it coming towards us. At first, I thought it was a Spitfire – one of ours – and then I saw the black crosses under the wings and I knew it was German. I remember standing there in absolute horror, thinking that the pilot was going to machine-gun the children.'

Carter could picture the scene: the schoolteacher staring upwards, the children playing happily in the sunshine and the plane with its black crosses and swastika tail swooping silently down on them.

'What did you do?'

'There was no time to do anything except shout a warning to the children. The plane was coming towards us so low that I thought he might hit the school. But he just cleared the belfry tower and it was then that I had the wit to realize that the pilot wasn't going to shoot at us but try to land in the cornfield.' Miss Burton paused and shuddered slightly. 'I can see it all happening again, as though it were yesterday. The children were playing about in the stubble, right ahead of the plane. I actually saw the pilot in the cockpit and he was waving to them, signalling to them to get out of his way. But when they heard me shouting and looked up and saw the plane they panicked and started running before it, scattering. It was the worst thing they could have done, of course. He had no hope of avoiding them.'

Carter said quietly: 'What happened then?'

'Well, I'm afraid I don't know how an aeroplane works, Mr Carter, but the pilot must have done something with the controls to stop it landing, to make it go up in the air again very quickly. It suddenly climbed up over the children and went on up until it was over the wood. Then, I think one of the wings dipped down and the plane fell straight out of the sky. It went down into the trees. I remember the ground shook beneath my feet.' Miss Burton tossed back the remains of her tea as though it were brandy. 'Poor man. He must have thought he was going to be all right until he saw the children. After that, he gave himself no chance – no chance at all.' Miss Burton set down her empty cup and saucer on the table beside her. '*That* is why I want you to put on record what that young man did and how he died. Even though it is forty years late.'

'There's something I still don't understand. How is it that nobody else seems to have known anything about the plane? Surely you reported it then?'

'Indeed I did, but not actually in person. And that was my mistake. You must realize, Mr Carter, that in 1940 the situation was exceptional for all of us. The battle was going on over our heads, but one carried on with the ordinary daily round as best one could. That Messerschmitt crashing was only one incident out of many during the war. As a teacher, of course, I did my best not to let the children's education be affected. After all, they were to be the generation that would have to rebuild a new world out of the old when it was all over.'

Some world, Carter thought. Aloud, he asked: 'Who did report the crash, then?'

'A boy called Roy Hutchins. I couldn't leave the children myself; they were terrified and crying and my assistant, Miss Thompson, was away with a cold – a very sickly creature with no stamina at all. The phone was out of order as usual, so I sent Roy. He was the oldest child in the school. Not a very pleasant pupil, I'm afraid – a bully and a braggart – but I chose him because he was the only one who was not frightened – on the contrary, he was the type who positively relish drama and disaster.' Miss Burton frowned at the memory of Hutchins. 'Also, he had a bicycle. I sent him off to the nearest police station with a handwritten message.'

'And then?'

'And then we went indoors and continued with our lessons. Arithmetic, if I remember correctly. I'm sure it was a Friday.'

Carter wrote it all down. In the middle of the Battle of Britain, with Germans falling out of the sky about her ears, Miss Burton had coolly carried on with arithmetic. He could see her taking her place again in front of her class, chalking up sums on the blackboard. Four plus three plus twelve equals what? What is three hundred times eight? If I share fifty-four sweets equally among nine children, how many will each one receive? Squeak, squeak goes the chalk as she writes away and the rows of tear-stained faces bend obediently over their wooden desks. Pencils are wielded laboriously in small fingers, heads scratched, fingers sucked, nails bitten and, gradually, the fear goes, receding before the comforting authority of Teacher. Someone giggles and is quelled with a look from the dais. If the Nazis had invaded England, marched into Fairfield and stamped all round the playground in their jackboots, Carter felt confident that Miss Burton would have insisted on finishing her class before dealing with them. But something else was puzzling him.

'Didn't the kids talk about the plane when they got home?'

'I told them not to, Mr Carter.'

'And they would have obeyed you?'

'Certainly. My pupils were properly disciplined. They always obeyed me. And they understood the reason. I told

145

them that on no account must they breathe a single word about the aircraft, because the Germans would want to know what had happened to it and their spies would find out if they so much as whispered one word to anybody. Careless talk cost lives in those days, Mr Carter. The children knew that. I also told them that there would be five hundred lines for any child who disobeyed or who went anywhere near the wood where it had crashed. Plane wrecks could be very dangerous, you know. There might have been live ammunition there.'

So the threat of five hundred lines had ensured forty years' concealment for the Messerschmitt and its luckless pilot. Carter thought wonderingly of the contrast in discipline at his own school. They would have been down there almost before the plane hit the ground. Miss Burton was speaking again.

'As a matter of fact, it wasn't the only excitement of the day. Later on there were a number of dogfights directly over the village and a piece of burning wreckage fell on to the cornfield and set light to the stubble. The weather had been very hot and dry and the fire spread very quickly. I had to stop our history lesson and evacuate the children from the school building. Fortunately, the fire was put out and no damage done. I think the children probably remembered that more than the plane.'

And I bet she remembers the lesson, Carter thought. Probably the rotation of crops with the fields done in coloured strips for each churl. Oats, barley and fallow.

'The Battle of Hastings,' Miss Burton said suddenly, as though she had read his mind. 'It's quite extraordinary how people still believe King Harold died from an arrow in the eye. Nothing will persuade them otherwise.' She looked at Carter consideringly. 'I can see you are still puzzled. But if you had been alive in 1940 you would understand much better. So much was happening. There was fighting overhead every day. The children were accustomed to war. We all were. One plane wasn't very important. There was too much else to think of and to worry about. The invasion, for one thing. England stood on the brink of defeat.'

146

A Foreign Field

We will fight them on the beaches . . . and in the hills . . . and in the streets. We will defend our island, whatever the cost may be. It went something like that, so far as Carter could recall. He began to see why the Messerschmitt hadn't rated too highly.

'Unfortunately, I hadn't realized that Roy Hutchins was a liar as well as a bully and a braggart,' Miss Burton remarked. 'He told me he had delivered my message safely to the police. Quite obviously, he had done nothing of the kind.'

And that would have made a lot more than five hundred lines if she'd found out, Carter decided. 'It's odd the Home Guard or whoever they were didn't spot the plane coming down.'

'Not necessarily. There was very little noise and the wood is deep down in the valley. They could easily have missed it. It didn't occur to me then, but it does now.'

'What about the people at Fairfield Hall? They would have been right in the front row, so to speak.'

'The house was shut up at the time. Sir John was away fighting in the navy and Lady Dalrymple had gone to stay with friends. I remember that quite clearly because before she went she left instructions that the children were to be allowed to play in the field, as usual, as soon as the corn had been cut.'

And her son, Phillip, had not even been born, Carter said to himself. Zoe had not existed – not by many years – and he had only been a Saturday night twinkle in his old man's eye. It had all happened a long time ago. Miss Burton, though, had supplied the answer as to why and how the fighter had ended up in the wood. Bob Simpson had got most of the rest right but for one thing: he had been wrong about the pilot. He was down there, buried with his plane, not living it up in Stuttgart. Another thought occurred to him.

'You didn't say anything at all about it to the police or anyone else in authority later on?'

She shook her head. 'And I neglected my duty there, Mr Carter. I admit that, and with regret. I was very foolish to trust

147

Margaret Mayhew

Roy Hutchins at all, but I was younger then and perhaps not quite so sceptical as I am now.'

'And you had other things to think about,' Carter said reassuringly. It was a shock to realize that she would only have been somewhere in her late twenties then. She was one of those people it was hard to imagine young.

'It was not only the war,' she answered. A day or two later I received an urgent message from the doctor who was looking after my mother. She had had a stroke and was very ill. I had to leave Fairfield immediately and go to Hampshire to look after them. My father was incapable of looking after himself, let alone my mother. He had never had to wash up even a teaspoon in his life, you see. My mother had learned to manage somehow, but she had been used to having servants to do everything in Ceylon. I stayed to look after my father while she was in hospital and when she came out I looked after them both until she was back on her feet and did what war work I could fit in. Miss Thompson had taken over the school here in my place. I've often wondered what sort of a job she made of it, with all her colds . . .'

'When did you come back to Fairfield?'

'Not until five years ago. My father died quite soon after the end of the war, but Mother lived on for many years, in spite of the stroke. In fact she had two more. Creaking doors, you see. She was never self-reliant again, though, and so I lived with her in the bungalow. I did some part-time teaching and after she died I became headmistress of another primary school in Berkshire. When I retired I decided to come back here. I always liked the village and this little cottage was up for sale. I've been here ever since and here I shall remain until I die.'

To join Ezrah, Josias, Ann, Hannah, old George Clark and the rest . . . Carter flipped over the cover of his notepad.

'I'd love to do this story, Miss Burton. But there are difficulties.'

'*Difficulties?*' Miss Burton sounded and looked as though she had never come across the word.

148

'Sir Phillip isn't too keen on us printing anything about the plane – and that's putting it mildly. And he's refused permission for any further excavation. On top of that he's apparently been upset by trespassers who've heard the rumours. I promised Lady Dalrymple I'd do what I could to scotch those rumours.'

'I see. Is that what you were doing in Mrs Jennings' shop?'

'Trying to.'

Miss Burton rose to her feet and stood with her back to the fireplace, beneath the trumpeting elephant. 'I am aware, of course, that Sir Phillip's unfortunate illness has made him frequently unreasonable to deal with – one can only sympathize with him and with Lady Dalrymple – but what exactly is his objection to this discovery being made public, apart from possible trespassers?'

'In a nutshell, Miss Burton, he doesn't want any more digging around on his land and, most of all, he doesn't want anyone digging up a German aircraft while they're doing so. His father was shot up by some trigger-happy German pilot when he was in a lifeboat in the Atlantic. It's coloured his thinking, as they say.'

'I remember the story. Mrs Jennings told me all about it when I came back to Fairfield, with many lurid details – mostly invented, no doubt. Very distressing for the family, of course, but these things happen in wartime. On both sides, I dare say. Personally, I don't believe in bearing grudges, Mr Carter, do you? Certainly not against a whole race indiscriminately and certainly not for nearly forty years.'

'I'm with you all the way, Miss Burton, but Sir Phillip doesn't see it quite like that at the moment.'

'Is he aware that there is a pilot buried with the aircraft?'

Carter put away his notebook and stood up. 'No one was aware of it until you said so – or only of the possibility. But I doubt if it would make any difference if there were twenty pilots.'

Miss Burton stared at him with eyes that shone with conviction. 'Of *course* it must make a difference. It's Sir Phillip's

149

duty to have the fighter properly excavated so that the pilot's body can be recovered and identified. That young man probably has relatives still living who have no idea where he is or what happened to him. They have a right to know, Mr Carter. And they also have a right to know that he died a hero's death. That is only fair. It makes no difference whether he was German or not.'

'Maybe you should trying explaining all that to Sir Phillip, Miss Burton.'

She squared her thin shoulders and lifted her chin. 'I intend to. He must be told everything and I can speak with some authority. I lost my only brother in the war, Mr Carter. He was killed in the desert. Both his legs were blown off by a mine and he bled to death because they couldn't reach him in time. I bear no ill will because it would be pointless. He died an honourable death, fighting for his country. And so did that German pilot. The difference is that my brother was decently buried in a marked grave.'

She saw him out of the cottage and called after him as he walked down the path between the neat ranks of flowers.

'In any case, if Sir Phillip wants to stop people trespassing in search of the aeroplane, the most sensible course of action is to remove it. And to do so publicly. He must see that.'

In Carter's view there was no 'must' about it, just a faint possiblity, given Miss Burton at full throttle. He was not sure quite what odds he would have laid on her succeeding where he and Simpson had so far failed.

Eight

Bob Simpson telephoned Carter at the office a few days later. He sounded slightly bewildered.

'We've got the go-ahead to excavate that Me109, Frank. I thought I'd let you know. Sir Phillip phoned me last night. Bit of a surprise after all that carry on.'

Carter stuck a cigarette in his mouth and fished around in his pocket for his lighter. 'What made him change his mind? Did he say?'

'No. He just said he thought we'd probably do a lot less damage in the end than a lot of trespassers. He said we'd better get on with it and take the plane away before he shot one of them.'

'No mention of a Miss Burton?'

'Who? What's she got to do with it?'

Carter told him. He heard Simpson grunt in amusement at the other end of the line.

'Piece of luck, that. You say she can't remember the date exactly?'

'It was early in September 1940 – around the sixth or seventh. She thinks it was a Friday.'

'She must have an amazing memory. Is she a reliable sort of witness?'

'They don't come any better.' Carter grinned to himself. 'She even remembers what poem they were doing in the English lesson that day.'

'"Tiger, tiger, burning bright"?'

'Wrong. "Quinquireme of Nineveh".'

Simpson sighed nostalgically. 'I used to know that one by

151

heart, too. I always liked the "Dirty British Coaster" verse best. I suppose it was easier to understand than all those galleons sailing about. You said this schoolteacher thinks she saw the pilot in the cockpit?'

'All but the whites of his eyes. She saw him waving to the kids to get the hell out of it.'

'Hmmm. I don't think I'll mention that bit to the MoD. She could have been mistaken. People think they see all sorts of things when there's an accident or disaster. You get as many different stories as there are witnesses. A plane's *supposed* to have a pilot, so they tend to see one.'

'If she got the rest right then there would have to have been a pilot onboard. The plane was coming down to earth and then suddenly went up in the air again before it did a nosedive. Unless that was done by remote control, somebody must have pulled the stick.'

'It sounds as though that's likely,' the surveyor agreed. 'But in this business nothing is proved till it's proved. Forty years is a hell of a long time to remember anything clearly. We can't really rely on her description of what happened, or on that rough date. It probably *was* some time in September because she remembers the corn being cut and the kids being out in the field, but that's about all we can say. It might easily have been later. It might not even have been 1940 at all. People muddle years. Even schoolmistresses.'

'In other words, we won't know anything for sure until you dig the rest up?'

'That's it. I'll look up what 109s are still missing from around that time. The sixth of September *was* a Friday in 1940, by the way.'

'So the old girl could be right on the nail?'

Simpson would not be drawn. 'We'll just have to wait and see. I'll let you know when we've fixed the day for the dig.'

He rang off. Carter leaned back in his chair and smoked his cigarette for a bit. Harvey was in Ken's office, griping away about something; he could hear the old hack's querulous and plaintive whine through the open doorway. He waited until the reporter had emerged, sour-faced, and then went in. He found the editor sitting behind his desk, equally sour-faced, and crunching noisily on a mint.

'God know's why I keep that senior citizen on here, Frank. He's past it. Less use than you and that's saying something.'

'It's your kind heart, Ken.'

'It must be.'

'And I've got some good news to cheer you.'

'You're leaving?'

'Not yet.'

'I thought you said good news.'

'The landowner's given permission to excavate that Messerschmitt. It looks like you're going to get a story out of it after all.'

'That's something, I suppose. Put that cigarette out, Frank. You're asphyxiating me. Can't you read the sign? Are you sure this isn't just another of your hunches?'

Carter stubbed out his cigarette alongside the little pile of neatly folded mint wrappers. 'I had it straight from the horse's mouth. Permission granted to the recovery group to go ahead.'

Ken ground away with his false teeth. 'We'll have to handle it right, Frank. We don't want to tread on any toes. We want to keep to the bare facts on the German side – recovery of the plane, name, rank and age of the pilot – if you can find all that out.'

'Miss Burton will be disappointed.'

The editor stared. 'Who the hell is she?'

Carter told him, and her story. 'In her view the pilot was a hero. But for him throwing in the towel at the last minute the kids would have been mown down. She wants us to say so.'

Ken swallowed the last bits of mint. 'Miss Burton is not editor of this newspaper, Frank. *She* won't have people ringing her up and writing a sackful of rude letters. The war may have been over some time but to the majority of our readers *no* German is a hero. The only hero is the chap who shot him

153

down. You'd better remember that. And you'd better find out who *he* was.'

Carter persisted. 'It makes a good story, though, if you think about it. Self-sacrifice always goes down well. Noble deeds are noble deeds, whoever does them.'

'Who are you trying to convince, Frank?'

'You, Ken.'

The editor unwrapped another sweet. 'Well, it won't wash. We'll give her account in amongst the rest, but I'm not having it plastered all over as the biggest thing since that Dutch boy put his finger in the dyke.' He put the mint in his mouth and worked his jaws. 'I wish to God it had been a Spitfire!'

When he had come out of Ken Grant's den, Carter rang Miss Burton. She answered the telephone in her deep, brisk voice. She was one of those people, he thought as he listened, whose voice exactly matched her appearance. Meeting people after only hearing them talk at the other end of a phone line could be a big surprise. Miss Burton, though, was everything she sounded.

'We're going to be able to print that story of yours about the German pilot,' he told her. 'Sir Phillip's changed his mind about things. I expect you know that. Was it all your doing?'

'I simply went to see him and explained what happened, Mr Carter. In the end I think he saw things differently.'

Carter smiled. Dame Slap had not lost her touch with recalcitrant males. He would have given a good deal to have been a fly on the wall at Fairfield Hall when she had been there.

'I'm in your debt, Miss Burton. I was as keen to use that story as you.'

'Then you can repay me by giving us much better coverage this year for the Fairfield fête,' she said promptly. 'I saw Mrs Armstrong-Avery today and she talked about you. I hear that you were at our last committee meeting – the one that I missed. Is that a true indication of your newspaper's interest or were you really at the Hall because of the plane?'

Silver tongues were wasted on someone like Miss Burton, but he could hardly tell her the exact truth – that he had really

154

been there to see Zoe Dalrymple again. 'I was after a story of some kind. I got co-opted while I was there.'

'I see,' she said with dry amusement. 'And agreed to help judge the fancy dress for your pains, I understand?'

'That's it.'

'You don't know any of the local children personally, I hope.'

'Not one.'

'Good. We have to be strictly impartial, you see. A photograph would be very nice. On the front page. Like Mayhurst had last year.'

'I'll try and make it *your* year this time, Miss Burton. Especially if you win the best-kept village competition.'

'*That* remains to be seen, but we shall certainly be doing our best. The judging last year was very *uneven*, to say the least.'

She hung up after a further brief exchange and, after a moment, Carter put a call through to Fairfield Hall. Zoe Dalrymple answered him.

'I'm glad you phoned, Mr Carter. Have you heard that Phillip has agreed to the plane dig after all?'

'That's what I'm ringing about. Bob Simpson told me. I hope your husband isn't too upset about it.'

'He *was* but he's been much calmer since Miss Burton talked to him. She told him an extraordinary story about the Messerschmitt – how she'd actually seen it come down over the school when she was teaching there in the war. Apparently, the pilot was trying to land in the field and then had to change course at the last minute to avoid the children playing there. He crashed into the wood.'

'I know. She told me about it too. I wasn't sure it would make much difference to your husband's feelings about Germans.'

'It didn't. I thought it was terribly sad, but Phillip didn't. He just said good riddance!'

'Then why did he agree to the dig after all?'

'He's terrified of Miss Burton. He hasn't the nerve to say

no to her about anything. It's amazing. She can always get him to do anything. Apparently she's just like the matron at his old prep school.'

'I remember him saying that. She has the same sort of effect on me. I'm back in the lower fourth with dirty knees and wrinkled socks.'

She laughed. 'I can see you as a small boy.'

'Not a pretty sight. I was a bolshie little so and so. Still am.'

'That's why Phillip likes you.'

He wouldn't if he knew I coveted his wife, Carter thought. Feeling guilty on all counts, he said: 'I hope this whole business hasn't given him too much aggro.'

'In a way it does him good to have something to get angry about. He gets so bored. This morning there were two men snooping about in the field below the house with metal detectors. Phillip fired the shotgun when he saw them – only into the air, but next time I think he'll aim *at* them. He's always been paranoid about trespassers.'

'I did try to stop the rumours.'

'I know. I heard you went and saw Mrs Jennings. She was awfully disappointed.'

'I wonder how she'll feel when she finds out it was a Messerschmitt. She'd set her heart on a Spitfire.'

'She'll come round to it when she hears what the pilot did. I've been thinking what it must have been like for him . . . to think he was going to survive and then realizing that he couldn't. Not without killing those children.'

'I don't expect he had much time to think about it. It must have been all over pretty quickly.' Carter paused. 'Are you going to come to the dig, Lady Dalrymple?'

'I'd love to – if I won't be in the way.'

'It's on your land. They can't stop you.'

'Phillip's land, not mine.'

But it will be, Carter said to himself, and when that happens, you'll be free. And I'm a louse even to think about it. Except that I'm not that much of a louse because you'll have moved

A Foreign Field

several more rungs up the ladder, way out of my reach. He said as matter-of-factly as he could manage: 'I'll be going myself to report on it so I'll pick you up beforehand. The site takes some finding in that wood.'

She began to thank him but he cut her short and put down the receiver more sharply than he intended. After that, he lit another cigarette, avoided Harvey's inquisitive gaze and, to stop himself thinking about Zoe Dalrymple, started thinking instead about the German pilot. He wondered what sort of a bloke he had really been. Had he been a hero, as Miss Burton maintained, or had the plane simply gone out of control and missed the kids more by chance than design? After all, the schoolteacher had said there was no engine noise. Just a rushing sound, she had described it as. How controllable was a plane with no engine power? He had no idea.

The clatter and buzz of the newspaper office went on around him. Two of the other reporters had just come in and someone was asking about a small ad; Brenda, traffic-stopping in fluorescent green, was taking details. Carter flicked ash on to the floor. When they dug up the pilot, what would they also be digging up with him? A mother thankful to have news at last of her long-lost son? A wife who had since remarried and didn't want to know? A sister who could barely remember her brother? As a newsman he'd go for the mother any day, for choice. A lot of readers were mothers and mothers of any nationality understood each other, especially about children. A sort of Mothers' Mafia existed that transcended every frontier and language. It was a long shot, though, that this particular *Mutter* would still be alive. The son, had he lived instead of plunging into Trodgers Wood, would probably have been over sixty now. Any mother was likely to be at least eighty.

Brenda had finished with her small-ad applicant and was coming over with a cup of coffee and Harvey, pecking away at his typewriter opposite like some scrawny old turkey, looked up and scowled.

157

Nine

The Messerschmitt dig took place two weeks later. Bob Simpson and his team had handled all the arrangements – notifying the Ministry of Defence, hiring a JCB and driver, and working out the best access route to the site. As he had pointed out, at the north-west side of the wood the road came reasonably close to where the plane lay and there was also an old track through the trees wide enough to take the machine and passing within fifty yards or so of the hollow. Because of the hot, dry spell of weather the ground was firm enough to use a wheeled JCB instead of a tracked one, which would be more manoeuvrable and make less disturbance.

Carter and a *Courier* photographer drove out to Fairfield early. The photographer had a bad hangover and was unenthusiastic, but Carter couldn't remember when he had been so eager to get to an assignment. When they called at the Hall, Zoe was already waiting for them on the doorstep. She was wearing a man's shirt, old jeans and gumboots and her hair was tied up in a wispy knot on top of her head. She looked about fifteen and as unlike a Lady as it was possible to look. Carter watched the photographer open his bleary eyes wide and do a double-take.

He got out and held the door open for her with an unaccustomed gallantry, ignoring the raised eyebrows of the photographer who had crawled into the back of the van and was watching with fascination. It was the first time, he realized, that he had driven with a woman beside him since the night he had killed Jan, and he did the half-mile round to the church as though he were carrying a load of nitroglycerine.

158

He said politely: 'Did your husband mind you coming to this?'

'He always minds me leaving him, for any reason,' she answered, smiling. 'But I think he secretly would have liked to come himself today.'

'Pity we didn't know that. It could have been arranged. If a JCB can get through so could something like a Land Rover to take his wheelchair.'

She shook her head. 'It would have meant a big fuss and he would have hated that. You can imagine. He's waiting to be told about it afterwards, though he'll still pretend not to be interested. And he'll be in a foul temper because Mrs Sweet is looking after him. She's known him since he was a child and says what she likes to him – still calls him Master Phillip and tells him to behave himself. He's dreadfully rude to her, but she doesn't seem to care.'

The cockerel – alone for once – was beside the lychgate as they drew up and he followed them through and up the church path, stepping out elegantly behind them.

'He's after your sandwiches, Joe,' Carter warned the photographer.

He and Zoe laughed as Joe, glancing over his shoulder, quickened his pace and the cockerel broke into a trot after him.

'Leave him alone, Mactavish,' Zoe called.

'Bluebeard would be a better name for him. What's he done with all those wives?'

There was a scuffling and flapping sound and they turned to see the wives jostling each other to squeeze through the part-open gate. They advanced in a faithful little band and Mactavish abandoned his quarry and led them off into the graveyard.

When they reached the stile, Carter thought that the view from it had never looked better. The field was full of buttercups, the trees were in their full summer glory and a bright thread of sea shone in the sunlight. The bullocks were lying down, chewing placidly and swishing their tails against the flies. As the three of them walked downhill towards the wood he looked up at the big house and saw its owner sitting in his wheelchair at the open window. Carter tried, but failed, to imagine what it must be like to know that one would never again be able to walk through a field on a summer's day.

He helped Zoe through the barbed-wire fence. They had no difficulty in following the track to the site since he and Simpson had beaten a way through. Simpson and his group were coming in from the north-west side of the wood, where the road came nearest to the buried plane. Carter kept a lookout for Tom and his dog but saw no sign of them, and when they reached the site only Glen and two others were there. Glen doffed his blue hat to Zoe.

'Bob's waiting at the road for the JCB. Shouldn't be long now.'

They chatted. Carter offered cigarettes round and lit one for himself. Zoe went and stood on the edge of the incline and stared down at the hollow, hands stuck in her jeans pockets.

'I can't believe there's really a plane there. There's no trace of anything at all.'

'If you look at those trees over there you'll notice some of the branches are missing,' Carter told her. 'They're all lopsided. The fighter did that as it came down. And if you look carefully you'll see there's a saucer-shaped depression in the ground. That's another sign. The rest of the evidence is underground, except the bits and pieces already dug up – and Tom's tail wheel, of course.'

Zoe looked up at the trees and then bent down to study the ground. 'I see what you mean. But I'd never have noticed it.' She looked up at Carter. 'If Miss Burton's right then the pilot must be here, too.'

'*If* she's right.'

They could hear the noise of the JCB approaching, the snap and crackle of twigs and undergrowth as it forged a way through the wood. It came into their view through the trees looking like some prehistoric monster with yellow jaws thrust forward. Bob Simpson had perched behind to guide the driver

160

A Foreign Field

and was shouting and waving instructions as the great beast lumbered along. Behind, in its wake, came a small lorry with another eight men onboard.

As the sun rose higher over the wood, the dig began. The monster's jaws extended out over the hollow and bit into the ground. A huge mouthful of leaves and earth was lifted into the air and disgorged on one side. A few more bites and Simpson motioned to the driver to stop. Patches of powdery blue were appearing – just as Carter had seen before at the hand dig. He watched the surveyor inspect the area carefully before giving the go ahead.

The bucket descended again and went on scooping out the earth in a steady rhythm. The noise must have frightened away every animal and bird for miles, Carter thought. And what would poor old Tom, wherever he was hiding, be making of it? Probably the last time there had been any disturbance in the wood had been when the Messerschmitt arrived and made what the Americans called an unscheduled ground-airframe interface.

Every load of earth tipped out was sifted through by the men who waited with forks and pickaxes and extracted and put aside anything they had found. The pile of crumpled, muddy aluminium grew steadily. Carter picked up one of the largest pieces and showed it to Zoe.

'Getting warmer all the time.'

Simpson and two of the men had climbed down into the hole and the surveyor waved to the JCB driver to stop. Working with spades and gloved hands and in several inches of black and oily water, they uncovered a large piece of metal protruding from the side. They lifted it out as tenderly as if it had been priceless porcelain and wiped away some of the mud. Simpson looked up at Carter and grinned delightedly.

'Nice bit of the fuselage here with part of the Luftwaffe cross showing.'

The prize was handed up out of the hole and given to Glen, who was busy washing the most interesting-looking finds in a red plastic bowl. He set aside a fistful of German bullets

161

and went to work on the section of fuselage. The black and white marking – one arm of the cross – emerged with startling clarity.

'Not much doubt about it now, Mr Carter, is there?

The JCB resumed its digging and more and more finds were salvaged from the dumped bucketfuls. There were more pieces of fuselage, more bullets and cannon shells, snake-like lengths of rubberized cable with coloured wires trailing from them like innards, and hanks of more wires covered with silver mesh. The digger was stopped several more times as larger and important things came to light: an oxygen bottle with the date 2.1.40 still legible on its casing and part of the cockpit door. The photographer's flash popped away.

Zoe was standing beside Carter. She said quietly to him: 'There's no sign of the pilot yet, is there?'

He looked down at her. 'Don't worry about it. Bob says it's never more than some bones – nothing gruesome.'

The smell of oil was strong now and the water lying in the hole had become viscous and greenish-black. The sides had scorch marks where the soil had been burned. Zoe went away to sit by a tree and Carter, finding a spare spade, helped search through the mound of excavated soil near the rim of the hole. It was he who discovered the first evidence of human remains.

The piece of cloth had been embedded in a lump of mud, well camouflaged. It was sodden, dirty and torn, but Simpson, who had climbed out to take a close look, identified it instantly.

'Part of his uniform. The jacket, I think. That looks like the edge of a pocket. And he was an officer, I'd say, by the look of the weave. The NCOs had much coarser stuff.' The surveyor felt the material between his fingers. 'This is very fine. Superior quality. We'll get Glen to give it a good soaking and take another look.' He glanced at Carter. 'He's here all right. More's the pity.'

As Simpson had predicted, the remains of the German pilot, when they began to find them, were pathetically few. The disinterred bones were handled with due respect and care and laid together in a separate black plastic bag. Carter watched thoughtfully.

That skull had a tongue in it, and could sing once . . . Alas! poor Yorick . . . The melancholy ponderings of Hamlet went through his mind, although in this case there was not even anything as recognizably human as a skull. Miss Burton would probably have come up with something much more bracing for the occasion. *There is a victory in dying well.* Or, better still and more appropriately: *Who is the happy Warrior? Who is he?*

Who indeed, Carter wondered. There was nothing to give them a clue yet, except that he had possibly been an officer. He went over to Zoe and crouched down beside her, resting on his heels.

'Are you all right?'

'Heavens, yes.' She brushed her fringe away from her eyes. 'I wasn't being squeamish. It's just that I didn't feel like turning it into a peep show – not when they were finding those remains.'

'There could be more, I'm afraid.'

'Then I'll stay here for a bit and you can shout if I'm missing any interesting parts of the plane.'

He left her by the tree and went back to the hole, which was now at least twelve feet deep. The JCB clanked on, its bucket streaming with water as it lifted into the air. Some interesting bits, as Zoe had called them, started to come forth from their watery grave. They dredged up part of an undercarriage leg, a rudder pedal, the oil temperature gauge and a length of tubing from the oxygen apparatus. And there was jubilation in the camp over the recovery of one of the fighter's guns, almost intact. It was all beginning to piece together, metaphorically speaking, Carter thought, although all the king's horses and all the king's men could never put the Messerschmitt together again.

More of the pilot's clothing was found. A bucketload of earth yielded up part of a fleece-lined flying boot and a wrinkled black leather glove. Simpson, beavering away down the

163

hole, passed up what was left of a rubber life jacket. Meanwhile, the pile of twisted wreckage grew higher.

They stopped for an early lunch, sitting round in the shade. The lack of air movement in the dense wood made it stiflingly hot and oppressive. The photographer produced a squashed-looking sandwich from his anorak pocket and ate it lying flat on his back, his camera bag still slung over his shoulder.

Zoe conjured a stick of French bread filled with lettuce and salami from a Marks and Spencer carrier bag, together with two cans of Coke. She broke the bread in half.

'Here you are, Mr Carter. I brought enough for two.'

He flopped down on the grass near her and accepted the offering, embarrassed. Any more of these jaunts and he must remember to provide for himself and not pinch other people's food. It was the old bad habit of just not bothering about it.

Zoe said through a mouthful: 'I can't go on calling you Mr Carter all the time. It's ridiculous.'

'The name's Frank, Lady Dalrymple.'

'And mine's Zoe – as you very well know.'

'I'm not sure it's going to trip lightly off the tongue. I'm not used to first-naming Ladies.'

She laughed. 'We're no different from anybody else.'

'I think *you* are. Most of the Ladies I've ever come across wouldn't stick by a sick and crippled husband for more than a week, let alone take care of him.'

She turned away and picked at the grass beside her. 'Let's not talk about that.'

'Why not? It's the truth. If it weren't for you he'd be in a nursing home.'

'That's the one thing he dreads. And the one thing I've promised him I'll never let happen. Not as long as I live.'

'I told you that you were different.' He rolled on to his stomach and took a bite of the bread. 'He's a lucky man.'

'I doubt if Phillip would describe himself quite like that,' she said. 'He's miserably unhappy most of the time. Dying very slowly, inch by inch, isn't much fun.'

'You could say we're all doing that – one way and another.'

A Foreign Field

'It's not quite the same though, is it? You can't compare it. Do you know, this morning he said that the death of the German pilot was too good for him because it must have been quick. I sometimes think his mind has become as twisted as his body.'

'Well, if it's any comfort to him the pilot might have been wounded before and suffered quite a bit.'

'Don't! Don't say that!'

'It was war. And it all happened a long time ago.' He picked up the bread she had put down beside her. 'Shouldn't you be eating this?'

She took a mouthful and then said suddenly: 'Look who's just arrived.'

Carter turned his head and saw Tom and his dog standing at the edge of the clearing by one of the trees. 'He seems to have decided it's safe to come out. Curiosity has got the better of him.' He gave the old man a wave and Tom nodded and grinned and lifted his mittened hand in reply.

Bob Simpson walked over to them. 'One of the lads found this. I thought you'd like to see it.'

He took something out of his pocket and gave it to Carter. It was a diary with a brown leather cover, soggy and dirty but undamaged. When Carter opened it carefully he saw, printed inside: *1940 und Januar 1941*. He looked at the name handwritten on the flyleaf.

'Martin Kern. That's our pilot, then.'

'Possibly,' Simpson acknowledged with his customary caution. 'But there's always the chance that the diary belonged to someone other than the pilot.'

'For pity's sake, Bob. People don't go carrying other people's diaries round with them.'

'It's still not conclusive evidence. And we won't have that until we find his dog tag – or the aircraft number. So far we've found neither.'

Carter turned another page. '*In Falle eines Unfalls*. What does that mean?'

'In case of accident,' Zoe said. 'I did German at school. I even passed my O level.'

165

Carter smiled at her. 'You're going to be useful. In case of accident, then, this bloke wanted someone called Barbara Karslemn to be notified. Address: Hamburg 27, Markannastrasse 72. He wrote it all down, just in case . . .'

He turned a few more pages. Disappointingly, Martin Kern had not been one for recording anything but the briefest notes. The diary had very few entries and these were only of two or three words. Two of them were evidently appointments. Zoe had leaned forward and was looking over his shoulder.

'*Schneider*, 11.0. That's tailor, I think. And *Zahnarzt* is dentist.'

Carter leafed through more damp pages. The diary was peppered with the name Barbara, written again and again, and, against June 3rd the German had put *Geburtstag von Barbara*.

'Barbara's birthday,' Zoe translated helpfully.

'She must have been some lady.'

After August 15th the diary was blank, except for some handwritten figures on a free page near the end.

'Radio call signs,' Simpson explained. 'He shouldn't have done that, of course. It was strictly *verboten*. Have you seen the interesting list at the very back?'

Carter looked. On the end page, where its English equivalent might have listed Bank and Public Holidays or the Sun's Risings and Settings or given a coloured map of the London Underground, there was a long and sinister list headed *Der Führer und die Reichsregierung*. The names of the German High Command in 1940 were printed below, beginning with Adolf Hitler and including Von Ribbentrop, Goering and Goebbels – names to send a shiver down the spine, even forty years on. He turned back to the beginning of the diary.

'Barbara Karslemn. It obviously must be the same Barbara written all through the diary. I wonder if she ever *was* notified. Odd not to have put his parents as next of kin. She wasn't his wife – not with that name.'

Simpson said smugly: 'Do you want to see what she looked like? This was tucked into the diary.'

He had delved into his pocket again and passed over a faded

166

and rather crumpled snapshot. Carter took it gingerly between finger and thumb.

The girl was standing and smiling into the sun and straight into the camera. All his imaginings of some smoky cellar-based Dietrich were dispelled. She was very young – not more than eighteen at the most – and with a natural, fair-haired prettiness. She was dressed in a patterned, short-sleeved blouse, a skirt and rather ugly sandals. What struck Carter most of all was the warmth of her smile: this was no posed shot, but a moment of real happiness reflected in the camera's eye. He turned it over. On the back she had written in a clear, round hand: *Meinem Liebsten Martin. Barbara.* He showed it to Zoe.

'No need to translate. Even I can get that.' He turned to the surveyor. 'Do you mind if I hang on to this for a couple of days? We may want to use it.'

'So long as I have it back.'

'You will. That's a promise.' Carter put the snap away safely in his wallet. 'Scout's honour. I'll make an enquiry or two through some old Fleet Street contacts. We might find something out about her. She might still be alive.'

'If she is she'll probably be a grandmother by now,' Simpson said. 'And she'll have forgotten all about Martin Kern. Whoever he was.'

'I thought us news hounds were supposed to be the cynics, Bob.'

The work went on. Apart from the diary and the scraps of clothing there was still no conclusive evidence of the pilot's identity. Carter watched impatiently as the slow process continued. Some parts of the wreckage were found to have manufacturers' labels, but these were no use for identifying the plane itself, however useful they might have been to British Intelligence in 1940. Looking for the dog tag was the equivalent of searching for the proverbial needle and Carter felt exasperated that the best hope, the Werke number, still eluded them. The men kept on sifting through the pile of spoils and even Tom had moved in closer and was darting in now and

167

again to pick up scraps of metal turned up by the others.

The JCB had stopped again. The sharp-toothed bucket had uncovered something that needed delicate handling and Simpson and two of his helpers probed gently with spades and hands. Carter and Zoe watched from the side of the hole as a sodden bundle was gradually unearthed. When it was lifted out and passed up they could see whitish material and a nest of black cords. The man next to Carter whistled.

'Cripes! It's his bloody chute. All in one piece, by the look of it. Bit of bloody luck!'

The parachute was spread out to dry on a patch of clear ground and the photographer stepped forward with his camera. The white silk was badly stained but otherwise intact.

'You could jump out of a bloody plane with that today – no problem,' Carter's neighbour commented. 'Bloody miracle, after all this time.'

'Bloody pity he didn't use it.'

'No chance, was there – not according to that schoolteacher woman. You have to be five hundred feet up to use a chute or there's a nasty mess on the ground. Got it all wrong, didn't he? Some kid, just out of the schoolroom, I expect. Just like our own lads. They all bloody soon learned, though, or they ended up like this one.' The man – older than most of the group – stooped to finger the discoloured silk at his feet. 'Poor bastard.'

Glen was busy washing up in his red plastic bowl. Someone had found the parachute release buckle and he was rinsing it as though it were Dresden. Carter weighed the heavy piece of metal in his hand. The instructions *Auslösen Drehen Dann Drücken* were stamped on the front. As the man had said, the pilot had had no chance to do any of that.

Glen was showing Zoe another find. 'Cigarette case,' he said laconically. 'Nice one, once.'

She bent her head closer over the flattened silver square. 'Aren't those initials? It looks like an M and a K entwined.'

Carter bent his head beside hers. 'I think you're right. In which case, that's another bit of proof that the pilot *was* Martin Kern. Unless he was a kleptomaniac.'

Glen grinned. 'Bob won't be satisfied with that. It's only what the police call circumstantial evidence, isn't it? Could just be coincidence.'

Zoe gave him back the case. 'Will it be returned to his family?'

'If we trace him and if he has one,' Glen said.

They left him to his washing-up.

Carter glanced at Zoe as they walked away. 'What's the matter?'

'Matter?'

'You're frowning.'

'Am I? Sorry, but I was just thinking that maybe it's wrong to have disturbed things. Perhaps it all ought to have been left alone. It seems a bit like grave-robbing. The cigarette case and the diary and the photograph all belonged to someone who's been buried here just the same as if he were in a cemetery. You wouldn't open a coffin and take out a dead person's possessions, would you?'

He stopped and turned to her, putting his hand for a second on her arm. 'That's not how you felt before. Don't you remember? You said how hard it must be not knowing what had happened to someone in the war? Well, they can't find out what happened to this bloke by leaving him and his belongings in the ground. The personal things will be offered to his relatives – Bob Simpson will see to that. He does it all by the book. As for the human remains, there'll be a decent burial in a marked grave with full military honours. And there'll be a public acknowledgement of the sacrifice he made. I'll see to that. So, it can't be all bad.'

'You know all the answers, don't you?'

'Only to some of the questions.'

The JCB was clattering away to and fro. They watched it for a moment and then Zoe said suddenly: 'Why did you leave Fleet Street, Frank?'

'I was thrown out. Fired.'

'Sorry. I shouldn't have asked.'

'Why not? I don't mind, so why should you? I'll tell you

why as well.' He lit a cigarette to give himself time. It was hard to talk about, even now, but he wanted to tell her. 'I used to drink too much – I told you that before. In the beginning it was just a hell of a lot, but not much more than many others in Fleet Street. Then, one evening I killed my wife.'

He heard Zoe's gasp above the noise of the digger. He went on doggedly. 'Don't worry, I'm not a homicidal maniac. I didn't kill her with my bare hands – though I might as well have done.' He drew on the cigarette and watched the JCB's long arm emerge from the depths of the hole. It must be working at full stretch now, he thought. 'We'd been to a party. I'd had a jar or two over the top. Jan wanted to drive but I wouldn't let her. It was raining and on the way home I took a corner too fast. The car skidded, went out of control and hit a tree. Jan was killed outright. She was four months pregnant.'

Zoe looked stricken. 'I'm so sorry. How dreadful for you!'

'Much worse for her, wasn't it? And the kid. *I* survived.' The bucket was tipping out its dripping load and the waiting men moved forward. 'If I'd had the guts I'd have finished myself off then as well. Made a proper job of it. Instead, I hit the bottle even harder.'

'You shouldn't blame yourself,' she said. 'It was an accident.'

'I blame myself because I was to blame,' he answered. 'The coroner at the inquest made bloody sure I hadn't any illusions about *that*. He had a lot to say on the subject and his only regret was that I wasn't going inside for it. Instead, I went back to the paper. I lasted a lot longer than I deserved to before they finally had to give me the boot.'

She said something that was inaudible against the noise of the digger. Carter was convinced that he had shocked and repelled her. He already regretted saying anything. After a few moments she spoke again, this time louder so that he could hear.

'What did you do then? After they fired you?'

'Any work I could find – washing-up, working on building

sites, serving in shops. I even worked in Harrods menswear department until I insulted a customer. I drank what I earned. Finally, I got ill and the quack told me that if I didn't stop drinking I'd be dead in a couple of years. He sent me to one of those clinics where they dry you out. You're never cured, they say, but I haven't touched a drop since.'

The JCB had stopped again and the men were crowding round the rim of the hole. Carter stubbed out his cigarette. He said, without looking at Zoe: 'Looks like they've found something interesting. Want to see?'

It was the engine. Carter, standing watching the struggle to uncarth and lift the heavy lump of metal, thought, somewhat poetically, that it was rather akin to finding the fighter's heart. The other fragments recovered had been interesting enough, but here was the part of the plane that mattered – the bit that had been alive, as much as its pilot had been alive.

Bob Simpson, once the engine had been safely lifted and landed like some big fish, clambered out of the hole to take a closer look at it himself. As everyone gathered round, he wiped away at the casing with a rag.

A faint gleam of metal showed beneath the dirt, growing and brightening with each stroke of the cloth.

'Not a patch on a Merlin,' someone growled disparagingly.

The surveyor raised his head. 'That's a lie, George, and you know it. There's nothing wrong with Daimler-Benz. Beautiful engines. Beautifully made.' He gave another careful wipe. 'A bit of work on this one and I reckon she could start up.'

Carter was sceptical. It seemed impossible that after forty years in its marshy grave that muddy hunk could ever burst into life again. Any more than its pilot.

He looked up to see that Zoe had gone to stand on the other side of the group and was talking to Dave. With difficulty, Carter returned his gaze to the engine. He regretted his confession more than ever. Why hadn't he kept his stupid mouth shut? Why blurt out something he hadn't spoken about to anyone for years? And then again, why the hell not? What difference could it make? So what if she thought the worse

171

of him for it? Nothing could really change between them because there was nothing *to* change.

He kept clear of her for a while, talking with the men and gleaning any useful information he could. They were a friendly lot – willing to answer questions and reminisce about past digs. Most of them had a story or two to tell and plenty to say about their hobby. Carter could find no common denominator among them, except for their enthusiasm for digging up old aircraft. As Simpson had told him, they were all ages and all sorts.

The JCB, grinding away remorselessly, delivered up more trophies. Part of the Messerschmitt's spinner, distempered yellow like the rudder, was recovered and, later, the propeller unit, bent and battered but almost complete.

Two more of the pilot's own possessions came to light: a small silver disc that had been the back of his watch and a thin piece of material, badly torn, which Simpson reckoned had been his scarf.

'A lot of the pilots wore them,' he told Carter. 'Apart from looking doggy they stopped the neck getting chafed.'

Carter fingered the muddy silk. It looked as though it had once been white. He tried and failed to visualize the man who had worn it round his neck as he plunged to his death. As yet he could not build up any clear picture of the pilot in his mind. His name was probably Martin Kern. He was probably an officer – if Simpson was right about the uniform cloth. He probably had a girlfriend called Barbara Karslemn – if the diary owner and the pilot were one and the same man. If Miss Burton was right, then he was also a brave man who had sacrificed his life for a handful of unknown, enemy children. If, on the other hand, Phillip Dalrymple was right, he was a vicious Hun who had been aiming for the children and screwed it up, killing himself in the process. He, personally, went for the schoolteacher's theory: she was nobody's fool and she had no hang-ups or axes to grind. But, when it came down to it, who would ever really know the truth?

'Still no luck finding the plane's number?' he asked Simpson.

The surveyor looked disconsolate. 'Not a bloody sign of it. Hell, we should have found it by now. It must be here.'

'What does it look like?'

'It's just a small metal plate screwed to the port side of the cockpit. Without it we're sunk for proper identification. This laddie'll end up in an "Unknown"' grave if we don't have some luck soon.

Carter looked across at the black plastic bag. 'What's the procedure?'

'I've already sent someone off to notify the police. They'll ring from the village.'

'And then?'

'The police will want to come down and see the site and the remains in situ. It's all evidence for the coroner's court. They'll take them away and they'll stay in the mortuary until they've been identified – if that's possible. Then an inquest is held and after that he'll be buried, almost certainly in Cannock Chase. The War Graves people moved most of the Germans up there after the war, unless the families preferred otherwise. But it looks like this one won't have a family to say either way. He'll be *Ein Unbekannter Deutscher Soldat.*'

'But that diary—'

'Isn't proof positive, Frank. I've told you. People *do* carry other people's possessions sometimes. They carry letters they're going to post for someone, for instance.'

'But not diaries, Bob. I just don't believe it.' Carter took the snapshot out of his pocket and looked at it again. The girl, Barbara, smiled at him from across the years. She looked a nice kid. 'I'll see what I can find out about her.'

'Don't expect too much,' Simpson warned him. 'I keep on saying it, but forty years is a long time. And Germany was a devastated country by the end of the war.'

'If you can't find the Werke number, Bob, couldn't you dig up a nice Iron Cross for me? To go with the diary and this photo.'

Simpson smiled. 'You'll be lucky! I've never found one

yet. And something tells me this was a new boy with no medals.'

'I get the same feeling. He just loused the whole thing up.' Carter put the photograph away carefully. 'Five quid says his name *is* Martin Kern and it's his diary and his cigarette case – and this is his girl.'

'I'm not a betting man, but I wouldn't mind if you were proved right.'

The surveyor went back to the digger. Carter smoked a cigarette and thought about the girl in the photo. He knew who he was going to ask to help find her.

Zoe appeared beside him. 'I've got to go now, Frank. Mrs Sweet will be wanting to get home.'

'I'll walk back with you,' he offered.

'There's no need. I'm on home ground.' She paused. 'Will you come and have supper with us, when you've finished here? Phillip will want to hear all about it – even if he pretends he doesn't.'

She had taken him by surprise; he had not been expecting invitations any more. The thought crossed his mind that perhaps she was feeling sorry for him, just as she had felt sorry for the German pilot. The thought wasn't a pleasing one. He didn't want pity – not at any price.

'If it's the food you're worried about,' she went on, 'I promise it won't be sardines again.'

'If you're sure it's OK . . .'

'Of course. You'll be doing us a favour.'

He watched her saying goodbye to Simpson and the others and knew he'd been a fool to accept. He should have settled for something at the Crown and Anchor on his way back instead of a supper spent looking across the table at a woman he wanted and could never have. She was speaking to Glen and he was smiling and nodding. She had a way with people – a natural and genuine friendliness that put them at their ease. There wasn't a vestige of the Lady Muck about her and yet she had real class. And he hadn't yet been able to bring himself to call her Zoe.

When she had gone, he put out his cigarette and went to lend a hand. The men were still searching painstakingly through the mound of earth, turning it over repeatedly and sifting through. Tom was sitting a short distance away, leaning his back against a tree. He was busy polishing something against his tattered coat sleeve and crooning happily to himself as he did so. The dog lay beside him, its muzzle on its front paws. As Carter passed him to fetch a fork the old man looked up and smiled and nodded. He held out his prize proudly. A piece of shiny metal winked against the black mitten.

'Spitfire! Boom! Boom!'

Oh God, Carter thought wearily as he trudged on. Isn't he ever going to get it right? He picked up the fork and as he re-passed the old man something made him pause to look again and closer. He saw then that Tom was holding in his palm the small metal plate bearing the serial number of the Messerschmitt.

It was half past seven by the time Carter arrived at Fairfield Hall. The photographer had left long before, hitching a lift back to Milton with one of the group. Carter had stayed on to help clear up and had been amazed by how quickly everything had been restored to order. The JCB made short work of refilling the deep hole and the hollow scarcely looked as though it had been disturbed. The police had arrived and taken away the pilot's remains and his possessions. The wreckage and tools had been loaded on to the lorry. Nothing had been left.

Zoe answered the door. She was wearing the same clothes as before, except that she had exchanged muddy boots for a pair of white gym shoes with a hole in the left toe. Considering his own bedraggled state, Carter was relieved. The most he had been able to manage was to change his boots for an old pair of shoes he had left in the van. When he apologized for his appearance she laughed.

'Did you think I meant top hat, white tie and tails?'

She showed him into a cloakroom off the hall where he

cleaned up as best he could in a marble basin the size of a small bath. When he had finished he stared at himself in the mirror with glum dissatisfaction. It was a long while since he had wasted more than half a minute on his reflection and he saw that the drinking years had taken their toll. He looked nearer forty than thirty. There were lines he didn't know he'd got and, God help him, already some grey hairs. He stood back a foot or two and the picture improved a little but one thing was unchanged. Phillip Dalrymple might be crippled but the several hundred years' breeding still showed – just as the obvious lack of it showed in his own face now.

He found the baronet out on the terrace, a glass of whisky carefully balanced on the arm of his wheelchair. The evening air was heavy with the sweet scent of roses and honey-suckle.

'A drink, Carter? Help yourself. Zoe is attempting miracles in the kitchen but I wouldn't raise your hopes too much.'

He followed the direction of the waving arm to the side table in the drawing room where he found a silver tray, two heavy cut-glass decanters and a small plastic ice bucket. The two glasses on the tray had yellow flowers and spots over them. The place was full of wild contrasts: pricless antiques and silver and crystal alongside plastic ice buckets and Woolworths beakers, with rickety garden furniture on a superb balustraded stone terrace.

He poured himself some plain ginger ale – a drink he had found convenient since people invariably assumed it also contained whisky. He had learned early on that not to drink made others uneasy and even resentful and that it was simpler to conceal the fact. He took his glass out on to the terrace.

Phillip Dalrymple raised his drink awkwardly. 'Your health, Carter. Don't bother to drink to mine. A waste of good whisky.' He took a long swallow and returned the glass to the arm of the chair where it balanced precariously. 'Well, sit down and tell me all. Zoe refuses to say anything. She says you know much more about it.'

Carter sat down on one of the cane armchairs. It had

developed a sideways list in its old age and he had to compensate by leaning hard to port.

'It *was* a Messerschmitt 109E. There's no longer any doubt about that. Bob Simpson and Miss Burton were right.'

'I'm not so sure about your friend Simpson, but I should have been very surprised if Miss Burton had been wrong. The plane wouldn't have dared be anything else. Have you got a cigarette on you?'

Carter produced his pack and lit one for the baronet and one for himself.

'They found a lot of the fuselage – all broken up, of course, but there was one bit with part of the Luftwaffe cross.'

'A load of old scrap, as I thought.'

Carter put away cigarettes and lighter in his pocket. 'Not quite. They recovered some other interesting things.'

'Such as?'

'All sorts of bits and pieces: the temperature gauge, an oxygen bottle, part of the undercarriage, not to mention the engine and the prop. There was a lot of stuff and in a pretty good state of preservation.'

'Which is more than can be said of me. Get me another drink, will you Carter? Whisky on the rocks.'

Carter took the glass and refilled it from the decanter in the drawing room, adding two ice cubes. He replaced the glass on the arm of the wheelchair and sat down again. The wicker creaked and tilted beneath him. He said casually: 'They found the pilot's parachute too. Undamaged.'

Phillip Dalrymple sipped at his whisky clumsily. Some of it splashed on to the flagstones. 'Did they indeed? And what about the pilot? Did they find him too – not quite so undamaged?'

Carter took a drag at his cigarette before answering. 'Yes, they found him all right. Or what was left of him. The police have taken the remains away.'

'Just think, Carter, our Nazi hero died without ever knowing that he had somehow managed to earn Miss Burton's approval. She gave him ten out of ten for behaviour.'

177

'I take it you don't rate him quite so high.'

'You know my views on all Germans. And they're unchanged by Miss Burton's story. She deluded herself. The Hun was aiming at the children and fouled things up by mistake. They thought nothing of machine-gunning civilians, you know. It became quite a habit in France. A nice little posse of English children in his sights would have been more than any German could have resisted.'

Carter shrugged. There was little point arguing. 'I don't suppose we'll ever know what happened exactly. Miss Burton seems to have been the only reliable adult witness. They'll be able to identify him easily enough because they found the aircraft serial number. It's all in the Luftwaffe records.'

'Very meticulous people, the Germans. I believe they kept records at Belsen and Auschwitz. Why can't they just put him in the nearest dustbin?'

Carter ignored this. 'There'll be an inquest, the same as for any other corpse found in this country.'

'I'd forgotten you were a press vulture. You'd know all about corpses and inquests, wouldn't you?' The baronet balanced the glass precariously on the arm of the wheel-chair again. 'Well, at least you've done me one good turn, Carter. You've removed the Hun and his plane from the bottom of my garden. I'm indebted to you for that. Have another drink?'

'No thanks – sir.'

'Odd sort of bugger, aren't you? I'd have thought you would have been sinking them like there are no tomorrows.'

'It's the tomorrows I'm thinking about.'

'Which is just what *I* never think about. Not if I want to keep sane. Can't have a sick body *and* a sick mind, can we? That wouldn't do at all. What do you think of my wife?'

The abrupt question and its change of tack took Carter aback. He said slowly: 'I think she's some lady.'

'Apart from her cooking and housekeeping, I agree with you for once. Marrying Zoe was the best thing I ever did, you know. Thank God for her! I couldn't do without her – even a few hours, like today, is hell. Get me another drink, will you?'

Carter made another trip to the drinks tray in the drawing room. Phillip Dalrymple's words had made him feel uneasy, even though he had nothing to feel guilty about. He poured out a stiff measure of scotch. There was something somewhere in the Bible about it being as bad to commit adultery in your heart as actually doing it – in which case he was as guilty as hell every time he looked at Zoe. He dropped two more ice cubes into the glass, took it outside and handed it over.

'By the way, they also found one or two things that probably belong to the pilot – apart from remnants of his clothes.'

'What sort of things?'

'A cigarette case. A diary. And a photograph. The police have the cigarette case and the diary, but I borrowed the photo – temporarily.'

Carter took the snapshot out and held it out. The baronet stared at it for a moment, holding it in his crabbed fingers. He turned it over. '*Meinem Liebsten Martin. Barbara*. My schoolboy German can just about manage that. This is the girlfriend, I take it? Or his wife? What did it say in the diary?'

'The owner's name was Martin Kern. We won't know for sure if he was also the pilot until he's been officially identified from records, but I'd stake my life it was him.'

'What did he put in the diary?'

'Not much, unfortunately. There were a couple of appointments – but nothing that told us anything about him other than his name and his girlfriend's. She wasn't his wife. Her full name was Barbara Karslemn and she lived in Markannastrasse, Hamburg. Her birthday was on June third. That's all we know for the moment, but she must have meant a lot to him. Her name was written on almost every page and he gave her as the one to be notified in case of accident. I'm going to make some enquiries and see if I can find out more – see if she's still alive.'

'Are you a romantic, Carter? Or is it just the scavengers of the press picking over the bones for some scraps of flesh?'

179

'Both.'

The baronet handed back the photograph. 'You'll find she's a fat old *hausfrau* now with twenty grandchildren. She won't even be able to remember his name.'

Zoe had appeared at the open windows. 'Yes, she will. Of course she'll remember it.'

'Zoe is a romantic like you, Carter. Aren't you, Zoe?'

She smiled. At both of them. 'I hope so. Dinner is served, gentlemen. In the kitchen.'

There was a startling improvement there. A valiant attempt had been made at clearing up. Things had either been put away or thrown away and in place of the Kim's Game on the table there was a brown cotton cloth, three places neatly laid and two candles burning – somewhat incongruously – in antique silver candlesticks. Carter, fingering the cutlery as he sat down, realized that it, too, was solid silver and crested.

Zoe had made no attempt, however, at any flights of culinary fancy. The supper was cold ham – not plastic supermarket squares but proper old-fashioned thick slices – homegrown potatoes, crisp, slug-free lettuce and tomatoes from the greenhouse. She had poured red wine into thin-stemmed glasses but Carter found, with gratitude, that his was Ribena. He caught her eye and smiled.

'The ham's very good.'

'Our local butcher,' Zoe said. 'He cooks it himself.'

'And thank God for him,' her husband added, raising his glass. 'Three cheers for Bert – or we'd starve. Cut it up for me, Zoe. After a day of Mrs Sweet I can't be bothered with anything.'

She leaned across to cut the ham into pieces for him and the simple service, performed willingly and without fuss, made Carter feel both jealous and compassionate. He drank some Ribena and looked away.

When she had finished Zoe asked: 'When will the piece appear in the *Courier*, Frank? I'm longing to see it.'

'As soon as I've got it all written up. I'll let you know.'

Phillip Dalrymple jabbed at a bit of ham with his fork. 'I

hope you're not going to write that Hun pilot up as the big hero.'

'I'll give the facts. Readers will judge for themselves quick enough.'

'Miss Burton's story is absolute twaddle – I told you. I'm surprised at her. She's a tough old bird, but she's got no sense.'

'I don't see that it's a question of sense,' Zoe said. 'It's what she believes happened. What she actually *saw* happen, after all. The plane was trying to land in the cornfield and when the pilot saw the children there he changed course and went out of control.'

Her husband let his fork fall with a clatter. His face, usually deathly pale, was flushed almost red. 'For Christ's sake, Zoe, whose side are you on?'

'There must have been decent, brave Germans too,' she went on stubbornly. 'There are good and brave people of every nationality.'

'Like the old saying goes, the only good Germans are dead ones.'

'Well, the pilot's dead all right, Phillip. And the war has been over a terribly long time. I know how you feel about what happened to your father, but I don't think he would have felt as bitter about something like that as you. It was war.'

'How do you know what he would have felt? You never even met him.'

'Nor did you, Phillip.'

There was a short silence. Oh brave, wise woman, Carter thought, waiting for the explosion. Phillip Dalrymple's flush had deepened ominously but, after a moment, he picked up the fork again.

'It's a fine thing to have a disloyal wife, Carter. Is your wife loyal to you?'

'She's dead.'

'So she is, I'd forgotten. Sorry. Accident, wasn't it?'

He avoided Zoe's eye. 'That's right.'

'Bad luck. But when she was alive, was she loyal?'

'Very. Except when she thought I was wrong.'

Margaret Mayhew

'How diplomatic of you, Carter! You should have gone in for diplomacy not journalism.'

'I don't think the Foreign Office would have had me, do you, sir? Not quite the right sort of background or school. Or redbrick university. Not really the thing at all.'

'You've got a bloody great chip on your shoulder the size of a house, haven't you, Carter? It's all different now, didn't you know that? Jack's better than his master. In a few years' time all our ambassadors will come from comprehensives and all the public-school chaps will be down the mines. Why did you go in for journalism anyway?'

'I was the English teacher's pet.'

'I hope for your sake that she wasn't anything like Miss Burton.'

To get as far away from the subject of the dig as possible, Carter proceeded to talk about his schooldays and then to regale them with a few Fleet Street stories and some about the *Courier*. Gradually, Phillip Dalrymple relaxed. The flush subsided and he looked more at ease than Carter had ever seen him. So, for that matter, did Zoe. The strained look had gone from her face and in the candlelight, her hair released from its topknot and her eyes shining beneath the ragged fringe, she was almost beautiful.

They finished the meal with fruit and cheese. Carter offered to help wash up but Zoe refused, insisting that the job could wait until morning. He passed the dirty dishes for stacking in the sink. Jan would have had kittens. She would never have left so much as a teaspoon unwashed overnight. Remembering that, he smiled.

Zoe made instant coffee in mugs and he carried the tray through for her, following Phillip Dalrymple's wheelchair as it squeaked through the house. They sat out on the terrace and watched evening turn into night. Carter, smoking and drinking evil-tasting coffee from a chipped mug with OXO on its side, felt at peace. From where he sat in the same creaking cane chair as before, he could watch Zoe unobserved from semi-darkness. She was sitting on the ramp outside the

182

French windows, her arms round her knees. The light from the drawing room shone on her face and he studied it with a lover's intensity, watching every movement, every small flicker of expression. A moth fluttered past him, drawn by the light, and brushed past her head.

From the shadows beyond, on the other side, Phillip Dalrymple said suddenly: 'Do you play the piano, Carter?'

The mere idea almost made him laugh. Pianos had been rarer than tigers where he'd been brought up. And playing them – had they existed – would have been rated roughly on a par with ballet dancing.

'Sorry, no.'

'Pity. I used to once. Before.' There was a pause. 'Zoe can manage the scale of C if you show her where to start, and something called "Stepping Stones" which she learned when she was six, but that is the extent of her repertoire.' The wheelchair squeaked gently in the darkness. 'If you can't oblige, Carter, then Zoe had better put on a record. Something soothing, to suit our mood – whatever that may be.'

She got up and went into the drawing room. Carter could see her shadow on the wall as she moved about. His host spoke again.

'There's only one thing I envy that German pilot for, Carter.'

Carter said uneasily: 'What's that, sir?'

'The manner of his death. It was quick. And it was clean. One minute he was a whole and healthy man and the next he was dead. No long, drawn-out process in between.'

'Most of us go through that process.'

'But some of us more than others. Have you got a cigarette, Carter?'

Carter lit one for him.

'I'll tell you something,' the baronet went on. 'If the process becomes too humiliating, I've every intention of putting a final stop to it. Finish. Over and out.'

'Is that cricket?' Carter said quietly. 'I thought the game was meant to be played until the last ball.'

'Not if you declare.' A spiral of smoke drifted towards

Carter. 'I always found cricket rather boring, actually. Rowing was more my style. Not so much hanging about. I don't care for that.'

There was the faint crackling sound of a rather old record from the drawing room, a rhythmic scratch-scratching, and then the voice of Vera Lynn floated out on the night air. 'There'll be blue birds over the white cliffs of Dover . . .'

Zoe had reappeared. 'It's one of your mother's, Phillip. I thought it was appropriate.'

'Did you?' he said sarcastically. 'Hardly appropriate to a Kraut. You should have put on "Lilli Marlene".'

Carter listened to the old song as it sounded out across the terrace and the lawn below, into the still darkness of the field and the wood beyond. Strange how evocative it could be about something he had never known. It made him think of air raids, shelters, rationing and uniforms; of soldiers going off to fight and coming home on leave; of Jesse and his Home Guard filling up sandbags and challenging the locals with ancient rifles; of barbed wire and bombed buildings and blackout; of ships sinking while men clung to lifeboats and of planes spiralling down out of the sky . . .

He stayed until late. Zoe had made more coffee and put on some more of her mother-in-law's old records. They listened to 'We'll Meet Again' and 'Room Five Hundred and Four', to Noel Coward speaking 'I'll See You Again' and Richard Tauber singing 'You Are My Heart's Delight' and to dance music played by Geraldo, Ambrose and Roberto Inglez. And Phillip Dalrymple talked about his childhood at Fairfield and his schooldays at Eton – his voice, for once, without rancour or regret.

And Carter watched Zoe.

At half past one he finally left. Zoe uncurled herself from the swing seat and went to see him off.

'Sorry I stayed so late.'

'I'm glad you did. Don't you realize how good you are for Phillip? I haven't seen him like he was tonight for a long time . . . It was almost like the old days. Thank you.'

She walked out on to the drive with him and stood with her arms folded across her chest. The stars were brilliant overhead.

'They found the plane's number, by the way. Tom had picked it up and polished it nicely. He was quite upset when they took it away from him.'

She smiled in the darkness. 'Poor Tom, but well done him! That means they'll know for sure whether it was Martin Kern or not.'

'That's right.' Carter opened the van door. 'Thanks again for the supper, Zoe.'

'Frank . . .'

He turned quickly. 'Yes?'

'Nothing. Except that I hope it *was* him. And I hope you find your Barbara. And that she remembers.'

He nodded, got into the van and drove away.

Mrs Eliot had switched off her television and gone to bed. When Carter let himself into his lodgings in Lime Grove the house was silent except for his landlady's snores. He smoked his last cigarette of the day, lying in bed and staring up at the River Nile and the map of Australia. But for once, geography was not on his mind. He was thinking about other things: the Messerschmitt, Martin Kern, the girl, Barbara, Phillip Dalrymple . . . and Zoe.

It was only as he stubbed out the cigarette and switched off the bedside light before drifting into sleep that he realized that it was the first time in six years that he had not been tortured with thoughts of Jan.

Ten

Identification of the Messerschmitt pilot was established through the Ministry of Defence and Luftwaffe records. As Bob Simpson had promised, with the aircraft serial number known, it was a relatively simple matter to trace and confirm that the pilot and the owner of the diary were one and the same. Leutnant Martin Kern was listed as having disappeared over Sussex on Friday 6th September, 1940. It had been his nineteenth birthday and his first – and last – sortie into combat.

Carter, once he had learned this, set the wheels of his own investigation into motion. Barbara Karslemn was not Kern's official next of kin. They had never married and her name did not appear on any records. He had to find her through other sources. He rang Don Clayton, an old Fleet Street colleague with a nose like a bloodhound who had since risen to the dizzy heights of assistant editor to one of the nationals and gathered about him those similarly qualified.

After the preliminaries, Carter said: 'Have you got a useful stringer in Hamburg, Don? There's a woman there I'm trying to trace.'

'Then you'll want Peter Smith. He's your man. He'll either do the job himself or put you in touch with one of the agencies over there for tracing missing persons. Very efficient, the Germans are at finding people. Mind you, they need to be since the last war. Hang on a tick and I'll give you his number.'

Carter hung on. He blew a kiss across the room to Brenda, who sent one back on the tips of vermilion-painted nails. He waited. Tantalizingly, he could hear background noises at the other end of the line – the clatter and chatter, the hum and throb of a big newspaper office. There was no denying that he missed it. At last, Don Clayton picked up the receiver again and gave him the Hamburg telephone number. Carter wrote it down.

'Thanks, Don.'

'You're welcome. Story in it?' The bloodhound's nose was twitching.

'Don't know yet. Could be a dead end, Don.'

There was a laugh. 'Not giving anything away, eh? Nice to know you haven't lost your touch, Frank. How are you keeping?'

'Fine. Great.'

'Still off the booze?'

'Temperance Carter's my new name.'

'Good for you. When are you coming back up to the smoke? About time you came out of the wilderness.'

'When there's a job for me.'

There was another rich chuckle. Carter could picture Don at his desk – overweight, rumpled and benevolent-looking. An appearance that concealed a shrewd, sharp and very tidy mind. There were no flies on Don Clayton. Not one. He'd help him back to Fleet Street, but only if it suited him and the paper and if he thought Carter worth it. He was not in business to be charitable to old crocks or down-and-outs.

'Come up and see me sometime, Frank. We'll talk about it.'

'I'll do that, Don. And thanks again.'

Carter rang off. He smiled wryly to himself. He had no illusions or false hopes about getting back into the big time. The door to Fleet Street had shut on him and was unlikely to reopen. Just the same, he had caught a strong whiff of it down the phone; the atmosphere had somehow filtered down the wire to him and brought back old memories. He brought his mind back to the present and reached out for the phone again.

It took six tries throughout the day before he finally got in touch with Peter Smith in Hamburg. The line was clear and he could hear every word. It was impossible, though, to tell

187

whether the stringer was English, German or what nationality. Like so many of them, he was probably bi-, or even trilingual and belonged to no single country. He spoke perfect English but in the slightly stilted manner of one who is constantly using other languages and has lost spontaneity.

'I could give you the name of an agency which might be able to help you trace this woman, Mr Carter, but I think it would be much better if I handled this myself. A great deal has happened in Germany during the past forty years and in wartime there was a lot of confusion. I have many friends and contacts. I should like a copy of the snapshot, although, considering the lapse of time, it may be of no use. Leave the matter with me. When I have some news I will contact you.'

Carter put down the receiver feeling restless and impatient. For two pins he would have gone to Hamburg himself even though he knew that if Barbara could be found the stringer would find her in a fraction of the time it would take him. He was surprised at how much he now wanted her to be traced, and not only because she would – as Phillip Dalrymple had so graphically described – put flesh on the bones of the story. It had become something more with him than the usual sniff round for the human-interest angle. He wanted to know what had happened to the girl in the photograph – not just for the readers but for himself.

Ken Grant, however, had no such romantic feelings.

'Never mind about her, Frank. Haven't they found the chap who shot the plane down yet? That's the one we're after. Get on to that surveyor of yours again and get things moving.'

But Bob Simpson had no news as yet. He was making a visit to the Records Office at Kew in two days' time in order to go through the RAF operational records and combat reports.

'It's a matter of searching and checking,' he told Carter. 'At least we know date, place and approximate time, but the trouble is that for every German aircraft shot down during the Battle of Britain there are, on average, three combat reports filed claiming the kill. Makes it tricky pinning it down to one man for sure. By the way, the inquest on Leutnant Kern is fixed for Tuesday week.'

'I'll be there.'

'The coroner's ordered a post-mortem.'

'Bit superfluous, isn't it?'

'They often do. If only to establish that the remains *are* human and not animal. It can help identification sometimes. Even a few bones can tell them if it's male or female as well as the height and age.'

Carter, remembering a particularly gruesome murder case he had covered years ago, could have told him that himself.

'Have they traced any next of kin yet, Bob?'

'Nothing doing. The Germans are still trying. If I hear anything I'll let you know.'

'I spoke to the bloke at the MoD myself and he didn't sound too hopeful. I've got a contact of mine on to following up the girlfriend in Hamburg.'

'The best of luck. But don't bank on it.'

Carter wasn't banking on anything, but he was hoping like hell and a feeling of optimism stayed with him throughout the day, despite less appealing distractions. Councillor Jackson was mercifully quiescent but pomposity raised its head in another form. The Member of Parliament for Milton Spa was attending prize day at a boys' public school near the town and it was Carter's lot to attend. He sat at the back of a hot and crowded hall, behind mothers in straw hats and fidgeting fathers in old school ties, and listened resignedly to the colonel's long exhortation to his audience to play the game fair and square, bat on a straight wicket and fight the good fight.

A meandering and obtuse commentary followed on the temptations life was likely to offer the sixth formers about to take their first unwary steps into the outside world. Unfortunately the MP, for all his straight wickets, was unable to call a bat a bat and skirted these pitfalls in such a roundabout way that Carter doubted if any of the leavers were able to identify the perils with which most of them would already have been perfectly familiar. So far as he could understand, wine, women and drugs were the three deadly dangers, with the Labour Party a close fourth. Like others round him, Carter was beginning to nod off when the colonel suddenly changed tack. He paused, put on his spectacles to consult his notes, removed them again and took a slow look round the hall.

'In 1940,' he began, 'this country stood alone against all the might of Nazi Germany. For several weeks during that summer our survival depended upon a few young chaps – many of them your age or very little older.'

The audience had gone very quiet as audiences do when they are really listening. The colonel's military stare passed along the rows, reviewing the troops.

'I should like to think that each and every one of you present here today, forty years later, would be capable and willing, if called upon, to do your duty the same as those few young men . . . To fight and, if necessary, to die for your country and in the cause of freedom. It is said that the youth of today have no ideals and are not prepared to defend their country – that nobody cares any more.' The stare turned to a glare. 'I don't believe this is true. You may never be put to the test, God willing, but if you are I trust you will not be found wanting. And I want you to remember one thing: we are all sitting here today, in this school and in a free and democratic country, because a handful of chaps just like you did care. Our future was in their hands then, just as your children's future is in your hands now.'

The old buffer had managed to get it right in the end, Carter acknowledged, as the warm applause reverberated round the hall. A short and sweet appeal to the heart strings, well laced with patriotism, had done it. And it would look good in print. He toyed with a few headlines. *MP challenges school-leavers.* Or *Schoolboys reminded of their debt and their duty.* Or *MP recalls sacrifice of the Few.* What would be the answer to the question they had been asked? Would they fight or wouldn't they? Nobody really knew.

The school was not all that far from Fairfield and Carter

made an excuse with himself that he might as well return to Milton that way and stop for some cigarettes at the village shop. He could find no excuse to call at the Hall. He had not seen the Dalrymples since the day of the dig, although he had spoken once to Zoe on the telephone when he had called to let her know that the Messerschmitt pilot had been identified. Unless it was by chance, he was unlikely to see her again before the fête, which was still nearly three weeks away.

He drove into the village by the same route he had first taken. The Bull was shut, but as he approached he recognized the bent, flat-capped figure of Jesse who was working with a sickle on some rough grass and nettles outside the churchyard wall. He looked up as Carter slowed the van and stopped.

'Afternoon to you, Mr Carter. Fine day.' Carter agreed. The old man began to sharpen the sickle's blade. 'I told you 'twere possible about that plane of Tom's, Mr Carter. Didn't I say so when Charlie wouldn't have it? Mind you, I didn't reckon on it being a *Jerry* plane. Somehow that *did* surprise me. Thought 'twould be one of ours, if it were anything. Old Tom was wrong about that.'

'Yes, he was.'

'Reckon you'd known that for some time, Mr Carter, but you weren't saying anything. I don't blame you. You've got to keep quiet about these things, I dare say, or you'd have every Tom, Dick and Harry nosing about.'

'Are you sorry it's not a Spitfire, Jesse?'

He shrugged. 'Don't worry me. I don't mind it being a Jerry plane . . . Only thing bothers me is how we missed it.' He put down the whetstone. 'But you should have heard some of them in the Bull. Took it personal, some of them did. You'd think the Jerry had done it just to annoy them. And Charlie still don't believe it. Never will – not if he was to see it with his own eyes. Stupid bugger! Real short he was with poor old Tom when he came in. Still, Tom's had a good few drinks out of it.'

'Glad to hear he's still around. I was afraid the digging might have frightened him away.'

Jesse shook his head. 'Not Tom. He might go to ground somewhere for a while but he'd always come back. Trodgers Wood is his home. He doesn't know anything else.'

Carter started up the engine. 'There'll be a piece about it all in the *Courier*. Front page.'

'I'll remember that.' Jesse was testing the sickle's edge with his thumb. 'Hope it won't bring the trippers here though. We don't want them and their litter, not with the competition.'

'Is that what all this is in aid of?'

'Just tidying up the edges. Making it all shipshape. The judges look at that, see. Care of grass, they call it. Counts for fifteen marks and last year we only got ten.'

'You'll get full marks this year, Jesse.'

'Hope so. Or Miss Burton'll have something to say to me.'

Carter grinned and drove off. Round the corner he stopped at the village shop but found it shut. He had rattled the door before he saw the CLOSED sign, half-hidden and only dimly perceived through the yellow cellophane over the window. He was walking away, back to the van, when he saw Miss Burton bicycling towards him. She stopped and put one brogued foot to the ground.

'Mrs Jennings is shut this afternoon, Mr Carter. It's her half day.'

'Not to worry. I just wanted some cigarettes.'

'Very bad for your health.'

'So they say.'

Miss Burton was looking at him with disapproval. Carter found himself almost shuffling his feet.

'I gave a statement to the police about that German pilot, Mr Carter. I understand there is to be an inquest. They tell me that he has been positively identified now as a Leutnant Kern.' She gave the rank its English pronounciation.

'That's right, Miss Burton. Martin Kern. Aged nineteen – just. It was his first sortie.'

She frowned. 'It seems very young. But of course they all were. Mere boys, hardly out of the schoolroom. Very sad.'

'The German authorities are still trying to trace his next of kin before he's buried.'

Miss Burton said sharply: 'I hope they bury him with full honours, as he deserved.'

'They always do. Don't worry.'

'And you're going to write a full account of what happened in your newspaper, Mr Carter?'

'As full as my editor will allow, Miss Burton. I'll write up your story just as you told it to me.'

'Hmmm. You can send me a copy when it comes out. I don't take the *Courier* any more. It's become very expensive and I have to watch every penny these days.'

'I'll do that,' he promised, smiling.

She rode away, pedalling along at speed, and Carter watched the ramrod-straight, typically English figure, and wondered if there had ever been a more unlikely champion for a member of Hitler's Luftwaffe.

The inquest on the German pilot was brief and undramatic. Only a small number of people attended – the pathologist, the police officer who had visited the crash site, Bob Simpson, representing the recovery group, and three or four others, including a couple of local reporters besides Carter.

Evidence was given, in turn, by those concerned, and Miss Burton's statement was read out. The post-mortem had established that the remains were human and of a young male, height approximately six foot. The coroner finally delivered his verdict. The remains were those of Leutnant Martin Kern of the Luftwaffe and he had been killed on active service on September 6th, 1940. Since it could not be said with absolute accuracy whether the pilot had died due to injury received in action before his plane crashed or at the moment of the crash itself, this ruling conveniently covered both possibilities.

Carter buttonholed Bob Simpson after it was over. The surveyor had more news.

'I've just been talking to the MoD bloke. Looks like there's no next of kin left alive. Apparently, Kern's father died before the last war began. He was an architect. His mother remarried in 1941 and then died in 1947. There were

193

no other children by either marriage and the stepfather died ten years ago.'

'Aunts or uncles? Cousins?'

Simpson shook his head. 'Both parents were only children themselves. They can't even come up with a second cousin once removed.'

'So it's Cannock Chase and only official mourners?'

'Almost certainly. It'll be the full treatment, of course, but it would have been nice to find a member of the family. No luck with Barbara, I take it?'

'Nothing so far. It'll take time.'

'Anyway, even if you did find her, she's not going to be that interested after all this time. She'll have a family of her own.'

'Probably.'

Simpson smiled. 'Haven't given up hope, have you? It's odd he gave *her* name and not his mother's in the diary. His mother was his next of kin, after all.'

'Perhaps there was a family row. It might have been over Barbara.'

'She looked a nice girl in that photo.'

'Maybe she wasn't good enough, class-wise. You know what mothers are like.'

The surveyor grimaced. 'I do. My mother-in-law didn't approve of me. She wanted Sally to marry a doctor. We hardly spoke and it wasn't until after Sally died that we finally got on. Stupid business!' He shook his head again. 'I'll tell you something else about that pilot, though, Frank. I took a piece of that cloth to someone I know in London who's an expert on uniforms and he said it was a tailor-made job, privately done. The material was superior to the normal issue for officers. And that cigarette case we found was solid silver. The Kern family must have been well-heeled.'

'That's probably what he was having done at that appointment with his tailor in the diary. Interesting.'

As he drove back to the office, Carter was putting together a picture of Martin Kern in his mind. He knew quite a bit about the pilot now. Apart from his rank, his age and his height, he knew that he had come from a well-to-do family, had been left fatherless in his teens and almost certainly quarrelled with his mother over his girlfriend. He had been something of a dandy, with his privately tailored uniform, his white silk scarf and his silver cigarette case, but, even so, he had picked an unsophisticated-looking girl like Barbara. And she had meant a hell of a lot to him. But that was all they were likely to discover unless she was traced.

When Carter reached the office he found a message waiting for him to ring Peter Smith in Hamburg. He felt a prickle of excitement as he put through a return call; it seemed like providence answering his prayers. The stringer answered the phone at once.

'I have some news for you, Mr Carter.'

'Great!' Carter reached for his pen.

The slightly stilted voice continued without emotion. 'Barbara Karslemn was a butcher's daughter. She died in Hamburg in 1945. Her home in Markannastrasse was flattened in a night raid. Her parents were also killed. Also a small brother.'

Carter felt like a deflated balloon. He found himself drawing a circle on the pad in front of him and criss-crossing the empty space with lines.

'That's that, then. Thanks a lot.'

'It's not quite all.'

Carter's pen stopped. 'Oh?'

'She had a daughter . . .'

'A *daughter*!'

'That is correct. She alone of the family survived the bombing.' There was a brief pause while the stringer consulted his notes. 'Born April fourteenth, 1941. Illegitimate. And, incidentally, Fräulein Karslemn named a Leutnant Martin Kern of the Luftwaffe as the father. It's on the birth certificate. He was killed in September 1940 – missing on a raid over England.'

Carter had torn off the doodled sheet of paper and was writing quickly on a fresh one.

195

'Anything else about her?'

'Oh yes.' The precise voice sounded suddenly amused. 'We had to follow quite a long trail, but we got there in the end. The child was christened Martina Barbara. She was put into care after her mother and maternal grandparents were killed. The paternal grandmother refused to acknowledge her.'

That figures, Carter thought. The architect's widow had found the butcher's daughter as dismaying a prospect as the Karslemn family had probably been delighted by her tall young son in his privately tailored officer's uniform. There would have been rows in the Kern camp from start to finish and any woman who had been able to reject the only child of her only son must have been a formidable opponent. Maybe she didn't believe it was his. Or maybe she didn't want to believe it. Either way, she was a tough lady.

'What then?'

'Later on she was fostered by a couple in Hamburg who eventually adopted her legally. After the war they emigrated to the United States, taking the girl with them.'

Carter caught his breath. 'Is she still alive?'

'Very much so. She is an actress and lives in Los Angeles.'

'What does she call herself now?'

'She still calls herself Martina and uses her first husband's surname professionally. Martina Drake.'

Carter's pencil stopped in mid-air. 'Not *the* Martina Drake?'

'The same.'

'I don't believe it! You're kidding!'

'I assure you that I am not, Mr Carter. I admit, though, that it surprised me, too.'

As well it might, Carter thought, and I bet he's already spilled the beans to the nationals. Martina Drake, film actress turned television comedienne, was the all-American girl – blonde, bubbling and squeaky-clean. Her comedy series, situated around her family, was shown all over the world and epitomized the American way of life, as most people in other countries imagined it to be. A luxurious open-plan house, a built-in kitchen, an ever-full fridge, a tolerant husband, two rebellious teenagers, a cute dog and nosy neighbours. And yet Martina Drake had been born, and nearly died, in the maelstrom and horror of wartime Hamburg and Nazi Germany.

'Are you sure about this? No chance of a mistake?' he asked.

The voice turned a little huffy. 'I verify my facts always, Mr Carter. It is all documented. Naturally, Barbara Karlsemn may have been lying or mistaken about the identity of the father of her child. We cannot be absolutely certain of that fact. But, whoever her father may have been, Miss Drake is unquestionably the daughter of Fräulein Karslemn.'

Barbara had been neither lying nor mistaken, Carter would have staked his life on it. The girl in her simple blouse and skirt and ugly sandals had not been the type, if he was any judge. She would have been faithful to her pilot. He would have meant as much to her as she had to him.

'Does she know?'

'Miss Drake? I couldn't say. I have not approached her myself. It was not necessary. In any case, at present she is away on vacation somewhere unknown.' There was a small cough at the end of the line. 'I understand that the body of a German Luftwaffe pilot recovered recently in Sussex has been identified by the authorities as that of Leutnant Martin Kern . . .'

There was no point in denying or concealing what Peter Smith obviously knew perfectly well anyway. 'That's right.'

'An interesting story, Mr Carter. Quite intriguing. No wonder you were so interested in tracing the lady . . .'

Carter rang off. There was no hope that the stringer would keep quiet. He had no loyalty to anyone or to any one newspaper and would sell the story wherever he could find a buyer. All of which meant that it would very probably break first in the nationals and pip the good old weekly *Courier*, plodding along like a carthorse, to the post. There might be a slight delay while the jackals hunted down Martina Drake in her holiday hideout, but that was as much as could be expected.

Carter sighed. He reached for his cigarettes. Ken was going to take some pacifying.

Eleven

As it happened, thanks to the fact that Martina Drake was holidaying on a small private island in the Caribbean – unusually inaccessible even to the gentlemen of the press – the story appeared in the nationals and the *Milton Weekly Courier* on the same day. The actress, run to earth and quizzed about her antecedents, had proved entirely, and admirably, amenable. Yes, she had known that her natural father had been a Luftwaffe pilot killed in the last war. Her foster parents had kept papers and letters salvaged from her mother's Hamburg home when it was bombed. No, she did not bear any grudges against the Allies for the deaths of both her parents. She had considered herself American for many years, though she had never forgotten that her roots lay in Germany and she was proud of the fact that her father had been a serving officer who had died bravely for his country.

Good for her, said Carter to himself as he read the *Daily Star*'s version. Thus she had neatly drawn any sting. He looked admiringly at the photo of the actress, smiling and relaxed beside her Caribbean swimming pool. She didn't look a day over twenty-nine and yet he knew she was knocking forty. Nice legs, nice figure, good teeth and groomed to perfection. It must be hard work being a star.

His own report, set out sedately on the *Courier*'s cover, cheek by jowl with summer fêtes, Scouts' camps and traffic accidents, made far less racy reading. For one thing, Ken – fearful as ever of legal repercussions – had insisted on only an oblique reference to 'a well-known actress, thought to be the next of kin'. No names, no pack drill. Let other editors –

the big boys – collect the libel suits. Except that he need not have worried. Martina Drake had had no intention of denying anything and had kept her lawyers on a tight leash.

Carter picked up the *Courier* from his desk. Ken's prim headline – *Discovery of World War Two Fighter* – had been no match for the *Daily Star*'s *Nazi Pilot Shock*. The rest could have been worse. There was a good photo of Bob Simpson holding the piece of fuselage with the black Luftwaffe cross and, beside that, a shot of two other members of the group holding the buckled prop. Another photo showed the Daimler-Benz engine in all its muddy glory. A fourth picture had the black leather diary open at Martin Kern's signature and below it was the snapshot of Barbara smiling into the sun. A nice touch that, Carter thought. Poignant was the word. Even the crustiest colonel might spare a second's sympathy. He reckoned that he had somehow managed the difficult feat of telling it like it was without treading on too many patriotic toes. Miss Burton's account was faithfully reported and due acknowledgment given to the pilot's sacrifice – more trouble with Ken there, but he had won the day. This was followed by a report of the dig, went on to say that it was hoped to trace the RAF pilot responsible for the 'kill', and finished with a timely reminder of the gallant feats of the Few in defending England from the might of Hitler's Luftwaffe.

He put down the paper and looked up to see Zoe standing in front of him.

'I'm terribly sorry to disturb you, Frank. You're busy . . .'

He stopped staring at her like a moron and jumped to his feet. 'Not a bit of it. Nothing doing, as you can see.'

Out of the corner of his eye he could see, or sense, his editor's distorted shadow swimming like a predatory fish behind the reeded glass of the half-open door.

'I shouldn't have come,' she said apologetically. 'But I was in Milton shopping and I wanted to say how much I liked your piece in the paper. About the plane.'

'You did?'

'Very much.'

'How about your husband?'

She smiled. 'What he likes is that it's over and done with.'

'No more trespassers?'

'Only one or two. People just wanting to gawp for the sake of it, but of course there's nothing left now for them to see. Only the place where it happened.'

Which was more than enough for some people, as Carter knew, but he didn't say so. The Great British Public loved gawping at places where things had happened. However, this particular place was conveniently inconvenient. And it meant leaving their cars and walking, which was more deterrent than a minefield.

'They'll forget all about it soon,' he told her. 'Last week's headlines are staler than last week's loaf. Did you see the nationals as well? About Martina Drake?'

She nodded and looked down at the copy of the *Daily Star* with its big picture of the actress. 'Mrs Sweet brought that one in for us to see as well.' She shook her head. 'I just couldn't believe it at first, Frank. It's like a fairy story. I haven't seen many of her shows – Phillip hates television and our set's a hundred years old and black and white – but she's world-famous, isn't she? And so American. Is she really that pilot's daughter?'

'So far as anyone knows, she is. She's certainly Barbara Karslemn's daughter and Barbara named him as the father. She was born after he was killed.'

'Yes, I read that. How on earth did they find out about it?'

He hesitated. 'I found someone to find out. Through Fleet Street. Someone in Hamburg.'

She stared at him. 'It *was* you, then? I didn't think it could be because you said so little about her in the *Courier* . . .'

'Editorial policy,' he said flatly. 'Gentlemanly discretion and all that.'

'You should be back in Fleet Street where you belong, Frank.'

'More my mark, do you think? Less gentlemanly?'

'*Much* more your mark!'

Harvey, looking as sour as little green apples, had begun to bang away at his typewriter. Carter glanced at his watch. He wanted her to himself.

'Come and have some lunch.'

'I don't think I've got time. Mrs Sweet's looking after Phillip, but I said I wouldn't be long.'

It was like being tied to a child, he realized, only worse. A child grew up and became independent. Her husband would only become more dependent, not less.

'Just a sandwich,' he persuaded her. 'There's a pub just round the corner. It won't take long.'

She gave in. 'Actually, I am rather hungry. If *you* can spare the time . . .'

The fish shadow was looming larger and blacker against the glass. Any minute now Ken would see to it that he couldn't. Carter grabbed the shopping bags that Zoe had put down and, taking her arm, steered her firmly out of the office, running the gauntlet of winks, nods, leers and, finally, Brenda's rounded gaze.

The Bunch of Grapes was a nice old Victorian pub with a good line in sandwiches and snacks. It was still too early for it to be crowded but not too early for Mike Tubbs to be well-established at the bar. Carter found an empty table in the far corner, well away from the chief sub. At the other end of the bar he ordered a glass of white wine for Zoe, tomato juice for himself and two rounds of chicken sandwiches. As he carried the drinks over to the table where she was sitting he still couldn't believe his luck . . . that she was there and that she had sought him out.

'Cheers!'

She lifted her glass in reply and drank. 'I needed this. How I hate shopping!'

'I thought all women were supposed to love it.'

'Are they? Well, this one doesn't.'

'Not even for clothes?'

She laughed. 'You can see I'm not interested in clothes. When Phillip and I were first married I tried to be. I went out

and bought the sort of clothes I knew everyone would expect
me to wear – tweed skirts, Jaeger suits, cashmere sweaters,
that sort of thing. I wore them to begin with and then after a
bit they just stayed in the cupboard. In the morning I'd find
myself putting on jeans and a sweater every time – unless I
had to attend some kind of function.'

'Like fête committees,' he said, remembering how she had
looked in her skirt and blouse. Different, but not necessarily
better. He thought of the studio portrait of her in her evening
gown and pearls that he had seen in the drawing room at
Fairfield Hall. That had been definitely worse – stiff, artifi-
cial and almost unrecognizable as the girl who sat opposite
him now.

'Like fête committees,' she agreed. 'When it comes to it I
can rise to the occasion. Anyway, it seems a shame to spoil
good clothes doing housework, and that's what I seem to
spend most of my time doing – or trying to do, I should say.'

'You look fine to me as you are,' he said with perfect truth.
'Stay that way.'

'That's nice of you. Phillip was right. You should have been
a diplomat.'

'I meant it.'

He lit a cigarette and wondered, as he watched her drinking
her wine, if she had any idea just how much he really did
mean it. Had she any clue at all how much he bloody well
loved her?

She lifted her head suddenly and caught his eyes and, just
for a second, he thought that she did know, that she knew
very well. But then she had turned away from him and was
rummaging in one of the carrier bags at her feet.

'I bought this sweater for Phillip. It's his birthday next
week. Do you think it'll be all right? I stood at the counter in
Wakemans for nearly half an hour trying to decide between
pale blue and moss green and in the end I bought a black
one.'

She pulled a V-neck lambswool sweater out of the bag and
held it up by the shoulders above the table.

'Very nice.'

'You don't think the pale blue would have been better?'

'No, I don't.'

'Or the green?'

'Definitely not. No way.'

'You don't think black's a bit . . . a bit *sombre*?'

Funereal was the word she subconsciously, or consciously, meant, Carter thought. He still thought she had made the right choice. Baby blue was no colour for Phillip Dalrymple. Black moods went with black sweaters. But he did not want to think about Zoe's husband and, to his relief, she was folding up the V-neck and putting it back in its bag.

'Have some more wine?'

She looked down at her half-empty glass and then at her watch. 'No, thanks. I really ought to be going soon . . .'

'They won't take long with the sandwiches. They're pretty quick here, but I'll chase them up.'

He went over to the bar, desperate for her to stay longer. Mike Tubbs flapped a hand in greeting from his stool at the other end but luckily turned back to his neighbour. The last thing Carter wanted was the chief sub lurching across to their table and making crude insinuations. Nothing, he knew, would be more guaranteed to make Zoe take flight. He turned on the charm for the benefit of the landlord's daughter who was helping behind the counter and she came up promptly with the two rounds of chicken sandwiches. He carried them back to the corner table.

'There you are, madam. Service with a smile.'

'Thank you. It looks marvellous.'

She ate without appetite or interest though, he noticed, as she had done on the other occasions when he had eaten with her. And she was too thin and too pale. The one good thing to be said about that studio portrait was that she had looked healthier. Maybe the photographer's cosmetic brush had painted out the dark shadows under her eyes. More likely they had come since her husband had fallen ill. Also, she had fallen silent, which was a bad sign.

'Penny for them?'

She roused herself. 'Actually I was just thinking how glad I was that it was *you* who traced that girl.'

'Barbara Karslemn. I didn't. I just asked someone to find out for me.'

'Same thing in the end. And but for you the plane would never have been found.'

'Wrong again. Tom knew it was there all the time. And it was Bob Simpson and his group who saw he was right and found where to dig. I wouldn't have known the first thing about it. In fact, I didn't even believe Tom to begin with. And I didn't really believe Bob either. If anyone takes the credit, it's Miss Burton. She persuaded your husband to let the dig go ahead.'

'I think she could persuade anyone to do anything.'

'She sure has a way with her.'

'I wonder how Martina Drake feels about it all. It must have been quite a shock for her.'

'I don't think she minded – or if she did she wasn't letting on. She knew about her real father anyway. The foster parents had told her.'

'Yes, I remember it said so in the *Daily Star*. Even so, Frank, I don't suppose she ever expected that he would be found. It's sad they never met. He never saw her and she never saw him.'

'It must have happened a lot in the war. The same as your husband and his father.'

'Yes. That's an ironic coincidence, isn't it? I wonder if that's occurred to Phillip.'

'I'll tell you another one. My birthday's on the same date as Martin Kern's – September sixth. The same date he died, too.'

'Virgo,' said Zoe with a faint smile. 'I don't know about the German pilot, but it doesn't seem to suit you.'

'What should I be then?'

'I'm not sure. Leo, perhaps. Or Scorpio.'

'Scorpions have a sting in their tail.'

205

'Not necessarily. But they're usually very strong-willed. Sometimes ruthless.'

Carter let that pass. 'What about you? What sign were you born under?'

'Pisces. We're hopelessly indecisive about everything – as you may have noticed.'

'I hadn't.'

The pub was filling up rapidly now and someone jostled Zoe's arm and spilled her wine. She dabbed at her knees with a paper napkin and then ate a small bit of the chicken sandwich.

'Did your father fight in the war, Frank?'

'Not him. He was too bloody canny for that! Made out he suffered from asthma and got himself a nice cushy job on the railways. According to Mum he spent most of the war in a hut in the sidings, drinking tea and reading the *Mirror*.'

'You come from Newcastle, don't you? I remember Phillip saying.'

'That's right.'

'You don't sound very much like a Geordie. I thought you were all supposed to be impossible to understand.'

'We are. But it's bad for business so I ironed out some of the accent along the way.'

'Say something in proper Geordie.' Zoe looked round for inspiration. 'Say "pass the salt please".'

Carter laughed. 'A proper Geordie'd be more likely to say gimme and no pass or please about it.' He shook his head. 'You've no idea. It's all light years from anything you've ever known.'

'That makes me sound very dull.'

'That's not what I meant. Different, that's all. And I wouldn't let it worry you – you haven't missed a thing, believe me.'

'Do you see your parents often?'

'Not if I can help it.'

'That's a pity.'

He smiled. In her upper-class world all children were supposed to love and honour their parents and visit them regularly. And all parents were supposed to be glad to see them – or at least pretend to be. It was the safe, cosy world of Christopher Robin going on for ever. God bless Mummy and God bless Daddy.

'Dad's an old rogue who never stops grousing and Mum was bloody glad to see the back of me. Six kids and a husband more out of work than in it – can you blame her? She wore herself out just keeping things going. When I left home at fifteen it just meant there was one less to worry about.'

Zoe was silent and Carter doubted if she had the blindest idea of what he was talking about. She would never have even seen a dole form. For her a house without a bath and an inside toilet would be unthinkable. He tried – and failed – to picture her in his parent's back-to-back with its curling brown lino, dingy net curtains and sour smell. Even with its shabbiness and messy kitchen, Fairfield Hall was a different world. Martin Kern had probably had much the same difficulty, only in reverse. His little butcher's daughter could have been equally out of place in Frau Kern's house in some smart quarter of Hamburg.

He said tiredly: 'Your childhood must have been a bit different from mine, one way and another.'

'I don't have the sort of golden memories I can see you're imagining. As a matter of fact, I was miserably unhappy most of the time.'

Carter lifted his head, surprised. 'No doting parents? I can't believe it.'

'They did their doting from a safe distance. I was looked after by a succession of ghastly au pairs and then packed off to boarding school at the first opportunity.'

'A select academy for young ladies?'

'Something of the kind.'

'What then?'

'Finishing school in Paris. Actually, I quite enjoyed that. I'm not too bad at languages.'

Which meant she was bloody good, Carter translated for himself. His own prowess extended to good morning, good evening and thank you in French, German and Spanish. If the postilion was struck by lightning and nobody spoke English he was in big trouble. He wondered suddenly whether Martin Kern had spoken any English or whether their conversation – had they ever met – would have been limited to three polite exchanges.

'What about when you were finished? If that's the word.'

'My mother wanted me to do the Season. I think she rather liked the idea of being a deb's mum and giving smart little lunch parties and sitting on ball committees. I wasn't quite so keen on the idea. In fact, I dug my toes in and refused point-blank to do it. There was the most frightful row but in the end they gave up trying to persuade me. Instead I went to do a secretarial course in Oxford . . . and met Phillip.'

Zoe drank some more wine. Carter said nothing but waited until she went on talking.

'We met at a party at Oriel – one of those when about fifty people are all squashed together in a room that really only holds about fifteen. The noise was terrific and you could hardly move.'

'I've been to them,' Carter said. 'Though not quite as classy.'

'I noticed Phillip at once. He was standing over by the window talking to a very beautiful blonde girl in a gold lamé dress, and he was easily the best-looking man there. In fact, he was the best-looking man I'd ever seen. You can't know how different he was. He was charming and amusing and so tall and fit that it was hard to imagine him ill with anything, let alone something so awful . . .' She put down her glass on the table between them. 'Anyway, after a bit he stopped talking to the blonde and came over and talked to me instead. Then he took me out to dinner. I remember that meal better than any other I've ever had in my life. The waiter gave us a table in the corner. We had smoked salmon and duck and masses of wine and by the time we got to the pudding I was so in love with him I thought I'd die if he didn't ask me out again. It can seem like life or death at eighteen, can't it?'

'It can at any age.'

'I've almost forgotten.' She gave a wry smile. 'I needn't have worried, as it turned out. He *did* ask me out again.'

'Bloody fool if he didn't.'

'We were married three years later, when he had got his degree. He was all set for the Foreign Office when his illness started.'

'Was it sudden?'

'No. He just began to realize that something was wrong. I remember we were staying at Fairfield one weekend with his mother and went out for a walk on Sunday afternoon. He kept complaining that he couldn't seem to pick his feet up properly – they sort of dragged and he kept tripping over little bumps on the ground. After that his feet started to feel numb and tingly and his hands trembled sometimes so that he couldn't write very well. Then there were other signs ... It was all terribly gradual and, of course, he refused to see a doctor for ages. I managed to persuade him to go in the end and they did all sorts of tests.' She drank some more wine, tossing it back quickly. 'When he was first told what was wrong he simply didn't believe it. I don't think I did, either. Not until much later on.'

Carter lit another cigarette. He knew she was talking more to herself now than to him and half of it he didn't want to hear, though he knew he had to listen. He wanted to pretend – just for now – that Phillip Dalrymple didn't exist.

'Isn't there any chance of a cure?'

She shook her head. 'Apparently not. At least, not in time for Phillip. They've tried all sorts of things – injections of liver extract, vitamin B, anti-typhoid vaccine, even arsenic ... and all sorts of different diets. None of them has done more than help for a bit. That's the worst part of it. Living without hope and with things getting more and more ghastly for him. You wouldn't recognize him from the man he was. I don't just mean his looks – those have gone, but that doesn't matter. His whole character has changed. He used to be so different. We were very happy together in the beginning.'

Carter didn't want to hear that, either, but he said quietly: 'It must be tough for both of you.'

She stared down at her glass. 'It's bloody tough sometimes, if you want to know the truth. And I get scared stiff that I won't be able to go on coping. I'm terrified that one day I'll let him down. I even dream of just running away from it all . . . going off by myself and leaving it all behind me. And I despise myself for even thinking of that.'

'Plenty of women dream of that even in normal circumstances, let alone yours.'

She half-smiled. 'I suppose they do.' She drank some more wine but the chicken sandwich remained half-eaten on the plate. 'I wish I believed in God – really believed. People manage to get through all sorts of awful things because they've got absolute faith, don't they? But I just don't seem to have much at all. Do you?'

'No. But that's just me. A very cynical old hack. Don't rule it out if it helps.'

'If we'd had children it might be easier somehow, I think. We'd have them to consider as well as ourselves. Life would *have* to be more normal. I was going to have a baby the year after we married, but I miscarried. It would have been six years old now.'

'The same age as Jan's,' Carter said, almost without thinking.

Zoe looked dismayed. 'I'd forgotten, Frank. I'm sorry. Here I am moaning on about my own problems when you've had enough of your own.'

'Self-inflicted. That's the difference.'

'Which must make it worse, not better.'

He let that pass. 'I only wish I could help.'

'You already have. More than you realize. Finding that plane made Phillip forget everything else – even if only for a while.'

'It made him angry as well.'

'Yes, but it was something different to be angry about, don't you see?' She looked at her watch again, a man's one that was too big on her thin wrist. 'I must have bored you to death, Frank.'

'You haven't.'

'And I really must go now. Mrs Sweet will be champing at the bit and Phillip will be in a foul temper if I'm much later.' She fumbled in her bag for her purse. 'How much do I owe you?'

'You don't. It's my treat.'

'Thank you. That's sweet of you.'

She began hurriedly picking up the carrier bags.

'Let me help . . .'

'No, honestly. They're not at all heavy and the car's quite near. I really must dash. Thank you so much for the lunch.'

She stood up and began to edge her way through the crush. He called after her.

'I'll see you at the fête on Saturday.'

She stopped and turned back to him. 'I'd forgotten . . . Please don't bother about it. We can easily find someone else to do the judging. It'll be the most awful waste of your time.'

'It's my newspaper's time,' he said. 'And I'd like to do it.'

She stood nonplussed, the bags in each hand. 'Well, if you're really sure . . .'

'I'm really sure. See you Saturday. I'll be there early.'

He watched her squeeze her way towards the door and then sat down again to finish his sandwich. He ate half-heartedly and with as little appetite as Zoe. Whether or not she knew or guessed how he felt about her, there was no way she was going to let him get any nearer. In the nicest possible way she had been trying to give him the brush off. He took another bite and chewed thoughtfully. And yet she had come to see him.

Carter was working late that evening when the phone rang. Brenda, somewhat reproachful since Zoe's visit, had abandoned her switchboard long ago and even Ken had gone home to his wife and orchids. Bob Simpson spoke.

'Picked up something earlier through the MoD that I thought you'd be interested to hear, Frank.'

'I'm all ears.'

'Seems Miss Drake has some pretty firm views on where she wants her father buried.'

211

'If it's not Cannock Chase she has to foot the bill, doesn't she?'

'That's right, but I don't suppose that matters much to her. She's quite definite that she doesn't want him put there.'

'Where then?' Carter asked with horrid visions of Forest Lawns flashing through his mind. What would American undertakers make of the remains of Leutnant Kern?

'She wants him buried at Fairfield, if possible. In the village churchyard.'

'*Fairfield*! That's a turn up for the books.'

'A nice turn up for your paper, if the rector agrees.'

Carter had already thought about that. If he hadn't been holding the telephone he'd have been rubbing his hands, thinking of possible headlines. *Hollywood star buries long-lost father in English country churchyard. Luftwaffe pilot laid to rest in English grave. Village honours gallant foe forty years on . . .*

Simpson was speaking again. 'She's supposed to be flying over in the next day or two to arrange things.'

'Thanks for the tip, Bob. Any luck with the RAF bloke who might have shot Kern down?'

'Nothing yet. I'll let you know if I find him.'

Carter sat thinking with satisfaction of All Saints, Fairfield. It was just the spot – the perfect setting for a poignant, tear-jerking, full-military-honours ceremony. Martin Kern would be buried in company with Ezrah, Josias, Ann and Hannah and assorted other villagers from over several hundred years.

'If I should die, think only this of me: That there's some corner of a foreign field that is for ever . . . Germany.' Except that Fairfield could only be for ever England and Martin Kern would lie for ever under an English heaven.

There was no need to find an excuse, consciously or subconsciously, to go back to Fairfield. It was all in the line of duty. Carter drove into the village the next day and drew up outside the rectory. It was one of the few post-war buildings there – a modern square box with a tiled roof and aluminium windows.

There was a square patch of lawn in front of the house and some snapdragons edging the concrete path leading up to the reeded glass door. A ginger cat sat washing himself near the step and ignored Carter completely. He pressed the buzzer. The rector himself answered, dressed as before in jeans and a sweater.

'Come in, Mr Carter. What can I do for you? Let's go into the study.'

Carter followed him into a small room overlooking fields at the back of the house. One wall was lined with crammed bookshelves, the contents stacked this way and that wherever space could be found. There was a modern teak desk across one corner, a two-seater settee with wooden arms and a dilapidated-looking armchair. Hugh Longman stepped over a plastic toy lorry lying on the parquet floor.

'Take a pew. The settee's more comfortable, you'll find. I always put difficult parishioners in the armchair – they're at a disadvantage and it gets rid of them quicker.' He picked up the lorry and set it down on the desk. 'Tell me, is this a professional call? If so, I'll sit behind my desk. If it's social I'll sacrifice myself and take the armchair.'

'Professional.'

'In that case . . .' The rector went round behind his desk. He removed a one-eyed, hairless, naked doll from the chair and sat down. 'I do wish the children wouldn't play in here, much as I love them. You've chosen a good time to call. My wife has taken them out for the day to visit their grandmother, otherwise our peace would be disturbed. This house has cardboard walls.'

'I'd have thought Fairfield would have an old house for a rectory.'

'It did once. It used to be at the other end of the village – a very nice Georgian pile with attics and cellars and wet and dry rot. It's set back from the road behind some trees, so you probably haven't noticed it. The church commissioners sold it off and built this instead.' Hugh Longman grimaced. 'It's easy to run and warm in winter, so I'm not grumbling. Let's just say it lacks romance. I'm sure I'd write better sermons in a panelled study looking out on to a croquet lawn.' He leaned his elbows on the edge of the desk and formed his fingers, appropriately, into a steeple. 'Now, tell me what I can do for you, Mr Carter. Is it spiritual or temporal?'

'A bit of both, I suppose. It's about the burial of the pilot of the Messerschmitt dug up in Trodgers Wood.'

'Ah! What else, of course? You were instrumental in finding the plane, weren't you? I remember our conversation in the churchyard. I must say I didn't believe it likely that it was there at all at the time, which was rather short-sighted of me. After all, in our professions we both know the impossible is always perfectly possible.'

Carter shifted himself sideways on the settee. If this was supposed to be comfortable he was glad he hadn't sat in the armchair.

'I didn't believe a word of it myself, to begin with. And it was the aviation group who did the recovery.'

'But it was *you* who took some notice of what poor old Tom had been trying to tell the village for years. If you hadn't, this pilot might never have been found.'

'We thought it was a Spitfire. Or at least, Tom did.'

'Spitfire, Messerschmitt – what's the difference? The pilot has been found, traced and will now have a decent, Christian burial. Which brings us back again to why you're here, Mr Carter. I can save us both time by telling you that Martina Drake has already written to me about the question of having her father buried at All Saints. The German Embassy and the Ministry of Defence have also been on to me – sounding out the ground, so to speak – and that's not meant as a pun, by the way. I don't know how *you* got to hear about all this, but I suppose that's part of your job.'

'What's your reaction to burying a German pilot in your churchyard, Rector?'

'Exactly the same as it would be if he were British.'

'What about the rest of the village? How do you think they'll feel?'

Hugh Longman unsteepled his fingers. He picked up the toy lorry and ran it backwards and forwards along the top of the desk. One wheel was missing and the lorry listed sideways.

'I hope this is off the record, Mr Carter.'

'Definitely.'

'Good. Because I don't want to find myself quoted in the *Courier*. The press are rather fond of clergy, one way and another, and my bishop wouldn't like it. Neither would the parochial church council.'

'You've discussed it with them?'

'It was raised at our meeting last night. Apart from the fact that burial space is getting scarce for the locals, I have to consider the feelings of my parishioners, a great many of whom took part in the last war.'

'And what *are* their feelings?'

'Mixed, in a word. And I'm not talking specifically about the burial. So far, the village in general hasn't heard about that possibility. But when they found out it was a Messerschmitt and not a Spitfire, a lot of the old Home Guard started sounding off . . . You can imagine.'

Carter could. The air of the Bull would have been even thicker than usual with reminiscences.

The plastic lorry rolled to and fro again. 'You can understand their feelings,' the rector went on. 'Some of them lost relatives and memories can die hard. Do you know that Mayhurst buried three German airmen *outside* the churchyard wall in the war because the villagers refused point-blank to have them buried inside.'

'I hope Fairfield is more generous spirited.'

'So do I. This country has always been very liberal in its views on such things – and quite right, too. I should like to think that our village will carry on that tradition.'

'Who has the final say?'

'I do. Or rather the law does, strictly speaking. Anyone who dies, or is killed, within the boundaries of this parish is entitled to be buried in our churchyard – assuming there is room for him or her. That is a common law right. It's not necessary to be a member of the parish. If some young man from another part of the country dies speeding through on his motorbike – which has happened – then he has a perfect right to be buried here.' The lorry was lifted into the air and dived down towards the desk top. 'Leutnant Kern, one might say, was speeding through in his Messerschmitt. I don't see that he should be denied the same right.'

'So you are going to agree?'

The rector smiled. 'On one condition.'

'Condition?'

'That Miss Drake consents to open our fête for us.'

The cunning devil, Carter thought admiringly. 'That's bloody clever,' he said. 'I'll guarantee you publicity before.'

'I rather thought you might. From the tone of her letter to me I feel confident that she will be only too glad to help. She is convinced that Fairfield is the right place for her father to be buried, close to where he fell. In my experience people tend to have strong emotional feelings about such things.'

'You don't believe then, like some people, that he should have been left where he was – with the plane?'

'No, I don't. I think he should be given a proper burial in a marked grave. And due respect paid, as it no doubt will be. The same applies to any serviceman, on any side.'

'It'll be full military honours.'

'So I gather.'

'And you'll officiate?'

'I'll certainly take part in whatever form of service is decided upon. And be glad to. I don't generally rely on information given in the newspapers, but according to Miss Burton this particular pilot was something of a hero.'

'She saw it happen.'

'Yes, I know. And you should have heard her in action at the parochial church council meeting yesterday. She demolished the opposition quite effectively.'

Carter grinned. 'Do they know about your condition?'

'Not yet. I only thought of it myself this morning. I must

say I thought it was rather a good idea. The fête is in aid of
the church bells and we need to raise more than eight hundred
pounds to get them back into working order. I don't have a
lot of time spare for watching the telly myself and I've never
seen one of her shows, but my wife loves them and I've a
feeling that Martina Drake might be a good attraction.'

'I think you'll reach your target, Rector.'

'So do I. By fair means or foul. And that should go a long
way towards soothing any ruffled village feathers. It also seems
to me to be a fair exchange. Leutnant Kern is given a last
resting place at Fairfield – and it's a very pleasant place, as
you know – and, in return, we get our church bells.'

'Very fair.'

The rector smiled. 'I'm glad you agree. But I'd be grateful
if you'd keep it under your hat for the time being. I'll bring
them all round to it gently.' He brought the lorry to a stop
and it tilted drunkenly to one side. 'You're going to judge the
fancy dress, I hear. Has anyone warned you that you're liable
to get lynched by all mothers whose children don't win a
prize?'

'Thanks for telling me,' Carter said.

After he had left the rectory he called at the Bull. Charlie was
wiping glasses behind the bar with a grey-looking rag. The
patrons, as usual, were lingering over their beers. Mactavish
and two white hens, as dingy as Charlie's drying cloth, were
pecking round the brick floor.

Jesse rose from the dimness of his chimney corner and
offered a pint. Carter thanked him and asked for a Coke
instead – it was a safer bet than the Bull's tomato juice. He
bought a packet of plain crisps and dropped a few crumbs
stealthily as he ate them. The cockerel quickly mopped them
up.

'Not come to find another plane for us, Mr Carter?' the old
man asked.

'Tom's one did me nicely, thanks, Jesse.' Carter ate another
stale crisp and let some more bits fall.

217

'Read all about it in the papers. You could have knocked me down with a feather when I saw that Jerry pilot had a famous American film star for a daughter. It took us all back a bit, I can tell you. Didn't seem possible for something like that to happen in a place like Fairfield. It takes a bit of getting used to.'

'What they can't get used to,' Charlie said witheringly, 'is the idea they missed seeing the bugger in the first place. I ask you! There's this bloody great Messerschmitt landing in the middle of the village and this lot didn't know a thing about it. I'd sooner you didn't feed Mactavish, if you don't mind, Mr Carter. It doesn't do to encourage him.'

'I told you, Charlie,' Jesse protested. 'Fighters were small planes. Tiddlers. And we couldn't have our eyes everywhere at once. There was a lot going on.'

The landlord snorted. 'Bloody lucky we weren't invaded, is all I can say. If Hitler had known about you, he'd've marched over toot sweet. Couldn't guard a chicken house, you couldn't.'

There were angry rumblings from the ranks. Jesse took his pipe from his mouth and said with dignity: 'Seeing as you were doing nothing but sitting nice and safe on your backside most of the war, Charlie, I don't see as you've any right to speak. I'll thank you to keep quiet about it. I always said it was possible there *was* a plane, seeing as how things were in the heat of the battle, which you wouldn't know about. I wasn't so surprised about *that* – nor were a lot of the lads – it was this American film star that surprised me.'

'TV star,' Charlie corrected. 'She hasn't made a film for years. Not since *Hearts and Flowers* back in the Sixties.'

'I don't remember that,' Jesse said. 'I haven't been to the pictures since 1955. I've seen her on the TV though.'

Charlie leaned heavily on the side of the bar. 'You don't believe it, Jesse, do you? Just because you read it in the papers?'

'Believe what?'

'That that Jerry pilot was her father. I ask you, is it likely? Of course not! It's all a publicity stunt, isn't it, Mr Carter?

218

They do things like that over there. Anything to be in the newspapers. Doesn't matter what it is, so long as it makes more people watch that show of hers on the telly. And *he* can't deny it, can he? What's left of him.'

'Makes more people drink your beer, doesn't it, Charlie?' someone said gleefully. 'Good publicity for you, too. All those trippers in here.'

'I can do without 'em,' the landlord growled. 'One drink and they waste my time asking a whole lot of questions like I was an information bureau.' He turned to Carter. 'We had two Americans in yesterday, wanting to see the plane. You'd think this was Disney World or something.'

'Wanted to know where the pilot was, too,' Jesse added, his pipe back where it belonged. The altercation with Charlie was evidently over and they were now back on common ground.

'I told them everything had been taken away and good riddance to it,' Charlie went on. 'I tell them all that, so perhaps we'll soon get a bit of peace.'

If only you knew, Carter thought, quietly drinking his Coke. If only you knew.

Twelve

O n the morning of the fête, Carter arrived at Fairfield Hall by eleven o'clock. He found the driveway blocked with cars parked at odd angles, their boots and doors left wide open for unloading. Faded red, white and blue bunting decorated the entrance, looking suspiciously as though it might have done service for Queen Victoria's jubilee. There was a bold handwritten amendment to the printed notice on the gate, announcing that the fête would be opened by the celebrated American actress Martina Drake at two o'clock. Carter had already seen similar additions to other posters dotted round the countryside. Apart from literally cutting the grass for the best-kept village competition, the locals had figuratively not let any grow under their feet so far as the fête was concerned. The rector's wisdom had prevailed.

Carter left the van outside the gates and walked up the driveway. The closer he got to the house, the more frenzied the activity. Women – and the odd male press-ganged into helping – were hurrying to and fro about their business like ants. And, as with ants, although there was a method to it all, it was not easily apparent to an outsider. Mrs Fortescue, his friendly sofa neighbour at the committee meeting, hailed him delightedly.

'Mr Carter, *could* you carry this box for me? I'd be *so* grateful. It's my back, you know. The doctor won't let me lift anything heavy. So silly really, but I feel I must do *exactly* as he says.'

He lifted the cardboard box, which contained a quantity of trailing greenery, and followed her. She trotted ahead, chattering away over her shoulder, her small bolster legs taking two strides to his one.

'Just a few little plants for the garden stall. I raise them myself in my greenhouse. They always seem to go well. I think people prefer *home-grown* things, don't you? And of course they're much cheaper than in the shops or those garden centres. And, though I say it myself, they're much better. Some of the things they sell in those places are half-dead already. Aren't we lucky with the weather? The year before last it rained cats and dogs and little fishes all day long. This way, Mr Carter.'

He followed her obediently round the side of the house and through the archway in the hedge. On the main lawn below the terrace the scene was being set – a typically English scene under an untypically brilliant summer sun. Trestle tables had been erected at intervals, coloured table cloths fluttered gently in the light breeze, produce and goods were being laid out, notices hammered in, sideshows set up. Amongst the small army of workers, Carter recognized several of the committee ladies, including Mrs Armstrong-Avery, who stood centre stage with arms outstretched like a policeman on point duty. Her voice could be heard above all else, commands ringing clearly across the garden.

'Not *there*, Mrs Hillman, if you don't mind. Your table is over in *that* corner. We must have the cakes in the shade. You are only allocated *one* table, Miss Plumb, not two. The other belongs to toys. Books are over there, Mrs Ayres – I'm afraid you'll just have to be in the sun. I think we should move that coconut shy much further to the left, Mr Nelson; it's too near the bottle stall and we don't want any confusion, do we? I hope your pony isn't going to go lame on us today, Mrs Allen. We're relying on you. Has anyone seen our treasurer? He's very late arriving.'

Beside Carter, Mrs Fortescue, exuding faint whiffs of April Violets, said breathlessly: 'Doesn't it all look lovely? It's going to be such a success this year – I know it. Such lovely weather and *such* a famous personality to open it for us. I

221

know I shouldn't say it, but it really does serve them right.'

Carter pushed a frond of greenery away from his face. He was looking for Zoe. 'Serve who right, Mrs Fortescue?'

'Mayhurst, of course. For holding their fête on the same day as us again. They keep on doing it and theirs is usually much bigger than ours. They can afford a marquee and a roundabout and someone well known to open it. But this year they've only got that funny fat little man with the bald head from that comedy on Wednesday evenings – I can't even remember his name – and *we've* got Miss Drake.'

Game, set and match to Fairfield. Carter smiled. 'Where do you want this box?'

She led the way across the lawn to a table on the far side, which was already laden with plants. As they approached, Miss Burton rose, genie-like, from behind the display, her arms full of cacti.

'Good morning, Mr Carter. Put them down there, would you, please? Thank you, Mrs Fortescue. Your plants are always welcome.' She looked down at the cluster of prickly and furry growths she was holding – some of them distinctly suggestive. 'I wish I could say the same of these things. I'm afraid I don't care for them at all.'

Carter kept a straight face and parked the box where he was bidden. After some more twitterings Mrs Fortescue moved off while he remained, moving plants around as directed. The offending cacti were banished to the back row, well hidden by taller and more graceful offerings. He arranged a group of herbs as decoratively as he could.

'What do you think of the news about your German pilot, Miss Burton?'

'Not *my* pilot,' she reproved him.

'Were you surprised when you learned who his daughter was?'

'*Nothing* surprises me any longer, Mr Carter.'

'Even so,' he persisted, 'it's pretty amazing the way things have turned out.'

'It's very useful,' she granted, tweaking off a dead leaf.

'For us, anyway. We should reach our target for the bells.'

'I'm sure you will. Martina Drake will be a big attraction.'

'So I'm told. I don't possess a television set myself, so I am afraid I have never actually seen any of her programmes.'

'You'll beat Mayhurst this year.'

'So I should hope! Pass me that variegated ivy please, Mr Carter. It looks untidy there.'

'Sad she never met her father. Or he her.'

'There is a great deal of sadness in this world. At least Miss Drake will have the comfort of burying him decently and with honour – something denied to many of the fallen.'

'And at Fairfield. What do you feel about that?'

She looked at him sharply across the trestle table. 'I hope this isn't an interview, Mr Carter. I'm much too busy.'

'I was just curious.'

'Then you will have to go on being "just curious". Would you move that pelargonium further back, please. It's a very poor specimen. It's probably one of Mrs Skinner's. We always have to reduce hers to get rid of them.'

Carter obliged meekly. As he did so the church clock struck half past eleven. He looked across the lawn and saw that Zoe had come out and was standing talking to Mrs Armstrong-Avery.

'Excuse me, Miss Burton.'

She nodded dismissively, then, as he was a few steps away, called after him.

'By the way, Mr Carter, there were two grammatical errors in that article of yours in the *Courier*: a split infinitive and a mixed metaphor.' Her stern features softened suddenly and unexpectedly into a smile such as she might once have awarded a deserving pupil. 'Apart from that, it was excellent.'

Mrs Armstrong-Avery greeted him expansively. 'Good of you to be here so early, Mr Carter. We're counting on plenty of coverage in your newspaper. Not *all* photographs of Miss Drake, if you don't mind. We mustn't forget that this is, after all, a village occasion. Some pictures of the children in their fancy dress would be nice – it always pleases the mothers. You do understand the judging rules, don't you?'

223

'I'll explain them to him later,' Zoe said. She smiled at him. 'It's quite simple.'

'I wish everything else was,' Mrs Armstrong-Avery said with feeling. 'It's been one crisis after another this morning. Our treasurer *still* hasn't arrived. And I don't know how we're going to manage without Madame Zara.'

Zoe caught Carter's querying glance. 'The fortune-teller. She's gone down with laryngitis and can't come.'

'We shall have to find a substitute somehow,' Mrs Armstrong-Avery insisted. 'If fortune-telling was printed on the posters, then it must be provided. Otherwise the public have the right to feel cheated and that would never do.'

Her eyes rested speculatively on Carter for a moment and he was afraid she was about to suggest him as an understudy. Then her attention was claimed by two stallholders bickering over a trestle table, each hanging grimly on to opposite ends.

'The battle of the tables,' Zoe said, as they escaped, walking away towards the house. 'It happens every year. Everybody tries to pinch everybody else's tables and there are the most awful rows before they all settle down.'

'I thought I was going to be seconded as a surrogate Madame Zara.'

'Like Rochester in *Jane Eyre* in a cloak and bonnet?' Zoe laughed. 'You're quite safe. You're much too useful as a gentleman of the press, let alone fancy dress judge.'

She walked gracefully beside him – so unlike Mrs Fortescue's bouncing, bolstered trot. Most upper-crust Englishwomen seemed to plod round like carthorses – if that wasn't insulting a carthorse.

'Tell me about these judging rules. What do I do?'

'It's quite straightforward. The children will be divided into two groups by age: up to eight and then from eight to twelve. Anita Fleming – she's a dentist's wife who paints a lot in her spare time – will be judging with you. Between you, you pick the first three in each group and they get the main prizes. The others all get a tube of Smarties as a consolation.'

'There's no overall winner for both classes?'

'No. The main thing is to keep everyone happy as far as possible. And, if you possibly can, try not to pick one that's just been bought from a shop – that's always unpopular.'

'The rector warned me I was in danger of being lynched by angry mums.'

She smiled. 'I heard you'd been to see him. Wasn't it a marvellous idea of his to get Martina Drake to come and open the fête?'

'It was blatant blackmail. Open our fête and I'll let your father be buried in our churchyard. Very clever.'

'I thought so, too. But I'm glad he's going to stay here at Fairfield. It seems so much better than some impersonal war cemetery with rows and rows of graves all looking exactly alike. Or being buried somewhere like Hollywood.'

'I'm with you all the way. But what about the villagers – that Dad's Army in the Bull, for instance? I bet they're not so happy about having a Luftwaffe pilot taking up a local plot.'

'I gather there have been a few mutterings. Charlie's dead against it, but then he's against everything. Anyway he's still considered a newcomer so his opinion doesn't really count. Phillip was furious, of course. He tried to persuade Hugh to change his mind, but he wouldn't.'

In the old days the parson would have done what the squire told him, Carter thought with interest. Times certainly had changed.

'And the rest of the village?'

'Most people seem to feel we owe the pilot something for what he did – or what he *didn't* do. They think it's a fair exchange, and you know how the British like to be fair.'

Thus spake the rector. Only from a slightly different angle. Carter said: 'Apart from not killing your schoolchildren, he'll get your church bells mended for you.'

'That's true.' Zoe stopped. 'How ironic, when you think about it! He was our enemy but he's done us more good than harm.'

'I don't think he had the bells of All Saints in mind when

225

he took off from northern France in September 1940, but that's the way things have turned out.'

They walked on up the steps towards the terrace.

'You're here very early, Frank. Are you hoping for an exclusive interview with the star herself?'

'If I can get it.'

'I warn you it might be difficult. We've had most of the nationals on the phone in the past week. I think they're all going to be here in force.'

'I'll bet.'

They reached the terrace.

'Her publicity man said she'd be here by half past one. He sounded quite unhappy about the whole thing, as though opening village fêtes was something he'd never heard of.'

'I think *she's* quite happy about it.'

'I hope she isn't expecting something like Chatsworth. Otherwise she's going to be terribly disappointed.'

'She'll love it all. It's so English.'

Zoe turned to look back at the lawn. The table dispute had been settled and some sort of order and harmony was emerging. The stalls looked amateurishly festive, the sideshows endearingly makeshift, flags fluttered bravely in the breeze and the gentle murmur of English voices reached them. Mercifully out of earshot, Mrs Armstrong-Avery stood with feet planted firmly apart in spirited conversation with the rector. From behind a screen of yew the ancient bell tower of All Saints watched and awaited the result of it all.

Zoe smiled. 'I see what you mean.'

Although she was friendly towards him, there was a reserve in her manner that had not been there before. Carter wondered if she regretted confiding in him in the pub when they had lunched together – much as he had regretted confiding in her at the dig. Or whether it was something else, something he had done. He said easily: 'Since I'm here so early, can I do anything else to help?'

'Actually, there is something you could do, if you don't mind. We always put some extra chairs out on the terrace –

the old people need somewhere to sit down. They're kept over in the summer house.'

'Consider it done,' he said.

On his way back across the lawn to the summer house he passed the rector, who had somehow eluded Mrs Armstrong-Avery and was banging posts into the grass with a wooden mallet.

'Good morning to you, Mr Carter. Ready for the fray?'

'You mean the lynching.'

'Whatever you do, don't give first prize to Samantha Jones. She won last year and they'll think it's favouritism.'

'I won't know which one she is.'

'Yes, you will. Blue eyes, baby-blonde curls and sickeningly coy. The Shirley Temple type. Her mother will be watching from the sidelines, front row. You'll feel her eyes upon you like a laser beam.'

'Thanks for the warning – and encouragement. What's this? The coconut shy?'

'No. This is bowling for the pig. I hope you're going to have a go.'

'I'm not sure what I'd do with a pig.'

The rector laughed. 'It's not a live pig any more. More's the pity. It's a side of bacon. Could you hold this post steady for me a minute?'

Carter obliged. Before he finally reached the summer house he had obliged several others several more times – moving a table, carrying another box, hanging out more flags, nailing up a notice. Most people seemed to know who he was and to have accepted him as some kind of honorary villager.

The summer house was a dark hut in the furthest corner of the lawn, half-hidden by rhododendrons. A card had already been fixed to the door: MADAME ZARA, FORTUNE-TELLER. 20P. Mrs Armstrong-Avery had not yet found her substitute sibyl, for inside there was no sign of any preparation. The folding canvas chairs, together with other garden impedimenta, lay cobwebbed and undisturbed. He brushed them down outside and carried them, four at a time, across to the terrace where he ranged them in line as though on the deck of a pre-war liner. On the lawn below, there was a fresh wave of activity. Mrs Armstrong-Avery had equipped herself with a megaphone, which she was testing enthusiastically and, to Carter's mind, superfluously. Catching her eye upon him, he slipped into the house through the open French windows just as she hailed him by name.

Phillip Dalrymple was beside the fireplace, reading a newspaper.

'She's after you, Carter. And she must be obeyed.'

'I didn't hear anything.'

'You can have sanctuary so long as you don't disturb me. I came in here for some peace and quiet. It's worse than ever this year and I hold you responsible for that. If you'd left that bloody plane where it was, we'd never have had all this fuss. God knows how many people will come and gawp at that frightful woman.'

'It's in a good cause.'

'The church bells, you mean? Sod the bells! They sound like hell anyway. Two solid hours of bell-ringing every Thursday night is what we're in for again – thanks to you.' The paper rustled as a page was turned clumsily. 'Christ, give me patience to get through this day. Zoe and Mrs Sour are in the kitchen making enough sandwiches for an army, if you want to make yourself useful.'

In the hall Carter passed the treasurer trotting through in a great hurry. He scurried off and Carter went down the passageway to the kitchen, where he was not surprised to find that chaos reigned. Every available surface area was covered with something – sliced loaves, butter, paste pots, cucumbers, lettuce, plates, cups, knives and spoons. In the middle of it all Zoe and Mrs Sweet – enormous in her flowered bungalow apron – were buttering bread and filling sandwiches on the table.

'Need some help?'

Zoe looked up. 'You could cut off crusts, if you like.'

He found a bread knife and stationed himself beside her at

the end of the assembly line. Mrs Sweet grunted – either with approval or disapproval.

'What's this lot for?' Carter asked after his third trimming operation. He cut the sandwich into four dainty triangles like the others.

'Teas,' Zoe explained. 'We sell teas at the fête, out in the old stables. The local WI do the cakes but we always do the sandwiches here on the day.' She struggled vainly with the lid of a new paste pot. 'Oh, *hell*!'

Carter took the pot from her and prised it open with a coin. He looked at the label.

'Sardine and tomato. Very nice.'

'I hope you like pilchard, too. And salmon and shrimp. I don't think I ever want to see any sort of paste again.'

They worked on and the piles of sandwiches grew steadily and spread themselves round the kitchen. At half past twelve the doorbell rang long and loud. Mrs Sweet wiped her hands on her apron.

'I'll see to that.'

'No, don't stop, Mrs Sweet. Who on earth could that be? Frank, could you possibly . . .'

Carter laid down his bread knife. 'I'll be the butler.'

'You don't look very much like one.'

'Nobody will know the difference these days.'

He went back to the hall and opened the front door with a grand flourish. Martina Drake stood there in living flesh and colour before him.

The big surprise was her height. She was tiny – much smaller than she appeared on the screen. And she also looked a good deal older. Despite that, she was still stunning. The warm personality and the star quality were present and correct, together with the short blonde hair, the bright blue eyes, the suntan and the dusting of freckles. She was wearing a white silk jumpsuit and a lot of very expensive gold jewellery.

'I'm early, aren't I?' She put out a hand heavy with rings. 'Do forgive me. I was so afraid we'd be late. Your country lanes! So pretty to look at, but how do you know which is

229

which? My driver lost the way five times before we found you.' She looked hard at Carter. 'We *are* in the right place now? Fairfield Hall, Fairfield, Sussex, England?'

'That's it.'

'Well thank heavens for that! I'm Martina Drake. Are you Sir Phillip Dalrymple, or have I got that wrong? In this country, believe me, I'm always getting things wrong.'

Her voice was rich and full of amusement. As she spoke she looked Carter up and down with frank appraisal.

'I'm not Sir Phillip,' he said, equally amused to be taken for a baronet. 'But this is his house. Come in.'

She stepped into the hall, followed by a man who had been standing close behind her. As he shut the door Carter saw the huge and gleaming Cadillac that had brought them parked grille to grille with one of the stallholders' runabouts.

Martina Drake waved a hand towards her companion, who was as swarthily dark and fat as she was fair and trim. He wore a thick, winter-weight overcoat.

'This is Gregor. He looks after things for me, but don't take too much notice of him. He's just here to spoil the fun if he can.'

Gregor remained silent and unsmiling. He reminded Carter of a Russian delegate at an international conference.

The actress was looking round the hall, drinking it all in – the antiques, the beautiful Indian carpet, the long-nosed aristocrat staring down at her from the wall.

'Isn't this just wonderful? Isn't it great, Greg?' She turned to Carter with almost childlike excitement. 'Do you know, I've never been inside a real English home before. When I'm in London I always stay at the Dorchester. They're very sweet to me, but it's no more English than Gregor. Know what I mean?'

Carter knew exactly what she meant. What he didn't know was what to do with her next. He was debating whether to risk showing her into the drawing room and encountering Phillip Dalrymple, who would almost certainly be far from sweet to her, when Zoe came out into the hall, paste pot in hand.

'I can't get this one open either, Frank . . .' She stopped dead.

Carter moved in quickly to make the introductions. He was not sure, having done so, whether Martina Drake had been surprised and disappointed not to be greeted by a grande dame in a diamond tiara and ballgown, or at least cashmere and tweeds, but if she had been, she was too good an actress and too polite to let it show.

'Pilchard paste! Imagine that! I just *adore* pilchard sandwiches!'

After that, it was easy. They returned to the kitchen where the actress, batting not a false eyelash at the disorder, sat down and demolished several pilchard sandwiches and two mugs of instant coffee. Gregor, still overcoated and unspeaking, accepted a sandwich and a beer and stood beside the sink munching morosely. Mrs Sweet, thrown momentarily into confusion by the presence of one of her favourite TV stars, recovered her senses enough to ask for an autograph – for her granddaughter, of course. Martina, with charm and good grace, immediately borrowed a gold pen from Gregor and wrote 'With Best Wishes to Sharon' on the back of an unpaid milk bill. Carter asked himself what Mrs Eliot would have made of it all and then decided that the transition from small screen to real life would have been too much for her. Dreams, after all, were usually best left as dreams.

From time to time figures passed and re-passed the window with studious casualness. The actress, eating her pilchard sandwiches, did not appear to notice – a technique presumably cultivated after years of being stared at by the public. She looked instead at Carter.

'May I ask who you are? We haven't been introduced.'

'Frank Carter. *Milton Weekly Courier.*'

'Stay where you are, Gregor, and don't be so stuffy! Wait a minute. Frank Carter. I remember that name. Aren't you the reporter who found my father's plane in the first place?'

Carter shook his head and explained.

'So this old man saw it come down,' she said. 'But *you* did

231

something about it. I'm so grateful to you. You don't know
how much this whole thing has meant to me. Be quiet, Gregor.
I'm giving Frank an exclusive. He deserves it. Ask anything
you want. Fire away.'

He did so, scribbling furiously in his notepad as she talked.
As she had promised, she held nothing back. She had known
of her true parentage since early childhood. Her foster parents
had made it known to her from the beginning. For one thing,
her mother had deposited a letter for safe-keeping with a
Hamburg bank, to be given to her when she was sixteen in
the event of her mother's death.

'At that time in Germany you expected to die,' she said
calmly. 'I was nearly killed myself in that bombing raid. My
father was already dead and I guess she wanted to make quite
sure I knew all about them. Give me a cigarette, Gregor, for
Christ's sake!'

Gregor moved forward with a gold cigarette case and lighter.
The actress tilted her head back to blow the smoke away and
shut her eyes for a moment.

'Sorry, Frank. This is still kind of hard for me to talk about
sometimes ... Don't try and stop me, Gregor. I *want* to.
Thanks, honey.' She acknowledged the saucer ashtray that
Zoe had found for her. 'My foster parents were wonderful
folks, see. Eventually, they adopted me and I was like their
own daughter. I couldn't remember anyone else so it must
have been tough for them when I was given that letter. Not
that it made any difference to how I felt about them. I was
just glad to learn about my real mother. I feel sorry for kids
who've been adopted and don't know. They must always be
wondering. Who was she? What was she like? Why didn't
she keep me? I *know* what my mother was like. She loved
me. And my father and she loved each other. When you're
sure of something like that about your parents you can't have
any real hang-ups – only regrets that you never met them.'

'What else did she say in her letter, Miss Drake?'

She gave Carter an old-fashioned look. 'A few other things.
Some of them private, Frank, so I'm not telling you everything.

What I can tell you, though, is that my father was a good, kind and brave man. And that they were going to be married just as soon as he came home on leave . . . Only he never did come home. Aw, stop making those long faces, Gregor! So I'm illegit! Who cares? *I* don't. And everybody knows by now anyway. I'm proud of my father and if it hadn't been for his goddamned stuck-up mother – *my* grandmother, come to think of it – they'd have been married long before. She couldn't take the idea of her son marrying a butcher's daughter. And, I guess, she just couldn't take the idea of me.'

'How do you feel about that?'

The actress shrugged. 'She was probably an old cow, but I never got to meet her, so who can say? I'm charitable and I guess it was her loss in the end. Maybe I'm not so proud of my grandmother, but I can tell you one thing you can get straight, Frank: I *am* proud of my father. He wasn't a Nazi. He was just a young guy of nineteen fighting for his country in a war that was none of his making. The same as our American boys and your British ones. And now I know just *how* he died, I'm twice as proud.'

'The letter from your mother would have been in German. Did you have to get someone else to translate?'

She wagged a finger at him. 'You're forgetting something, Frankie. I spent part of my childhood in Germany and my adoptive parents were German. We spoke the lingo together as a family even after we went to live in America. When I went to school I soon learned English as well as anyone else, but I've never forgotten my native tongue. If my parents came back from the dead, I could talk to them in their own language.'

'Did they speak any English, do you know?' Carter asked curiously. It was something he had wondered before about Martin Kern.

'I doubt if my mother could, but my father was very well educated, by all accounts, so I guess he'd have been able to speak some.'

It probably meant that he'd spoken it pretty well. He and Kern could have had quite a chat.

'Have you been back to Germany since you emigrated, Miss Drake?'

She shook her head decisively. 'Never. It's no longer the country my parents knew, nor my foster parents, and I don't remember too much about it myself. Besides, I'm kept pretty busy working in America.'

'What made you decide to have your father buried here in Fairfield?'

'That's a tough one to answer, Frank. I just figured that maybe this was the right place for him to stay, close by where he'd already been lying for forty years. He'd never been to America, so far as I know, so why take him all the way back there? And his folks in Germany are all dead.'

'Why not Cannock Chase – the official German war cemetery in England?'

'Well, I guess I just didn't fancy the idea. I've seen some of those places in pictures and I reckoned he'd be just one more cross among a whole load of others. I thought if he was buried here it might make some kind of sense, because he is already a part of the history of Fairfield. I also figured that the English wouldn't mind too much. What do you think?'

Carter smiled at her. 'I think you're dead right.'

'Gregor here thinks I'm crazy. I tell him I don't care what he thinks. It's none of his damned business. On the way here we stopped by that old church in the village and went into the graveyard. As soon as I saw it I knew I was right. It was so quaint and peaceful. It was just perfect.'

She zipped open her white leather purse. 'Here's something else for your exclusive, Frankie. 'It's only a copy, so you can borrow it if you like. The original was with my mother's letter and I keep that safe back home. It's the only picture I have of my father.'

The black and white photograph was the twin of the one of Barbara Karslemn. Background and light were identical and so was the subject's smiling pose. But, instead, of the young girl, Carter found himself looking at a young man dressed in the smart uniform of a Luftwaffe officer. So at last he now knew what Martin Kern had looked like. He had already known him to have been tall; now he saw that he had been slim, flaxen-haired and good-looking in a typically German way. But there was none of the swagger of the typical Luftwaffe fighter pilot and the smile was as shy as Barbara's had been. The two photos had obviously been taken, one after the other, on the same occasion – probably just before Martin Kern went off on his first and last sortie. They must have swapped: he had taken hers with him and she had kept his. He passed the snapshot to Zoe and Mrs Sweet peered curiously over her shoulder and made tutting noises.

'Did your mother leave a photo of herself as well?'

The actress shook her head. 'She only seemed to think of my father. I guess that was typical of her. If it had been me I'd have left a stack of the best shots of myself I could find. Maybe I inherited some of my paternal grandmother's personality – kind of tough.'

Martina Drake, of course, would hardly have been likely to see the *Milton Weekly Courier* with the snapshot of Barbara. It had been missing from the big nationals, who had concentrated on the big star herself. Carter felt in his wallet.

'This belongs to you, Miss Drake. It was found in your father's diary at the site of the crash. He had it with him when he died. I hadn't yet got around to handing it back to the authorities or they would have given it to you.'

'For heaven's sake, Gregor, where are my glasses? I can't see a thing.'

Gregor unearthed a pair of diamanté-decorated glasses from the white purse and handed them over. The actress put them on and stared at the snapshot of her mother.

'I guess she's just like I always imagined – pretty and kind of shy-looking and nice.' Her voice trembled a little. 'Excuse me, folks, but it's kind of hit me . . . They already gave me his diary and a cigarette case. And now this . . .'

Zoe said solicitously: 'Would you like a drink, Miss Drake?'

'Honey, that's the best idea I've heard in hours. A whisky sour and I'll be like new again.'

235

Before she could go off to fetch the drink and before Carter could ask the actress about her forthcoming television plans, there was the sound of squeaking wheels approaching. Phillip Dalrymple charged into the kitchen.

'What the bloody hell's going on here? Who are all these bloody people, Zoe? They're supposed to stay out in the garden, not come crawling all over the house.'

There was a short, sharp silence. Then, right on cue, Martina Drake rose to the occasion. With an actress's instinct she had sensed the role required and played it to perfection. The exuberant, expansive American manner was subtly toned down several decibels and her natural warmth would have been hard for any man to resist. Carter watched in admiration.

'You must be Sir Phillip. I'm Martina Drake and I'm so pleased to meet you at last. What a wonderful home you have and what a privilege it is for us to be able to visit you like this. I understand your family has lived here for generations. I should *love* to hear its history.'

It was cleverly done. And, more to the point, she completely ignored the wheelchair, speaking to Phillip Dalrymple exactly as though he were a normal, healthy, attractive man and without a trace of the talking-down that invalids and children alike deplore. By the time Zoe had returned with the whisky, this particular invalid, if not actually eating out of the actress's hand, was at least not biting it.

Later, looking back over the whole day, Carter realized how much the star had contributed to its success. She had done far more than just make a speech. From the moment when, in front of a huge and record crowd, she had declared the village fête open with as much enthusiasm as if she had been making an announcement at the Hollywood Bowl, to the time when, three hours later, she drove away in her Cadillac, waving through the back window, she had held the stage totally and seen that the crowds not only came and saw, but spent their money as well. As the music of the silver band trumpeted out across the gardens, she circulated like royalty at a garden

236

party, the centre of a moving throng of worshippers, flash bulbs popping from press and public to illuminate her progress.

She went from stall to stall and sideshow to sideshow in turn, Gregor one step behind, unsmiling and still overcoated in the hot sun. She bought a chocolate cake from the country larder, a hand-knitted penguin from toys, a cactus (much to Miss Burton's chagrin) from garden plants, a hideous china bowl from the white elephant stall and a tattered volume of English poetry from the books. And, as she did so, she encouraged others to follow suit, exclaiming and enthusing over everything she saw so that the satellites felt either obliged or inspired to open their purses and wallets with reckless abandon. Even the local MP, who had never been known to buy anything, was seen wandering around with a raffia table lamp.

At the bottle stall she won some South African sherry and waved it aloft as though it were a magnum of champagne. At the coconut shy she scored a bullseye first go. She rolled pennies, bet on the guinea pig race and went to have her fortune told by Madame Zara, who had mysteriously managed to take up residence in the summer house. She emerged, brushing cobwebs out of her hair, and smiling broadly.

'She says great things are in store for me next year, folks! Isn't that nice to know? You should all try it. She'll only tell you the good things.'

Best of all, from Carter's point of view, she presented the prizes for the fancy dress. This meant that there was no unseemly argument about the judges' decision, only subdued mutterings and a few muffled sobs.

Mrs Armstrong-Avery had announced the event through her megaphone loudly enough for anyone not stone deaf to hear from anywhere within the village boundaries and, in case anyone had still failed to pay proper attention, the band had begun to play 'The Teddy Bears' Picnic'. A crowd had gathered round. Carter, who would far sooner have been down in the woods with the teddy bears and well away from it all, stood in the centre of a ring of entrants with Mrs Fleming, the dentist's wife, at his side. Dressed in a drooping peasant skirt, smocked blouse and fringed shawl, his co-judge was clearly going to go for the artistic angle. Carter, grimly watching the straggling parade of reluctant – or plain recalcitrant – under-eights had made up his mind to take Zoe's advice and concentrate on the genuine home-made look. He assessed the contestants carefully as they trailed past him and reduced the number to four possible winners: a pirate, complete with tricorn hat, black patch and kitchen foil cutlass; a Little Red Riding Hood with a crêpe paper cloak and raffia basket, a Mad Hatter with a ticketed top hat and tea cup, and a white-faced clown with orange wool hair, baggy cut-down trousers, Dad's braces and long cardboard toes attached to his shoes.

Mrs Fleming had sunk to her knees and was crouching now, studying the contestants intently at eye-level, rather like a judge at a dog show. Carter stood with his arms folded and hoped he was looking half as authoritative. The mothers, who had pushed their way to the front row, were encouraging or cajoling their children, as required. Red Riding Hood suddenly spoiled her chances by bursting into tears and running to clutch at the skirts of a stout matron who promptly slapped her hard and sent her back into the arena. Carter wavered between the clown and the pirate for first place. He caught the rector's sardonic eye upon him and remembered his warning about Samantha Jones of the blonde curls and blue eyes. The pirate, wielding his cutlass with gusto, was all too obviously male, but the white greasepaint and orange wool wig of the clown could well have concealed last year's winner and made it impossible to tell even whether it was a boy or girl. He searched the front ranks for a laser-beam stare and encountered at least half a dozen that could have qualified for the rector's description.

The dentist's wife, at last, rose from her dog-show crouch and consulted with him in hisses. To Carter's relief she had decided on the pirate and with little more time wasted they settled on the clown and Red Riding Hood for second and third places. Red Riding Hood dried her tears with a handkerchief from her basket, Martina Drake presented the prizes as though handing out Oscars, and the winners did a final lap of honour while the winners' mothers beamed. Carter relaxed momentarily. Across the lawn he could see Phillip Dalrymple in his wheelchair watching from the open French windows with his binoculars. Even at a distance he could tell that this was the only part of the day that the owner of Fairfield was enjoying – and that was at Carter's expense.

The first round over, it was the turn of the eight- to twelve-year-olds. There were fewer competitors and most of them looked as unenthusiastic about the whole affair as their juniors. Only one, a Little Bo Peep in mob cap, laced bodice and starched blue muslin, showed any real sign of eagerness. She tripped daintily round the ring, crook in one hand, toy lamb in the other, blonde hair curling from beneath the mob cap. As she passed Carter she slowed to a near stop and smiled sweetly up at him. She did not spend quite so much time passing Mrs Fleming. Without turning his head, Carter could feel a mother's eyes boring into his back. He looked enquiringly towards the rector who nodded as discreetly as a bidder at Sotheby's.

Mrs Fleming did not appear to have even noticed Bo Peep. She had remained standing for the seniors, resting her chin in one hand with her head a little on one side.

They came together and conferred in whispers.

'The sweep, the Egyptian mummy and the pilot,' she hissed.

'In that order?'

'Definitely. Don't you agree?'

To question her judgement seemed almost *lèse-majesté*, but Carter had taken a liking to the Battle of Britain pilot in his fake leather helmet and cling-wrap goggles. The Egyptian mummy was nothing more than a parcel of white crêpe paper.

'I think the pilot's better than the mummy.'

Mrs Fleming shook her head vehemently, long jade earrings a-jangle. 'Oh, *no*! The mummy's far better. Can't you see? It's a really *original* conception. And the line is so good.'

239

Carter gave way to superior knowledge. 'What about Bo Peep then?'

'Oh, *her*! The costume's all wrong. Visually it's a disaster. And that dreadful toy lamb . . .'

The sweep was a popular win and received his prize grinning from sooty ear to sooty ear. The white parcel was second and the pilot third. Little Bo Peep lost her smile as well as her sheep and flounced sulkily from the ring.

The rector took Martina Drake off to the stables to have more pilchard sandwiches, an iced fairy cake and a cup of WI urn tea.

Carter sought out Zoe, who was helping to man the garden plants stall. She smiled at him across a half-empty table.

'Well done with the judging. You got it right.'

'Thanks to Mrs Fleming. How are things?'

She ran her fingers through her fringe, looking pleased. 'It's marvellous! We seem to be doing terribly well. We've already made over seventy pounds on this stall alone, thanks to the star attraction. She's been wonderful. She even bought one of our cacti and after that everyone bought the rest.'

'Very handy for putting on Gregor's chair next time he sits down.'

'He is pretty grim, isn't he? Like one of those Russian generals at the May Day parade. Now what are *you* going to buy? We haven't much left.'

Carter chose a trailing ivy. He would probably forget to water it but if he took it to the office then Brenda might be persuaded to take it under her wing. Zoe wrapped it up in newspaper for him.

'Have you had your fortune told yet?' he asked her.

'Yes, I did, as a matter of fact.' She began rearranging the remaining plants.

'Who did they get to do it in the end?'

'That would be telling.'

'Is she any good?'

Zoe moved an aspidistra to the other end of the table.

'I don't think you'd find it very interesting.'

'I might. If she just told me the good things. What did she say to you?'

Zoe had turned away from him to attend to a customer. 'That would be telling, too.'

He walked back across the lawn, carrying the trailing ivy. The band had gone off to have their tea, leaving their instruments on their chairs. He decided against joining the crush in the stables and had a couple of turns instead at bowling for the pig. Then he bought a raffle ticket from Mrs Jennings of the shop.

'You never know your luck, dear, do you? And they're ever such nice things.'

He had a go at rolling pennies and took a turn at the hoopla and then found himself near Madame Zara's lair. A stout woman he recognized as Red Riding Hood's mother came out, looking pink and flustered. Intrigued, Carter knocked at the summer-house door.

Inside, the house had been darkened still further by tacking pieces of black material across the windows. Mingling with the lingering fustiness of damp canvas there was a faint, sweet smell that he vaguely remembered from somewhere.

The rickety table had been set in the centre and spread with a thick cloth. On it a night light burned in a saucer and behind it sat Madame Zara, a shadowy and unrecognizable figure draped in scarves and shawls, her face veiled.

'Come in, please, and shut ze door.'

Carter obeyed. The accent was gloriously false French. He decided that he was going to enjoy himself. The fortune-teller spoke again from behind her gauze veil.

'Please to sit down. And to hold out your hand.'

A chair had been placed on his side of the table. Carter shut the door and groped his way to it, stubbing his toe against the croquet box.

'Ze left hand first. Zat is ze past. Your right hand is ze future. We will look at that after.'

Carter put down the trailing ivy plant and the table rocked gently. He put out his left hand and Madame Zara took the tips of his fingers in hers and turned his palm towards the night light, peering at it closely. He waited, amused.

'I see much suffering in your past . . . Not a happy childhood . . . For a while everysing was better and zen zere was a tragique accident . . . Ze death of a loved one . . . Much sorrow.'

Carter had stiffened.

'Please not to move your hand. Keep it just so or I cannot see what it will tell me.' Madame Zara nodded. 'So . . . much sadness in your past. Always you blame yourself for zis accident. But you must not do zat. Not any more. Zat part of your life is finished and soon you will begin to forget. Ozzer people will help you to forget. I see a stranger . . .'

If he had not been so stunned by what she had told him already, Carter might have asked cynically if the stranger was a dark one. But he was taken aback. Apart from Zoe, he had told nobody in the village about Jan and his past and Zoe was the last person to gossip.

Madame Zara hitched her shawls closer round her shoulders and, again, the familiar scent reached his nostrils as she bent forward towards his palm.

'Zis stranger zat I see . . . He is, I sink a foreigner . . . Not English. He is come from across the water. Somehow he will help you to forget . . .' She moved the night light a little closer and shook her head. 'But zis is very odd because I sink zat zis foreigner was dead a long time ago, back many years, before you were born. Somehow his life is joined with yours . . . I see anozzer tragedy . . . A plane, a wood . . .'

Carter relaxed. She'd been reading the papers. He asked curiously, wondering what she would manage to think up: 'How's this foreigner going to help me?'

But, again, she shook her head. 'Zat I do not know. Zat, perhaps, may lie in ze future. Please to give me your right hand now.'

Carter changed over and she bent to his right palm for a few minutes without speaking.

'Aaaaah! Zis is *much* better. Zere is happiness in store for

242

you ... but not quite yet. You must be patient.' The stage French took on sing-song, Indian overtones. 'I see a woman. You love zis woman but it is a forbidden love. It cannot be. Not now. Perhaps some day. Some day she may be ze one who will bring you ze happiness ... I cannot say this for sure. Before zat you will go away. Zere will be much sings happening to you ... I see a big city ... crowds ... success ... all good sings for you. You will have a long life and, in ze end, everysing will come right.'

She covered his hand for a moment with her own, head bowed as though in deep concentration. Then she released it.

'Zat is all I can tell you. And zat will be twenty pence.'

He paid her and went out into the bright sunlight. Someone else brushed close past him to go in for their turn. He lit a cigarette and was annoyed to find his hand trembling as it used to do when he'd boozed. He stood for a moment by the rhododendrons, collecting himself. Since he did not really believe for one moment in Madame Zara's ability to see into either the past or the future, Zoe must have told someone about him and the story had got around. Not surprising in a village this size, but surprising that she had said anything to anybody. He put away his lighter. The fortune-teller had avoided answering his question, but, when he thought about it, the foreigner had *already* helped him. Martin Kern had not only given him his front-page story, but also a lot else to think about since – including, and most of all, Zoe.

Carter frowned. No one but himself knew how he felt about her so there was no chance of gossip there. Forbidden love was probably a useful phrase fortune-tellers trotted out most of the time, knowing it would be a pretty safe bet with a lot of people – though the forbidden angle might have gone out of fashion a bit. He smiled wryly. It would be nice to believe in all the good things she'd rattled off for the future, even if the immediate prospect didn't sound so hot. *In ze end everysing will come right.* Whoever Madame Zara was – and he was sure as hell going to find out – he hoped her long-range forecasting was accurate. He realized, suddenly,

243

that he had left the ivy plant behind on the table. It would
have to wait. Madame couldn't be disturbed in the middle
of a session.

After her tea in the stables, Martina Drake finally departed.
A large crowd assembled in the driveway to see her off and
she made her exit amidst loud cheers. Before climbing into
the car she had singled out Carter, standing beside the rector,
for a final word.

'I won't forget what you've done, Frankie. If there's
anything else you want to know . . .'

She winked and disappeared into the maw of the Cadillac
and Gregor followed her. As the big car drew away she turned
and waved through the rear window until she was out of sight.
Carter and the rector waved back with the rest. The crowd
dispersed slowly.

Hugh Longman said admiringly: 'A wonderful woman!'

'Some dame,' Carter agreed. 'No problem now with the
church bells.'

The rector rubbed his hands. 'At the treasurer's last count
we were well over the fifteen hundred mark. There'll be more
than enough for the bells *and* the damp patch in the chancel
roof. And that's not all. Miss Drake handed me this over the
tea table just now – to be used for the benefit of the parish,
as we see fit.'

He took a piece of paper from his pocket and showed it to
Carter. It was a cheque for one thousand pounds.

'Are you keeping your side of the bargain?'

'Certainly. The funeral is all arranged and will take place
on Wednesday week. Two p.m.'

Carter made a note.

The rector folded away the cheque. 'I've given him a very
decent plot. Like I said, it was a fair exchange.'

Now that the star turn had gone, the crowds began to thin
out. The band played on but to a much diminished audience. Carter wandered through the house. He passed the
treasurer counting away happily in his counting house, and

found Phillip Dalrymple still sitting very unhappily in the drawing room, his face even more drawn and pale than usual.

'Get me a whisky, will you, Carter? When the hell are all these bloody people going to go?'

Carter poured him a stiff one. 'They're starting to leave already.'

'Thank God for that!' The misshapen hand clawed at the whisky tumbler. 'I can't stand much more of it. They've been up here on the terrace looking at me through the windows as though I were something in a zoo. I made faces so they went away in the end. And that Armstrong woman's been bellowing like a foghorn all afternoon.' There was a pause to drink the whisky. 'I saw you doing your stuff at the fancy dress, Carter. Didn't look as though you were enjoying it much! And you picked the wrong one. I'd have given it to the Eskimo.'

Carter couldn't even remember an Eskimo.

'The judges' decision is final. Especially Mrs Fleming's.'

Phillip Dalrymple shuddered. 'That ghastly woman! All sandalwood and Indian cotton. And she paints the most hideous pictures you can imagine. Dawn over the Downs . . . that sort of thing.'

'What did you think of Martina Drake?'

'Hmmph! Not bad. If you like American women. Which I don't.'

'She's just handed over a thousand-pound cheque to the rector for the parish.'

The baronet raised his eyebrows. 'Is that the going rate for a grave now? I must remember to put more in the collection on Sundays or Hugh might not find room for me when it's my turn. Though, come to think of it, I think I'll arrange to be buried elsewhere if the churchyard's going to be full of Huns.'

Mrs Armstrong-Avery's voice could be heard booming from the lawn, announcing the raffle draw.

'Got a ticket for that, Carter?'

He'd forgotten for the moment that Mrs Jennings had sold him one. The blue slip of paper, number 333, was in his trouser pocket.

'This could be your lucky day!' Phillip Dalrymple mocked him.

Carter remembered the list of prizes from the committee meeting. 'I hope not.'

Mrs Armstrong-Avery's voice rang out. 'Pink ticket, number 465. The bottle of sherry!'

There were loud cheers and some applause as the winner stepped forward.

'Green ticket, number 239. The box of fruit!'

More applause. Carter watched uneasily from the French windows as a bashful villager staggered off with a huge cellophane-wrapped container.

'Yellow ticket, number forty-five. The teddy bear!'

This time there was laughter and hoots of derision as an even more bashful Jesse from the Bull went to receive the monstrous pink plush bear.

'Blue ticket, number 333. The bedjacket!'

Carter considered defaulting, or even absconding, but remembering that Mrs Jennings had carefully written his name and address on the back of the draw ticket, he knew there was no hiding place or escape. Collecting a lemon-yellow hand-knitted bedjacket with satin ribbons and dainty bows was not an easy thing to do with any grace, but he managed it somehow. Mrs Armstrong-Avery beamed and Mrs Jennings looked gratified.

'I told you so, didn't I, dear? You never know your luck. You'll have a nice present for your lady friend.'

He passed Jesse who was clutching his teddy bear; the old man shook his head in sympathy.

'Mug's game, this is, if you ask me, Mr Carter. What are we going to do with this lot, you and I?'

The band had finally stopped and were packing up their instruments. The stallholders were clearing away the few remaining unsold items and dismantling the trestle tables. Carter went to help Zoe with the garden plants stall.

'You wouldn't like a bedjacket, I suppose?'

She laughed. 'No, thanks. I haven't reached that stage yet. Try someone else. It would look good on Mrs Armstrong-Avery.'

'I don't think the colour's quite her.'

'Did you have your fortune told?'

'Too right, I did. Who was she?'

'Can't you guess?'

'Not a clue. Zoe, you didn't by any chance tell her anything about me, did you? About what I told you . . .'

She looked up. 'Of course not. I haven't said a word to anyone.'

'I didn't think you would. But she got pretty close to it.'

'I promise you, Frank, I haven't told anyone.'

'I believe you. It's bloody odd, though, because—'

He was interrupted by Miss Plumb of the dancing classes, pleading coyly for his help with her table.

'So good of you, Mr Carter. It's just a *teeny* bit too heavy for me, all on my own.'

He ferried several more tables and made himself generally useful. Gradually, the lawn was cleared and the garden almost restored to normal. The band and their chairs had gone and only a few remnants from the sideshows lay about the grass. There was the sound of cars revving up, the shriek of crashed gears and the crunch of the driveway gravel. Carrying the hoopla takings into the house for the treasurer, Carter met Mrs Fortescue in the hall. She wagged her finger at him.

'I have something of yours, Mr Carter. Had you forgotten?'

She gave him the trailing ivy plant in its newspaper wrapping and, as she did so, the sweet scent in the summer house clicked into place in his mind. April Violets and Mrs Fortescue! Looking at the plump and pleasant features and the tightly permed hair, he found it hard to believe that she had been the one behind the sinuous shawls and veils of

247

Madame Zara. He remembered the yellow bedjacket, tucked beneath his left arm.

'And I have something for *you*, Mrs Fortescue, if you'd like it.'

She accepted delightedly. 'So useful for the winter. And *that* will soon be here before we can turn round. Thank you, Mr Carter.' She winked laboriously at him and it was the second wink he had received that afternoon. '*Sank* you, very much.'

He watched her trot away on her bolster legs. He'd probably never know how she'd known what she'd told him. Maybe it had just been lucky guesswork or maybe there was more to Mrs Fortescue than met the eye.

He stayed until the last car had gone away down the drive, helping to clear up. Zoe offered him a supper of leftover sandwiches and multicoloured fairy cakes. They ate them in the kitchen, which had been more or less tidied up by Mrs Sweet before she had gone off, proudly bearing her autographed milk bill. Carter dried the remaining plates and cups while Zoe washed.

'What was the grand total in the end?' he asked.

'Not counting that marvellous cheque, we made two thousand, one hundred and twenty-two pounds and fifty-three pence. It's double the highest we've ever made before. Or ever will again, I expect. Miss Burton says we've lost our chances of winning the best-kept village competition. Apparently, the cars parked all over the place and the green's in a dreadful mess. And there's litter everywhere. But who cares? It was worth it.'

'There'll be more mess on Wednesday week, after the funeral. It's bound to attract notice.'

'I suppose so.' Zoe rinsed a cup absently and passed it over. 'He looked nice in that photo – the German pilot. Not a bit like one always imagines them. And awfully young.'

'They were all awfully young.'

She rinsed another cup. 'It's lucky they can't see the brave new world they died for – our people, I mean. I don't believe they'd think much of it, do you?'

'This is still a free country, remember. But for them it might not have been.'

The day had obviously exhausted Phillip Dalrymple. He looked deathly pale and tired and Zoe went off to help him get to bed. Carter lit a cigarette and waited for her, giving himself the excuse that there might be more he could do. When she finally reappeared she looked very tired, too.

'Anything else to be done?'

'You've already done more than enough, Frank. I don't know how we'd have managed without you today.'

'What about all those chairs still out on the terrace. Do you want them back in the summer house?'

'Oh, lord! I'd forgotten them. If you can bear it . . .'

'I can.'

She went out to the terrace with him and together they folded the chairs and carried them in twos across the lawn to the summer house. Dusk was settling over the garden and a bat flittered above their heads. After the noise and activity of the afternoon it was quiet and peaceful.

Madame Zara's notice was still pinned to the door. Carter laughed and took it off.

'I'd never have guessed it was Mrs Fortescue.'

'How *did* you guess?'

He told her. 'I still can't work out how the hell she knew so much about me.'

'Just luck, I expect,' Zoe carried two chairs inside and stacked them against the wall. 'It's how you interpret what she says that's the trick, isn't it? I mean, the same thing could apply in different ways to different people.'

He followed her in with two more chairs. 'Like shouting: "Fly, all is discovered!" And everyone makes a run for it.'

'Something like that. What did she have to say about your future? I hope it was nice things.'

'Well, it was a whole lot better than the past. It seems I'll be off to the big city. It's all going to happen for me.'

'I always thought you'd go back to Fleet Street in the end, Frank,' she said seriously.

He took a chair from her and stowed it away in the far corner. 'I haven't got there yet. And on present showing it doesn't seem too likely . . . You haven't told me what she said about you.'

'Oh, the past was easy for her – she knows a lot about me.'

'What about the future?'

'She didn't say much.'

'What *did* she say?'

'I'm not going to tell you.'

'In case it might not come true? Or in case it does?' he persisted.

'Both.'

It was getting so dark in the hut even with the door open that Carter lit Madame Zara's night light. They finished carrying in the chairs and put them away.

He looked down at Zoe and removed a cobweb from her hair.

'I think the spider's there too. Stand still.'

He extricated the insect carefully and set it down on the table.

'Is it all right?'

'All legs present and correct, so far as I could tell. I can't remember how many they're meant to have . . . Zoe, I love you. I can't help it.'

She stayed motionless, her head still bent.

'And now,' he went on, 'you're going to tell me ever so politely to go and jump in the lake.'

'We haven't got a lake.'

'You should have. Every self-respecting baronet should have a lake.'

She lifted her head. 'This particular baronet has rather lost his self-respect. I'm all he has left.'

He said heavily: 'I know. Sorry I spoke. Forget I said anything. I should have kept my bloody mouth shut.' He blew out the night light. 'Well, that's it, then. I'll be off . . .'

Zoe spoke again in the darkness, very clearly. 'I love you, too, Frank. And I can't help it, either.'

He turned, disbelieving at first, from the doorway. Then he moved slowly towards her. When he kissed her it was as good as he had dreamed it would be. He kicked the door hard shut behind him and, with it, shut out the outside world.

Thirteen

B ob Simpson's voice was jubilant.
'I think we've found him!'

For a moment Carter's own mind was blank. The Tuesday panic was on and the office in chaos around him. The chief sub, in an ugly and stone-cold-sober mood, was shouting obscenities, the clatter of typewriters was deafening, the phones were ringing non-stop and Brenda, most unusually, had just burst into tears and was sobbing into the switchboard. He put a finger to his free ear.

'What did you say, Bob? I didn't get that.'

'I said, we've found him. The RAF pilot who shot down Leutnant Kern.'

'Great! How did you manage it?'

'The old process of elimination. Working through combat reports. I had to sift through quite a pile of them. In most cases the wreckage of enemy aircraft shot down on September sixth, 1940 was accounted for and known. I got quite excited about a Hurricane pilot's report out of Tangmere, but the Messerschmitt went into the sea off Bognor, he says, and he saw the pilot get out before it sank.'

Ken Grant had stuck his head out of his office doorway and was making urgent signs at him. Carter turned away.

'So?'

'So, it looks like Pilot Officer J.S. Mackintosh is our man. Out of Biggin Hill. Want me to read his report?'

Carter cradled the receiver under his chin and reached for his pencil.

'Go ahead.'

'Here goes.' The line suddenly crackled infuriatingly as the surveyor read out the pilot's report in a flat monotone. Carter, straining his ears above the racket around him, missed some but got most of it.

'While on patrol . . . flying at twenty-seven thousand feet . . . seven Me109s approaching about one thousand feet below, heading south-east . . . attacked the rear aircraft, from astern, firing a four-second burst at two hundred yards' range . . . saw smoke coming from the top of the engine and glycol from the radiator. The enemy aircraft went into a steep dive. I followed him down in order to fire a second burst, but the gun jammed . . . the 109 appeared out of control, although the pilot made no attempt to bail out . . . attacked from the rear by another enemy aircraft and climbed to take evasive action. I subsequently lost sight of the damaged 109.'

'He never saw it actually hit the deck, then?'

'No, but I'm pretty sure it was our 109. It all fits. Day, time and place. I've spoken to Mackintosh on the phone and he remembers it all very well. He says the plane was a dead duck and would have landed somewhere in the area.' The line crackled loudly again. '. . . often wondered exactly where it *did* come down. Sussex is his home county. He knows it well.'

'Where does he live?'

'A village called Mayhurst. Do you know it? Funnily enough it's only a couple of miles or so from Fairfield.'

'I know of it. They're bitter rivals. As far as I can make out it goes back to the Dark Ages. How did you find Mackintosh?'

'In the phone book. Simple as that. He finished the war as a squadron-leader by the way – DFC. He was invalided out. He sounded a very interesting bloke.'

'Can you give me the address, Bob? I'd like to go and see him and get his story, in time for the funeral next week.'

'Long Meadow, Tinkers Lane.'

'Is he willing to talk?'

Simpson laughed. 'They always are.'

*   *   *

253

The editor had gone back into his office and Carter slid out before he could reappear. He had been going to tell Simpson about the photograph of Martin Kern but the line had begun to crackle again and he decided that it would keep until he saw him at the funeral. More important, for the moment, was to get to see Squadron-Leader Mackintosh before Ken sent him off on some fool's errand. The editor's interest in the story of the fighter had waned and he had looked on Carter's exclusive with Martina Drake with wary suspicion, as though it might prove too heady stuff for the *Courier*'s readers.

'This isn't the *News of the World*, you know, Frank. We don't need the intimate revelations of Hollywood stars – just straightforward facts about what's going on in and around Milton Spa. If our readers want that sort of thing, they go and buy a different paper. I know you Fleet Street boys think you know all the answers but you've still got a lot to learn. Now, about that next council meeting. I don't want any more misrepresenting Councillor Jackson, so watch it! Make sure you get what he says word for word – nothing more and nothing less – and then we can't get it wrong, can we?'

On his way out, Carter chucked Brenda under the chin but for once she failed to respond and turned away, sniffing into a pink tissue.

He drove through Fairfield on the way to Mayhurst. It took him out of his way but the village seemed to draw him like a magnet. The success of the fête had certainly left its mark. The litter had been cleared but the grass verges had been gouged deep by careless parking. The green had been turned into a battlefield and someone had picked all the salmon-pink geraniums from outside the Bull.

As Carter passed the gates of the Hall it had taken all his self-control not to turn the van into the entrance, drive up to the front door and knock. That was all it would take to see Zoe again. Except for one small thing: he had given her his word that he would stay away. So, he had slowed the van to a near stop, and then he had driven on.

Mayhurst was a great deal easier to find than Fairfield and

it was larger. It was also pin neat. Their fête might have raised only eight hundred pounds or so, but the village had not been ravaged in the process. The green looked like a prize lawn, the hedges were trimmed to a leaf, flowers bloomed to perfection in every garden and the pub – the Rose and Crown – must have been the pride of the brewery. It was the antithesis of the Bull. Clean, well-kept and welcoming. The window boxes were overflowing with bright flowers and Martini umbrellas sprouted in a little garden at the side. Not one crisp packet, sweet paper or cigarette butt marred the scene. Carter surveyed it all with a sour eye and was gratified to see that the church was a Victorian redbrick monstrosity. They could scrub every gravestone and trim every blade of grass with nail scissors, he thought, pleased, but that, at least, could never match its ancient rival at Fairfield.

He passed a shop that looked like a miniature Fortnum's and found Tinkers Lane. Unlike in Fairfield, every road here was clearly marked. Long Meadow was a bungalow at the end of a row of identical bungalows. He parked the van in a small lay-by and walked up the path. Door chimes ding-donged behind frosted glass. Carter waited and looked about him. This peaceful, orderly and almost suburban place was an ironic retirement for a man who forty years ago would have been blasting the enemy out of the skies, and who had known the whole heat of bloody battle, the flames, the fear, the deaths . . .

A distorted figure appeared behind the frosted glass. The door opened and the shape resolved itself into a grey haired woman who was as neat as her surroundings. She was small and spare with blue eyes and she wore a rather old-fashioned cotton dress and a single row of pearls. She smiled and Carter realized that she must once have been very pretty.

'I wonder if Squadron-Leader Mackintosh could spare me a few minutes?' Carter went on to explain his business quickly, before she could think he was selling encyclopaedias or brushes.

She smiled even more.

'I'm sure he could. Give him half a chance and he'll talk about the war all day. In fact, he's been talking about it ever since Mr Simpson phoned him. Fancy them finding that German plane he shot down. We'd read all about it in your newspaper, of course, but he didn't put two and two together until those people got in touch.' She opened the door wider and stood back. 'Come in, please, Mr Carter. I'm Mollie Mackintosh. I was in the WAAF myself in the war – that's how Johnnie and I met. We didn't marry until after it was all over, though. When he finally got out of hospital.'

Carter stepped into a narrow hallway. The fitted carpet was a sunny, golden colour and there was a bowl of yellow and pink roses on a side table beneath an oval mirror. It looked comfortable and well-kept. A decent home for a hero.

'He's in here.' Mrs Mackintosh opened a door. 'It's supposed to be our spare bedroom but he's taken it over as his study. He doesn't call himself Squadron-Leader any more, by the way. Just plain mister.' She announced him cheerfully. 'A Mr Carter from the *Courier*, dear, to ask you about that Messerschmitt.'

She ushered him through and closed the door after him. Carter found himself in a small, square room that reminded him of the rector's study in its pokiness, its view over the fields and the large quantity of books on shelves. Instead of toys, piles of books littered the floor, to be negotiated like rocks in a river.

A man was seated at the desk beneath the window, in front of a portable electric typewriter. He was surrounded by more books and scattered papers and, as Carter entered, he was pecking laboriously at the typewriter keys with two fingers. He finished a word and turned.

As Phillip Dalrymple had once put it, after years in Fleet Street nothing could shock or embarrass Carter any more; he was immune to most human conditions. Even so, the ex-pilot's appearance took him aback for a moment.

His face had been hideously burned. Heaven knew how many painful operations and what miracle of plastic surgery and patience had rebuilt the nose, the lips and the eyelids to something ressembling the originals. The result, though, could not be described as anything other than horrifying – a grotesque mask of patchwork skin and slits. By contrast, his silver hair grew thick, wavy and normal, giving some clue to the man he must once have been. He stood up and his mouth twisted into what was clearly intended to be a smile. He held out his hand.

'Glad to meet you, Mr Carter.'

The hands had not escaped either: both bore obvious burn scars and the fingers of the right were slightly curled. He lifted a pile of books from a chair.

'Sit down, please. Excuse the mess. I'm trying to write a book – about the war, believe it or not. Hardly original, I know, but I felt I had to get it down before I was too old to remember a damn thing about it.' Again, the twisted smile. 'Trouble is, it's harder than I thought. More to it than just putting down a lot of words. You have to get it all right, and after forty years it takes some doing. The old brainbox isn't what it used to be, for one thing.'

He sat down again at his desk and fumbled in a drawer for cigarettes, which he offered to Carter. His voice was pleasant and as cheerful as his wife's – another part of him that had remained untouched. They lit up.

'I believe Bob Simpson of the aviation archeology group has already spoken to you about the Messerschmitt 109E found in Trodgers Wood near Fairfield.'

'That's right. He reckons it's the one I shot down on September sixth, 1940. By the sound of it he's probably right.' The cigarette rested awkwardly in the corner of the slit-like mouth. 'Forty years is a long time to remember anything well but, as a matter of fact, I do happen to remember that particular one rather well. I got shot down after it myself through sheer bloody carelessness. Bailed out all right and lived to fight another day, but I lost the Spit. I didn't get this little lot till later on in the war, when I wasn't quite so lucky. I got trapped in the cockpit longer than was good for me. By the time I got out and fell in the drink I was rather well done. Still, I survived. I can see, I can talk, I can walk. And my wife thinks I'm the handsomest man she knows.'

Carter smiled with him. He was already getting used to the disfigured face. He wondered, though, how long it had taken its owner to get used to what he confronted daily in his mirror.

'Bob Simpson read out your combat report to me, sir, from RAF records. He says the date, time and place all add up. It looks like it was your kill.'

The pilot had turned away and was searching among the papers on a table beside him; presently, he unearthed the copy of the *Courier* with Carter's story of the discovery and the dig on the front page. He looked at it for a moment.

'Bloody odd to think of that 109 hidden away in that wood all those years, from that day to this. Leutnant Martin Kern, aged nineteen. Still wet behind the ears, as I thought. Well, I was only twenty-one myself. You were almost past it at twenty-five. We used to look down on the old men of thirty with their cushy ground jobs. The reverse of peace-time, when age and experience get respect. Youth was all in those war years.' He tapped the newspaper. 'There were lots like this one. Thousands of 'em on both sides. A few flying hours under their belts, a couple of goes with the guns and, hey presto, they were operational. Most of them didn't stand a chance. Nice-looking girlfriend. Sad for her. Sad for a whole lot of people, the whole bloody thing.'

Carter felt for his wallet. 'I've a photo of him that his daughter let me have – if you'd like to see it.'

'Know your enemy! As a matter of fact, I've seen him once before – at a distance.'

He took hold of the snapshot carefully with his burned fingers and turned it towards the light.

'Handsome chap, wasn't he? Looks a decent sort and if that story of the children in the paper was true, he *was*. Most of them were, I think. It was a civilized battle, for the most part – if war can ever be called civilized. Single combat can breed respect for your opponent, though you tried not to think about him too much as you did your damndest to shoot the bugger down!'

Carter, who believed in letting people talk, prompted him quietly: 'You said you remembered it clearly. Would you tell me about it? There's been a lot of interest in the plane. Our readers would like to have the full story.'

'Not surprising considering who the pilot's daughter is. Mollie's a great fan of hers. She wanted to go to the Fairfield fête to see her open it but we had one of our own here and she was helping with the teas or something.'

'She'll get another chance at the funeral next Wednesday, two o'clock. He's being buried at Fairfield.'

'Is he, now?'

'His daughter's special request.'

'Some corner of a foreign field . . . She's probably right. After all this time he should stay there. He's become part of the place.' He handed back the photograph and got up from his desk to stand at the window, looking out, hands in pockets, eyes raised to the sky. 'It was a day just like today, you know – warm, sunny, clear. We'd taken off from Biggin mid-morning, I think, and cruised about a bit. We were somewhere over Milton Spa when we saw these bandits below us – a whole *Staffel* of ten or eleven 109s on their way home in a hurry. We peeled off and I went for the straggler. He was a sitting duck. I don't think he even saw me until it was too late. Piece of cake.' The pilot opened the window wider and leaned out, staring upwards into the blue. 'Must have all happened somewhere up there. Queer to think of it now. I could see the kite was badly damaged – there was white smoke coming out and all the usual signs. But I followed him down to give him another burst, just to make sure. Then the Spit's guns jammed on me and I couldn't do a bloody thing. There I was, flying alongside this 109, just astern of him, and wondering why in hell the chap inside didn't bail out before it was too late.'

'Do you think he was injured?'

Johnnie Mackintosh turned away from the window. He

shook his head. 'I couldn't say for sure, but I don't think so. He didn't look it and I saw him pretty clearly. He had his goggles up and he turned and looked over his shoulder at me. I could see he was only a sprog. A real greenhorn. I remember he had a white scarf round his neck . . . Used to wear a red one myself, still got it in a drawer somewhere. The poor sod must have thought he'd really had it then. I could have blown him to bits.'

'Would you have done?'

'Too bloody right! I'd have made damn sure the plane was properly finished off. He'd have done the same in my shoes. As it was, I just signalled to him to get the hell out of it.'

'But he didn't?'

'Maybe he couldn't, or wouldn't. It was his first time out, wasn't it? He was just a sprog and probably too shit-scared to move. That happened when you were new to the game. After a bit you got more used to it and bailed out bloody fast if you had to. The best trick was to flip the kite on its back and fall out – that saved a lot of climbing about and getting tangled up in things. I parted company with three Spits like that before the last one didn't want to let me go.'

'You said you were shot down yourself right after shooting down Leutnant Kern.'

'That's right. As I said, I was too damn careless. Getting that 109 had been too easy and I wasn't paying proper attention. One of his pals came after me and I had to climb bloody fast to get away. Then another one of them joined in and they chased me all over the shop. They got me in the end. I had to take to the skies and landed in a duck pond on some farm.' He smiled. 'The farmer's daughter was very pretty and made me a very nice cup of tea.'

'So you never saw what happened to the 109 you'd shot down?'

'I was otherwise engaged. One thing I can tell you, though, is that he must have come down near there. That kite wasn't going to fly much further.'

'As a pilot, do you think the schoolteacher's account makes

sense? That Leutnant Kern was trying to land in the field and crashed because of avoiding the children?'

'Certainly. From what she said he was coming in without power, pulled himself up to avoid the kids, stalled and just fell out of the sky.'

'Otherwise he might have landed safely?'

'He had a nice big flat field in front of him, didn't he? Plenty of room. If it hadn't been for the kids running about I think he'd have put down all right. As it was he couldn't risk it without doing them a whole lot of damage. Picture it for yourself, Mr Carter. A ton of metal coming out of the air, bits of it maybe flying about as it hits the deck, wings going along like a scythe . . . Leutnant Kern would have known all that when he sized up the situation and that's why he chose the alternative. He might have got away with it, but he didn't. Bloody bad luck!'

Carter thought of Phillip Dalrymple. 'You don't think he was planning to shoot up the children?'

'Good lord, no! The poor bugger was trying to get down in one piece, that's all he was planning. That's all any pilot in that situation would have been trying to do.'

'A brave man.'

'Anyone who got into a plane to fight in those days had to be brave – same as anyone who went off in a destroyer, or a submarine, or a tank, or fought on any battlefield. But I don't think it was a conscious bravery. You just did it because it had to be done. Precisely how you fought your own particular part of the battle depended on you, I suppose. Leutnant Kern did it his way.'

'Like the song says.'

'Like it says.'

Carter consulted his notes. 'You said you were shot down on two other occasions, apart from the one on that day and the final one.'

The pilot smiled his lopsided smile. He stubbed out his cigarette in the ashtray on his desk. 'I got to be quite a dab hand at hopping out of planes. Twisted an ankle one time and nearly got shot up by the Home Guard on another, but apart from that, no damage. I just got myself back to base and went up again as soon as possible.'

'Until the last time.'

'Until the last time. There was no going back to base then. I spent two years in and out of East Grinstead – one of McIndoe's guinea pigs – and God knows how many return visits ever since. The thing that really got me all those months when I was lying in a hospital bed was that I was missing the whole show. I'd have given anything to be able to walk out of there and jump back into the nearest Spit.'

Carter, who had been writing quietly as the pilot spoke, looked up. 'You'd have done that? In spite of your injuries?'

Mackintosh laughed. 'Ask any Spitfire pilot and he'll tell you that flying one was the nearest thing to heaven.'

The gulf was wide, Carter though regretfully, between the man who had known war and active service and the man who had not. 'You never got back to flying then?'

'Not in wartime. When I was more or less patched up to their satisfaction, they gave me a desk job. I filled in forms in triplicate and dictated memos for a few years before they finally decided to retire me. I'd injured my back as well and that was still giving me problems. Mollie had married me in spite of everything, bless her, and we came to live here. We're both Sussex born and it suits us.'

'Don't you find it a bit quiet?'

'I can see you don't know much about village life, Mr Carter. It's not a bit quiet. If you want to be quiet, go and live in a big city. When we came here the vicar said it would be ten years before we were accepted, but we'd only been here a few months before we were approached to take on all sorts of things. Mollie has a finger in every pie and I'm treasurer of this and secretary of that . . . I may not be an oil-painting but I can still count on these fingers. There's always something happening: bring-and-buys, coffee mornings, committees, council meetings . . .'

'But no flying?'

The slit mouth stretched into another smile. 'I didn't say that. I fly whenever I bloody can.' He held out his scarred hands and flexed the fingers. 'These don't look so good but there's nothing wrong with them when it comes to handling the controls, and my eyesight's still twenty-twenty. I'm a weekend pilot at the local club. Can't afford anything else.'

'Never been back in a Spitfire then?'

'As a matter of fact, I have. An old RAF friend of mine – wealthy sod who made a fortune out of nuts and bolts – keeps a collection of old planes. He's got a Lancaster, a Lysander, a Hurricane . . . and he's got a Spitfire. He's let me fly it a couple of times, when he's feeling generous.'

The pilot unhooked a framed photograph from the wall near his desk. 'That's him there, third from the left, and I'm the lazy bastard lying down on the right. That was taken at Biggin in August 1940.'

Carter looked at the black and white picture. The scene was an English summer day in the country with oaks and elms in the background and grass and sunshine. Only this was no picnic. In the middle ground stood a Spitfire and in the foreground, sitting or sprawling in a group on the grass, were seven young men wearing Mae Wests over their RAF uniform. They were all smiling or laughing, as though without a care in the world. There was no sign of stress or fear. The wealthy sod sat leaning casually against an upturned chair, his arms folded across his chest. He was dark-haired, fresh-faced and looked as though he should have been playing for the school first eleven. The lazy bastard on the right was leaning back, resting on his elbows, his long legs crossed at the ankles, his face tilted up towards the sun. He was good-looking in a thoroughly English way, with thick and wavy fair hair.

'Almost as handsome as the chap I shot down, wasn't I?' Mackintosh said drily.

'May I borrow this to use in the paper?'

'If you like. So long as you let me have it back, safe and sound. It's my only copy.'

263

'That's a promise.' Carter looked at the photograph again. 'What happened to the rest of them?'

'The other five were all killed. Bill and I were the only survivors of that little bunch. Two of them bought it the day after that was taken. The others lived a few months longer. We were lucky.'

Lucky was not a word that would have come immediately to Carter's mind to describe anyone who had endured what Johnnie Mackintosh must have endured. But that was the way the pilot saw things himself.

'Do you bear any grudges for what happened?'

The scarred fingers touched his face. 'Do you mean for this? Good lord, no! What's the point? I'll tell you something, Mr Carter, though I don't expect you'll understand. They were the best years of my life. There was an intensity of experience – a bit like being high on drugs, I suppose. Of course, we were scared. I used to be sick as a dog waiting to scramble. The only time you felt safe was under the blankets at night. When you had to get up it was like leaving a cocoon. It was all bloody frightening, but it was more exhilarating than anything I've ever felt before or since. You lived for the day and the Devil take the morrow.'

He shrugged. 'You're not a pilot yourself, are you? Damned hard to explain what it's like to someone who's not. Ever read a poem called "High Flight"?'

'I'm afraid not.'

'Chap called Magee wrote it. A Yank pilot serving with the Canadian Air Force, as a matter of fact. He was killed in a Spitfire in '41 and they found the poem afterwards in his papers, scribbled on the back of an envelope. Talked about slipping the surly bonds of earth and dancing the skies on laughter-silvered wings . . . I can't quite remember it all properly, but it's pretty powerful stuff.' He went on tentatively, quietly, gradually remembering more. 'Sunward I have climbed . . . and done a hundred things you have not dreamed of . . . wheeled and soared and swung . . . through footless halls of air . . . topped the windswept heights with easy grace where

264

never lark nor even eagle flew . . . trod the high, untrespassed sanctity of space . . . put out my hand . . . and touched the face of God . . .'

There was a moment's silence. Breaking the spell, Mrs Mackintosh opened the door and came in with a tray of coffee and biscuits.

Later on, as he left, Carter said: 'Will I see you at the funeral next Wednesday at Fairfield, sir?'

The pilot smiled and nodded. 'Oh yes, Mr Carter. I'll be there.'

Fourteen

It rained hard on the morning of the funeral, but by the time Carter and a *Courier* photographer drove into Fairfield, the weather had cleared up. The clouds were dispersing and there were already small patches of blue sky.

Other pressmen and TV news cameramen were making use of such facilities as Charlie was grudgingly prepared to supply at the Bull. Carter and the photographer joined the crowd in the bar. The regulars had been summarily displaced and the landlord, overworked and overwrought by the invasion of foreigners, was banging tankards and glasses down on the counter and snorting like a baited bull. Fancy requests for ice, lemon or peanuts were being brusquely rejected. God help anyone, Carter thought, who asked him for sandwiches.

Soon after one they began to move outside. Cars were now parked all round the village green, as well as on it, and other visitors had swelled the invasion numbers. Photographers fiddled with their cameras, reporters stood around smoking and talking together and some of the villagers were emerging from their houses. There was an atmosphere of expectancy and even Charlie could be seen peering out of the pub doorway.

As the contingent from the RAF arrived, the sun came through to light up the scene. The bearer party and the armed escort party assembled smartly by the lychgate in readiness. Two senior RAF officers and a young WAAF emerged from a staff car and two representatives from the German Embassy, both also in uniform, arrived. The group stood waiting together and were presently joined by another plain-clothes official whom Carter deduced was from the Ministry of Defence. They were doing Martin Kern proud.

He could see Bob Simpson parking his old Sunbeam Talbot away on the far side of the green and, presently, the surveyor walked across to join him. He was carrying a wreath of red and white chrysanthemums. Carter felt rather ashamed he had not thought of the same thing.

'From all the group,' Simpson explained. 'The lads like to pay their respects.'

Carter showed him the photograph of Martin Kern and he studied it closely.

'Good-looking bloke. No wonder she fell for him.' He looked at the crowd by the lychgate. 'I see they're pulling out all the stops for him. That's as it should be. I suppose a lot of them are just waiting to see the daughter, autograph books at the ready. I hope they don't spoil it.'

The rector had now arrived, in company with an RAF chaplain and their white surplices stood out against the sombreness of the uniforms. Both men were too young to have known anything of the war that had killed the man they were about to bury.

As the church clock struck two the funeral cortège came slowly into the village – a black hearse carrying the coffin and a black limousine carrying the chief mourner. There was an excited murmur from the crowd. The photographers pressed forward. Martina Drake was wearing a simple and very elegant black chiffon gown and carried a sheaf of white roses. She looked composed, dignified and very beautiful. Gregor hovered two paces behind her, wearing his overcoat. The officials moved forward to greet her.

Carter took his eyes from her to watch as the hearse door was opened and the coffin, draped in the West German flag and crowned with a single wreath of white flowers, was lifted carefully on to the broad shoulders of six bare-headed airmen. Six pall-bearers – officers of equivalent rank to the dead pilot, with black armbands on their sleeves – moved into position, three on each side of the coffin. The escort party and their officer, arms reversed, took up their place. When all was ready, the procession, led by the rector and the padre, moved through the open lychgate and up the brick pathway. At the top of the path they turned to cross the scythed grass, past old George Clark and his jam jar of bright cottage flowers and past the east wall of the church where the two white doves cooed softly from the chancel roof, to the open grave in a quiet corner, which looked down on to Trodgers Wood: Leutnant Kern's corner of a foreign field.

The cameramen pressed forward, outflanking the onlookers to get the best vantage points. Carter stationed himself at the front and scanned the rows of faces. There was Jesse and the old Home Guard, all dressed in their Sunday best even though it was Wednesday. Mrs Jennings, who had shut up shop for the afternoon, was wearing a shiny black straw hat that had probably done service for the passing of Mr Jennings. Mrs Fortescue dimpled at him from among the committee ladies who included Mrs Armstrong-Avery, massive in pale grey and pearls. Miss Burton stood a little apart, severe in a tailored suit and felt hat. Carter searched for Zoe and found her at last, near the back and on the opposite side. He guessed that she had slipped in at the last moment from the side gate that led from the Hall garden to the churchyard. She was alone – not that he had expected Phillip Dalrymple to come to see the German buried. He caught sight of Mollie Mackintosh, also alone, and felt an acute, if unreasonable disappointment that her husband had not kept his promise after all.

The actress stood at the foot of her father's grave; the two priests at its head. Carter heard the escort party leader give the command 'Rest on your arms reverse' and the men bent their heads over their rifles as the committal began.

Carter's experience of funerals had been limited to grim suburban cemeteries and crematoriums. This was different. Uplifting, he supposed, was hardly the word, but it was certainly not depressing. It struck him simply as very fitting and he watched it with a sense of satisfaction.

The six airmen who had borne the coffin from the lychgate

now retired and their place was taken by the six officers who gently and solemnly lowered the pilot to his final rest. The familiar words were spoken over the grave by Hugh Longman.

'For as much as it hath pleased Almighty God of his great mercy to take unto himself the soul of our dear brother here departed . . .'

Dear brother, dear enemy and dear God, what a bloody waste of thousands of young men like him in all the wars before, since and still to come. Carter shifted his weight to his other foot. The RAF chaplain was speaking now in halting, schoolboy German. He could see Mrs Jennings' white handkerchief a-fluttering and Mrs Fortescue quickly wiping away a tear with her gloved hand. Miss Burton stood solid and expressionless as a rock while Jesse, his cap removed for once, was rigidly at attention. A movement by one of the trees at the back of the crowd caught Carter's attention and he caught sight of Tom's unshaven, bright-eyed face peering round from behind the trunk, the dog's feathery tail just visible at the foot.

Earth rattled down on the coffin. The six officers, their task complete, filed one by one past the grave, saluting it in turn before they marched off. The escort party raised their rifles and as the three volleys shattered the quiet of the country churchyard the white doves fluttered in panic into the sky.

As silence returned, the RAF bugler stepped forward. The Last Post rang out through the village and down across the fields and the woods. Reveille followed and, as the last note died away, another sound could be heard, perfectly on cue. The sound of an approaching aircraft. The sound of a Merlin engine.

All heads lifted as the Spitfire came into view, skimming towards them above the trees. It roared low over the church and soared up above the tower, climbing high into the air and banking so that it was outlined against the blue, wing tip to wing tip. It seemed to hang there for a moment, suspended in space and eloquently beautiful, before it turned to dive and pass over them once more. And as the fighter did so it rolled slowly in salute.

269

Carter felt his throat tighten. He could picture the pilot's disfigured face and imagine the burned hands on the controls. Johnnie Mackintosh had kept his promise after all and paid his own respects to the man he had shot down forty years ago in the best way he knew.

He watched the plane fly away. Jesse was right: it was small. A tiny machine dancing through the skies. But it was also a symbol of victory and freedom and triumph over evil. And, to people like Johnnie Mackintosh, a symbol of things that he, Carter, had never done or dreamed of.

Martina Drake half-knelt to lay the bouquet of white roses on her father's grave. The young WAAF officer marched up to place a wreath on behalf of the RAF, saluting smartly before she turned to march off. She was not unlike Barbara Karlsemn, Carter thought. Fair, young, pretty and a nice-looking girl. One of the German officers came forward to put down his wreath of red and yellow flowers and to salute his compatriot. Then it was Bob Simpson's turn to pay the respects of his group. To Carter's surprise, Jesse suddenly detached himself from the crowd. He was carrying a bunch of summer flowers, probably picked from his own garden. The old man stood bare-headed and stiffly at attention for a moment before laying down his tribute to his former enemy.

It was all over. The bearer party and the escort party were marched off to their vehicles. The other RAF officers took their leave and the two Germans drove away. The crowd began to disperse, filing singly past the grave as they went.

Carter went up to Martina Drake. He told her who had piloted the Spitfire and her eyes filled with tears.

'I guess that's the nicest thing of all,' she said. 'The best tribute he could have had.' She held out her hand to him. 'Thanks for telling me, Frankie. Goodbye and good luck.'

Carter also said goodbye to Bob Simpson, Mrs Jennings, Mrs Fortescue and even Mrs Armstrong-Avery. Tom had vanished, together with his dog, in his own magical way. Miss Burton accosted him.

'A decent service, Mr Carter. Properly done.'

A stout, middle-aged man in a check suit came up to them. 'Remember me, Miss Burton?'

Glacially: 'I'm afraid I do not.'

'Hutchins is the name. Roy Hutchins. I used to be at your little school here. Way back in the war.'

His former schoolteacher gave him a withering look. 'Oh yes, I do remember you.'

His laugh was as loud as his suit. 'Not one of your best pupils, eh? Still, I've done all right for myself since.'

Miss Burton turned to Carter. 'Mr Hutchins was the one I sent to inform the police of the Messerschmitt coming down. The one who failed to deliver my message.'

He looked injured. 'I delivered it, just like I told you, Miss B. And when I read about it in the papers, I said to myself, I said, that must be the ruddy Kraut who tried to kill us all that day. So I said to myself, as I was in the area on business, I'd come along and take a dekko at the old place. I haven't been back for years.'

'You remember what happened clearly?' Carter asked.

'I'll say I do. Nearly copped it, didn't we? You don't forget something like that in a hurry. We were out in the cornfield, all us kids, and this bloody great Nazi plane – excuse my French, Miss B. – with crosses and swastikas all over it came zooming down straight for us.'

A bully and a braggart, Miss Burton had called him. But, to be fair, to a small boy the fighter must have looked big and terrifying.

'I should not have described it quite like that,' Miss Burton said coolly. 'Zooming is not a word I should have employed. The plane was coming in slowly and the pilot was simply trying to land.'

'Land, my eye!' her former pupil said disrespectfully. 'He was going to take a potshot at us, that's what. He came straight towards us, very low, like I said. And I could see that Nazi bloke – same one they've just made all this hoo-ha about – sitting with his finger on the firing button.'

'You must have had remarkable eyesight, Mr Hutchins,'

271

Miss Burton observed. 'I'm afraid I couldn't actually see that far into the cockpit myself.'

Her sarcasm was wasted on him. He was warming to his story.

'I ran like hell, I remember. All us kids did. You should have heard the screaming and yelling. Then I threw myself to the ground. He went right over us, no more than a few feet above my head. I thought we were gonners, but the guns must have jammed on him, or else he'd run out of ammo.'

Carter glanced at Miss Burton. Her face was set. 'That's what you reckon happened, Mr Hutchins?' he asked.

'That's what *did* happen, mate. All that sacrifice bit is a load of rubbish, if you'll pardon me saying so, Miss B. Blooming disgrace, burying him like this – and *here*, of all places. They used to shoot up civvies on their way back, didn't they? Strafe anything they could. This bloke was going to kill us kids and then go home for lunch. Only he messed it up and killed himself instead.'

'According to Miss Burton, the pilot had no engine power. He would have found it a bit difficult to get home for lunch, or anything else.'

Hutchins shrugged. 'I wouldn't know about that. Maybe he turned it off to come in quiet and surprise us. He must have had some power because he climbed right up after that. Before he went down in that wood.'

Miss Burton had had enough. 'If you will excuse me, Mr Hutchins, I have other things to do.' She turned away.

'Okey-dokey. Not to worry. Here's my card. I've got my own little business now, so give us a tinkle some time and I'll come round and see you. No charge. Free estimates.'

She looked at the flashy card as though it were something pornographic and then returned it.

'Thank you, Mr Hutchins, but I shall not be requiring double glazing. Goodbye.'

Hutchins stared after her as she walked off. He was too thick-skinned to recognize her disdain or understand it.

'Rum old bird! A real gorgon in the old days. I never forgot anything she taught me, you know, so I suppose I should be grateful for that.'

'It doesn't add up, Mr Hutchins. If you reported the Messerschmitt crash to the police that day, why didn't they act on it? The site was never investigated.'

Roy Hutchins laughed. Life seemed one long laugh to him. 'Told a fib there, didn't I? Well, wouldn't you? She still puts the wind up me, and that's a fact.'

'What happened then?'

'Lost her message, didn't I? Must have dropped out of my pocket when I was biking along. I went back to look for it but when I couldn't find it I reckoned I'd leave well alone. She'd have had me doing lines till the next Christmas. And it was only some bloody Kraut who'd tried to shoot us kids up. I was buggered if I was going to get into trouble because of *him*.'

Miss Burton had picked the wrong one there and Roy Hutchins was as capable of telling lies now as he had been in 1940. Carter declined the offer of the double-glazing card and removed himself from Ron Hutchins' orbit. He felt the same aversion to him as did Miss Burton, and yet he admitted that although truth was said to be the daughter of time, in this case, no matter how much time passed, it could never be known for sure. According to Hutchins and Phillip Dalrymple, the *leutnant* had been a Nazi murderer, bent on killing innocent children. Miss Burton, however, maintained the exact contrary. The pilot had died to save them. Luckily for Martin Kern it was Miss Burton's version that was on record.

And Carter knew which one he believed.

He hurried to catch up with Zoe as she was walking away. The photographer would have to wait for him.

'Can we talk a minute? I've got something to tell you.'

She hesitated and then nodded, walking beside him as he took her away from the church, down to the old, wild part of the graveyard where Jesse's scythe had not reached and where faceless tombstones leaned half-hidden in the long grass. Beyond an iron paling fence, the green and pleasant Sussex fields rolled on towards the Downs and the English Channel.

Zoe sat down on one of the gravestones, hands in pockets, head turned towards the view.

'That Spitfire,' she said. 'I cried when it came over. Did you know it was going to happen?'

'No. It was the pilot who shot Martin Kern down. Squadron-Leader Johnnie Mackintosh. When I went to see him he told me about some rich friend of his who owned a Spitfire and let him fly it sometimes. He promised he'd come to the funeral today, but I never guessed he meant like that.'

'It was the nicest thing he could have done.'

'All's well that ends well.'

She scuffed at the ground with her toe. 'I think so. It's all over. Finished and done with.'

He knew that she was no longer talking about the German pilot.

'Phillip will never know, Zoe. I'll keep my promise and stay away. In fact, I'm going away altogether. That's what I wanted to tell you.'

She lifted her head. 'Where?'

'London. Back to Fleet Street. An old mate of mine rang me yesterday. He's a big name now on one of the nationals. He's offered me a job – if I want it.'

'Take it, Frank. You must. It's where you belong.'

'Back in the big city, like Madame Zara foretold.' He took hold of her hands and pulled her to her feet. 'Listen, Zoe, I love you. And I'll take the job because I do. I can't stay near you and not see you.'

Tears were unshed in her eyes. 'There's no other way. Not with Phillip.'

'I know that. That's why I'm going.'

He kissed her for a long while and afterwards she pressed her face to his shoulder for a moment. Somehow she pulled herself together and smiled.

'Goodbye, Frank. And good luck with the new job.'

He watched her walk away between the gravestones, out of his sight and out of his life.

Ken Grant said sourly: 'You'll be back. If I'll have you. Which I won't.'

'Come on, Ken. Be fair. You'll miss me.'

The editor looked up with humourless eyes. 'Too big for your boots, Frank, that's the trouble with you. It's all the same with you Fleet Street lot.' He unwrapped a mint and stuck the sweet into his mouth. 'I've had Councillor Jackson on the phone again today. Didn't like how you reported that last meeting. You couldn't even get that right, could you?'

Carter said what he felt the councillor could do.

'You'll have to watch your step, Frank. That sort of talk won't get you very far.' False teeth crunched on mint shards. 'Got yourself too wrapped up in that plane business over at Fairfield, you know. It was only a German fighter, not the Titanic.'

'I think it was pretty important.'

'To you, maybe. They didn't win that competition anyway, did they, in spite of all that fuss. Not even a mention in the ratings. Mayhurst won again, didn't it?'

'Depends how you look at it.' Carter lit a cigarette. 'One thing's always puzzled me, Ken. Why in hell did you ever hire me in the first place?'

'God only knows, Frank. God only knows. And you can take yourself and that filthy weed out of here while I'm trying to remember.'

Brenda sniffed loudly and dabbed at the corners of her sooty eyes with a rainbow-coloured tissue.

'It won't be the same without you, Frank. Lot of dreary old sods, they are. Not a laugh out of them half the day and pissed out of their minds for the rest.'

Harvey was glowering from across the room. His resentment had trebled since he had learned of Carter's departure to London, even though he had always wished him gone. Carter patted Brenda's shoulder.

'Come on. Cheer up. It's not as bad as that and you know it.'

She pulled a face. 'I know I'll miss you, that's what.'

'Your mascara's run.'

'Bloody stuff's supposed to be waterproof. Cost me a fortune. I'll sue them. It says on the box you can swim in it.' She wiped away the black smudges. 'Oh well, all good things come to an end, as my mum always says. Though I never see why they should.' She put the crumpled tissue away and ranged blue-painted talons over the typewriter keys. 'Got to get on with this. His lordship wants it double-quick.'

'Look after the ivy for me, will you?'

The trailing ivy he had bought at the Fairfield fête had flourished under her care and was spreading itself over the windowsill.

'If you like.'

He turned again from the door.

'I'll see you around, Brenda.'

'No you won't.' She looked up at him sadly. 'Best of British.'

Mrs Eliot displayed a good deal less regret at his going than Brenda had. She seemed totally indifferent to whether he stayed or went and whilst he was explaining and offering rent in lieu of notice, half her attention was still on the happenings in *Coronation Street* taking place tantalizingly out of her view behind the sitting-room door. She kept her head cocked in that direction.

'It's all the same to me, Mr Carter, when you go – so long as you leave the room tidy and respectable. I've no complaints, except for the smoking. My husband never did, you see. I don't like the smell of it about the house. Otherwise you've been satisfactory.' She applied her eye to the crack of the part-open door. 'I dare say I'll find another lodger quick enough. Someone nice and quiet. I don't like a lot of noise and comings and goings.' The programme's signature tune started up. Mrs Eliot looked agitated and dismayed. 'Oh dear, oh dear! You've made me miss the end, Mr Carter. Now I won't know what's happened.'

Carter went slowly up the stairs to his first-floor room. He packed his few belongings, chucking them anyhow into an old suitcase. When that was done, he looked for the last time round the room, at the cheap post-war furniture, the shrunken curtains, the long crack in the ceiling and the damp patch. He wondered if the next tenant would notice the Nile and Australia as he, or she, lay in the sagging, lumpy bed. Perhaps whoever it was would be better at geography. The other night he'd worked out where Cairns was and thought of the name of another river: the Darling. The whole class at school had sniggered at that one. For all its bare ugliness, he would remember this room kindly. In it he had somehow finally laid the ghost of Jan to rest.

He closed the lid of the suitcase.

Epilogue

He lost his way several times before he finally remembered the road and found himself driving up that same narrow lane between the great beech trees, as he had done on his first visit to Fairfield. This time, though, the trees were bare and the car was not an overheating, rattling newspaper van but his own fast, smooth-running two-seater.

He stopped at the top of the rise and looked down at the village below. In winter it had a naked air. The little huddle of houses around the square-towered church stood out clearly, denuded of their summer camouflage. He could see the pub, the green, the pond – a cold grey now – the schoolhouse belfry. And the big house with a white hoar of frost on the lawn.

He waited there for several minutes, smoking a cigarette and remembering that summer. Since then things had mostly gone his way. As Madame Zara had predicted, he supposed, he had done pretty well for himself. And on the surface he had changed – for the better, he hoped. He'd rubbed off a few more rough edges and taken on some of the polish that goes with success.

He continued looking down at the village. In the four new years of world-shattering violence and upheaval that those church bells had rung in since their restoration, he would have staked his life that nothing much would have changed in Fairfield. The patrons of the Bull would still be sitting round, quietly quaffing their pints, and jumble sales, coffee mornings, whist drives, dancing classes, fêtes, harvest festivals and carol services would have come and gone in peaceful rotation.

He stubbed out his cigarette, drew in a deep breath and

278

drove on downhill. It was all exactly as he remembered. The absence of litter and the neatness of the verges meant that Miss Burton must still be alive and kicking. And the presence of Mactavish and three scraggy boilers meant that all was well within the Bull. Fairy lights and fancy menus had been kept at bay. If he were to open the door of the public bar and walk in – as he had done that first time on that hot summer's day – he would find Jesse puffing away at his pipe in his corner, Charlie presiding short-temperedly at the bar, and the rest of them probably still swapping tall yarns about World War Two. He would drink flat Coke and eat a packet of stale crisps, dropping a crumb or two surreptitiously for Mactavish. Then Tom might come in, the black and white dog slinking at his heels, to sit and nod and wink at his table. He would have some story to tell. The Queen might have been in the church-yard again, or Prince Philip might have bought a quarter of toffees at Mrs Jennings' shop.

He parked the car, but instead of going into the pub, he walked over to the lychgate and went up the brick pathway into the churchyard.

Some things, he knew, *had* changed.

He passed Ezrah, Emma, Florence Mary, Hanna and old George Clark whose eight children and sixteen grandchildren had chipped in to buy a marble headstone enscribed: 'In Loving Memory of Grandad'. There was still a jam pot full of flowers.

The frosty grass felt crisp beneath his feet as he crossed to where the German pilot lay in his quiet corner of a foreign field. The headstone there was plain and simple.

MARTIN KERN
6.9.1921
6.9.1940

At the foot of the stone there was a vase of red roses. Florist's roses. Sent, he guessed, by the daughter.

He stood there for a moment, hands in the pockets of his tweed overcoat, collar turned up against the cold. He was looking down at the grave of someone who'd died forty-four summers ago – a stranger whom he had never met, but who had helped him all the way along the line. No Martin Kern, no Messerschmitt, no story, no stringer, no Don Clayton, no return to Fleet Street. He hoped that what he had done had been a fair return and that the pilot rested in peace.

Nearby there was a more recent grave with a larger, grander headstone.

PHILLIP HENRY JOHN DALRYMPLE
Born 6th July, 1944
Died 14th February, 1984
Remembered for his courage

The same might be said of both men, he thought. In life they would have been inseparably divided, but in death they lay close together and had earned the same tribute.

He left the churchyard and went back to his car. At the entrance to Fairfield Hall there was a For Sale sign. He had expected that. He had known that she would leave.

The announcement of Phillip Dalrymple's death had been in the papers ten months ago. Later, there had been an inquest. The baronet had died from an overdose of pills and the coroner, giving a verdict of accidental death, had ruled that he had taken too many by mistake. Carter had not believed that. Phillip Dalrymple had done just what he had told him he would do – cash in his chips when he'd had enough. Zoe had known it, too. And she had blamed herself. He knew what it was like to feel guilt for another's death – even though, in this case, there was no cause. Her letter in answer to his own had been formal and very distant. When he had telephoned she had politely refused to see him.

So now he drove very slowly and apprehensively up to the house. It had a desolate air – as desolate, he suspected, as its remaining occupant must be.

He stopped the car and got out. The stone walls that had been covered by a creeper in summer were bare and a deep drift of dead leaves had accumulated against the side of the house. Through the archway in the hedge he could see the lawn where the fête had been held. And he could see the dark little hut by the rhododenrons where Madame Zara had read his palm and where he had made love to Zoe.

He had given her time. Kept away for as long as he could. He had done what he knew was the 'decent' thing. Chance had played its part in his life. If he hadn't turned off the main road that day four years ago, taken wrong turns and developed a leaking radiator, he would never have come across Fairfield, stopped at the Bull, or heard Tom's story about the Spitfire. But this time he had come here deliberately. And he wasn't going to leave anything to chance any longer.

He reached out and pulled at the brass bell. It pealed through the silent house and then stopped. He waited, listening to the wind coming across the fields. Then he heard the sound of her footsteps.

She opened the door and stood there in old jeans and a sweater that was too big for her, much as she had been when he had first seen her and mistaken her for the au pair. Carter smiled. He knew now by the way she was looking at him that Madame Zara had got it smack on the nail.

In ze end everysing would be all right.

Author's Note

Although it has remained unpublished until now, I wrote this story some years ago when I was living in a village in southern England in an area where the Battle of Britain had been fought overhead during the summer of 1940. Many planes, British and German, had crashed to earth during the fierce conflict, and their wreckage had often stayed buried for years after the war – in some cases with their pilots or crew.

During the Eighties a number of these sites were located and excavated by World War Two aviation enthusiasts, the recovered wreckage ending up in museums and in private collections and any identified human remains given an official military burial with full honours. There were opposing views about this. On the one hand the next of kin were often relieved and comforted by the discovery and by a proper and fitting burial, and their feelings were shared. Other people, however, felt that the crash sites were war graves and should be left undisturbed. In the end, the government forbade any further excavations.